WE WILL
RID THE
WORLD
OF YOU

I0525243

Also by Scott Burr

BUMMED OUT CITY

WE WILL RID THE WORLD OF YOU

A NOVEL BY

SCOTT BURR

The Artless Dodges Press
www.TheArtlessDodgesPress.com
Cleveland, Ohio

We Will Rid the World of You: A Novel
Copyright © 2020 Scott Burr
ISBN-13 978-0-9907227-1-7
ISBN-10 0-9907227-1-6
Published by The Artless Dodges Press
Cleveland, Ohio
www.TheArtlessDodgesPress.com

Layout and cover design by The Artless Dodges Press

Front cover image by mistress_f from Rome, Italy
Agnostic Front
CC BY 2.0 (http://creativecommons.org/licenses/by/2.0)
via Wikimedia Commons

Back cover image by Adrián Cerón
Own work
CC BY-SA 4.0 (http://creativecommons.org/licenses/by-sa/4.0)
via Wikimedia Commons

For my teachers, with gratitude.

PART
ONE

HEY THERE, folks. How's it going? Let's start the show.

If you're just tuning in for the first time, Hi there, hello, how are you? I'm your host, Dexter Anthony Foster, and I'll be taking you through until we're done here or until I run out of pages or until they come and get me, I guess. I'll be taking you through until whatever comes next.

We've got a great show for you tonight. I know I say that all the time, but tonight I really mean it. Tonight's show is something special. Tonight we're doing something we've never done before. So tune in, turn on, hunker down, strap in. Do whatever you need to do to prepare yourself. I know I have.

No calls, tonight. No contests, no news, no requests. No Danger Dave at the console. Tonight it's just me. Tonight it's all just me.

Tonight's show is brought to you by Jonathan Upasaka, I guess.

Tonight's show is brought to you by Bhakti and Ananda and Drishti. It's brought to you by Teacher. It's brought to you by Logan Hazelette, by Ricky and Chad and Danger Dave. It's brought to you by Dan and Eileen Foster. It's brought to you by everything. The All that is the All is not separate from the All that makes the All. Tonight's show is brought to you by Bethany Katherine Alpern. Thank you. Thank you to the All that is the All and the All that makes the All. Thank you.

Full and honest. Okay, let's do it. It's all yours. This shattered jumble, this fucking wreckage, is all for you.

IT'S LATE November, 2014. Dave tells me that we have to be in early, that there's a meeting for all the show runners, but when I get to the station there are streamers hanging from the ceiling and a big sheet cake in the common room and everyone is there to slap me on the back and shake my hand and say, Holy shit, congratulations, can you even believe it, ten years, Goddamn.

The cake has a pair of faces and a microphone next to the words *CONGRATULATIONS DEX AND DAVE! TEN YEARS OF ASSAULTING THE AIRWAVES AT WXYY*, and a set of dates like on a tombstone, all done up in colored frosting.

Tommy from the morning show points and says, "Hey, look at that. It looks just like you."

Kyle the intern wants to know how it feels.

Dave hands me a coffee. The Bailey's is all at the bottom. I swirl it around to make it mix.

"How does it feel?" I say. "It feels like drunk driving yourself home, and being surprised when you actually get there."

People laugh. Tommy shakes his head.

"You know they have a name for that," he says. "Right? You do know that, right?"

Denise, the new girl in reception, has started in, cutting pieces and tipping them onto plates. The chin has already disappeared, and now the mouth is going. The chocolate inside makes it look like the cake man is sinking into something, like he's being sucked down. I sip the coffee and I nod.

"Sure," I say. "I call it 'Tuesday.'"

WE ALL meet up later, at a bar down the street. Dave gives the bartender twenty bucks to unlock the jukebox. Somebody puts down for some pitchers. I buy a shot for everybody. Somebody proposes a toast. We raise our glasses to ten more years. Everybody is talking, laughing, having a good time. The music is up loud. We push tables out of the way to make a space for dancing. We jump around, sweating in our layers. Denise grabs me and we dance to a few songs. Tommy works his way around with the pitcher, filling glasses.

It gets late, gets boozy. Dave says he has to get home. He gives me a hug, tells me he'll see me tomorrow. Other people have already disappeared. The diehards huddle up and make a plan. Somebody suggests another bar down the street. We get our coats. Out on the sidewalk the wind blows the falling snow into our faces and down our collars. Denise walks with me, hugging my arm with her arms and pressing her cheek against my shoulder. At the corner she looks up at me, her teeth chattering and her eyebrows bunched together and her eyes slitted against the wind and I can feel her hot, moist breath on my chin, can see the snowflakes that are collecting in her hair standing out sharp against the red dye and the black roots.

And it's all so stupid. This moment, this party, the thing it's celebrating. Everything that's about to happen and all of her reasons for it. This guy she thinks I am, this thing she's impressed by. I want to be far away, want them to just go and do whatever they're going to do and live their lives and leave me alone.

I tell her to wait, tell her to hang on for a second, and I work my arm free from hers. I jog back down the street and I turn in down an alley. She calls my name, asks me where I'm going. Somebody else tells me to come back, says we're almost there. I don't stop, though. One side of the alley is a brick building, the other is a parking garage. I climb over the low concrete wall and I move past the few cars and across the empty spaces. I go over into the stairwell and I go up. It's like being in another universe, after all the wind and snow outside. The painted cinderblock is bright and smooth and my footsteps echo loud. The staircase seems to go on forever. Finally I reach the top. I go across the empty pad, over to the edge by the street, and I lean over and look down. I can see them all there. They're standing now in a little cluster at the mouth of the alley. Denise is hugging herself, shuffling around in her stupid shoes and her ridiculous skirt. Kyle is trying to talk to her, moving in as she moves away. I can hear Eric and Cynthia singing the last song we all danced to, laughing and mixing up the words.

Tommy cups his hands in front of his mouth and calls down the alley, calls my name.

I swing a leg over, work my way around, sit facing out. I kick my feet and watch the big snowflakes fall past my shoes. And I call down to them. I wave and laugh when they figure out where my voice is coming from, when they finally turn and look. Denise's hands go to her mouth. Kyle steps backwards off the sidewalk to get a better view and a dark-colored van has to brake hard and swerve to keep from hitting him. The driver blares the horn as the tires slide and catch on the slushy road. Denise is yelling up at me, telling me not to move. I pinwheel my arms, kick my legs, shout and pull a stupid, panicked face. I laugh at their alarm. I laugh and laugh.

"Don't move," Denise yells. "Don't you move one inch."

Tommy and Eric have already disappeared inside. Kyle and Cynthia and Denise go in after them. With everyone gone everything is quiet again. I stop laughing. I watch the snow go down and down and down. The empty white-covered street stretches out like a cloud.

I raise my glass to ten years. Ten years, and ten more after that. You do one thing and then you do another thing and then you do another thing and you think it's all just for now, just for a while, just until you get the real thing going again. Then one morning you go into work and there are streamers hanging from the ceiling and a sheet cake in the common room, and there's your face made up in frosting and dates like on a tombstone. Like a prank somebody is pulling. Like some kind of joke. They're going to jump out any minute now and say that it's all pretend, that you're still young, that there's still time. That you're not turning forty a decade into a career you never chose.

I raise my glass high, reach it out. I reach it out and out. Ten years. I'm laughing again. It all just seems so funny.

LATER, THOUGH, Denise sets me straight. The next day she stops me in the hall and she tells me that it wasn't funny, what I did, that it wasn't funny at all.

"You really scared us," she says. "You really scared me."

I'm too hungover to care, too hungover to think. I shrug. "That's why it was funny," I say.

She frowns, shakes her head. She opens her mouth to say something but then she closes it again without saying whatever it was. She looks up at the ceiling, blinks something back. She gives a dry little humorless snort.

"You know people ask me what you're like," she says. "When they find out that I work here they always want to know if you're actually as much of a dick in real life as you are on your show. And I always tell them that you're not. I always tell them that you're totally different in person. That the way you are on the show is just a character. That really you're a totally decent guy." She laughs, shrugs. "I guess that shows you what I know," she says.

After Eric and Tommy came and got me down the party was pretty much over. You could just feel it. The energy had shifted. Standing out in the cold had taken something out of everybody, too. I insisted that we keep going, though. I was all fired up. It was my party, I told them. It was over when I fucking said it was.

They humored me. Or at least they didn't fight me. At the next bar I ordered shots, but nobody wanted them. Tommy did his and so did Kyle, but I ended up doing mine and Eric's and Cynthia's. I don't know what happened to Denise's. Maybe I drank it. Or maybe it was somebody else at the bar, I don't know. At least I can't imagine that Denise drank it, not after all that.

Sometime after that somebody was putting me in a taxi, and sometime after that I was home and I was standing in my bathroom and I was looking at myself in the mirror. I was looking at my face and I was thinking how strange it was that it was my face, and then I was waking up on the bathroom floor. I was still in my clothes, still in my coat, even, and I'd thrown up in the tub, even though the toilet was right there.

I push my fingers up under my sunglasses, push my fingertips into my eyes. "I don't know what to tell you," I say. "I'm like one of those actors. I stay in character all the time. That's how committed I am. I'm the fucking De Niro of drive-time radio."

I drop my hands. She's still looking at me. She keeps looking at me. Then she nods. She gives another little snort, smiles a tight-lipped smile. She holds up her hands.

"Fine," she says. She takes a step to the side, steps around me, keeps going. "Whatever," she says, as she goes past. "My mistake."

I turn, watch her go, watch her short little angry steps. Then I go down the hall to our office. Dave is there. He swivels around in his chair, holds out his hands.

"And here you are," he says.

"Here I am," I say. I sit down on the couch and I lay back against the cushions. I feel like I could fall asleep right here. I raise my head back up and I look at him. "Why," I say, "where am I supposed to be?"

He shrugs. "I don't know," he says. "I hear all kinds of things. I hear you tried to jump off the top of that parking garage over at Euclid and 8th."

I'm still sitting half-slouched on the seat. I make myself sit all the way up, sit forward. I rest my elbows on my knees and let my head hang. I can feel my blood pounding behind my eyes. I shake my head. "I didn't go up there to jump," I say, "I went up there to get away from Denise."

Dave laughs. He holds up his hands. "All right," he says. "If you say so."

"I do say so," I say. "Why, what are people saying?"

He shrugs again. "I don't know," he says. "I heard Tommy tell somebody that he had to pull you in off the ledge. That he really thought you were going to do it."

"Tommy's full of shit," I say. I raise my hands, point around at the walls and the desks in the shitty little broom closet where they let us keep our stuff. "And anyway," I say, "why would I kill myself, when I have all of this to live for?"

Dave laughs again, but it's not real. It's the not-all-the-way-real laugh he does on the show when I say things that may or may not be funny, may or may not be clever. It's his schtick for my schtick. He stops laughing and leans in.

"Look," he says, "it was just a stupid thing that management wanted to do. You know. Show everyone that they pay attention to these things. Show how much they appreciate the talent. It doesn't have to mean anything. It's not like, I mean, it's just a number. It's just a round number. It doesn't have to mean anything."

I push my sunglasses up on my head and blink at him. "I know that," I say. "Why are you telling me that?"

"I just mean it's not worth getting worked up over," he says.

He waits for me to say something back, but I don't. He sits back and he holds up his hands again.

"Okay," he says. "Never mind. You're good, I get it. Enough said."

It's pretty clear that it's not enough said, though. He's still got a vibe, a funk, an aura. It's in his look, his tone, his body language. I let myself drop back into the cushions.

"Come on," I say. "What? What is this?"

He shakes his head. His expression is open, blank, innocent. "Nothing," he says. "Never mind. Forget I said anything."

He doesn't quite finish what he's saying, though, doesn't quite get it all out, because I'm talking again.

"What?" I say. "What do you think? Tell me what you honestly think. Do you seriously think I was going to jump off a fucking building because I've been doing this for ten years?" I say, "I was fucking with those guys, okay? That's it. If you'd stuck around you would know that."

He waits until I'm finished, waits for a second after I'm finished to make sure. Then he says, "All I'm saying is, there's no reason to get hung up on it. Okay? It's just a stupid office party."

"I'm not hung up on it," I say. I'm talking louder, now, have been talking louder, and it's making my temples throb. "I'm not even talking about it," I say. "You're the one who keeps bringing it up."

He's got his hands up again. "Fine," he says. "That's fine. I get it. You're over it. Never mind. Forget I said anything."

I'm going to say something back to that, but then I don't. It feels like there's no point, like getting him to really let it go is going to take all the energy I have. I lean back, lay my head back on the cushion. I stare up at the ceiling. The fluorescent light is like a thousand needle points in my brain. I close my eyes, put my sunglasses back on over them.

"What are you even talking about?" I say. "I don't even know what you're even talking about."

He's turned back to what he was doing before I came in, but now I hear him get up and I hear him go over and I hear the door close. It's a relief. The constant low noise from outside was making everything worse. I hear him come back over and sit back down.

"Look," he says again. "I'm fine, here. I'm good with this. I could do this for another twenty years and be fine. That would be just fine with me. I don't need this to be anything more than what it is."

He lets that stand. I tip my head up and look at him.

"And?" I say.

He shrugs, looks down. "And I know that this isn't really what you saw yourself doing with your life," he says. "And I could see how, that being the case, you might not love being reminded of the fact that you've been doing it for a decade."

I let my head drop back again. "And so you thought that maybe I meant it," I say, "when I climbed up on top of that parking garage."

"I don't know," he says. "I didn't know what it was about. So I figured I would ask."

There's still light getting in, light making its way through my sunglasses and my eyelids. I push my fingers in under the glasses and I make it dark, as dark as I can.

"I'm fine," I say. "I was just drunk. Okay? I was drunk and Denise was hanging on me and Kyle was being Kyle and I just wanted to see the look on their faces. Okay? That's it. I'm fine."

I tilt my head, push up my sunglasses, blink my eyes clear. I look at him. He's looking at me. He's working something around in his mouth, something he never ends up saying. He looks past me to the clock on the wall, looks down, shrugs. He nods toward the door.

"We'd better get in there," he says. "It's getting to be about that time."

WHETHER HE'S right on not, whether I really meant it or not, that night is the start of something. It isn't good. Drinking too much on weekends turns into drinking too much four or five nights a week. It turns into me ripping into callers, baiting people for no reason. It turns into me picking fights in bars, talking shit and causing scenes, getting thrown out. It turns into me going home with women I don't even like.

These women, they all say the same thing.

They all say, "Wow."

They all say, "I can't believe it's you."

They all say, "I can't believe Dex Foster is actually standing in my apartment."

To them I say, "Please, for fuck's sake, don't remind me."

THIS GOES on for weeks, goes on through the holidays and into the new year. Dave gets worried.

"What are you doing to yourself?" he says. "You can't keep this up. You're not a kid anymore." He laughs. "Shit," he says, "you're not even a young adult anymore."

I'm cupping cold water from the bathroom sink onto my face and over my head, cupping it into my mouth. I work the water around with my tongue, push it between my teeth, spit.

"Thanks," I say. "Thanks for that. Really, I mean it. Thank you for bringing that to my attention."

"I'm serious," he says. "I don't know where you think this is headed, but from here it doesn't look like it's anywhere good."

I nod. He's right. I know he's right. But the show only takes up so much of my time. There are so many hours left, hours and hours and hours, and it's there for all of them. It's there when I go to bed and it's there when I wake up in the morning. It's the song I can't get out of my head, the one where—the second it's finally gone—it just happens to come on the radio. I see my reflection in a window, or I see an old photo, and there it is.

"I mean it," Dave says. "Maybe you need to talk to somebody. Or shit, I don't know. Maybe you should see about going to a meeting, or something."

I rinse my mouth again, spit. Water runs down my face, off my chin. I hold up a hand at him. "Please," I say, "I don't need a lecture, okay? Not from you."

"Not from me?" he says. "Is that a joke? Why not from me?"

"Because," I say. "Because you don't know anything about it. Because you've got Katie and the kids and your whole little domestic sunshine island over there."

"Oh, right," he says. "I don't know what it's like for you, is that it? I don't know what it's like for you, but you know everything about what it's like for me. Right? Is that it? Have I got it now?"

His voice is suddenly loud, and practically every flat surface in this bathroom is tiled, and the combination is overwhelming. It's like somebody hitting me over the head with something unforgiving.

"Stop," I say. "Just stop, okay? Just stop."

"I'm worried about you," he says. His voice is back down, back normal again. "I'm concerned for you well-being. I'm not trying to be up in your shit. You're an adult, you can make your own decisions. I get that. It's just that sometimes we need an outside perspective on these things."

I turn off the tap, pull a long sheet of paper towel from the dispenser, dry my face and hands. "Thank you," I say, "but I'm fine. I've got it. I'm dealing with it."

He nods. "Okay," he says. Then he says, "What are you doing tonight? Why don't you come over for dinner? Katie's making spaghetti and she always makes too much and the kids won't eat it if it's been reheated."

I wad the paper towel, throw it at the trash can, miss. I shake my head. "I think I need to just go home," I say. "Just watch a movie, or something. Check out for a little bit."

He shrugs. "Okay," he says. "Suit yourself. But the offer stands if you change your mind."

WE DO the show. We do a bit about some roadwork going on downtown that seemed a lot funnier when we were coming up with it and we give away a pair of tickets to see some band I've never heard play the Agora and we play some music and we take some calls. I give some guy a hard time about some shit he says about some local politics thing, make fun of something some woman says about some actor. Then it's over. Dave asks again if I want to come for dinner, but I tell him Thanks, no. I tell him I meant it before, that I really am going to go home and make it an early night. At home I toss a frozen pizza in the oven and kill time while it cooks. I watch something on YouTube, watch something else. I put on some Minor Threat and I pick up one of my guitars and I play along. I play one song, play another. I try to just relax, to slip out of this moment and into that forever moment of the next note and the next note and the one after that, that place where nothing is really lost or taken because nothing is ever over, not really, not when you can wind it back and start again, that place where it still feels like there's a point, like putting in time is still taking you somewhere, somewhere you want to be. I can't do it, though. It doesn't work. Three songs in I'm still there, still in my head. So I get up and I turn off the music. I go into the kitchen and I turn off the oven, too. I leave the pizza where it is and I get my coat and I get in my car and I drive over to this bar I know. I go inside and I sit there at the bar and I think, That's it. Dave's right. I can't do this anymore. I'm done. I think, I'm going to get up off this stool and I'm going to pay my tab and I'm going to go home, and tomorrow morning I'm going to go in and tell them. I'm going to tell them that I'm done, tell them that I can't do this anymore, tell them to find somebody else. I'm going to get off this stool and I'm going to go home and I'm going to write it all out, write out exactly what I'm going to say, and when I wake up in the morning it'll be there and I won't even have to think about it. It'll be there, ready for me. All I'll have to do is go in and read it. I think, That's what I'm going to do. That's it. That's the plan. I'm going to do it after I finish this drink. After I finish this one. After I finish this next one, I'm going to go.

But I don't do it. I don't do it after that drink or the one after that, and it keeps getting later and later. I think I've still got time, think I've still got a handle on it, think I've still got it straight in my head, what I want to say and how I want to say it, but then the bartender rings the bell and it's like I wake up and I realize that I don't, that it's too late, that it's all a mess.

There are only a few of us left, now. There's the bouncer at the door and there's a couple off in one of the booths and there's the drunk who lives upstairs and who cleans up after the bar closes and then there's me and the woman who's been hovering around me all night and the man who's been hovering around her.

"Hey," the man is saying, now. "Hey, I'm talking to you."

I turn on my stool, swivel around to look at him, and I laugh. I laugh right in his face.

The woman moves in, puts herself between us.

"Stop it," she says to the man. "Just stop."

He won't stop, though. He doesn't want to stop. He has something to say, something he wants me to hear. He can't say it yet, though, because I'm still laughing. I'm laughing and laughing.

The bouncer comes over. He doesn't hurry. He holds up his hands, showing the palms. His fingers are loose, relaxed. "All right," he says, "let's cut it out."

"Him," the man says. He's pointing at me. "You tell him."

The bartender is watching us. He moves to the switch, turns on the lights, claps his hands.

"That's it," he says. "Drink up. It's time to go."

The bouncer stays close. He leans against the bar. The man just stands there. He doesn't look at me, doesn't look at the woman. He looks at the bouncer, looks at the bar, looks at his shoes. The couple in the booth slide out, get their coats on, head for the door. The drunk starts sweeping up. I finish my beer and I go get my coat off the bench seat where I left it. When I come back the woman has a hand on the man's arm and is talking to him. I move farther down the bar and I wave the bartender over and I close out my tab. Then I go out. I'm not a dozen steps down the sidewalk, though, before the woman catches up with me. She takes my arm. The man is right behind her.

I turn around to face him, walk backwards as I say, "What? Do something, then. Do something."

He doesn't do anything, but he doesn't stop either. He keeps following us. He looks from me to the woman. His eyes are red, puffy, slitted, angry. The woman pulls me to a car. She unlocks the door, puts me inside. Then she goes back to the man. I watch them in the sideview, watch her say something and him say something back. Then she comes back. The man just stands there. The woman opens the door and gets in, turns the key and starts the engine.

"Sorry," she says.

I shrug. The world outside starts to move. The falling snow slants past us. The man's reflection gets smaller and smaller. I lean my head against the window. The cold glass feels good against my skin. I close my eyes and I drift off. I come awake in the parking lot, come awake to her shutting off the engine. We get out and go inside. Her building is old and too hot from the radiators and the whole place smells like old carpet and everyone else's dinner. Inside the apartment there's a girl asleep on the couch and the woman gives her some money and she leaves. We go down the hall and past a couple of closed doors to the bedroom. The woman takes off her coat, takes off her shirt, puts her arms around my neck. With her cheek to my cheek and her mouth close to my ear she says something I don't understand, something that doesn't make any sense, until I realize that she's making a joke, making a reference to this bit that we do on the show, letting me know that she knows. She kisses me and she makes the joke again, then again and again until I stop her, until I tell her that I got it the first time. Her bedsheets smell like Febreze and her bed is too soft and at some point in the night she steals most of the covers so that even with the loud-ass hissing radiator I wake up in the morning cold, shivering, with my head throbbing and my stomach sick and my mouth tasting like stale cigarettes and shitty beer and shots I don't quite remember doing.

The woman isn't there. I dig around for my pants, hunt down my shirt and my coat, get dressed. I go out and back down the hall and she's there in the kitchen. She's pouring cereal into bowls and there are two kids sitting at the counter and when I walk in everyone turns and looks at me.

"Oh, fuck," I say. Then I say, "I mean, shit. I mean, sorry."

The kids look back at their cereal. The woman shakes her head, clears her throat.

"It's fine," she says.

One of the kids, the smaller one, the girl, looks at me again and frowns. "Who are you?" she says.

"This is Dex," the woman says. "He's on the radio."

"Why is he here?" the girl says. She's talking to her mother but her eyes are on me.

The woman looks at me. I point to the door.

"I'm going to get going," I say.

The woman frowns, shakes her head again. "It's okay," she says. "Let me get these guys off to school and I'll drive you."

I'm already across the room, though, already working the deadbolt and opening the door. I turn to look at her, turn to wave.

They're all looking at me, now, her and both kids.

"It's fine," I say. "I'm good. I'll see you. Take care," and then I go out and I pull the door closed behind me.

I GO downstairs, go outside, try to get oriented. I go down the street until I can read the signs on the corner. And it's funny. I could be almost anywhere, really, but I'm only a few blocks from the station. It would literally take longer to wait for an Uber than to just walk over. So that's what I do. I figure I can get Kyle or somebody to give me a ride back to my car. Denise looks confused when I get off the elevator but I don't stop to explain what I'm doing there. I go past her, past reception, through the doorway and down the hall. I don't make it very far, though. Around the first corner I get stuck behind a whole line of people coming out of the common room. They're all sweaty and red-faced and they're all decked out in get-fit gear, yoga pants and shorts and teeshirts. I have to stand there and wait for them all to pass. There're a fucking million of them, different techs and producers and people from accounting and ad sales all moving slow, all relaxed, all talking and laughing together. Finally they're all out. The last in line, this girl I don't know, turns to close the door and she sees me standing there and she shrugs and shakes her head.

"Sorry," she says. "You're too late. It's over. You missed it."

And maybe it's just that I didn't sleep very much or maybe it's the hangover, or maybe I'm still part-of-the-way drunk or it's something else, but for whatever reason for one second I completely forget how shitty I feel, forget about being annoyed by the people taking forever to get out of the hallway, forget about looking for Kyle and getting back to my car. I forget about the woman making the same joke over and over, about the way her kids looked at me, about the party and the sheet cake with the tombstone dates. For one second, looking at her, I forget everything. I forget my own stupid name.

"Shit," I say, "I am?" I say, "Late for what?"

HER CLASS, apparently. I don't know anything about it, but it turns out there's some new health and wellness program that the owners started up for the new year, some new deal with the station's insurance provider, some better rate for companies that encourage their employees to be more fit and active, some new way for the station to save money, and there are all of these different programs and incentives that go along with it. Like there's a weight-loss contest and a four-week juice cleanse group, and special deals for us at a bunch of healthier-choice restaurants around town, and a special cheap membership option for us at the 24-hour gym down the street, and—as it relates to what's happening here—a deal with one of the local yoga studios for a staff instructor to come in and lead a basics yoga and meditation class in the common room a couple mornings a week.

Like I said, it's all news to me. I skipped the meeting where they announced the program and I don't really read most of the mass emails that management sends out and I don't keep social media contact with the station or with anybody who works at the station. Standing there in the hallway I have no idea what's going on, no idea what I'm too late for, no idea what she's talking about.

She looks me over, shakes her head again. "And here you are," she says, "all ready to go. What happened? Did your alarm not go off? I hate that. That's the worst."

She's giving me a hard time, feeding me a setup, but my brain isn't working. It's spinning its tires, running sludge through its gears. I nod, open my mouth, but all that comes out is, "Yeah, no, totally, yeah."

She nods. She pushes some sweat-stuck strands of hair back from her forehead.

"Well, okay," she says, "Heidi is back on Thursday, and then it might be Heidi or it might be me covering again on Tuesday, but either way somebody will be here. So you can try again then."

I'm still nodding. My brain feels loose in my skull, feels like it's sloshing back and forth, hitting bone. "Sure," I say. "Yeah, okay."

"Okay," she says. "Maybe I'll see you Tuesday, then."

"Sure," I say, "maybe Tuesday."

"Okay," she says. She turns to go.

"Wait," I say.

She stops, turns back. She looks at me.

"You're done?" I say. "I mean, you're done with what you were doing? You're leaving now?"

She nods, frowns. "I was," she says. "I am."

"Great," I say. "Do you think you could give me a ride?"

THAT'S BETHANY. That's how we meet. One random thing chases another random thing chases another random thing chases me into the station at a time I'm never there, a time I never would be there, not ever, not for any reason. And she's there covering for Heidi and she's coming out into the hall as I'm coming through and I ask her for a ride and she thinks it's funny. She asks me where I need to go, tells me that she's headed that way. We go out, go past Denise, ride the elevator down. Her car is parked one street over. I tell her we can shortcut through the parking garage down the block, but when we get there there's a police car blocking the entrance and a cop leaning against the hood. He holds up a hand and shakes his head as we walk up.

"Sorry," he says, "I can't let you in."

"We're not parked here," I say, "we're just cutting through."

He shakes his head some more. "I can't let you cut through, either," he says. "You've got to go around."

"Why?" Bethany wants to know. "What's happening?"

The cop shrugs. "Suspicious vehicle," he says. "Somebody saw something and said something. It should be cleared pretty soon, but you know how it is. These days you can't be too careful."

Bethany is watching him, nodding. "No," she says. "Absolutely. You can't be too careful."

We go around, find her car. She has to move stuff off the seat before I can get in, some clothes and some shoes and a bag. She throws it all in the back. We get in and she starts the engine and we drive around, past where the cop's still standing.

"Wow," she says. "That's kind of scary."

"It's probably nothing," I say.

"I know," she says, "but I mean, just the thought that it could be something."

"Yeah," I say, "but it's not. There's like a ninety-nine point nine percent chance that it's not. No terrorist is looking at Cleveland and saying, Oh, yeah, there it is. That's the target. The whole point for those guys is to do something in a place where people actually give a shit about what happens there."

She laughs. "That's terrible," she says.

"It's true," I say. "Trust me. I'm an expert on how little anything that happens here matters."

IT'S TEN minutes to the bar, and I talk the whole way. I just don't shut up. I don't even know what the fuck I'm saying, after a certain point. It's like being on-air, like a reflex. She thinks it's funny, though. Or at least it seems like she does. She acts like she does. She laughs at the nonsense coming out of my face. So I just keep going. When we get to my car I ask if I can buy her breakfast somewhere, just to say thanks for the ride, but she shakes her head. She can't, she says. She's got another class to teach at ten, back at the studio. She says she'll take a raincheck, though. She asks for my phone and she puts in her number and she calls herself and she hands my phone back.

"There," she says, "now I'll know it's you."

I get out and I stand there by my car in the inch-deep film of slush that covers the parking lot as she drives away. Then I open my door and I get in. The windshield is completely iced over, and not just on the outside. There's a film of frost covering the entire inside surface. I go at it with the Drug Mart loyalty card I had sitting in the cup holder. It flakes off all over the dashboard, where it melts.

IT'S CLEVER. It's a good move. You call yourself from their phone and they think they're getting your number, when the reality is that it's so later you know it's them calling and you can not answer. You can even block their number right from the start. You can make it so you never have to deal with them at all, ever again.

Or at least this is what I think. This is what I tell myself, what I project. That she doesn't want me to call her. That she gave me her number for the same reason she gave me a ride: because she's a nice person and I put her on the spot like the asshole that I am. That I should just forget about it, just move on.

The thing is, though, I kind of can't forget about it. I kind of can't move on. I keep wondering. For two days, three days, four days, a week I'm hung up, distracted. I'm up in my head, off somewhere else. I forget callers' names, forget what we're talking about, flub ad copy, miss hour breaks. I'm thinking about her, about her number in my phone, about what I would say if I called. It's ridiculous. It's laughable, really. It's like being fucking fifteen again. I know it's ridiculous. But it doesn't change the fact. The thing is, all of the women I've dated in the past seven or eight years have all been the same woman, basically. We'd get together and they'd complain about the same things. This one's boss is an idiot, this one has to go to court over some unpaid parking tickets, this one's kid needs braces. This one's ex is shorting child support by having his boss pay him overtime under the table. Being with them is the same as being by myself. It's just more of the same grey, Cleveland bullshit. Not like her. Not like those twenty minutes with her. Which sounds absurd. I know it sounds absurd. I don't even know her, don't know anything about her. But it doesn't make any difference. Realizing that doesn't make any difference.

It's all making me half crazy, is the point. Going around like this is making me nuts. So I call her. Finally I just call her. I tell myself that it's not really even about seeing her: that it's about getting to something definitive, about playing it all the way out to the end so I can stop wondering. That's how I get myself to actually press the buttons. I'm really not even expecting her to answer—I'm ninety-nine percent sure she's not going to—but she does. And I'm basically too surprised to say anything stupid. I'm too surprised to say anything obnoxious. I ask her if she wants to have dinner with me and she says yes.

WE MAKE the date, get together, go out. We go to this Thai place she wants to try and we eat and we talk. She tells me about herself. She's twenty-four, she's the youngest of three, she was raised in the suburbs outside Pittsburgh. Her father runs a consulting firm, her mother volunteers, her brother and sister are both much older.

"I was a late arrival," she says. "Which was great for me. Like I totally recognize how great it was. My parents were kind of done parenting, by the time I came along. I was eight when my brother graduated from high school, and by then it was just over. I got away with everything. It pissed my brother and sister off so bad."

Her brother's an executive for a brokerage firm in Boston, now, married with two kids. Her sister's a corporate lawyer in Paris.

"Wow," I say, "Paris."

"I know," she says. "She's always telling me to come visit, and I still haven't made it happen. It's embarrassing. But I'm going to. It's the number one thing on my list. Mark my words, I will see Paris before I die."

She's been in town for less than a year. Before that she was in Chicago with her college boyfriend. They moved there right after graduation. He had a job waiting for him at his family's company and the company made it easy, paid all of their moving costs and part of their rent. It paid for their shared gym membership, even.

"It was kind of crazy," she says. "It was like being on one of those rides, you know? Like all I had to do was keep my arms and legs inside the vehicle."

They talked about getting married, about looking for a house. It all just seemed like the next thing. Their friends—the new ones in Chicago and the old ones from college—were getting engaged and making down payments. And it made sense. They'd been together for a long time, been living together for a long time. They got along with each other's families, their families got along with each other. Still, somehow it kept not happening.

"It never felt like it wasn't going to happen," she says. "But it also never felt like, Okay, now. Let's go. This is what we want to do. This is the next thing. We can't do anything else until we do this."

It got to be a joke, almost. They couldn't meet up for drinks without somebody making a comment. Was he worried she was going to say no? Even his parents gave him a hard time.

"So finally we sat down and we were like, Okay, we need to just do it," she says. "We went to the jewelers and we picked out a ring and then we went out to dinner and he proposed. It was funny. Everyone around us thought it was this big, romantic surprise, and here we both knew it was coming. It felt like we were playing a trick on the restaurant to get free champagne."

At first it seemed fine, she says. It didn't seem like anything. But a month later she called it off.

"It was weird," she says. "There was no real moment. I mean there wasn't a moment where he did something or where he said something or where we had a big fight, or anything. It was like I just sort of slowly realized that everyone around us was way more excited about this thing than I was. Like we would go out for drinks or we'd go hang out with our friends and these girls would all want to talk to me about all of this stuff, and I kind of didn't care. Or, it wasn't that I didn't care. But it was like how I felt about us getting engaged in the first place. It was like, Okay, sure, fine. But after we did it and I saw how excited everybody else was I started feeling like, Wait, maybe this isn't how this is supposed to feel. Maybe I should really, really want to do this, if I'm going to do this. Maybe it shouldn't just be the thing that happens because it feels like the next thing. And then I started noticing how all of these other couples were all sort of laying the groundwork for becoming these people and for living this life that I was never really all that interested in. Like where you get married and you buy a house and you move out of the city and you have some kids, and then your life becomes about raising these kids and keeping the house nice and making sure the landscaping looks good, and then the kids grow up and the kids graduate and they go off to college and they go off and get jobs and you take some trips and you volunteer and you play tennis or whatever, and that's it. That's your life. And I started thinking about these couples who lived on our street back when I was growing up, and I started realizing that they were probably only a few years older than I am now. All these couples who seemed so established and so set, where you just knew that you could leave and come back ten or fifteen years later and they'd be exactly the same. Same house, same job, same friends, same hobbies, same opinions, same everything. Like they're there right now, and they're exactly like they were back when I was ten." She stops, holds up her hands. "And I know," she says. "I know how that sounds. I know that sounds really shitty and judgmental, and that's really not how I mean it. That's not what I'm saying. What I'm saying is that if you're going to do that, if you're going to make that life, then you should be really excited to make that life. Those things should be the things that you can't wait to do. Like all those friends we had back in Chicago? Super excited about that life. My brother and his wife? Totally living the life they want. And I think that's great. I'm really happy for them. For me, it just wasn't what I really wanted to do. It's not where I was at." She frowns, chews her food, shakes her head.

"The really messed-up thing," she says, "is that, if we hadn't gotten engaged, we'd probably still be together. Like realistically I feel like there's a really good chance that we would still be together. Or if we got engaged and then we got married right away. If we just went to the courthouse and did it. And it's crazy because once we split up it was like, Oh, right. No way. Like once I stepped back it was obvious. It was obvious that it wasn't the right thing. I could sort of see it at the time, but I couldn't really see it until I got all the way out of it. Then it was like, Of course." She looks down, shrugs. "And I feel bad," she says, "because it wasn't even him. It wasn't like he did anything wrong. It wasn't his fault. He's a really great guy. He's a genuinely decent person. He didn't deserve what happened. And he was totally blindsided. I mean, he was one of those people who was way more excited about it than I was. Once we got engaged he started really getting excited about everything. So it wasn't fair to him. But." She shakes her head again, looks at me. "I don't know," she says. "Maybe that sounds crazy. Does that sound crazy?"

"Which part?" I say.

She shrugs again. "The part where I blew up my whole life and pissed off everybody I knew based on what was probably a pretty unfair estimation of what most people's lives are like," she says.

I laugh. "I don't know," I say. "I don't think so. I think you're probably right. I think that's the way it goes, for a lot of people. A lot of people start off with one idea about what their life is going to be and then they sort of drift into something else and the next thing they know ten years have gone by. It's like all of a sudden they're this whole other person. And you don't know whether that's just the way things go or whether you're supposed to actually do something about it. You don't know whether, if you did something, it would make any difference. If anything would actually change or if you'd still be you in a different outfit with a different haircut, or something. So, no, I think you were right."

She's nodding, now. "Exactly," she says. "That's it. That's exactly it. You drift. Because the thing is, back before college, back before I met Andrew, I had all these ideas about what my life was going to be like. I literally had journals with actual checklists of things I was going to do before I turned thirty. And not just like, Go to South Africa or Go backpacking in Peru, or whatever. Things like, Fall in love. Have your heart broken. Get stranded in a foreign country. Experience God." She laughs. "I know," she says. "I really did, though. I'm totally serious. I can show you. All that stuff is somewhere in my parents' basement, still. But then I went off to college and I met Andrew and I started hanging out with these people and it was like I sort of let them all convince me that all of that was kind of stupid. I mean, I didn't tell them about it. It wasn't like I told them about it and they were mean, or anything. It was just their attitude. It was their whole deal. Like the future they saw for themselves, that version of life, was real life. That was what real adult people did. And I think I just sort of let myself get carried along with it. I think I sort of let myself get convinced that they knew something I didn't know about how I was supposed to be."

"So," I say, "that's how you ended up here?"

She nods. "Pretty much," she says. "I didn't have any real reason to stay in Chicago and I figured I'd just keep running into people if I stuck around. I was thinking about going out to Portland or I was maybe going to move back home, and then I kind of randomly found this job in Hudson and so I split the difference and I came here." She shrugs. "I guess I didn't really split the difference," she says. "I don't know. It just seemed easy. It seemed easier than moving out west and it seemed better than actually living at home. I didn't want to just move back home and I didn't feel like there was any reason to be in Pittsburgh if I wasn't living at home. So, Cleveland. I figured I'd give it a year and see what happened."

"And so?" I say. "How's it been?"

She frowns, nods, shrugs again. "It's been all right," she says. "I mean, it wasn't great in the beginning. But it got better. One thing was I'd never moved anywhere on my own, so there was a lot of practical stuff that I hadn't thought of that I had to figure out, and that kept me pretty busy for a while. It was a good distraction." She laughs. "It's kind of funny," she says. "I had this little thing I kept repeating to myself, in the beginning. Anytime I felt like I'd made a huge mistake I would just tell myself that I'd done a great job and I'd done exactly the right thing and I'd made exactly the right choice. I would have these moments where I felt like, if I stopped saying it, I was going to suddenly realize that I'd made this colossal mistake. Like a hole was just going to open up under my feet and swallow me. Anyway, the point is, one of the ways I knew things were getting better was that one day I realized I wasn't doing it as much."

Even still, she says, it wasn't easy. Her parents weren't much help, either. They couldn't understand what her problem was. They thought she'd lost her mind. Her mom actually tried to get her to see someone, offered to pay for it. Which wasn't really a surprise. Her mom really loved Andrew. It was the same with her brother. Her brother thought she was crazy. Her sister was more under-standing. She talked to her sister a lot, in those first couple of months.

She looks down at her plate. "Like I said," she says, "eventually it got better. It got easier. I kind of made myself go out and get involved in stuff. I went to a couple different churches. I checked out a bunch of the MetroParks. I joined a running club. I joined this adult kickball league with some people from this bar near my apartment. I started doing a lot of yoga. And then I did the yoga teacher training, and then I started teaching some classes, and then Heidi asked me to cover that class at the station on Tuesday, and now we're here." She laughs, shrugs again. "That's it," she says. "That's me." Then, her expression changes. She frowns, looks down at her plate. She looks up at me through her eyebrows. "There's something else I should probably tell you," she says.

I frown, but I'm kind of laughing, too. "Oh no," I say. "What is it?"

"Back when I first got here," she says, "back before I quit that job in Hudson, for those first few months, I listened to your show *a lot.*"

I'm pretty surprised. It just isn't what I was expecting. I'm not sure what I was expecting, exactly, but it wasn't that. "Wait," I say. "Seriously?"

She sips her wine, nods, shrugs again. "Yeah," she says. "The thing is, I kind of decided where I wanted to live based on proximity to things I thought seemed kind of fun and interesting, and not on what was close to where I was working, so I had this massive commute. So every day until I bailed on that job you had at least one very dedicated listener making her way north on 271." Then she laughs, because I'm pulling my hands over my face. "What?" she says. "What's the problem?"

"Nothing," I say, "but you could have told me."

She's still laughing. "I could have told you?" she says. "Why? Are you embarrassed? Are you embarrassed that I've heard your show?"

"I'm not embarrassed," I say. "But if I'd known you were the kind of person who listens to my show I would have thought twice before I asked you out."

She laughs at that, too. "Oh, really?" she says. "What's wrong with the people who listen to your show?"

"Nothing," I say. "The people who listen to my show are fine. They're great. I love my audience."

She frowns. She's still laughing, though. She holds up a hand. "Hang on," she says. "A lot of people listen to your show. It's not just me. It's a lot of people."

"Yeah," I say, "a lot of people in Cleveland."

"Come on," she says. "It's a good show. People like it. Do you think people would like it if it wasn't good? It's a good show."

I look at her and I shake my head. "No," I say. "No, it's not. Thank you, but it's not."

"Well, I like it," she says. "I think it's good. How about that? Doesn't my opinion count for anything?"

I keep looking at her as I nod. "Sure," I say. "It counts. It counts for plenty. It counts a lot."

She narrows her eyes at me. "Right," she says. "Okay. No, it really sounds like you mean that. That sounded really heartfelt."

"Fine," I say. "Tell me what you like about it, then. What do you like about it?"

She shrugs. "I don't know," she says. "Can't I like it? Am I not supposed to like it? Am I not bitter and jaded enough to like it?"

"Wow," I say. "Okay."

She's laughing again. "Come on," she says. "It's just funny. You're funny. You guys are funny. The little back-and-forth you do. You're cute together. It's kind of comforting."

"It's comforting," I say.

"It's comforting," she says. "It reminds me of when I was a kid and my brother would be home from college and my parents would make him babysit me and drive me around and stuff. I'd end up hanging out with him and his friends and they were all so cool and in-the-know and over it. It's kind of like that." She shrugs again, holds up her hands. "I don't know," she says. "As someone who was new in town and who had no friends and who was working in an office with a bunch of people she could not connect with on any level, it was nice to just have that time on my drive home. It was nice knowing that your show was going to be there when I got in my car at the end of the day." She sits back. "So, that," she say. "That's why I like it. Is that okay? Is that a good enough reason?"

"Wow," I say. "Okay, sure. Yes. When you put it like that, yes."

Neither of us says anything after that. Neither of us says anything for maybe a minute. I don't know what to say. I really do feel kind of embarrassed that she's heard the show. Everything we've done seems so stupid, now. I don't know why. It's never mattered before. I feel like I want to explain how it is. I feel like I want to explain how you start out and you do one thing and nobody gives a shit, and then you do something else and people respond to it, and pretty soon you're doing that thing twenty times a day, every day. And then you keep doing that with different things, you keep trying different things, until a decade on you look at what you're doing and you don't even know what it is anymore. You look in the mirror and you hardly recognize yourself. You're talking like somebody else and you're thinking like somebody else, making somebody else's jokes with somebody else's attitude. And everyone expects you to be this guy, now. The audience and the owners and the sponsors all want you to keep being this guy. And what are you, then? Not a person, exactly. You're a creature, a creation. You're everybody's creation.

"So," I say, "do you still talk to your ex?"

She frowns, looks down at her plate, shakes her head. In the beginning there were some late night drunk phone calls, she says, some social media stalking, but she made herself stop all of that.

"It wasn't fair," she says. "It wasn't fair to either of us. I mean, he was a big part of my life. He's someone I care about and he's someone I'd like to be on good terms with, maybe not now but someday, and I felt like that definitely wasn't going to happen if I kept doing what I was doing. I was going to ruin any chance of that, doing what I was doing." She shrugs. "It's funny," she says. "My mom still thinks we're going to get back together. Every time I talk to her she asks me if I've talked to him. She's got this tone, like she knows something I don't know. Like she knows it's coming. I don't know what it's going to take to convince her." Then she stops. She looks at me, frowns. "Oh God," she says. "You don't really want to hear all of this, do you? You don't want to hear all of this. You don't want to hear about my ex." She laughs. "You tell me something," she says. "Tell me about one of your exes, so we're even."

I shake my head. "You don't want to hear about my exes," I say.

She nods. "Okay, then," she says. "Tell me something else. Tell me something terrible. Make me sorry I said yes to this."

I look at her. I think about the things I could say, the things I could tell her. I raise my glass. "Don't worry," I say. "Hang out with me long enough, and sooner or later you will be."

I DRIVE her back to her building. She tells me she had a good time. She leans across the center console and we kiss and then she gets out and I wait while she goes inside. Then I go home and I drink a couple more beers on the couch and I fall asleep watching some movie I've seen at least ten times before. I'm not really watching it, not really paying attention. I'm thinking about her, about what she said, about what I said.

I call her a few days later. We meet up, get a coffee at Presti's, walk around Little Italy. She tells me about the class she's teaching, about the book she's reading, about the meditation retreat she's thinking about going on. We walk around for almost an hour. Then I have to go to work. I tell her I'll call her later. We kiss by the car and then she stands and waves as I drive away.

I call her after the show. We make plans and we go out again. We go out again after that, and again after that. We go to some restaurants and we go to some movies and we use station comp tickets to go to some shows. I go and I wait with her while she gets her car worked on. She comes to Target with me and she helps me pick out a new rug for my entryway. She comes over and cooks dinner, tries out recipes for stuff I've never heard of, uses cookware I forgot I even owned. When she sleeps over she sleeps in my favorite Misfits teeshirt, sleeps facing away from me but with one hand reaching back to rest against my hand or my wrist or my forearm or my hip. In the morning she goes out into the living room and she does yoga in the lit rectangle where the sun comes in through the sliding glass doors off the patio while I make coffee. I lay in the filter and I scoop in the grounds and I pour in the water and I listen to the little sounds her hands and feet make on the carpet, the little sounds her breath makes, as she shifts and moves.

WE SIT on the couch, drink the coffee, eat cereal, watch TV, until it's time for her to leave.

"I'll call you later," I say.

"I may be busy," she says.

"I'll leave a message," I say.

We're standing in the entryway, now. She's dressed, got her coat on. She's got her arms around my neck. She shakes her head.

"I may be too busy to listen to your message," she says.

"Wow," I say, "you're really busy."

"I am," she says. "You're lucky I find any time for you at all." She moves in to kiss me, then stops. "You could always come with me," she says. "Then you wouldn't have to call me. I'd be right there."

This is her new thing. For the past couple of weeks she's been making these comments, pushing me. She wants me to come to a class, wants me to see what she does, wants me to see where she works, wants me to meet her friends. And she thinks it would be good for me, too, thinks I might feel better if I had a regular practice, even one day a week.

I just can't see it. It's not my thing. It's about as far from my thing as anything I can think of. I shake my head. "We've talked about this," I say.

She shrugs. "So?" she says. "We can talk about it some more. We talked about it then and we're talking about it now."

"Okay," I say, "so take what I said then and apply it to now."

She groans, sags on her arms. "Just tell me why," she says. "Tell me why you don't want to go. Give me one good reason."

"I've told you," I say. "It's not my thing. It's your thing and that's great, but it's not my thing."

She's already back up, though, already talking again. "Okay, yeah," she's saying, "but the thing is that you don't know that it's not your thing because you've never done it. You don't know that it's not your thing because you don't even know what it is."

"I don't have to do it to know that it's not my thing," I say.

"No?" she says. "You don't? Why not? How do you know?"

"Because I know," I say. "I know because I know. I don't need to get thrown out of an airplane to know that that's not my thing, either. I don't need that. Just like you know that yoga is your thing and golf or racquetball or boxing or whatever isn't."

She shakes her head. "I don't know that," she says. "Maybe those things are my thing. I can't say that they're not my thing. Maybe I would be super into golf. Maybe golf is my thing."

This isn't going anywhere. "Come on," I say. "Wouldn't it be weird? I mean wouldn't it be kind of weird, having me in your class?"

She frowns. "I don't think so," she says. "Why would it be weird? I don't think it would be weird at all. I think it would be great."

"I'll think about it," I say.

She gives me her most pained look. "Come on," she says. "Just one class. Come to one class, and I promise I'll never bother you about it ever again."

I can imagine this going on and on, imagine us doing this for weeks, imagine us doing this until she gets pissed, until she stops bringing it up but it's still there all the time, unsaid in the background. With other women at other times in my life it's the sort of thing I would have used to let them know where we stood, to let them know exactly where this thing with me stopped.

"So I come to one class," I say, "and that's it? We don't talk about it ever again?"

She nods. "Promise," she says. "Cross my heart."

"And there's no chance that you're going to take me at my word and believe me when I tell you that this isn't my thing and just let this go," I say.

She shakes her head. "Never," she says.

I sigh, shrug. "Okay, then," I say. "Fine. Sure. One class."

She grins. "Really?" she says. "Seriously?"

"Yes," I say. "Fine. Yes. Let's do it."

She's still grinning. "Now?" she says.

I shrug again. "Sure," I say. "Now or whenever."

She kisses me, lets go. She goes down the hall and she starts putting on her shoes. She doesn't untie them first, doesn't open them up. She works in her toe, mashes in her heel. She leans against the wall, digs with her finger at the place where the heel got folded under, digs until the flap comes free. She looks back at me. She's still grinning. "It's going to be great," she says. "You're going to love it. I promise. You'll see."

I FOLLOW her to the studio. We park and I wait by her car while she gets her stuff together. Then we go inside. Bethany introduces me to the woman at the front desk and the woman at the front desk shakes my hand and says it's nice to finally meet me. She says she's heard a lot about me. She gives me a form to fill out and a waiver to sign. While I'm doing that Bethany digs around and finds a mat for me to use. She shows me where I can leave my shoes and my coat. I take off my shoes and my coat and my socks and I stuff them into one of the empty cubbies and then Bethany opens the door and we go into the space.

The space has its own energy. The lights are low and there's some sort of ethereal music playing over the sound system, something tonal and arrhythmic. The ten or twelve people already inside are all sitting quietly, all waiting. Bethany whispers that I can set up anywhere there's room and then she leaves me there. She goes up to the front, welcomes everyone, thanks us all for coming. Then she starts the class.

I find a spot and I roll out my mat and I try to follow along, try to do what the people around me are doing, but it doesn't go very well. I have no idea what I'm doing, no idea what any of the poses are, and on top of that I'm in pretty bad shape. I haven't done anything more physically demanding than moving a microphone or lifting a beer in probably eight years. Five minutes in I'm panting, shaking, pouring sweat. I can feel my heartbeat running up the sides of my neck and into my jaw, feel it throbbing behind my eyes. By the time that part of the class ends and she brings us down into the meditation I'm wrecked. I'm too tired to move, too tired to think. I lay there on the mat in my pooling sweat feeling empty, feeling hollowed out, feeling blasted down to almost nothing. Feeling like Dex and all of his shit are something separate from me, something I'll get back to later or put back on when I walk outside, like a coat or a sweatshirt.

Then that's it. She guides us through the meditation, directs us to center ourselves in the breath, and then she brings us to sitting and she thanks us for coming. She puts her palms together in front of her heart and she bows to us. Everyone else does the same thing back and I do it, too, and then it's over. People gather up their stuff and they head for the door. Bethany follows the last of them and then she comes over to where I'm still sitting and she kneels down. She pushes some sweat-stuck strands of hair back from her forehead and she looks at me. Her face is flushed, glowing, happy.

"So," she says, "what'd you think?"

I GO back. I wake up the next morning feeling like somebody pushed me out of a moving car, like I fell down a flight of stairs, but I go back anyway. I go back again and again. Pretty soon I'm at the studio at least three days a week. I'll even go to someone else's class, if I can't make it to one of hers.

It's funny, I guess. I mean I must look ridiculous, in there with all the yoga hipsters and the old yoga hippies and the housewives, panting and sweating and shaking while they all center themselves and open their chakras and achieve Zen, or whatever. I know I must look like a complete idiot. But the thing is, I kind of don't care. Being exhausted like that is like somebody hitting the mute button on all the noise inside my head. For the time I'm in class and the hour or so afterwards I feel like a different person, almost. Outside of playing music I'm the closest to at peace that I can ever remember being.

Bethany and the other instructors, they all tell me the same things. They all say I'm keeping too much tension, that I need to relax. They tell me that I shouldn't fight the positions, that I should try to learn how to work with them. I nod and agree, tell them that I'm working on it, but the reality is that I'm not. The reality is that I don't actually want it to feel easier or better. I want it to feel like I'm doing something my body hates, something it can't possibly sustain. I want my breath to go all hot and dry and worthless, want my blood to turn acidic and burn in my veins. Somewhere past all of that is the calm center, the place where Dex and all of his stupid bullshit fade down to a whisper. Where there are no regrets or missed chances, no bad history. The place where I'm barely there, where I'm almost gone.

"Don't fight it," they tell me. "Work with it. Just breathe."

I nod. I unclench my gritted teeth, fill my useless lungs. "I know," I say. "I am. I will."

THAT'S HOW it is, all through the slushy ass-end of winter and the slushy beginning of what it feels like is never going to turn into actual, real, full spring. We hang out, run around, stay in and binge shows, and three days a week I'm there in class. And she's right: I do feel better. And it's not just in the ways you'd expect, either. It's not just that I'm sleeping better or that I have more energy or that my body feels better. It's stuff like the fact that I'm not getting as worked up about things, not getting totally emotionally derailed by random, meaningless bullshit. I don't go off on rants about how the world and society and people are dumb and fucked up every time some stupid little inconsequential thing happens. I don't make it the whole focus of our dinners out when the waiter or the bartender or some other diner does something that otherwise would have annoyed the living fuck out of me. I'm different on the show, too. I'm different in what I say about the news, different with callers. I let people have their say a little bit more. I'm more restrained with my responses. It's not just in my head, not just me who thinks this, either. Other people notice. Callers actually comment on it. A few people call in just to tell me that I sound like I'm in a good place, that they're glad for me, that whatever I'm doing I should keep it up. Guys at the station, Tommy and some of the other guys, give me shit about it. They want to know what happened to Dex, want to know who's the pussy-whipped replicant. And honestly, even that doesn't bother me. It doesn't bother me the way it would have before. I'm glad, almost. Part of me is glad that I seem different enough for people to notice. Part of me is glad that I seem like somebody else.

The point is that for the first time in what feels like a really, really long time I actually feel kind of good about things. It feels like things are all right, like things are just working. Then one night in mid-April Bethany comes over and it's obvious right from the second she walks in the door that she's got something on her mind, that there's something she's not telling me.

"What?" I say, finally. "What's up? What is it? What's your deal?"

She won't tell me, though. She shakes her head, says it's nothing. And it really freaks me out. She's never like this. It sets my head running. I think all kinds of things. I think about everything I said on the show that afternoon, about what she might have heard. I think about all the stuff she told me on our first date, all the stuff she said she wants to do with her life, all the stuff that's a million miles away from epicenter-of-fucking-nothing Cleveland. I think about her ex, even, about her mom being convinced that they'll get back together sooner or later, and from there I just go off. I think about all the yoga bros she's around all day at the studio, about all the people everywhere, all the people in the world that it would make a hell of a lot more sense for her to be with than me.

"Come on," I say. "Just say it. You're making me nuts."

She's chopping a carrot. She's making soup. She sets down the knife and she turns to me. She's got her mouth set in that way she does when she's upset or excited or nervous, the lips pulled in and pressed together in a crooked, indecipherable line. She crosses her arms and shrugs. "I talked to my mom today," she says. "It's my dad's birthday next week and she's planning this big surprise party for him and she wants me to come."

I laugh. I don't mean to, it just comes out. I'm just surprised. It's so far from anything I was thinking. "What?" I say. "I mean, okay. Great. Your mom's throwing a party for your dad. That's great."

She doesn't laugh. She cocks her head to the side and she looks at me. "It is," she says. "It's going to be really nice. Everybody's going to be there. My sister's going to fly in and my brother's driving in with his family and a bunch of my aunts and uncles are coming."

I'm nodding. "Okay," I say. "And so what's the problem? You don't want to go?"

She shakes her head. "No," she says, "it's not that. I do. I am. I'm going. I'm planning on going. I told her I'm coming."

"Okay," I say. "Great. Sounds good."

Then neither of us says anything. We just stand there, looking at each other. It feels like she's going to say something else, but then she doesn't. She shrugs.

"Okay," she says. "Fine. Never mind. Forget I said anything."

She turns back to the board, picks up the knife.

"Hang on," I say. "Wait. Come on. Come back. I don't get it."

She puts the knife down again, harder this time. She turns back to me. She's got her annoyed face on, now, the same face she gets when she talks about Heidi switching classes so she doesn't have to wake up early, about people who are going to the restaurant next door taking all of the studio's spots in the lot.

"What?" I say. "What's the issue? Just spit it out, already."

She leans in, speaks slowly. "My mom is throwing a surprise party for my dad," she says, "and she wants me to come, and I want to go, but I would really like it better if you came with me, but I don't know where we are when it comes to stuff like meeting each other's families, and so I don't want to ask you and make it weird if you don't want to go, but I can't find out whether it would make it weird until I ask you, so now I guess I'm asking you."

I'm surprised. I might be stunned, actually. Stunned might be the more accurate word. It's just so far from anything I was thinking. "You want me to come with you," I say.

"Yes," she says.

"You want your family to meet me," I say. "You want me to meet your family. You want us to meet each other."

She holds up her hands, the fingers spread, like, There it is. "I mean, is that a problem?" she says. "Is that all right? Is that weird? Is it too much? Because I don't know. You tell me. I don't know."

"I mean, no," I say. "No, it's not weird. It's not too much."

She lets her hands drop. She nods. "Well, okay," she says.

"No," I say again. "I mean, no, it's great. That sounds great. Yes. Let's do it. Let's go to the party."

She's still nodding. "Okay," she says. Her voice is flat, even, over-casual. She shrugs. "Great," she says. "Cool. Whatever."

"Great," I repeat. "Cool. Great."

She turns back to the cutting board. She finishes off the carrot she's been working on and she starts in on the bok choy. I leave her there and I go out into the living room. I post up on the couch, turn on the TV, flip around through the channels. I'm not even registering what I'm looking at, though, not even really trying to find anything. The last time I met somebody's parents it didn't go very well. I was maybe twenty-eight or twenty-nine and the girl was right around the same age and she had that thing where you could just tell that she felt like the dance was ending and she still hadn't found a partner. We went out to a pretty decent restaurant and her parents asked me a bunch of questions while the girl picked at her food and fidgeted and made little comments to try to make what I'd just said sound better than it actually did. Afterwards sitting in her car in the parking lot she started crying, started yelling at me, started asking me what the fuck was wrong with me.

"Why can't you just be pleasant?" she wanted to know. "You act like it's some sort of insult when people expect you to just be pleasant and normal and to just have a conversation like people do."

"What do you want?" I'd said. "You want me to just sit there and make chit-chat about, Oh, yeah, wow, the fucking Browns aren't doing very well this year. The fucking Cavs. Boy, that construction on 480."

She looked at me, her whole face and body and being and energy somehow focused down to the knotted furrow between her eyebrows. "What the fuck are you saying?" she said. "Yes, that's what I want. Yes, normal people do that. Normal people who aren't fucking assholes can do that when their girlfriends ask them to for the duration of one fucking dinner."

I opened the door and got out. "Fuck this," I said. "Fuck your parents. Fuck you." Then I slammed the door and walked away. I heard the car start, heard her tires on the asphalt as she backed out of the spot, and then the engine revved and got louder and she blasted past me, so close that I could feel the wind off her sideview mirror clip my elbow. I watched her taillights go across the parking lot, watched her turn out onto the road, watched her drive away, and that was the last time I ever spoke to her. She called once and left a message saying that she was going to throw away the stuff I'd left at her apartment, and that if I wanted it I could come and get it off the curb, but I didn't bother.

There's nothing on. The middles of some movies I've already seen or don't want to watch, sitcoms, college basketball, the news. The FBI has arrested six people in Minnesota and California in connection with what they say is a terrorism investigation; a telecomm millionaire won the election for prime minister in Finland; somebody had plans to attack a couple of churches in and around Paris, but fucked up and shot themselves in the leg before they could get going. In their apartment police found jihadi literature and more weapons and the plans for the attacks. Hillary Clinton is headed to New Hampshire; airfares are expected to drop this summer.

Bethany comes in, sits down, leans into me. I put my arm around her shoulders. She takes the remote. She goes into the TiVo, scrolls through the stuff she's recorded, puts on an episode of *Gray's Anatomy*. It starts up somewhere in the middle, where she left off last time. We sit like that until the soup's ready. We watch another episode while we eat. I eat too much, or maybe something in the soup doesn't agree with me, because later I can't sleep. I lay there awake, with my stomach knotting up and turning over on itself. It goes on like this all night. The next morning in class I'm only half-awake. I do the positions and I try to do the meditation but my mind keeps wandering. Afterwards Bethany asks if I want to go grab a coffee before her next class but I tell her I can't, that I slept like shit, that I think I need to go home and go back to bed before I do the show.

At home I still can't sleep. I stare at the ceiling for forty-five minutes before I finally give up. I get out of bed and I go in and I take a shower. Standing there under the water I try to just let my mind go blank, let my thoughts dissolve, let them wash off me into the tub and down the drain. I really try. And it kind of works, too. I can feel something inside me relaxing. It's not all the way there, but it's a lot better, by the time the water runs cold.

A FEW days later we go to the mall. It's Bethany's idea. I need some new clothes. The party is going to be kind of fancy, and I don't have anything nice. Or I do, actually, but it's all pretty old and none of it really fits me anymore. Between all of the yoga and the fact that I'm not drinking so much anymore and the fact that I'm eating a lot better since I'm eating with her so much of the time I've lost something like fifteen pounds, and everything I dig out of the closet and put on looks ridiculous. It all looks like somebody's hand-me-downs, like somebody else's stuff. So we go to the mall. We go to one of the big department stores and she stands in the dressing room with me while I try on the clothes she picks out. And it's strange. The stuff she picks out is all stuff that I never would have picked for myself, and standing there looking at my reflection in the big tri-angled dressing room mirror it's like I'm looking at somebody else. It's not that dramatic, maybe, but it's something along those lines. It's like that at first glance. You get used to yourself, get used to looking a certain way, and then you change a few things and suddenly it's all different. And maybe it shouldn't come as a surprise, but somehow it still is. I end up getting more than I need, a few shirts and a jacket and a vest and a couple pairs of pants and some shoes. I put it all on my card and then we go back to my house and she makes me try it all on again, has me make different outfits, do a fashion show, and a few days later we get all dressed up and we drive to Pittsburgh.

The party is at her parents' country club. They reserved the whole place. There are over a hundred people there. We sip white wine and eat hors d'oeuvres off little plates and we mingle. People are all smiles when they see Bethany. They want to know how she is, what she's doing now. They tell me how they've known her since she was just this big. They ask what I do, act impressed when I tell them. We shake hands, say it was nice to meet each other.

I meet her family, meet her parents and her brother and his wife and kids and her sister and some of her uncles and aunts. Her brother gives me a hard time about my outfit, her sister tells me she thinks I look nice. Her mom nods and smiles when she shakes my hand, nods and smiles at everything everybody says.

I imagine what they're all thinking, imagine them all thinking that I'm wrong for her, too old for her, imagine them all thinking about her ex and wishing that things had worked out differently and that he was here instead of me. I raise my glass to them, raise my glass to her dad. "Thanks for including me in this," I say. "Happy birthday."

Her dad shrugs, laughs. His face is flushed, happy. "At this point," he says, "what's one more year?"

Her brother says, "It's okay with me if we all want to stop counting." He's looking at me as he says it. Then he looks away. He points across the room to where his kids are running around, weaving their way between people and climbing under tables. "I just mean, it's crazy," he says. "With the kids and everything, it feels like it all keeps going faster and faster."

"I know," I say. "They just did this thing at the station, this surprise party because we've been doing the show there for ten years. I didn't even realize how long it had been. It was like, Whoah, wait, how did that happen? Like I got out of bed one morning and stepped through a black hole, or something."

Bethany has twined her fingers into mine. "Dex has the number one drive-time show in Cleveland," she says.

Everyone is looking at me, her brother and his wife and her sister and her parents and the aunt and uncle who were standing with them when we walked up.

"Wow," says her brother. "That's impressive. What's your secret?"

I shrug. "You know what they say," I say. "It's like everything else. Give the people what they want."

"Yeah?" her brother says. "And what is that? What do they want?"

I feel Bethany's fingers tighten on mine as I say, "You know. The same things they've always wanted. Bread and circuses. Stocks in the town square. Public executions."

IT FINALLY winds down. We help her brother and sister carry decorations and centerpieces and presents out to their mom and dad's car while their mom and dad sit at one of the tables, talking to the last few guests. Then it's all over. We say our goodbyes. Bethany hugs her parents, hugs her siblings. She wishes her dad a happy birthday. Everybody shakes my hand, tells me it was nice to meet me. Bethany's sister tells Bethany she's got to come visit, Bethany says she's going to make it happen. Then we go out. In the car Bethany leans across the center console and she kisses me on the cheek.

"What was that for?" I say.

She shrugs. "Just, you know," she says. "Thank you."

I shake my head. "Thank me for what?" I say.

She shrugs again. She nods back toward the building, toward the party that just was. "For this," she says. "For coming with me. I know it was a lot."

I shake my head again. "It was fine," I say. "It was no big deal."

She frowns. "It was, though," she says. "It was a big deal. It was a big deal to me."

I don't know what to say to that. I hold up my hands. I look at her. "I'm glad it was good," I say. "I'm happy that you're happy."

And I am, too. I really, actually, am.

She leans across and kisses me again, on the lips this time. Then she sits back. She stays turned in her seat, though, stays facing me. She's got this look on her face like there's something else she wants to say, something more. She keeps not saying it, though. We sit like that for what feels like a long time. Probably it's only twenty or thirty seconds, but it feels like longer. Then she yawns, and that sort of breaks it. She pulls her coat tight around her, shoulders down into the seat.

"Oh my God," she says. "Will you hate me forever if I fall asleep? I'm so beat."

I shake my head. "No," I say. "It's fine. I'm good."

She settles in and closes her eyes. I turn the key and I start the car. I pull out of the lot and down the drive, past the gate and out onto the empty road.

Out away from everything I have this feeling, this sense, of us: of us together, of us like something elemental, a concentrated point of energy moving in the big empty dark.

And I want to tell her things: want to tell her how sometimes we would drive all night from one gig to another, from one city to another. How we would finish our set and pack up our stuff and get right back on the road. How we would get the biggest coffees the gas station had and just power through. I want to tell her about how Logan could never do it, how he couldn't make himself stay awake, how the times he tried he was all over the road. I want to tell her about how Danny was okay for a little while, but then one time he fell asleep and we almost wrecked. He missed a curve and drove us off into the median, the van and the equipment trailer and everything. After that he wanted somebody to stay up with him and keep him company, but Paul and I figured that if you're going to do that then you might as well just be the one driving. After that it was always either me or Paul, when we had to drive all night.

I want to tell her all of this—I'm going to tell her all of this—but then I look over and she's already asleep. So I don't say anything. I watch the road. The pavement makes a hypnotic gray-black blur in the headlights' beam. The highway goes on and on. It's after one, getting closer to two, by the time we finally pull in. Getting out of the car and walking up to the house we're the only thing moving. The only sound is our shoes crunching on the trampled-down snow. Inside we leave the lights off as we get undressed and get into bed. Bethany tucks herself in against me, pulls the covers up.

"Goodnight," she says.

And then she says something else, something that gets muffled by the pillow and the blankets, something that I don't quite hear.

"What?" I say.

She doesn't answer me, though. She's already asleep again. Or at least she's pretending to be.

I lay there. I want to fall asleep but my thoughts keep jumping around. It's that thing where you're exhausted but at the same time your mind is wide awake, where you're weirdly alert, where your thinking is smooth and fast and operating with what seems like insight and precision but you know that it's all wrong, too: that in the morning you're going to look back and see that all of the insights you had and all of the conclusions you reached are nonsensical, ridiculous, absurd.

I expect it to go on like this, expect this to go on for hours, but then the next thing I know it's morning and she's kissing me good-bye, telling me she didn't set an alarm and she's going to be late, telling me she'll see me later, and she's running out the door.

I hear her car door close, hear the engine start and run, hear the sound get faint as she pulls down the driveway and out onto the road.

I lay there missing her. Or at least I wish she wasn't gone. I wish I'd tried to make her stay. We could have hung out, done nothing. We could have wasted the morning together. I get up and I go in and make the coffee. Standing there at the sink I remember some of what I was thinking while I was laying awake. It doesn't seem as absurd as I'd thought it would. Or at least it doesn't seem any more absurd than anything else. It doesn't seem any more absurd than the fact that I am who I am, now. I pour in the water, change the filter, scoop in the grounds. I flip the switch. Then I go back into the bedroom and I collect my new clothes from where I left them on the floor. I really do like them. I think about how I must have looked in them, how we must have looked together. I hang up the jacket, put everything else in the hamper. Then I go in and check my email. In with all the spam are maybe six or eight new messages from listeners letting me know about bits of pop culture gossip they're worried I may have missed. Some singer got busted for not paying her taxes, some movie star is breaking up with some other movie star. I make some notes, figure out what I'm going to say about all of it on the show. I really lean into it, really get snide and shitty. By the time I'm finished I'm not thinking about the party, about how we looked together, about what she said or didn't say when we got into bed, anymore.

THEN IT'S the end of May, and her lease is ending, and the renewal her landlord wants her to sign has her paying another seventy bucks a month.

"That's bullshit," I say.

"I know," she says.

"So what are you thinking?" I say.

She shakes her head. "I don't know," she says. "Seventy is kind of a lot for me right now. And I don't really love the apartment. It was just the first kind-of-okay place I found when I moved here."

"Sure," I say.

"But then," she says, "on the other hand, it's like, would moving even be worth it? Because what else am I going to find? Is there anything else decent that's in this area and that's available right now and that's going to be any cheaper?"

"Yeah," I say. "No, you're right."

She crosses her arms, shrugs. "I don't know," she says again. "One of the girls from the studio is trying to move out of her parents' house, and we talked about her maybe moving in and us being roommates, but I'm really not sure I want to do that. My apartment is technically a two bedroom, but it would be pretty tight with two people there. And I don't know that I really want to live with some-one who's a year out of college."

"Sure," I say. "Yeah, no, that's a whole thing."

"And," she says, "even if we did decide that we were going to be roommates, realistically we would probably want to try to find a big-ger place anyway, and then we'd be right back where we started. So it pretty much defeats the whole purpose."

"Right," I say. "Yeah, totally." Then I look around and I shrug and I say, "You could always just move in here."

I don't really think about it before I say it, I just say it. It kind of just comes out.

She's been pacing around. Now she stops and she looks at me. "Wait," she says. "What?" She cocks her head to the side. "You're not really suggesting that," she says. "I mean, right? Or are you really suggesting that?"

I kind of can't look at her, with the way she's looking at me. I look around again, look at the sink and the dishes drying in the rack and the refrigerator and the cupboards I still haven't updated and the linoleum I haven't updated either and I shrug and I say, "I mean, yes? Sure? Why not? You're over here all the time anyway."

It's true—she's sleeping over most nights and she's basically taken over a whole shelf in the bathroom and she already has clothes in the closet—but it's still not how I meant to say it. It's not how I meant for it to come out. I look at her and I shake my head.

"That's not what I mean," I say. "I don't mean. I just mean. You know what I mean."

She nods. She's watching me. "No," she says. "I mean, no, I get it. I get what you meant." Then she doesn't say anything for a minute. She looks around, looks back at me. "I mean, yeah," she says. "That could be, I mean, that would work. If that's, I mean, if that's what you want. If that's cool with you. If you're good with that."

I can feel heat running up my throat, up into my jaw, up the sides of my face. I try to make my voice relaxed, try to make it casual-sounding as I say, "No, totally. I'm totally good with it."

She thinks about it. Then she frowns. She looks at me and she shakes her head and she says, "I don't know. Wouldn't I be totally invading your space?"

I sort of laugh. "I mean, yeah," I say. "Yeah, but that's kind of the idea, isn't it? I mean, isn't that kind of the point?"

She's still looking at me, watching me. There's a smile tugging at the corners of her mouth. "I don't know," she says again. "I mean, I guess. I guess it's sort of the point."

"Well, okay," I say. "Okay, then."

Then neither of us says anything. We just stand there, looking at each other. Then she shrugs.

"Okay," she says. "I guess, I mean, yeah, okay. Let's do it. I'll move in. I'll move in here. With you."

I can feel my heartbeat running up the sides of my neck, feel it throbbing under my tongue and behind my eyes as I say, "Okay. Great. Okay."

She pushes herself up from where she's been leaning against the counter and she comes over and she hugs me. With her arms around my neck and her cheek pressed to mine she says, "Okay." Then she lets go. She steps back. "I'm going to go call my sister," she says.

She goes out into the living room, goes down the hall into the bedroom. I stand there in the kitchen. Then I go out into the living room and I stand there looking around at the walls, at the TV and the furniture. I can hear her talking, but from where I'm standing I can't make out any of what she's saying. Her voice is just a warm garble, rising and falling.

"Hey, Bethany?" I say. "I'm going to go call Dave. Dave's got a truck. I'm going to see if he'll let us borrow his truck. Maybe I can get one of the interns to help. I'll see if we can do it this weekend. If we get a few of us we can hammer it out."

Then I go do that. I don't wait for her to say something back. I'm not expecting her to. I didn't really say it loud enough for her to hear me. I don't know why I said it at all. I'm not thinking very clearly. My thoughts are all kind of swimming around. I cross the living room and I go down the opposite hall to the room where I have my stereo and my computer and my guitars and amps and everything. I go inside and I close the door and I lean back against it and I shut my eyes and try to breathe like we do in yoga, try to breathe in slow and hold it and breathe out slow and hold it. I try to do the visualization where you imagine that you're standing in the middle of an empty field, the one where you feel yourself floating on the surface of a calm mountain lake. It helps. After a minute I feel better. I push myself up and I get out my phone and I call Dave.

"Holy shit," Dave says, when I explain why I'm calling. "Dex motherfucking Foster. I never thought I'd live to see the day."

"It's not even like that," I say. "It's this thing with her landlord. Her lease is up and her landlord wants way more money."

"Oh," Dave says, "right. I see. I get it. You're moving in together because of her landlord. Because it's less money. Right. My mistake."

"Whatever," I say. "Fuck you."

He laughs. "Really," he says. "I think it's good. It's a sign of real personal growth. And it's good that now you'll have somebody there who's young and who can look after you when you fall and break your hip or throw your back out, or whatever."

"Wow," I say. "Thanks. Thanks for that."

"Seriously, though," he says, "I think it's great. I think it's going to be really good. I'm really happy for you. Honestly."

"Thanks," I say again.

"Now all you have to do is not fuck it up," he says.

I don't say anything back to that. I'm going to, but then I don't. I'm looking around at my stuff—at my '86 Strat and my '78 Tele and my Ovation American LX Custom Elite, at my Fender Hot Rod Deluxe and my Vox Pathfinder, at the bookcase behind the Salvation Army desk set where I've got my records and tapes and CDs, my rare imports and bootlegs, my signed copy of *Get in the Van* and my collection of back issues of *Slug and Lettuce* and *Black Market Magazine* and *HeartattaCk*, at the closet by the garage sale recliner where I've got boxes filled with old photos and xeroxed show fliers, with teeshirts and patches and pins from bands we played with or went to see, with demo tapes and dubs from studio recordings we never used, with LPs and EPs and other merch we didn't sell—and it's like I get hypnotized by it all, or something. I don't know how to describe it. It's like it all sort of blends together, or something. It changes in my mind from being a bunch of separate things to being one thing, one whole that includes me, too: that includes the guy it all belongs to and who belongs to it.

"Dex," Dave says. "Dex? Hello? Are you there? I was kidding."

I snap out of it. I shake my head, blink it away. "Right," I say. "Don't fuck it up. No problem. How hard could that be?"

Dave laughs. "Oh shit," he says. "This is going to be good. This is going to be amazing."

"All right," I say. "Can we just focus on the issue at hand, please? Are you going to loan me your truck or what?"

"Sure," Dave says. "Whatever you need."

"Thank you," I say. "Jesus Christ."

After I hang up with Dave I stand there, looking around. Everything looks normal again. I almost can't even remember what felt so weird before, can't remember what the feeling was like, what it was about. I keep looking, trying to feel it again. It doesn't come back, though. So eventually I give up. I open the door and I go back out. Bethany's there in the kitchen. I tell her what Dave said. We make the outline of a plan. Then we talk about dinner. We talk about going out, about going somewhere nice, about celebrating, but in the end we just go to one of our regular spots. Bethany gets the same thing she always gets, and so do I. Then we go home. We drive back to my house and we go up the walk and we go inside. And it's strange. It's different, somehow. Bethany plops down on the couch and she turns on the TV and a minute later I go in and join her.

"What were you doing?" she says.

"When?" I say.

"Just now," she says. "Before you came over."

"Nothing," I say. "Taking off my coat."

She sits up slightly, turns, looks at me. "Really?" she says.

"Yes," I say. "Why?"

She shrugs and settles back, nestles in against me. "It just took you a while," she says.

"Did it?" I say. "That's all I was doing." Then I say, "Why, what did you think I was doing?"

She shrugs again. "I don't know," she says. "Planning your escape. Figuring out how to tell me that you made a mistake, that you've changed your mind."

On the TV, some celebrity is struggling to learn a complicated dance sequence. She keeps stumbling over the same transition, the same couple of points. The choreographer is clapping the beats, calling out the steps. I think about what Dave said, about not fucking this up. I think about a half-dozen different shit-ass things that I could say, a half-dozen shit-ass things that Radio Dex would say. After she went in and turned on the TV I stood there in the front hallway. I needed to take off my coat and hat, needed to take off my boots, needed to wipe up the snow and water I had tracked in, but I didn't do any of that. I just stood there.

It was weird. It was like being back at the first day of school, or something. You're standing at the threshold of something and you're trying to get a sense for what you're stepping into, only you can't. You don't know what it is you're stepping into, so you can't get a sense for it. If you had a sense for it then you wouldn't need to come up with a sense for it. But because you don't, you do.

I lean and I kiss the top of her head. I can smell her shampoo, smell the incense they had burning in the classroom, smell her smell underneath it all. "Don't worry," I say. And then that's all I say. There's nothing I can think of that would make it any better, and so many things that would make it worse. It seems like enough, though. Or at least she doesn't ask again. She doesn't press the point.

On the TV, the celebrity starts to get it. She puts together a dozen steps, makes her way through a tricky transition, before she loses it. With each successive shot she's getting better and better. We never see what it all comes to, though. By the time she's done rehearsing and she's ready for the show we've both fallen asleep.

SHE MOVES in. She leaves her shit everywhere. She leaves her yoga mat by the door, leaves her shoes clustered in the front hallway, leaves clothes and books and other random shit on practically every flat surface. Almost anywhere I look there's evidence of her living there. Everywhere I look there are traces of her.

The room with my stereo and my guitars and everything, the room she calls my office, she leaves alone. We don't talk about it, she just does it. I assume that that means that she gets it, that this is her leaving me some space, but that just goes to show you what I know. When what happened later happened and she started talking about changing things around it caught me off guard, it kind of blindsided me, and probably it shouldn't have. Realistically it shouldn't have. If I hadn't assumed what I assumed, if I hadn't let it go unsaid, if I'd thought about it for two seconds and realized that her leaving that room alone probably had nothing to do with leaving me some space but just had to do with the fact that that room was already pretty full of stuff, and also that it was out of the way of everywhere she spent most of her time in the house, down a hall she never went down, it wouldn't have come as such a surprise. It wouldn't have caught me so much. Or at least I don't think it would have. I don't think it would have turned into such a thing, if I'd known from the beginning how it really was.

The point is, it's an adjustment. The whole thing is an adjustment. It's a new experience for me. I've never lived with anyone before. I've had roommates, but I've never done this. I've never lived with someone I'm in a relationship with. After high school, when me and the other guys in the band I was in moved down to Nashville, I spent two years without a room of my own. I slept on the couch in the living room of the house we rented. I kept my clothes and stuff in a pile in the corner. After we broke up and the other guys left I split my nights between a few friends' couches and the backseat of my car and a cot in the back of one of the venues where we played. When I moved back to Ohio I slept on a mattress in the basement of a house some high school friends were renting. When that ended I moved into the cheapest apartment I could find. I was on the road a lot of the time anyway, so it didn't really matter what my place was like. By the time I finally got somewhat settled and started living someplace decent I was almost thirty, and by then all of the women I met and dated had their own lives. I mean they all had decent places and the kind of furniture you hang onto. They were all past that phase where you're moving every twelve months anyway, where ninety percent of your shit is thrift store shit that you just donate back or throw away. At that point it would have been more likely that I move in with one of them, just based on who was more established, and it wasn't like I was going to do that. It wasn't like I was going to give up having my own space, no matter how shitty the place was. Not that it ever got to that point, with any of them. Not that it was ever that serious.

But it's good. For the most part it's really good. For the most part it works. We hang out, read books, watch TV. We do yoga in the living room, do yoga on the patio, do yoga at the studio. She talks me into reading a book on meditation, talks me into attending a couple of workshops. We go to a workshop where a woman in a black bodysuit teaches us how to engage the deep abdominal muscles in a half-dozen poses, go to another one where a guy with a ponytail and a prayer-bead necklace talks for two and a half hours about using your practice to listen to the Universe. We sleep late on Sundays, take turns making dinner. We rearrange the furniture and buy a new toaster. Pretty soon it's been a month already, and then two and then three. Pretty soon it's September already, and the summer is over.

Some people we know from the studio, one of the other instructors and her husband, invite us over. They're having a big, end-of-summer potluck. The other yoga instructors and their boyfriends and girlfriends and husbands and wives and partners and some students and their plus-ones are all going to be there. The instructor and her husband only live a few blocks from us, so it's easy. We get a bottle of wine and Bethany makes a vegetarian lasagna and we walk over.

I'm not sure what to expect—I'm not expecting much—but it turns out to be quite a party. It's a pretty big group, maybe twenty-five or thirty people. We stand around in the backyard of this house eating cedar plank salmon and quinoa salad off of paper plates, talking over music piped in through bluetooth speakers made to look like part of the landscaping. Bethany doesn't drink much and I haven't been drinking much either, but for whatever reason—

maybe because it's the end of summer or maybe because it's just wine and we're not driving or maybe for some other reason that has nothing to do with any of that—we do. We drink kind of a lot. People keep opening bottles, keep passing them around, keep topping us off. The sun goes down and the hosts build a fire in the fire pit on the patio and we sit around it and somebody brings out a bowl and starts passing it around. It comes to Bethany and I watch her face in the lighter's glow and then it comes to me and I breathe smoke and watch it rise, watch it go up with the embers from the fire through the trees still full of leaves to the stars high up overhead.

I have that feeling you get sometimes at good parties, that feeling like you're inside the best place in the world, inside the best moment in the world, that feeling that everyone is so nice and that it's a miracle, somehow: that you've stumbled across this remote tribe of the only nicest people in the world.

Finally it gets late. Bethany leans her head on my shoulder. "How are you doing?" she says.

"I'm good," I say. "How are you?"

"I'm good," she says. "I could be ready, if you're ready."

"I could be ready," I say. "Either way. Whatever you want to do is fine. If you want to go then we can go."

She raises her head, looks around, looks back to me. "I think I'm ready," she says.

"Okay," I say. "Sure. Let's go."

We get up, say our thank-yous and goodbyes. We leave them all there by the fire and we walk home. We start making out on the porch, keep it going as we move inside. Bethany says we should just do hand stuff, because we're out of condoms, but between the wine and the pot, and with how great things are going and how right it feels, we don't end up just doing hand stuff. And a few weeks later Bethany starts crying over every sad song that comes on the radio and every touching scene in every movie we watch, and after a week of this she goes to the drug store and gets one of those pee-on tests, and you can guess what it says.

PART
TWO

IT'S A fucking disaster, as far as I can see. It's not what I signed up for. Even setting aside the obvious issues—setting aside the age difference, the fact that by the time our kid would be out of high school I'd be in my sixties, almost, while she'd only be a few years older than I am now, and setting aside the fact that we haven't been together that long, and setting aside the fact that—despite the books she's read and tried to get me to read about owning your intention and emotional honesty and effective communication—we haven't had anything even approaching a big, where-is-this-thing-going conversation—there's still the basic fact that I never wanted kids, never wanted to be somebody's father. There's still the basic fact that I really have no interest in seeing the other side of that coin, in opening up that can of worms.

The thing is, though, Bethany's thrilled. She's beside-herself happy. She's all in, right away. She doesn't leave room for a conversation, even. Before she's even had the confirmation appointment with the doctor she's already told everybody at the studio. Before she's even had the appointment I've got people coming up to me after class congratulating me, telling me they think it's great, telling me they're so happy for us. She's already bought or put on order a dozen books about prenatal nutrition and natural childbirth and birthing traditions in different cultures, has already started building a library on the kitchen table. She's already flooded my inbox with links to articles and blogs that she thinks I need to read, already floated the idea of us trading in our cars for something newer and safer, already thrown it out there that, really, the thing that makes the most sense is for us to turn my office into a nursery.

AND IT doesn't stop. I figure that it's going to taper off, that it can't keep up like this, that there's going to be a break, but apparently it's not and it can and there isn't. It just goes on and on, goes on for weeks. For practically all of October it's one thing after another. There's always some new thing she wants to tell me or talk about, some new plan or assignment. This book we have to read, this class we've got to take, this documentary we need to watch. It's just endless. I lay in bed at night and I try to get a handle on it all, try to talk myself down. I try to tell myself that it's going to be all right, that what Dave and everybody says is probably true, that kids are the best thing that can ever happen to you and that once it happens I'll understand. That everybody worries about what kind of parent they're going to be, that it's totally normal, that having shitty parents doesn't mean you're going to be a shitty parent. That it doesn't mean that everything is fucked. And that anyway, what else was I going to do? What else was I going to do with the next twenty years? Host the show? Hang out? Get older? That I'm lucky, really. That I ought to consider myself lucky. That a better person would consider himself lucky. That this is a gift. And that either way it is what it is, now. One way or the other it is what it is. It's going to be what it's going to be. I lay there and I try to get my arms around it, try to get my head together. I lay there and I feel her next to me and I think, Fuck me. And it goes around and around. And in the morning she leans over and she kisses me and she tells me the next thing we need to do, the next thing on the list. And I nod and I smile and I say, "Okay."

AND MAYBE that would have worked. Maybe that would have kept working. Maybe I could have managed it. If that was the only thing, if it was just Bethany and everything involved with that situation, maybe it would have held together. But the thing is, it's not just that. I'm running around on no sleep and heroic doses of caffeine and the bullshit naturopathic Maalox knockoff they sell at Whole Foods and I get an email from the station's Listserv saying that the owners are calling a meeting, that they need everybody to be at the station at ten o'clock on Friday morning. It doesn't say what it's about, just that it's important and that everybody needs to be there.

It's funny. Despite what the email says, I still probably wouldn't go. Under normal circumstances I wouldn't go. Like I said I try to skip as many of the station meetings as I can, try to skip any that don't have to do with me specifically. But the thing is, with the way things are now, I'm looking for any excuse to get out of the house. Bethany's already got other teachers covering some of her classes and so she's around more, around in the mornings, around so we can talk and plan and pack up and rearrange things. So I go. I'm not expecting much. But it turns out to really be important. It ends up being good that I'm there, in the common room along with every-body else, when the owners get up on chairs and announce that, due to mounting financial pressures, they'll be transitioning ownership and management of the station to GlobalOne Media, effective imme-diately.

I don't see it coming. I honestly don't. Not in a million fucking years. Yes, it's true that there have been rumors going around, but that's nothing new. There have always been rumors. When your station's one of the last locally-owned stations in the entire region there are always rumors. It feels like you're always right on the brink of going under, of selling out. It's something you get used to. It comes with the territory. It's part of the charm. I knew what I was in for from day one. My first contract was only for eighteen months, and not because the station didn't want me for longer. The owners told me flat out that they couldn't guarantee anything beyond that. They said they didn't want me to feel like I was in some sort of contract limbo if I wanted to keep my ear to the ground, keep an eye out for another gig. But even still, it's not like you can live like that. It's not like you can go day after day for ten years thinking that the whole thing might end tomorrow. Sooner or later you start trusting that it's going to be there. You just do. You can't help it. You start taking it for granted. You start thinking it's impossible that one day we're going to come in and it's just going to be over, signed and sealed, just like that.

So it's a shock, is what I'm saying. I'm stunned. That's the only word for it. I'm fucking stunned.

There's this new guy there with the owners—this generically handsome, blonde, young-executive type wearing distressed jeans and a suit jacket over one of those graphic tees, the kind with eagles and open-mouthed skulls and all that other fashionable tough-guy bullshit—and the owners introduce him as Chad and they say that Chad's going to be our point man for the changeover, and that if we have any questions we should direct them to Chad. And Chad gets up on a chair and he waves to us and he thanks us for having him and he thanks the owners for that introduction, and then he launches into this big speech about how he's super excited to be here and how he can't wait to meet and speak with each of us individually, how he doesn't want us to think of this as GlobalOne *buying* the station so much as GlobalOne *investing* in the station, because the reality is that GlobalOne believes in our programing and our voice, that it was our programming and our voice that put us on GlobalOne's radar in the first place, and that what GlobalOne really wants is to help us take that programming and that voice to the next level. He tells us that we should be really proud of ourselves and the work we've done, and then he starts clapping and the old owners start clapping and everybody else starts clapping, too, because what else do you do when the guy who's apparently your new boss wants you to clap?

I look at Dave. Dave isn't clapping. Dave is pulling his hands over his face.

"Jesus Christ," he says. "If they're going to fuck us in the ass, they could at least buy us dinner first."

I'm not clapping, either. My hands are in still in my sweatshirt pocket. I shrug. "What's the problem?" I say. "They're investing in the station. They like the voice. They're excited to work with us. You don't think they're excited to work with us?"

Dave snorts at that. "Sure," he says. "Go ask Flipper and Gill over at WNTO. Ask Carl Potts at WLVY or Rick and Lois at WBYZ. Go ask them how excited GlobalOne was to work with them. Go ask them how much GlobalOne valued their unique voice." He pulls his hands over his face again, rubs his temples, shakes his head. "Goddamn," he says, "I need a drink. You want a drink? Let's go get a drink."

WE DUCK out, go down the street to the bar on the corner. Dave orders beers and while the bartender is off getting them he turns to me and he says, "This is it, man. This is the two-minute warning. If we're going to do something then we need to do it. If we're going to do something then we need to do it now."

"Our numbers are good," I say. "The advertisers love us. They'll back us."

Dave snorts again. "You want to bet on that?" he says. "You want to go all-in on the fucking advertisers?"

The bartender brings the beers. Dave tips his back. The glass he sets back down is half-emptied. He holds up six fingers.

"There," he says. "You see that? You know what that is? That is the number of months it takes on average for a bought station to become fully integrated into the purchasing conglomerate's *broadcasting package*." He makes big quotation marks in the air with his fingers around 'broadcasting package.' He says, "That's the average amount of time before every single time slot has been *reformatted to fit the current broadcasting vision*." He drops the air quotes and picks up his glass. "And bear in mind," he says, "that's the average. If one or two shows manage to stick round for a year or more, that skews the number. Typical lifespan post-takeover is more like four months." He tips back the glass, drains it, plunks it back down. He turns the hand that was holding the glass into a pointing finger and he jabs it into my shoulder. "So if I were you," he says, "I might take that into consideration. I might think about what that means for me and what's going to be going on in my life four or six months from now."

I shake my head. "Bullshit," I say. "Where did you even get those numbers? How do you know that? Is that something you actually know, or are you making it up? Because it sort of feels like you're making it up."

Dave is waving to the bartender, pointing at his glass. He looks at me and shrugs. "No," he says, "I looked. I looked it up when we lost BilCo Siding last year. Katie got really freaked out and we had a serious, down-to-business talk about it. Like, Let's not just hope for the best. Let's know what the fuck it actually looks like if this happens." He frowns, shakes his head. "And anyway," he says, "what does it matter? I mean, call it eight months. Call it a year. The point is that sooner or later that's where this is going. You know that's where this is going. Plus or minus a quarter, that's where this is headed."

"Okay fine," I say. "Call it six months. Nobody else has our numbers. You said some shows ride it out. What makes you think we can't ride it out? What makes you so sure we won't just get absorbed into whatever new lineup they come up with?"

The bartender is off at the taps with Dave's glass. Dave is leaning over the bar, watching him.

"Sure," he says, without looking at me. "No, sure, you're right, we could be fine. It's all just speculation, at this point. I'm just speculating about what could happen. About what's *likely* to happen. But no, you're right, I don't *know* what's going to happen. So let's not even worry about it. I'm sure it'll be fine."

I don't need this shit right now. I don't need any of this. I'm fucking exhausted. I sit down on a stool. "All right," I say. "Jesus Christ. What are you suggesting we do, then? You know of anybody else who'll pick us up? Everybody else is corporate, too."

The bartender is back with Dave's beer. Dave takes another long drink and shakes his head.

"That's not what I'm saying," he says. "I'm not talking about us finding another station. I'm talking about going independent. I'm saying we need to start a podcast."

I laugh. You have to understand, there's this thing about podcasting. Back in the beginning, back when podcasting first became a thing, there was this attitude that it was for guys who couldn't hack it in real radio, guys who weren't good enough to actually have a show. That it was a way for those guys to play pretend, basically. And it's not that I'm unaware of the fact that it's not like that anymore, really, not that I'm unaware of the fact that there are some podcasts that are kind of huge, now, it's more that I haven't really thought about it. It's more that I never really revamped my original take.

"Come on, man" I say. "A podcast? Seriously?"

Dave holds up his hands, the empty one and the one holding the beer glass. The new beer is already two-thirds gone. "I know," he says, "but just hang on a second. Hear me out. Don't write it off. It's not like how it used to be. It's a whole different thing, now. It's a huge market. I looked into it a little bit. Katie wants to do this thing, maybe. Like, listen to how crazy it is living with all these kids. Funny stories and shit like that. Funny things the kids say. It doesn't matter. The point is, based on what I'm seeing, even if we only carry a quarter of our current base, we can still pull decent ad buys. Not what we're making now, but decent." He's getting excited. He finishes his beer, thunks the empty glass down on the bar. He waves to the bartender and turns back to me. "And," he says, "think about this. Think about the fact that we wouldn't have to answer to anybody. That we wouldn't be limited by any regulatory body's guidelines. And think about the fact that we would own our own content. It would be ours to bundle or redistribute or anthologize or whatever." He pushes me on the shoulder. "I mean, fuck, man," he says. "Six months from now Bethany won't even have had the kid yet. Do you seriously want to just wait and see what happens? You really want to trust that they're not going to drop us right as your girl's about to give birth? You want to start off parenthood with no steady source of income?"

He's getting in my face. Or maybe it just feels that way. I lean back and I hold up my hands.

"All right," I say. "Jesus, fuck, enough already."

Dave leans back. He sits down on a stool, swivels to face front. He swivels to follow the bartender as the bartender comes for his glass and goes away with it. I lean on the bar and I stare straight ahead and I find my reflection between the bottlenecks. All the weight I lost has hollowed out my face, hollowed out my cheeks. I almost don't even look like me. Or maybe it's just the lighting. I look away, look down at my beer. I raise my glass and take a sip.

"All right," I say. "Just for the sake of argument, what's your vision for this thing? We can't play music on a podcast. We can't really do call-ins. What does that leave? Me talking? What's our content?"

The bartender is bringing back Dave's glass, but Dave doesn't see it. He's already swiveled back, already locked in on me again.

"No," he says, "exactly. I thought about this. This is the whole thing. As far as I see it, we've got two things. Thing number one is, interviews. People love your interviews. Those segments are always really strong. We always get a lot of response to those segments. So that's one thing. That's one big piece. And then the other piece is you telling all your different stories about playing gigs and being on the road and all that shit. People love that stuff. And think about it. Here we are with this whole thing about how Cleveland is the home of rock 'n' roll, right? It's the rock 'n' roll capital of the world, right? But who's out there who actually came up playing music in the scene? Playing gigs in the Flats before all of those places closed? Besides you there's nobody. Nobody else who lived it and who can tell that story is doing it. Nobody else is broadcasting it, and nobody's podcasting about it."

I take another long sip, shake my head. "I've told those stories," I say. "I've told them all a thousand times."

Dave shakes his head, waves that away. "So what?" he says. "Tell them a thousand more times. There are literally millions and millions of people out there who haven't heard them. It's a podcast. It's not local radio. You can be in fucking Calcutta and get the same shit."

"Yeah," I say, "but why the fuck is somebody in Calcutta going to give a fuck about some gig I played in the fucking Flats back in nineteen fucking ninety-seven?"

"I don't know," Dave says. "Why do people do anything they do? Why is anybody interested in anything?"

We're practically yelling, now. The bartender is watching us. I catch his eye and nod that it's okay. He goes back to what he was doing. Dave swivels around and leans on the bar, leans his head on his arms.

"What?" I say. "What's your deal right now?"

He groans. He raises his head and looks at me. "I didn't tell Katie about the rumors," he says. "I didn't tell her that the station was maybe getting sold. When I tell her what happened it's going to be totally out of the blue."

"Okay," I say, "but so what? I mean, there were always rumors. Were you supposed to tell her every time there was a stupid rumor?"

He winces, closes his eyes, shakes his head. "This was different," he says. "It felt different. You know it felt different."

"I don't know," I say. "I mean, maybe it did. I don't know. I've been kind of distracted."

He waves that away. "It doesn't matter," he says. "The point is, I need us to have the wheels in motion on this thing before shit starts falling apart. I can't tell Katie that we've been cancelled and not have anything else lined up. Okay? Because she will fucking divorce me."

I probably need to tell you more about Dave, so you really get the picture. Dave and his wife Katie have four kids under the age of six. In the time I've known him he's gone from being a fairly unrepentant man-child to knowing the names of all the Disney princesses. He's also the first person I told about Bethany when we first started dating, the first person I told about us moving in together, the first person I told about her being pregnant. He's the first person to congratulate me, to tell me how great he thought it was, to tell me how incredible it was going to be. It's because of all of this that I laugh, that I assume he's joking.

"Come on," I say. "Over that? That doesn't even make sense."

He isn't joking, though. He shakes his head. "I don't know," he says. "I honestly don't even know anymore." He picks up his new beer, sets it back down. "You have no idea what it's like at my house," he says. "I mean, don't get me wrong. I love Katie and I love the kids and everything, but Jesus Christ. It's like a fucking CIA black site over there. It's like they're constantly dreaming up new ways to try and break us. I don't think I've actually had a full night's sleep since Tristan was born. I don't think I've had seven uninterrupted hours of sleep once in the past six years. That shit changes you. You don't think it does, but it does. Katie has said things to me in anger that I have never heard anyone say, ever. Vicious things. And I'm not even being funny. If I come home and tell her that I lost my job and I don't have anything else lined up, I honestly don't know what she'll do."

"Yeah, okay," I say, "but why this, then? Why not do commercial editing or sound design or whatever? You're the one with actual technical skills. There have to be jobs out there for you. There have to be better options than us doing a podcast on fucking spec. What you're talking about is a total gamble. It's a shot in the dark."

He isn't having that, though. He shakes his head, waves his hands. The beers are catching him. His motions are getting big, getting loose.

"No," he says. "Fuck that. I've done that bullshit. This. This is the thing. It's got to be this." He looks at me. His eyes are intense, searching, pleading. "Come on," he says. "Can't you see it? Don't you understand what I'm saying? This is how we do what we're good at and actually own it. This is how we do it for us. Like back in the frontier days when you could just go out and stake a piece of land and then that would be your land. All you needed was the fucking balls to go do it. That's this, right now. This is that, for guys like us. This is the way. This is the way we really do something."

And I do see it. He has a point. At least in that moment it seems like he does. Still, it's a lot. It feels like a lot. I shake my head. "I don't know," I say. "What makes you think we're not going to do a bunch of work and spend a bunch of money and end up nowhere? What makes you think that in two years we won't be sitting here having this same conversation, trying to figure out what to do now that we're twice as fucked as we were before?"

He shrugs. "Nothing," he says. "Absolutely nothing. You're right, that could totally happen. It could totally go down that way. Or we could be sitting here toasting the fact that we just hit ten thousand subscribers. We could be toasting the fact that we just landed our first major sponsor. That we just broke into the top hundred in the iTunes rankings. It could be that. Think about that. Just take a second and imagine that."

I don't really know what to say to that. I sip my beer. "All right," I say, "let's say we move forward on this. What does that look like?"

Dave grins. Like he's got me, now. Like he's made the sale and now we're just hashing out the details. He sets down his beer and he holds up his hand, the five fingers splayed. "Okay," he says. "The way I see it, we need five things. We need the equipment. We need a space, maybe somewhere at your place for right now, because there's always at least one kid screaming at my house. We need a website. We need a name. And we need a really big, kick-ass, make-people-sit-up-and-take-notice guest for the first episode."

And as soon as he says that, before the words are even all the way out of his mouth, I know what's coming. I know what this has all been leading up to. And maybe I should have realized it sooner. Maybe if I'd been getting enough sleep I'd have realized it sooner. Maybe it's at least partially my own stupid fault for not realizing it sooner, is what I'm saying. But one way or the other right then I feel like he tricked me, like he brought me into this under false pretenses, like this is a fucking trap.

"Oh fuck off," I say.

He waves that away. He nods. "I know," he says. "But hang on. Wait a second. Listen. I know. But listen. We have to go as big as we can for the first episode. We have to make a statement. If we do that then hopefully we can convert a decent chunk of our audience right there. We get those people to subscribe and then we use those numbers to attract other guests which gets us more subscribers which attracts advertisers, and on and on like that. That's how this thing works. I didn't make it this way, I'm just telling you how it is. And so you tell me. If you're thinking about who we can potentially book and you're being honest and you're not hung up on some other bull-shit, you're just thinking in terms of pure celebrity status, who is the biggest name you can think of?"

I laugh. I've been laughing through most of what he just said. It's just funny. I shake my head. "I haven't talked to him in years," I say. "I don't have any contact information for him. And even if I did, even if I could get ahold of him, I don't think I'd count on him being in a big hurry to do me any favors."

Dave nods. "Right," he says. "No, I know. I get it. And I get that it's a sore subject, or whatever. And I'm sorry, okay? I'm sorry for bringing it up and I'm sorry to ask. But hear me out. Nobody has heard anything from Logan in what, five years? There's been no mu-sic, no news, no nothing. There was that DUI in 2012 or 2013 or whatever, but that's it. So what's he been doing? Where's he been? Is he making music? Is he doing something else? You're curious, right? And if you're curious, don't you think other people are curious, too? And while you're thinking about that, think about this. Anybody else, any other musician or celebrity or whatever, they would be doing our show to promote their tour or their new album or whatever. Our show would just be another stop on the press junket. They'd do our show and then go do a hundred other shows just like our show. Give the same answers to the same questions on a hundred other shows. But with Logan, it would just be us. You see what I'm saying? He's not promoting anything. He's not selling a tour or an album. It'd only be us." He stops, picks up his glass, looks inside, sets it back down. He shrugs. "I mean, plus," he says, "who knows what he'll say? It doesn't seem like he's all that concerned about maintaining any sort of public image these days. It could be crazy. And think what it would be like. Take yourself out of it for a second and really think about it. Imagine the two of you back together in the same room. If you were somebody else, wouldn't you want to listen in on that? Because who knows what's going to happen? Maybe you'll yell at each other, maybe you'll tell stories and shit, maybe you'll make plans to do a fucking album together. Who knows? You don't know. But you're curious. Aren't you curious? You have to admit you're a little bit curious. You have to admit there's something there."

I don't say anything to that. I kind of can't, almost. I stare straight ahead at the mirror and I lift my glass and I finish what's left. Dave finishes his too and he waves the bartender over. The bartender comes and takes our glasses and goes away.

"Look," Dave says, once the bartender's gone. "Probably he won't even get back to us. Probably we won't even reach him. We'll get some manager or somebody and they'll tell us they're going to pass the message along, and then they won't. But that's literally the worst thing that can happen, right? The worst that can happen is that we don't hear anything. So I say we reach out, at least. Right? It can't hurt to reach out."

I keep not looking at him as I shrug and say, "Sure. Right. Can't hurt. Can't hurt you."

Out of the corner of my eye I see him hold up his hands.

"Hey, listen," he says. "I'm just the messenger. If you don't want to do this, that's fine. If you want to go find some other job, if you want to go dig ditches or sell vinyl siding or something, that's fine with me. All I'm saying is, if we're going to do this, then we need to do it right. We need to give ourselves the best chance for success. We need to stack the odds in our favor. And all of that shit, whatever happened between you and Logan, that was all a long time ago. That's all ancient history. So I'm just saying that maybe, in light of our current circumstances, in light of what's happening now, in the fucking present, maybe it's time to swallow your pride and let that shit go a little bit and see if we can't do something positive with the cards we've been dealt."

I pull my hands over my face, shake my head. I watch myself do it in the mirror. "Shit, man," I say. "You know you don't know what you're talking about, right? You don't know the first fucking thing about it." I swivel around, turn to face him as I say, "You know that, don't you? You know that, right?"

The bartender has brought our beers, but neither of us makes a move to take them. We just sit there, looking at each other. Then Dave gets up. He digs some bills out of his pocket and he counts them out onto the bar. He watches himself do it, watches the money, watches his hands. He nods.

"You're right," he says. "I don't know anything about it. But you know what I do know something about? Putting on a solid show. Producing quality content. Attracting and maintaining an audience." He folds what's left of the wad and stuffs it back into his pocket. He raises his new beer and he takes a drink. Then he turns back to me. "You want to know something else?" he says. "You want to know something else I know about? Being a parent. Having other human beings whose health and safety and wellbeing depends on me staying on top of my shit." He raises the new beer again, but lowers it without drinking. "I mean, Jesus Christ," he says, "have you never thought about any of this? Have you never thought about what would happen if we got dropped? About what you would do if you couldn't make the payments and the bank took your house? About how you would live? You've thought about this, haven't you?"

I have, but it's been a while. It was a long time ago, before all of this. And even then, it probably wasn't very realistic.

Dave nods. He already knows what I'm going to say. Or what I would say, if I was going to say anything.

"Yeah," he says. "No, I know. You'll go back to living on PBR and Top Ramen, right? Sleep in your car, crash with people you meet at shows? You know you're not twenty-five anymore, right? I mean, you know that, right? Shit, you're not even thirty-five anymore. Listen to me. Take a second and really listen to what I'm telling you This whole punk rock, I-don't-give-a-fuck, you-can't-make-me-do-anything-I-don't-want-to-do, self-destruct thing, it's over, man. It's done. Dig it a grave and fucking bury it."

I've had enough. I turn back to the bar, center up on my beer. I shake my head. "Whatever, man," I say. "You can think whatever you want. You can think whatever you want to about me or my attitude or the way I live my life."

He deflates, a little bit. Out of the corner of my eye I watch him sag. He leans into the bar, holds up a hand.

"All right," he says. "Look, I'm sorry, okay? I didn't mean for it to come out like that. I'm not trying to insult you or piss you off or anything. I'm not trying to be an asshole. We're in the same boat. I'm trying to do something about it." He leans in, pushes my shoulder. "Come on," he says. "You know what I mean. I'm just saying, we need a plan. We need to be proactive, here. We can't just sit around and wait to see what happens. We have to do something."

I don't look at him. I keep staring at my beer. I've been working my way around the glass with my thumbs, wiping away the condensation. I've been watching the bubbles, watching to see which ones rise and which ones don't. I nod. "Okay," I say. "Yeah, I know. Sit down."

"Okay," he says. He sounds relieved. He sits down.

I can feel him wanting to say something else, something more, but he doesn't do it. After a second he swivels around to face the bar, and we sit there like that for a while.

I want to explain, want to make him understand, want to make him see that it's not ancient history. I want to make him see that it's still happening, that it's happening right now. That every morning I wake up still in Cleveland it's a little bit what's happening. It's right there on the tip of my tongue. I never manage to come out with it, though. I'm still thinking about what to say when the bartender turns on one of the TVs and starts flipping through the channels, and the empty bar gets suddenly loud with snippets of ads and newscasters talking and other random shit. So instead I close my eyes, press my fingers into my eyelids. My fingertips are cool, almost cold, from the glass. It feels so fucking good. I could stay here, just like this.

"Listen," Dave says, "just think about it, okay? That's all I'm asking. Just think about it."

There are starbursts going off inside my eyelids, inside my head, globs of yellow and orange and white. Out in the world there's a low interest rate on a new car and a two-for-one dinner deal. I nod without dropping my hands. "Okay," I say. "Sure. Okay. I'll think about it."

I feel him lean away. The bartender has stopped on a news show. ISIS is advancing into Syria, taking control of towns around Aleppo. The anchor sounds serious, really concerned. The next story is some unrelated bullshit. The anchor perks right up again. The bartender flips the channel. A gameshow contestant named Trisha makes a guess.

"Think about it," Dave says again. "Just remember. Six months."

I DON'T want to think about it. I don't want to think about any of it. I want things to go back to how they were before, back when everything was simple. Back when even my problems were simple problems.

I go get something to eat and then I run some errands and then I do the show and then I go home. Bethany is there and she has a lot to tell me. She found a teacher in Cincinnati who offers a prenatal yoga certification, and she wants to know if I'll do it with her. She talked to Katie at the studio, and Katie told her about the doula she used when she was pregnant with Frankie, and she already called and made an appointment for us to go and meet her. And she found the perfect color to paint my office, this creamy green that's one of the color options for a shirt she likes in the new Lululemon catalog. She already went to Home Depot and checked, and the man there said he could match it exactly.

"It shouldn't take very long," she says. "We can do it in a day, the man said. As soon as you get your stuff out of there we can do it. Maybe next weekend. I can get someone to cover for me and we can hammer it out."

"Sure," I say. "Right. No, it shouldn't take very long."

We eat some vegetarian stir fry dish that Bethany made and we watch most of a documentary about the birthing practices of a remote tribe in the Amazonian rainforest and then we go to bed and I lay there imagining things. I imagine all kinds of things. I imagine Bethany getting fed up with me, deciding that she has to do what's right for her and the kid, and going off somewhere. Back home, maybe. Or somewhere out West. I imagine becoming one of those middle-aged guys with an ex and a kid he never sees. I imagine Chad turning out to be a huge fan of the show, imagine him offering us a better contract, taking us national through the GlobalOne network. I imagine Dave and me doing a podcast, imagine it getting big, imagine us making a lot of money. I imagine the money making things simple again. I imagine it all going wrong. I roll over and close my eyes, roll back and open them.

I lay there and I listen to Bethany breathing. I try to imagine it as breath for two people, try to imagine that it's three of us here, now. I can't do it, though. I just can't see it. It's too abstract. I always come back to the same sense of us, the same sense of me. I try for a while, and then I give up. I go back to imagining other things.

I imagine a lot of things. I get lost in things, turned around in things, until I can't tell which thing would be better and which thing would be worse. Until I think, Well sure, maybe at the time, but in the long run. Until I think, Wouldn't it be better if? Until I think, Maybe we would all be better off.

IT TURNS out that it doesn't really matter, though, what I think or what I want. It turns out it doesn't really matter what I think is better or worse. When I get to the station the next day Dave is there pacing around in the hall and he tells me that Chad wants us to come in and talk to him for a few minutes before we go on.

"It's probably nothing," I say. "It's probably just him putting faces with names."

"Sure," Dave says. "Right. Sure."

We go down the hall to the common room where Chad has set up a workspace. Dave stops and knocks on the open door and Chad looks up and waves us in. He comes over and meets us, says our names as he shakes our hands.

"Dave," he says. "Dex. Thanks so much for seeing me. I really appreciate you guys making the time."

"Sure," Dave says. "No problem."

Chad's got some roller chairs that he must have commandeered from one of the offices set around the big folding table they keep for lunch trays and signup sheets and stuff like that. It's the table they used for the cake at our ten-year party, actually. Now it's covered with Chad's laptop and his phone and some big binders and folders and printouts on GlobalOne letterhead. You almost can't see the table, there's so much there.

Chad sees me looking at it and waves a hand. "Don't worry about this stuff," he says. "This isn't about you." He points to the chairs and we all sit. "This isn't any kind of formal meeting, or anything," he says. "I'm just trying to get a few minutes with everybody so we can all get introduced, get on the same page, see if I can answer any questions, that sort of thing."

"No," Dave says. "Yeah, no, that's what we figured. We were just saying that it's probably just a faces-with-names thing."

Chad's movements are loose, easy, relaxed. He leans back in the chair, spreads his arms. He looks from me to Dave and then back to me again. "Well great, then," he says. "So what can I tell you? What have you got? Questions? Concerns? Anything?"

Dave is shifting around, crossing and uncrossing his arms and legs. The chair's wheels rumble on the linoleum each time he moves. He uncrosses his arms, pushes himself up, crosses his arms and legs again. He glances at me, looks back at Chad, shrugs and shakes his head.

"I mean, no," he says. "I can't think of anything." He looks at me again. "Can you think of anything?" he says. "I can't think of anything." He turns back to Chad. "I think I'm good," he says. "I mean, we're good. I think we're good."

Chad lets that hang, watches Dave fidget around for a few seconds before he nods. "No," he says, "I know. I get it. It's a lot. It's like, Whoa, hang on, what's happening here?" He holds up his hands as he laughs. "Seriously, though," he says, "I'm with you guys on this. I'm playing catchup like you wouldn't believe." He starts picking things up off the table and setting them back down, binders and folders and stacks of paper, to show us how much he's got to deal with. "And this is only part of it," he says. "I've got about a million hours of audio files sitting on a hard drive back in my hotel room that I haven't even started on."

Dave laughs. I don't. It doesn't seem like a joke to me. Maybe it is. Dave glances at me and he stops laughing. He coughs and clears his throat.

"Wow," he says. "Sorry. That sucks. I mean, that's a lot."

Chad is moving things out of the way, now, clearing a space. He shrugs. "It's work," he says. He sets his elbows on the place he cleared and leans in. Like he's going to level with us, now. Like he's going to cut the shit and clue us in. Like he's our friend in this whole thing. "Listen," he says. "All of this—this whole meeting-with-everybody thing—it's as much for me as it is for anybody else. It's a way for me to get a sense for where everybody's at. You have to realize how it is. I was in Milwaukee this time last week. Three weeks before that, I was in St. Louis. I get dropped into these situations and it's like, Okay, here it is, you figure it out." He shrugs again. "The thing is," he says, "my job is pretty simple. Or at least it's pretty simple in theory. I come in, assess, figure out what isn't working, make a plan for how to fix it. And the way I do that is I start with the assumption that places work when they work for the people who work there." He slows that down, emphasizes each word, as he looks back and forth between us. "So, basically," he says, "my job is to try to understand who isn't happy and why they aren't happy, and then try to figure out what's going to make them happy. A job well done for me is when you're happy, the station is happy, my bosses are happy, your listeners are happy." He counts us all off on his fingers. "Everybody's happy," he says. "That's pretty simple, right? But the thing is, I come in when people's whole world has been rocked. Everybody's thrown and back on their heels and guarded up. Which is totally understandable, but it makes it pretty damn difficult for me to have a genuine conversation with anybody." He laughs and holds up his hands. Like, What are you going to do? He lets his hands drop, leans back in. "So, really," he says, "what I'm saying is, anything that you can tell me— anything that's going to help me get a better sense for things here, a sense for your show, a sense for how it fits into the lineup, for how the whole thing fits together, or maybe how you feel like it doesn't fit together, or anything that would make it fit together better—anything like that would really help me. It would really help me do a better job at my job, which means me doing a better job of making everybody happy."

Dave has stopped fidgeting around. He's sitting completely still, now, slouched down in the chair with his arms crossed high up on his chest. He looks at me without moving his head, looks at me with just his eyes. "Sure," he says. His voice is tight, thin. He looks back at

Chad. "No problem," he says. "Sure. Whatever we can do. Whatever we can do to help."

Whatever Chad gets from Dave's posture or his tone or his overall demeanor, he lets it go. He nods. "Yeah?" he says. "Well great, then. Fantastic." He leans back, opens his arms wide. "All right, then," he says. "Go for it. Hit me. I'm all ears."

IT'S KIND of a blur, what happens next. I'm there in the room but I'm somewhere else, too, so I only get it in chunks. As soon as Dave starts talking about the show—about the different segments and recurring bits we do, and the interviews we've done over the years— Chad fixes him with a look like he doesn't understand a word of what Dave is saying, like he's never heard a radio show in his life and he can't imagine what one would be like, or why anyone would listen to one, and all of sudden I know for an absolute fact that Dave is right, that we're going to get dropped, that we need to do something and we need to do it yesterday, last week, last year. That we need to get going on it right fucking now.

"Jesus Christ," Dave says, once we're back out in the hall. "Shit, we'll be lucky if we make it to New Year's."

"You're right," I say.

"Fucking A right I'm right," Dave says.

"No," I say, "I mean about the other thing. You're right about us needing to do something."

We're walking, now, headed for the booth, but when I say that Dave takes hold of my arm and he stops us and he says, "So wait. What does that mean? What are you saying? I'm right about us needing to do something. Does that mean you're good with what we talked about? The whole thing? Meaning that you'll do the thing? You'll reach out?"

I nod. "I'll reach out," I say, "but I'm not promising anything. I can't promise that he'll even get back to me. Not even to tell me to fuck off."

Dave shakes his head. He's grinning, though. "No," he says. "No, of course not. Just reach out. Reach out and see what happens, and we'll take it from there."

IT'S TRUE, what I said. I don't have any contact information for him. The best idea I can come up with is to call his parents. It's funny. I haven't talked to them since before Logan left, but I still know their number. It's still in my head. Or, I should say: I still know their number at the house where they were living back then, back when Logan and I were playing together. I don't know if they're still there. I don't actually know if they're still around at all.

Logan's mom answers on the third ring. She's surprised to hear from me. She says it's good to hear my voice. It's strange. We were pretty close, for a while. Back when Logan and I were playing together I spent a lot of time over at their house. We were all living in Kent and they didn't live that far away. Maybe forty-five minutes. Logan's mom would feed us and do our laundry, that sort of thing. She liked taking care of us. Logan's dad was great, too. He was always interested in what we were doing, where we'd been, how things were going for us. I spent a few holidays with them, even. I'd almost forgotten about it. I hadn't thought about it in years.

Logan's mom asks what I've been up to. I tell her about the show. She doesn't know about it. She mostly listens to NPR, she says. She says she'll listen for me now that she knows.

I tell her why I'm calling. She doesn't have a number for Logan either, though. For a long time, she says, when The Loose Ends were getting big and then after, he was constantly changing it. Somebody would give his number to somebody else and they would give it to somebody and then he would have people he didn't know calling him all the time. For a while he kept her updated, she says, but finally he stopped. It got to be too much. He would give them one number and then have to call three or four days later to give her a new one. She's got an email address for him, though. She gives me that. I thank her, say it was good talking to her. I tell her to say hi to Logan's dad for me. She wishes me luck with everything. We say goodbye.

I take the address she gave me and I go and I write the email. I write, Hey Logan. It's been a long time. I hope you're well. I write, I've got this podcast I'm doing. We're just starting out. I write, If there's any way we can get together, maybe even just have a phone conversation or something, you'd be doing me a really big favor. I write, I feel like you owe me at least that much, but then I erase that again as soon as it's written. I write, I hope to hear from you. And I hit send.

PART
THREE

I THINK I probably need to break in, here. I think I probably need to
cut in and explain. I don't know that what I have to tell you next will
make as much sense if I don't. I don't know that you'll understand. If
I don't go back and explain then you'll only have half of the story. If I
don't go back and explain then you won't know how it was, really.
You won't know what things mean. So bear with me, here. Stick with
me for a second. Hear me out. Then you can decide. Full and honest,
right? Full and honest. Here you go. This is that. This is my full and
honest. This is everything. This is everything I've got.

I'M MOPPING behind the line when Dylan comes out of the back and
tells me that he's almost done with the trash and that he's going to a
show after we're finished here, and do I want to come?

Dylan and I have been working together for maybe six weeks, and we go to the same school, but apart from work stuff and seeing each other in the hall between classes and at lunch we don't really interact. We don't hang out. For one thing he's a sophomore and I'm a freshman and for another thing he's got his own group of friends and for a third thing I don't really hang out with anybody. If I'm not at school or at work I'm either hiding out at the library or I'm off in the woods or I'm alone in my room.

"A show," I say.

"A show," he says. He takes the cigarette from behind his ear and tucks it into the corner of his mouth. He shrugs. "You can call your parents," he says, "if you need to."

There's no point in that. There'd be no debate around the subject. There's no question of getting permission. I'm only allowed out this late because it's work. I shake my head. "No," I say. "I don't need to."

He nods. "Great," he says. "We leave in three minutes."

DYLAN AND I don't hang out, but there is one thing that connects us. After the bakery is closed, after the door is locked, while we're cleaning up, the owner lets Dylan play whatever he wants over the stereo system. The stuff he plays is always loud, fast, aggressive. It fills the space, takes over. There's no ignoring it, no pretending it isn't there. It's the whole thing. It's what's happening. Even still, it takes me almost two weeks to say something. It takes me almost two weeks to ask him what it is, to tell him that I like it.

He looks at me. "Yeah?" he says.

I nod. The truth is that I've never heard anything like it. It's like the opposite of everything I've ever heard, somehow. It's the opposite of this whole stupid town, the opposite of my whole stupid life.

Dylan nods. "It's Black Flag," he says. He's tossing the bags of day-olds, throwing them from the middle of the line down to the trashcan at the end. He's tossing them without looking, still facing me. He misses and a dozen dinner rolls spill out and go skating across the laminate flooring. He doesn't seem to notice, though. He doesn't seem to care. He keeps nodding. "Rollins is the man," he says. "Rollins is a fucking God."

After that, whenever we work together, he makes a point of telling me what tape he brought, who it is and where they're from, his favorite song, if he's ever seen them play. He makes a point of telling me the crazy shit they've done on stage, the crazy shit they've done in their lives.

Apart from that, though, we hardly talk. During work he stays in the back prepping the next morning's bake while I work the line, serve the customers. When he tells me that he's going to a show and asks me if I want to come it's the first thing he's said to me all night.

WE FINISH up, get our coats. Mr. Cooper walks us to the front, locks the door behind us. We cross the parking lot to Dylan's car. It's a huge old sedan, like the kind my grandparents drive. The door is a mile long and only opens part of the way in the space between Dylan's car and the next one over. I have to squeeze through, have to turn sideways to get in. Inside smells like cigarettes and wintergreen air freshener. The bench seat sags under and behind me. Dylan turns the key and puts it in gear, pulls out of the lot. I can hear my heart beating in my ears, feel it pulsing along the sides of my neck and up into my jaw as the lighter button pops, as the first threads of Dylan's cigarette smoke reach my nostrils. As The Germs strain the car's speakers. As the town accelerates to a blur outside.

The show is at some house in South Euclid. We park down the street and walk over. The band is set up in the garage, the audience is clustered in the driveway. The music is louder than anything I've ever heard. It's louder than thought. Dylan pushes his way in, pulls me along behind, and before I can even think to hesitate we're in,

Scott Burr

we're part of it, we're swept up in it. Bodies press in and bodies hold me up and hands reach and pull me to my feet when I fall. Someone's shoulder smashes my nose, someone's elbow splits my lip. For the first time in my life I taste my own blood. It tastes elemental, tastes like life happening. Our breath and our heat rise in a cloud that catches in the headlights shining on the scene. Time ends and begins and ends and then dissolves into the sprinting present. I forget myself and remember and forget again. I die and am reborn.

And then the music stops, and the people around me are moving with a different energy. There are blue and red lights flashing from somewhere, flashing against the house and the garage and the fence posts and the faces and the backs of people, and Dylan's hand is grabbing my shoulder and his voice is in my ear, and he's telling me to run.

WE HIDE out in the bushes in a backyard a block over, me and Dylan and a few other kids from the show, all of us hunkered down and huddled in our jackets. We smoke cigarettes and make jokes and we slap each other's shoulders to stay warm. Then Dylan and I make our way back to Dylan's car, and Dylan drives me home.

I go up the steps and I go inside. My parents are there waiting, my mother on the couch and my father in his chair. They both stand when I come in. My mother puts down the magazine she's been reading, my father closes his book and takes off his glasses.

My mother says my full name. She asks me where I've been. She wants to know what happened to my shirt, my pants. She wants to know what happened to my face. "We were worried sick," she says. "Did you even think about that? Did you think about that at all? Did you even think about us?"

I look at them. I give them the look I've seen Dylan give Mr. Cooper, when Mr. Cooper wants to know why the baguettes aren't done yet. The look is blank and bottomless, beyond care or concern.

My father shakes his head. "Well," he says, "wherever you were, I hope you had a good time. I hope you had a really good time, because it's the last good time you're going to have for a while." He points down the hall. "Go to bed," he says. "Right now."

I go. I go into my room, change out of my clothes, get into my pajamas. I go into the bathroom and I brush my teeth. The foam I spit into the sink is tinted pink. The medicine cabinet mirror shows my split and swollen lip. It's all mine. I turn out the lights and I go back into my room and I get into bed. I lay there reliving it, trying to recapture it, trying to live inside the noise and the feeling. I lay there all night, too wired to sleep, and the next morning when I get to school Dylan is there by my locker and he tells me to come with him.

I follow him down to the stairwell by the art room and they're all there, all the kids you can't miss, the ones with the Mohawks and the combat boots and the safety pins in their ears, the ones I've seen smoking in the parking lot and giving each other stick-and-poke tattoos in the bathroom. Dylan introduces me around. They wave, say hi. One of the girls—Charlotte—asks Dylan what happened, asks him if the cops fucked with us. Dylan shakes his head.

"We bailed pretty quick," he says. "We ended up hiding out in somebody's yard for like half a fucking hour."

The bell rings, but no one moves. Dee makes a face and hugs her stomach.

"Oh God," she says. "I've got the worst cramps. This is bullshit. You shouldn't have to go to school when you're on your period. It should be against the fucking law."

The other girls agree. One of the guys—Justin—asks what people are doing later. A couple of them are maybe going to the movies. Gwen wants to go, but she's supposed to go to dinner with her family. It's her grandma's birthday.

"I may skip it," she says. "It depends on where they go."

Everybody nods. That makes sense, we all agree. She shouldn't go if they're going someplace shitty. Then Trevor stands up, says he has to go. He can't get another demerit, he says, or they'll stick him in Saturday school. It's like a signal. People start gathering their stuff, start splintering off. Dylan tells me he'll see me later and disappears up the stairs. Charlotte and Gwen head out. My first class is way off at the other end of the building, and it takes me a long time to get there. Mr. Miller has already taken attendance, is already up at the board and into the lesson, by the time I open the door.

He looks surprised, looks concerned, when he sees me. "Dex," he says. "What happened? Are you all right? Did you miss the bus?"

I give him nothing. I stand there in the doorway and I shrug.

He looks at me. For a minute we just stand there, looking at one another. Then something seems to resolve itself. Some question seems to find its answer. The muscles along his jaw flex and set. He nods toward my seat.

I walk past him, go sit down. I don't hurry. I take my time.

The other kids are watching.

Mr. Miller goes over to his desk, opens the book, erases what he's written. He brushes away the eraser crumbs, holds the pencil over the page. "Mr. Foster," he says. "I'm marking you down as being here on time, as long as I have your assurance that this won't become a habit."

He looks up from the page, looks up at me. He wants an answer. The other kids are turned in their seats. I've been chewing the swollen spot on my lip and the scab has started to come loose, has started to crack and bleed. I can feel blood running down inside my mouth, feel it spreading in a tacky film across my lips.

I've never been anything before, never been anything but what I was told to be, and what has it gotten me? Nothing. Nothing like this. Nothing like the gravity of their attention, their anticipation. This feeling like warmth and goodness and light.

I smile my biggest smile, smile my gritted teeth at all of them. I unclench my jaws to speak.

It's too late, though. Mr. Miller doesn't have time for this. "I'll take that as a yes," he says. He marks the page and closes the book, moves back toward the board. "Where were we," he says, "before we were interrupted?"

The class turns its attention back to him. Most of them do, at least. Angela Richards is still turned in her seat, still looking at me. I meet her eyes. She makes a face.

"You know your lip is bleeding," she says. "It's pretty gross."

I stick out my tongue, run it over the spot, run it back and forth.

Her look changes, intensifies. She looks sick. She recoils. "Oh God," she says. "You're disgusting."

I lean in toward her, nod. "Yes," I say. "Yes, I am."

AFTER THE last bell I go out and Charlotte and Dylan and Trevor are there in the parking lot, sitting on the hood of somebody's car, and Charlotte sees me and waves me over. She nudges Trevor, moves over to make a place for me on the hood. I go over and I sit with them. The wind is cold but I can feel their warmth through my jacket. I can smell their cigarette smoke and the mouthwash they use to cover it.

Dylan leans out from the line, asks me if I'm working.

"Yeah," I say. "Every night this week."

"That blows," says Charlotte.

I shrug. "It's okay," I say. "At least this way I don't have to be home."

Trevor laughs. "I hear that," he says. "My parents fucking suck."

Justin walks up, waves a hand at us. "All right you punks," he says, "get the fuck off my car. Do you want me to call the cops?"

We laugh and move. Justin unlocks the door, gets in, starts the engine. Kristin and Dee come running up. They stand by the passenger door, shivering in their miniskirts. Justin leans across and pops the lock pin. They open the door and fold down the seat, climb in back.

Justin leans across, looks at me. "What are you doing?" he says. "You going into town? You need a ride?"

I look at Dylan. He and Charlotte and Trevor are already moving off across the parking lot toward the woods behind the track. Dylan turns with a cigarette held tight between his lips, walks backward as he raises the lighter. He cups the flame, blows smoke, waves a hand. "Go with them," he says. "I'll see you down there."

"Sure," I say. "Okay. Cool."

I get in, close the door. Justin pulls out ahead of the line of buses. He steers with his knees as he cracks the window and lights a cigarette. He nods at the floor at my feet.

"There should be some tapes down there," he says. "Put something on."

I move my bag and dig into the space. I come up with Social Distortion and Minor Threat and Dead Kennedys, bands I only know because of Dylan. I slip one into the deck and Ian MacKaye's vocals crackle through the speakers.

Trevor nods, grins around the cigarette. "Good choice," he says. "Fuck yeah."

Dee is telling Kristin about something that happened in class, some comment that got her sent to the office.

"Whatever," Kristin says. "Everybody knows Mr. Yancy is an asshole. Even his own kids hate him. He's going to die alone. He's going to end up as one of those guys they find a month later, all rotted into his fucking couch."

They laugh. We all laugh. Justin guns it through a yellow light, pulls out onto the main road. The houses we pass, the mailboxes and signs and telephone poles, begin to blur as we pick up speed. Dee slaps her palms against the seatback, drumming along as the chorus builds.

"Fuck yeah," she says. "Fuck yeah. Let's go. Let's fucking go."

AND JUST like that, I'm with them. I'm part of them, now. Like it's been decided. It's that simple.

We hang out in different people's basements, sit in cars in parking lots. We take over the sidewalk in front of the gas station in town, take over corner booths in coffee shops until the owner or the manager or whoever tells us that we're too loud, that he's getting complaints from the other customers, that we have to leave.

We hang out in the stairwell by the art room, smoke cigarettes in the woods behind the gym. We give each other haircuts and make each other mixtapes. We pierce each others' ears and give each other scars.

And we go to shows. We go to lots and lots of shows. We scrape together cash if we need tickets, run scams to get in if it's eighteen-and-over. We sneak in the back, mark Xs on our hands. We hide from the bouncers and disappear into the crowd. There in the hot loud dark all of the bullshit in my life fades down to nothing and I dissolve and am absorbed, become part of the sound and the movement and the energy, and afterwards I stand out in the parking lot with my ears ringing and my clothes soaked in sweat feeling hollowed out and formless, like something new and undefined, just spat out by the universe.

And it's all fucking amazing. It's like the sun shining on me for the first time in my life.

I stop doing homework, stop doing chores. I stop getting to school on time and I stop coming home when I'm told to. Whatever they want me to do, whatever it is, whoever they are, I stop doing it.

And my parents freak out. They can't understand. What's wrong with me? They did everything right. They do all the predictable shit. They yell at me, punish me, take stuff away. They take me to see doctors and they put me on meds, put me on other meds when I won't take those. They say they're going to send me to boarding school, say they're going to send me to this paramilitary summer camp for wayward teens that my dad read about. They try to bribe me with things they think I want. They go back and start over, cycle through strategies. This goes on for probably two years before they finally just give up, give in, start leaving me alone. By then I've made it easy for them, though. I stay out of the house as much as I can. By the end of sophomore year I'm sleeping at other people's houses four of five nights a week. I keep clothes in my locker, keep a toothbrush in my backpack.

And I learn to play guitar. Like, really play. I borrow somebody's mom's classical acoustic that she doesn't play anymore until I have enough money saved up for something else. I get Justin to drive me to the pawn shop in the next town and I buy a decent Tele knockoff and a shitty amp for two hundred bucks. Other kids know how to play a little bit and they show me things. I watch and I learn at shows. I buy records and I sit with them until I can play along, note for note.

And people start to notice. They ask me to play with them, ask me if I want to start a band with them. They ask me to sit in with their band, ask me to join their band. From the beginning of sophomore year on I'm playing all the time. I'm either in school or at work or I'm playing with whatever band I'm in or I'm at a show or I'm asleep. That's it. That's my whole life.

The first band I'm in is called Ratf*ck. A kid named Ben is the lead singer. It's his band, really. We practice in his mom's garage while his mom's at work. We learn half a dozen Black Flag songs and a few by The Who and Iggy and the Stooges and The Kinks. We practice for a couple months and then we play a couple of gigs, one at a party at somebody's house and one at this country bar where Ben's mom knows the owner. It's funny, really. There are deer heads and mounted antlers and beer signs on the walls and then there's everybody we know, moshing around in the middle of the dance floor and trying to stage-dive off the eight-inch riser. It seems like a good start to us, though. We're talking about doing another show, maybe working on some originals, but then Ben's mom gets moved to part-time and Ben has to start working more and we can't practice as much. We never really break up, we just stop playing. It's just as well for me. I've got other things brewing. Right after that I get asked to join this group called The Reviled, which is a step up, because The Reviled is already an established group. They've been around for awhile, have actually played real shows at actual venues. They need me because their guitar player is moving out of state. I'm with them all through the rest of sophomore year. All of my first real venue shows are with them. It's my first experience having a real gig calendar and a real practice schedule, my first time getting paid to play music. We didn't get paid for the country bar Ratf*ck show. The owner was doing Ben's mom a favor. Then Tommy the lead singer and Eric the drummer both graduate, and that's it. We play together through the summer, but it's not serious anymore. They're already on to the next thing. Tommy's moving down to Nashville and Eric's going off to college in Indiana. Once they're gone me and Mike, the bassist, start our own group. We ask our buddy Adam to sing and we get Justin to play drums. We call ourselves The All-Arounders. We play together through junior and senior year, all through the summers. We play a lot of shows, get really sharp. We win a battle-of-the-bands thing put on by one of the local stations, get our winning song recorded and played on the radio. It really feels like something. By the time we all graduate we've got a handful of decent originals and a few more passable originals and a dozen or so really tight covers. By now Tommy from The Reviled is working at a venue down in Nashville and he tells us that we need to come down, that the scene is really good, that he knows all the owners and can get us gigs. He tells us that there are industry people all over the place, that groups are getting signed left and right, that if we want to really try to take a run at this thing then we should do it there.

My parents don't argue with me anymore. They don't argue with me about this, either. They stay in the house while I pack up my car, this piece of shit Oldsmobile that belonged to Lisa's grandfather and that I bought from Lisa's parents when her grandfather died. They come outside when I'm ready to go. My mom comes out into the driveway, hands me a cooler full of sandwiches. She kisses me on the cheek, hugs me goodbye.

"Be careful," she says. "You can call us. You can call us, if you need anything. If you need help, or anything. If anything happens."

"Sure," I say. Behind her, over her shoulder, I can see my dad still standing on the porch. He's examining the paint on the railing, picking at loose flakes with his fingernail. I turn back to her. "Sure," I say again. "Okay. Sure. I will."

IT DOESN'T work out. It seems like it might, but then it doesn't. After a year and a half we've built up a decent following and we're playing every weekend and we've got a demo that we're handing out and sending around, but it's not enough. The other guys feel like we should be farther along by now. They feel like we've been here long enough, like we've played in front of enough people. They feel like if we haven't tipped yet then we're not going to, like if it was going to happen then it would have happened already. They feel like it's time to call it, time to bail, time to pull the plug.

I tell them that it takes time, that we need to keep pushing, keep doing what we're doing, tell them that they're all pussies and traitors and posers, tell them that if they leave then our fucking friendship is fucking over. It doesn't matter, though. Nothing I say makes any difference. By the time they tell me what they're thinking it's not a discussion. By the time they tell me what's going on, the decision has already been made.

THEY LEAVE and I stay. I'm going to start another band, going to show them that I don't need them. I'm going to make it big and I'm going to do it fast and with the same material. I'm going to show them that they made a huge fucking mistake. I do probably two dozen sessions with different guys from around the scene, trying different combinations of people and material. None of it works, though. It just doesn't come together. It all sounds like shit to me. Six weeks later I've still got nothing.

With them gone and no gigs I can't pay the rent. I bail on the lease, move my shit into my car. I sleep on people's couches, sleep in the backs of venues where I know the owners. Some nights I sleep in my car, sitting up in the front seat because there's no room in the back with my guitar and my amp and all my other shit in there. I live on candy bars and cheap beer and ramen noodles and cigarettes. At night I go to shows, get fucked up, yell at the band. I punch walls and threaten people, get kicked out. I get a reputation. Bars stop accepting my fake ID, venues stop letting me in. To me it's just more proof that Nashville sucks, that the scene here is bullshit and has always been bullshit. That if Nashville didn't have its head up its own ass we'd have a deal and I'd still have a band. I get fed up and I say Fuck It and I drive back to Ohio. I move in with some guys I know from the scene. They're going to school at Kent and they're renting a house in town and they've got an unfinished basement I can crash in.

IT SUCKS. I thought I was out, thought I was gone and going places. Being back in Ohio feels like being nowhere. It's embarrassing. I feel like a joke, a poser, an asshole. I feel like a failure.

I tell everyone that I'm not staying, that I'm only going to be here for a month or two, that I'm going to get a job and save some money and then go someplace else. I met a lot of different people down in Nashville, I tell everybody. I met guys in different bands and fans of different bands who came through from a lot of different places, D.C. and Chicago and Boston and Philadelphia. I'm going to save up some money and then reach out to them and figure out which place is right and then go there.

"I just need to see where I can really get something going," I tell people. "Once I do that, I'm gone."

I GET a job at the deli in town. I work six days a week, making sand-wiches and running deliveries. It gets to where I can always smell mustard and pastrami, can always smell fake smoke and industrial cleaner. It all soaks into my clothes, my car upholstery, my body. It leaches out through my pores.

I start playing with a couple of student bands. We play campus parties and bars in town. We play alt rock covers, play a smattering of whatever random bullshit drunk college kids want to hear. The guys I play with are decent, but they don't really give a shit. They're all taking classes, working toward degrees. They're all working toward making some other kind of life. None of them are trying to really do something. To them it's just a way to make money and blow off steam and get attention.

I reach out to the people I met, try to make plans. Somehow nothing ever comes together, though. The timing isn't right, the op-portunity isn't there. I can't stay with this guy because his cousin's sleeping on the couch I would be sleeping on, can't stay with this other guy because his girlfriend just moved in. This band already found a new guitar player, this guy already formed a new group. The weather turns to shit, something breaks on my car. My one Chicago contact moves to Seattle, my one D.C. contact is hitting the road. They give me other numbers, give me names of other people to call, but nothing comes of any of it. One guy isn't sure what his roommate is doing, if he's staying or going, and another guy already sublet the room I'd be staying in. It's just one thing after another.

I think about just picking a place and going, about packing up my car and driving to Chicago or Boston or D.C. with no plan and nothing set up. I feel like I have to do something, like there's some kind of expiration date on this whole thing, a point after which I become the guy who works at the deli in town who's still kidding himself that one day he's going to do something, going to start a band and make a run, who's clearly found his place in the world even if he doesn't realize it, even if he can't admit it to himself. But then I imagine how it would be, imagine going to one of those places and working to get established and build something only to have it all fall apart again, and I don't do it. I go to work and I take the orders, go to practice and play the gigs. I go back to the house and I lay on the basement floor on my borrowed futon mattress with my headphones on and the volume cranked up as high as it'll go. And eight months go by, just like that. Before I even know it, eight months of my life just disappear.

THEN ONE night my housemates and I go to this event on campus. Some speaker is there giving a talk about the Gulf War's impact on the region's social and political climate. Or it's something like that. We're not really there for the talk, we're there for the free food and wine they're supposed to have at the reception afterwards. We're sitting there waiting it out when this kid in the audience stands up and starts yelling. He just goes off, ranting about interventionist politics and American colonialism and petroleum cartels. He goes on and on. It's kind of incredible. The speaker can't get a word in edgewise. The head of the department that's hosting the talk has to come up to the podium to try to calm things down. He doesn't do any better than the speaker, though. The kid just won't stop. Finally the department head just gives up. He waves to the campus security officers posted by the door. The kid is pretty well landlocked, though. He's right in the middle of a row, and he's got people with him. The kids in the seats around him get up and get in the way. They're all yelling, too, yelling about censorship and the Bill of Rights. Other kids have started yelling back, though, telling them to shut up and sit down and let the speaker finish. The room just erupts with people trying to shout over each other. Then campus security gets through and gets a hand on the kid. They more or less have to drag him out. He doesn't stop yelling the whole way. He's still yelling when the doors close behind him. By now it doesn't even matter that he's gone, though. The talk is effectively over. The audience is all yelling and the speaker has left the stage. The department head has gone off somewhere, too. More campus security officers have arrived and they're trying to go after anyone who looks like an instigator, but with everyone yelling you can't really tell who's who anymore. You can't even really tell what anyone is saying. It's pandemonium, a total breakdown of the proceedings.

My housemates and I are all losing our shit. We're dying laughing. We keep looking at each other and cracking up. It's too ridiculous.

"Holy shit," I say. "Holy shit, that's the best thing I've ever seen. That's the best thing ever."

Brian is wiping his eyes. "Oh my God," he says. "Oh my God, that fucking kid."

"What the fuck even was that?" I say. I can hardly talk, hardly breathe. My chest hurts from laughing. I feel like I'm going to be sick.

Kyle leans across. "That was Logan," he says. "He does this kind of shit all the time. I had a class with him last semester. He used to pick a fight with the professor over fucking everything. We used to take bets on how long it would take him. And I'm not talking poli sci, either. It was fucking art history." He looks toward the door and shrugs. "Honestly," he says, "I can't tell if the kid's brilliant or fucking retarded. I'll say this for him, though: He's not boring."

IT'S FUNNY at the time, but it also doesn't seem like that big a deal. It honestly doesn't make that much of an impression. And I feel like this is something you should know, because later the label's marketing team comes up with this whole thing about how Logan was this big undergraduate dissident, always walking out of class in protest and challenging his professors and getting up on his soapbox in the campus center, how even before The Loose Ends he was speaking truth to power and shaking up the system and making the establishment nervous. I was there and I'm here to tell you that that's ninety percent bullshit. It's ten percent truth and ninety percent embellishment. Yes he did that stuff, but apart from the fact that he was disrupting the peace it wasn't like anybody that mattered at Kent really gave a shit. Nobody gave a fuck about anything he did. He wasn't making anybody nervous. He wasn't Che Guevara. He wasn't starting a revolution. He was another kid who went off to college and got political and got all worked up about CIA intervention in South America or social injustice or racism in inner city policing or whatever. I'm not saying that he wasn't earnest about it, I'm just saying that this thing they created made it seem like a bigger deal than it actually was. He had a reputation, maybe, but so did the girl who could fit a whole beer can in her mouth. That's the sort of level we're talking about, here. That's the scale. We leave the talk and I honestly don't think about it or Logan again until a few days later when I'm walking across the campus and I see him sitting on a bench outside the administration building, smoking a cigarette and staring at the ground.

I go over and I sit down next to him. Even now I can't tell you why. Whim, I guess. I ask him what he's doing. He looks at me for a second before he nods up at the building.

"Fucking meeting with the fucking S-DAC," he says.

I shake my head. "What the fuck is the S-DAC?" I say.

"The Student Disciplinary Action Committee," he says.

"Shit," I say. "What for?"

He shrugs. "I made this speaker look like an asshole," he says.

"That thing the other night?" I say. "The Gulf War guy?"

He nods, blows smoke. "Last time they told me that next time it would be serious," he says, "and this is the next time."

I reach for the cigarette. He hands it across. I take a drag, blow smoke.

"What does that mean?" I say. "How serious is serious?"

He shrugs again. "I don't know," he says. "Last time they seemed pretty pissed."

It's a joke, somehow. It's funny. I laugh smoke. He laughs, too. I pass the cigarette back.

"Whatever," I say. "That shit was classic. If they can't appreciate that then fuck them."

He nods, waves the cigarette. "Exactly," he says. "Fuck them."

We don't say anything for a minute. We just sit there, passing the cigarette. It's good, though. It's good, somehow. Sitting there I start to feel better. Coming across campus I was feeling really shitty, really pissed off and down. When I came upstairs Brian was there in the kitchen, and right away he started giving me a bunch of shit about some beer bottles that I left on the counter. I didn't see what the big deal was, but he was all worked up. It was a whole big thing for him. How I was a shitty housemate, how I had no respect for other people's space. How they were doing me a big favor, letting me stay with them, and I couldn't even show them the barest fucking minimum of courtesy. It was unbelievable. It was bullshit. He totally blindsided me. Finally I had to just walk out. He was right about them doing me a big favor, so it wasn't like I could tell him to go get fucked, but I also couldn't deal with him. I wasn't going to just stand there and take it, just let him rail at me. So I left. I was so fucking upset. It was just one more fucking thing. One more big Fuck You from the universe. But sitting there on the bench with Logan, with the kids all rushing to class around us, I'm almost glad it happened. Most times I would be in a hurry, running late for work. Because of Brian, though, I left early. Because of Brian I don't have anywhere to be for another half an hour. And stupid as it sounds, that's enough. It's like for the first time in the whole time I've been here I don't have the feeling that I'm supposed to be somewhere else.

Logan passes me the cigarette. We're getting down to the end.

"So what'll you do?" I say. "I mean, if they kick you out?"

He shrugs, shakes his head. "I don't know," he says. "Maybe Greenpeace? Something like that? Or go out to the West Coast for a while? See what's going on out there?"

I hold out the last of the cigarette. "What about music?" I say. "You ever think about singing in a band?"

I don't really think about it first, I just say it.

He looks at me, frowns. "Why?" he says. "You starting a band?"

I'm still holding out the cigarette. I shrug. "I don't know," I say. "Maybe. You want to be in it?"

He doesn't move, doesn't take the cigarette. He's still looking at me but he's not frowning anymore. He shakes his head. "You haven't heard me sing," he says.

I shrug again. "That's all right," I say. "You haven't heard me play."

He doesn't say anything for a minute. He just keeps looking at me. Then he takes the cigarette. He takes a drag, leans and spits, drops the butt into the place and grinds it in with his heel. Then he stands up. I think he's going to leave, think he's going to just walk away, but he doesn't. He moves around in front of me and he goes down in his pocket and he comes up with a pen and he takes my hand and he starts writing something on the back. He nods up toward the building.

"I've got to go do this thing," he says. "If I'm still enrolled here tomorrow, maybe we can do something."

I can feel the pen tip digging in, can feel the veins and tendons and whatever else all rolling under the skin. I look up at him. "Sure," I say.

He finishes, caps the pen. He goes around and goes up the steps. I watch him open the door and go inside. Then I look down at my hand. I had imagined the pen tip cutting into the skin, imagined it leaving ink on what's underneath, imagined whatever he wrote staying as some kind of fucked-up tattoo forever, but it didn't. There's just a number.

I CALL him the next day. He doesn't answer when I ask how the meeting went. He just asks when I want to get together. One of the kids in his crew plays drums, he says. We could meet at his house and work though some stuff. So that's what we do. Logan calls the kid, Danny, and sets it up. We get together and we work our way through a twelve-pack of shitty beer and we riff on *Death or Glory* and *Johnny Too Bad* and *Blitzkrieg Bop*. It works pretty well. It works more than it doesn't. By the second or third time through it all sounds all right. Logan's voice isn't the best, but there's something to it. There's an intensity. It's interesting. We play for a couple of hours, play until the beer is gone. By then we're already talking about the next time, about when it's going to be, about what we're going to play then.

WE MEET up again a few days later, play some more. We just drop right into it. We talk about how to make this a regular thing, about what works with everybody's schedule. We talk about finding a bass player. We make up a few tear-off-tab ads and we put them up around town, in the deli and in a few bars and on the bulletin boards in the student center. We get some calls, meet some people, try out some arrangements. We think we're going to go with one guy and then we think we're going to go with another guy, and then Paul comes in and it's an easy decision. It just works with Paul. He just gets it. We do a few sessions playing different covers and then I give everybody copies of our All-Arounders demo and we start learning those songs. Logan brings in some stuff, too, some lyrics that he's written, and we noodle around on those. We build up a few ideas. I've got my one housemate Kyle's cassette recorder and I set it up in the driveway facing us and we record a few of the All-Arounders songs and a few different versions of the ones with Logan's lyrics and for the next few days I drive around listening to it all over and over and over again. By the time we get together again I know what to do, know what changes to make and what to keep and what to get rid of. We bring it all together, run it all through, and it's fucking solid. Just like that. It works so well it's almost funny. Between that material and the covers we've got enough for a set. We make another shitty tape of our best stuff and I make copies and I hand them around to people I know at different bars and venues in town and then I call and bug the people in charge of booking until they listen to the tape, until they put us on the schedule.

WE START playing out. People really respond. It's crazy, almost. It just moves. Practically every gig we play gets us another gig. It goes out in all directions. Within a couple of months we're playing a bar show or a campus event or a frat party practically every weekend.

We dial in our stage work, figure out our set list, hash out new material. We come up with songs and we figure out where they fit. All things considered there isn't much to do. The core dynamic or architecture or whatever you want to call it is there pretty much right from the beginning. Everything just falls in place around Logan. He's the hub of the whole thing. You can't not watch him, can't not follow his lead. We get consistent on our execution and then Danny gets a friend of his who works in the school's audiovisual department to record a set and we send that tape around to venues in Akron and Columbus and Youngstown and Cleveland.

Things start happening really fast. After recording our set Danny's AV department friend gets really excited about us, wants to manage us. He starts calling around, starts booking us gigs at other colleges and venues down in West Virginia and across into Pennsylvania and New York. Pretty soon we're on the road at least two weekends a month, sometimes more. The weekends we're in town we might play three or four shows, splitting Friday or Saturday night or both between opening at one venue and headlining at another.

We call ourselves Counter. It's my idea. Counter as in counterpunch, counterattack, counterstrike, counterinsurgency. Counter as in being fucking against. I make us a symbol—a capital C, x'd out —and I start leaving it carved into tables and scratched into payphone booth plexiglass and written on venue walls. Sometimes around it I'll write song lyrics, lines from poetry, quotes I like. I'll write, Smash it up til there's nothing left, write, Do you wanna be a prisoner in the boundaries they set you?, write, You will never rid the world of us. We will rid the world of you. I tattoo the symbol on the inside of my wrist with a sewing needle and the ink tube from a ballpoint pen. I do the same for Logan and Paul and Danny. Same pen, same needle. Like blood brothers, we say. Like soldiers for the cause, a guerrilla unit behind enemy lines. A force to be fucking reckoned with, bound together through whatever comes.

We do the whole thing. We pool money from a few gigs and we book some studio time and we record a demo and Phil, Danny's AV friend, sends it around. Some people from some labels come to see us play and we sign a tiny deal with a tiny independent out of Akron and we put out a single that gets some college radio play. Phil pushes that, gets us booked into some bigger college-town venues. We start playing shows where kids we've never seen before know our song, call it out by name, sing along when we play it. We go back into the studio and we record the rest of the album and the label puts it out. They get it reviewed in independent magazines and newspapers, push it out to radio stations all over the country. They send somebody around to our shows with a trunk full of cassettes and CDs and teeshirts they had made.

We do a mini-tour of the East Coast. We stay on the road for a month. I quit my job and Danny and Paul go on official academic hiatus and Logan drops out. Phil sends the merch guy the label sent with us off on random errands while he takes us to meetings he's set up with reps from different bigger indy labels in Boston and D.C. and New York. The reps all tell us they love us, love our sound, love the single. They say they're going to talk to their people and let us know. We shake hands and leave and that's the last we hear from them. Phil tells us not to worry, though, that it's just a weird time, with mainstream alternative morphing into pop rock bullshit and Napster fucking up the whole business model.

"Everybody's waiting to see what everybody else does." he says. "Nobody wants to be the first one out on the ice. Once the landscape settles down a little bit everything will get easier. Until that happens we need to just keep doing what we're doing."

So that's what we do. We build up some cash reserves and we clear the schedule for three months and we hash out and record another album. The label puts it out and we go back on the road. We tour some venues in the upper South, pass back through Ohio and take another lap around the East Coast. The response is solid and the shows are good but it all feels like a repeat, somehow, like we've done it all before. We're playing the same far-away venues for the second or the third time, recognizing waitresses and bouncers. We need something to happen, need something to tip us onto the next level. We need a national act to pick us up as an opener, need one of our new songs to land in mainstream radio rotation, need somebody with a following to mention us in an interview. It feels like we're right there, right on the cusp of something, but it keeps not happening. Eight months later we're still playing the same-size rooms, drawing the same-size crowds. We're getting airtime on the same stations that played us before, selling the new album in the same stores that sold the first one.

We get together without Phil, have practices where we just sit around with our instruments and talk about what to do. It's bullshit, we all agree. What's happening is bullshit. We're fucking good, the albums are fucking good. The response we're getting, the energy around us, it's all right there. Phil could be doing more, should be doing more. The label should be doing more. We should be bigger by now, should be farther along.

"Fuck it," Logan says. "Let's get out of here. Let's go out to L.A. They'll love us out there. I'll bet you money."

We don't really consider it, though. We don't have any contacts in L.A., and we've still got shows scheduled here. Besides that, Paul's girlfriend gets upset when he goes away. If we went out to L.A. he'd probably want to bring her with us, and then we'd have to wait for her to finish her semester at nursing school, and it would be a whole big thing.

WE KEEP going, keep grinding. We keep playing gigs, keep waiting. And then we're staying at this shitty motel outside of Albany while the mechanic Phil found works on whatever's wrong with the van this time and Logan turns on the TV and there it is. It's on every channel. We're watching it live when the second tower falls.

Nobody says anything. We just sit there on the shitty bottomed-out motel mattress and we watch.

And just like that, it's over. It's all over, somehow. Everything that was before is over. Everything is like a bad imitation of itself. It's all different, even the stuff that's the same. A week and a half later we play a show down in Cincinnati and people come out, drink beer, jump around, sing along. They hang out afterwards and they invite us to parties and it's all like it was before, only it's not. You'd swear it was the same, if you didn't know.

IT DOESN'T last. Whatever strange combination of cultural momentum and outright denial carried us through the immediate aftermath fades fast. Crowds start shrinking, gigs start falling through. Album and merch sales drop off. Interviewers want to know what we think about dissent during wartime, about punk rock in the age of terrorism. It's all fucked up. Logan's locked into an ongoing rant about Bush and Orwell and the Patriot Act and Danny's expressing more and more apprehension about being around crowds and Paul's girlfriend is too upset to go to class. She was fine through the end of the semester, fine until Christmas, and then she just fell apart.

"It was the families," Paul says. "It was thinking about all of those families at Christmastime."

There's other stuff, too. The situation with the label is turning to absolute shit. It's been a long time coming, but now it's happening all at once. The core guys are all leaving or are already gone and the guys who are still there don't seem to give a shit about much besides looking cool and being seen, besides getting to tell people that they run an independent label. Most of them weren't even part of the company when we signed on. Phil thinks he can use it as grounds to renegotiate, to make them either commit to doing more for us or let us go, but he isn't making much progress. He can't get a meeting, and when he finally does it gets wrapped into another meeting with a few other bands' managers where nothing really gets discussed, where nothing gets ironed out or resolved.

It may not be all the label's fault, actually. Phil's focus is a bit divided these days. Phil's wife is pregnant with their first kid and Phil has started picking up shifts again at his old job at Kent.

"You have to understand," he says. "It's not that I don't love managing you guys. And it's not that I don't believe in you. But you know how it is. It was one thing when it was just me. It didn't matter if you guys didn't play out for a month. It didn't matter if I had to pretend I wasn't home when the landlord came for the rent. But I can't ask Lisa to live like that. Not with a fucking baby. They're counting on me. I've got to do what's right. You guys can understand that, can't you?"

It's not like he's quitting altogether, he says, but if we find somebody else, somebody who can really focus on us and who can go out on the road, he wouldn't hold it against us if we hired them on. He feels like there's a good chance Kent is going to try to bring him back full-time, and if that happens he doesn't feel like he's in a position to turn them down. "I don't know if you guys really appreciate the hit I took coming on to manage you," he says. "It's been great, don't get me wrong, but it's not exactly a nine-to-five with benefits."

AND THEN there's Danny. Danny's been glued to the news since it happened and Danny's convinced himself that the next attack won't be big, won't be like the last one, that it'll be a bunch of ground-level attacks on small targets, all coordinated to go off at once.

"Think about it," he says. "They're not going to try the same thing twice. They know everybody's on high-alert lookout for all of that shit. They know steps have been taken. But small venues and night clubs and stuff like that, they all have minimal security and a high target density. Somebody with an automatic rifle or a fucking suicide vest could do massive damage, and who's going to be there to stop it? The bouncer at the door? The bartender? Are you fucking kidding me?"

We don't want to hear it, though. Nobody does. But Danny's adamant. He wants us to rehearse evacuation procedures, wants us to come up with a codeword for if we see something going wrong in the crowd. He wants to get a gun and rig a holster into his drum kit so he'll have it there in case he needs it. He starts walking venues before shows, walking through audiences, reporting back to the bouncers about anything or anyone he thinks they need to know about or keep an eye on. He's reading a lot of right wing websites, emailing us links to articles he thinks we need to read.

We're hoping that he'll calm down once some more time passes, that he'll get better, but he doesn't. He keeps getting worse, actually, keeps getting more extreme. In his language, in his suggestions, in his expectations. Finally it reaches a breaking point. He just refuses to go on. We're playing this venue outside of Indianapolis, this place we've played a few times before, and half an hour before the doors are set to open Danny decides he doesn't like the setup. This place has the stage set up in the loading bay and there's a garage door directly behind the drum riser, and to Danny this is a big red flag. To Danny this an easy access point, a place where anybody who really wanted to could force their way in, no problem, and then the whole thing would be wide open. Never mind the fact that nobody wants to force their way in, the fact that this place has shows at least three nights a week and nothing has ever happened, the fact that we've played here three times already and nothing has happened at any of those shows. Never mind the fact that nobody gives a fuck about a couple hundred punks in the middle of fucking Indiana. None of that makes any difference to him. Nothing we say does any good. His mind is made up. Which all would be enough on its own, but to make matters worse Phil isn't there to help us sort him out. Lisa's going to have the baby any day now, so Phil's stayed at home with her. We have to call him from the fucking manager's office. We end up standing around the desk trying to triangulate a conversation between Phil on speakerphone and the manager who's running around trying to make sure everything else is set and Danny who won't even come into the office to be part of the conversation.

It's a complete debacle. Finally we get Danny and the manager both in the office, and they hash it out with Phil. Even that ends up being kind of fucked up, though. Danny wants two more bouncers posted by the garage door during the show, and the manager tells Danny that if he's got to call in and pay two more guys then it's coming out of our end, and Danny says fine without even checking with us first or letting Phil weigh in. It's just total nonsense. And to top it all off, he won't come out for any encores. He just refuses. He says the deal was only for the standard set. Never mind the fact that the bouncers the manager brought in for him are still right there, still posted right where he wanted them. Never mind the fact that nothing even remotely suspicious has happened. Never mind the fact that everything is fine.

It's all just totally unacceptable. It can't stand as a precedent. How are we supposed to schedule shows, let alone a tour, let alone anything, when we don't know whether he's going to pull this same shit again? So I call a meeting. We get together in the practice space we've been using and I let Danny have it. I just go off. About how he's acting like an asshole, being totally selfish. About how we're supposed to be a team, a unit, a fucking tribe. About how he needs to get his shit together and make a decision, needs to figure out whether he wants to keep doing this or not. About how, one way or the other, he's out of the band if he ever pulls anything like that ever again. I really lay it out, really draw a line in the sand. And no, I don't check with Paul or Logan first, don't check to see if this is how they want to handle it, but the thing is that I really feel like I don't need to. I really feel like we're on the same page about this, like we all see things the same way. Like we're all trying to keep this thing going, all trying to figure out how to keep this thing together. That's totally where my head is at. So I genuinely don't see it coming when Logan stands up in the middle of everything—in the middle of me talking, even—and says that he has an announcement to make, that he's moving to L.A., that we can all come with him or not, can keep Counter going and try out there or not, but that either way he's going.

I think he's kidding. Or maybe I don't. Probably I don't. Probably there's no way I actually think he's kidding. Even still I say, "Funny, Logan. That's funny. You're really funny."

He shakes his head. He looks at me. "I'm not joking," he says. "I'm serious. I really mean it. I'm going."

I meet his look. "Bullshit," I say.

He shakes his head again without looking away. "It's not," he says. "I've already got my ticket. Thursday. I'm leaving Thursday."

I can't look at him anymore. I close my eyes, press my fingertips into my eyelids. It took six hours to get us back from where we were in Indiana and I did all of it. I was so pissed at Danny I couldn't have slept if I tried. By the time we pulled into town I'd been driving into the sunrise for an hour and I was even more wide awake. I called the meeting for that afternoon, figuring I'd get some sleep first, but then I didn't. I got into some other shit, and before long it seemed like there wasn't much point. Before long it was getting to where, if I went to sleep, I would pretty much have to wake right back up again.

I drop my hands, look at him. "Wait," I say. "What? What the fuck are you even saying right now?"

It's his turn to look away. He shrugs. "I just really feel like those are the people we need to be in front of," he says. "I really feel like those are the people who are going to get what we're about."

I can feel Paul and Danny watching us, but I keep my eyes on him as I say, "Okay, but because of what, though? Based on what knowledge of the scene out there are you making that statement?" Then I say, "No, wait. Hang on. Never mind. Don't tell me. I know. I already know. This because of Jade, right? This is because of Jade's bullshit," because for the past couple of months Logan's been hooking up with this art student, this chick who calls herself Jade even though her real name is Mallory or Melanie or something like that, and the whole time she's been hanging around she's been telling Logan how great he is and what a big deal he's going to be, and how he needs to get out to L.A. because everybody out there is going to love him. Never mind the fact that she knows fuck all about L.A. Never mind the fact that she grew up in fucking Wisconsin.

I feel like she's probably also been telling him that he's better than the rest of us, that we're all holding him back, that he should ditch us and go out on his own, but I've never really worried about it. For one thing she's not the first chick to say that type of shit and for another thing Counter's been together for years, at this point. Logan's only known her for a couple of months.

Logan shakes his head. "No," he says. "It's not because of that. And anyway, it's not bullshit. She's right. It's a good idea."

I barely let him finish, though. I'm talking again before the words are even all the way out of his mouth. "Listen," I say. "Jade doesn't know shit about L.A. Jade doesn't know shit about shit. She's a fucking fan. She's a groupie. You're taking career advice from a fucking groupie?"

His look changes. It's a warning, now. "Hey," he says. "Come on."

The thing is, though, at this point I don't give a shit. I've been awake for something like thirty-six hours and I've been significantly pissed off for at least half of it. All of the momentum I had going into Danny, all of the focused outrage, is shifting gears, now, is tuning in on Logan's frequency, and stuff just starts coming out. I'm not even in charge of it, really. I hear it for the first time right along with everyone else.

"What?" I hear myself say. "What do you actually think? Tell me what you actually think. Walk me through it. I want you to walk me through your actual idea of how this thing goes. We load all of our shit into the van and we drive all the way across the fucking country, out to where we don't know anybody, with no management, and then what? The West Coast Fairy Godmother waves her magic wand over us at the state line and all of our dreams come true? Listen to me. Listen to what I'm telling you. Nobody out there is going to give a shit, okay? There are a thousand bands like Counter in L.A. A fucking hundred thousand. I've done what you're talking about. I thought if we went down to Nashville that was just going to be it for us. I thought somebody was going to offer us a deal for just showing up. I promise you that if we go out to California we'll be doing exactly the same thing we're doing now, only we'll be doing it with no contacts and no fan base and way more competition and way more expenses and for way, way less money." Then, I laugh. "I mean, Jesus Christ," I say. "Are we actually having this conversation? Because of something your fucking fuck buddy said? Do you seriously think that going to California is going to solve anything? Are you actually that fucking stupid? Jesus Christ, how did I not know you were this fucking stupid?"

I have more to say, but I don't say it. I have to stop. I'm out of breath. My heartbeat is hammering along the sides of my neck and up into my jaw and I can see black spots swimming in the air around and in front of me. I look over at Danny and Paul, look for them to back me up or jump in, look for them to agree at least, but they don't. They don't even look at me. They look around, look somewhere else, look down at the floor.

"So what?" I say, finally. "That's it, then? Just like that? We're done? We're broken up? Is that what's happening? Because I just want to be clear about what's happening here."

It isn't Logan who answers me, though. It isn't Danny, either. It's fucking Paul.

"He's right," Paul says. "You know he's right. You know we've got to do something. We've got to change something. Otherwise it's just going to keep being this."

"Okay," I say. "Fine. That's fine. Let's change something. I'm good with that. I'm open to changing something. What do you want to change?"

Nobody says anything, though. Nobody says anything until Paul says, "I mean, I think that's what Logan's saying. I think that's what he wants to change."

Danny's been sitting back with his arms crossed. Now he shrugs and sits forward. "Put it to a vote," he says. "All in favor of the move, raise your hand."

Logan raises his hand. Danny keeps his arms crossed. Paul leaves his hands in his lap. Danny looks at me.

"Well," he says, "there you go."

I barely hear him, though. There's some kind of noise in my ears, some kind of hissing, some kind of sonic blur that's been steadily growing as I stand there. My field of vision is narrowing, too. Like my brain is shutting down. Like something won't compute. All these years of pushing, of grinding, of almost getting over and the gnawing frustration when we don't, and now this. Now Logan's stupid fuck buddy and her stupid ideas. Now Danny's stupid paranoid bullshit, his stupid smug certainty. Now Paul and his fucking surrender. For a second I have this vision of me just going off, going at them, of kicking Danny in his teeth and grabbing Logan by the throat, of telling Paul to fuck off back to his girlfriend and all of her fragile, melodramatic bullshit. For a second it almost feels like I'm going to do it, too. But then I don't. I don't do anything. I just stand there like a fucking asshole until Logan says, "The tickets Jade got us are for Thursday. You've got time. You've got time, if you want to think about it."

From somewhere far away I hear my own voice. "Don't worry, asshole," I hear myself say. "I'm not going to be thinking about anything else."

I DON'T get a ticket, don't change my mind. I don't talk to Logan, either, even though he tries. Even though he calls and leaves messages saying that we should go get a beer, go get a coffee, saying that we should get together. Saying that he doesn't want to leave with things the way they are. That Thursday he calls and leaves one more message saying that the bus leaves at ten-forty, saying that I should just throw some shit in a bag and grab my guitar and get a ticket and walk away from everything. Saying that it would be some real rock 'n' roll shit, the kind of shit that makes legends.

I don't do it. Besides everything else, besides everything I said to him and besides the fact that I'm still pissed and that the thought of spending three days on a bus with Jade makes me physically ill, I can't just go. I've got other shit to do. I've got other commitments in town. For maybe a year now I've had this gig at Kent's radio station, playing punk and ska and reggae records in the nine-to-midnight slot a couple nights a week, and after I left the meeting I called the station manager and I asked him what he thought about giving me more time, about having me do my show more often. I figured, Fuck it. I figured, Fuck them. I've got my own shit to do. I figured, Who the fuck needs them? So at ten-forty on Thursday night I'm not thinking about getting on a bus, about going to California. At ten-forty on Thursday night I'm sitting in the booth listening to Desmond Dekker sing about waking up and slaving for bread, about his wife and kids getting packed up to leave him. At ten-forty on Thursday night I'm thinking about Logan failing hard, about him realizing he fucked up, about him being so fucking sorry he didn't listen to me.

AND THAT'S it. That's it for almost a year. For almost a year, I don't hear anything. I do my show, hang around town. I sit in with a couple groups but I don't play out. I don't see Danny, don't see Paul. I start sort of vaguely wondering if maybe pretty soon I'm going to run into Logan, if it'll turn out that he's finally split with Jade and gotten frustrated with L.A. and come back, but it keeps not happening. Then one day I go into the station and there's a new CD on the pile and I put it on and I hear his voice.

I think about throwing it away, about breaking it into pieces, about pretending it never came. I don't do it, though. For one thing I know that it wouldn't make any difference. The CD wasn't sent to me personally. If it's sitting in our promo pile then it's sitting in dozens of other promo piles in dozens of other stations across the country. So I listen to it. I listen to it all the way through. I kind of can't help it. I've got this weird sort of sick curiosity about it. And it's not bad. I want to hate it, but I don't. The really fucked-up thing is, though, that the three songs on that little promo disc aren't any better than what we played in Counter. A lot of Counter's stuff was better, actually. Listening to it it's kind of like Logan is standing there saying, See? I told you. I told you Counter could have been big out here. I told you you should have come. It's like he's standing there saying, See? I told you so.

I DON'T break the disc and I don't throw it away, but I'm happy enough to bury it in the rotation. I'm happy enough to let it fade into the background. But then the full album comes out, the self-titled one, and their one song gains some traction on mainstream alt-rock radio, and people start calling in to request it. At first it's just here and there, but pretty soon it's more and more. Pretty soon it's all the time. I'm doing the show five days a week, now, so it feels like I'm constantly being asked to play it. It feels like I can't get away from it, like Logan's new bullshit is the soundtrack to my life. Still, I don't say anything. I introduce the song, give the band and the track name, and that's it. I don't say anything about how the guy singing lead used to sing lead for my band, about how Counter fans might recognize his voice, about how I'm pretty much the whole reason he's even doing music in the first place. I figure I can last it out, figure people get sick of songs, figure this'll be their one high point and that'll be that. But it's not. The label starts pushing another song off the album and pretty soon people are calling in to request that one, too, and it just keeps going. Day after day, week after fucking week, there's just more and more and more. They play Conan, play fucking *SNL*. Finally it's too much, already. It's making me sick, keeping it in all the time. It's giving me stomach problems, keeping me up at night. It's all just such unbelievable horseshit. How everybody thinks they're so great. How everybody thinks Logan is so great, thinks the album is so great. Which it isn't, even. It isn't that great. It's fine. It's okay. It's got some kind of catchy songs and some kind of clever lyrics, but when you get right down to it it's nothing special. It's just more derivative post-Green Day pop-punk bullshit. And to top it all off, all of the best stuff on the album is just re-worked Counter material. All of the best songs are just retreads of songs that I basically co-wrote, and what am I supposed to do with that? Am I supposed to just not say anything, just keep my mouth shut, forever? So finally I've had enough. I crack, or whatever. I start talking about it on the show. I start doing this thing where I go on a little rant every time I'm about to play one of their songs. The funny thing is, though, people like it. They really respond. It starts to become its own thing. People call in to request the songs just to wind me up. Clips of me yelling get passed around online. The show's audience actually grows, and the station manager reworks the schedule to give me another hour.

I have to work to fill the time. I start doing more call-ins, start telling more stories about being on the road. I work some contacts and I do some interviews. People respond to all of it. It's kind of crazy. Pretty soon I'm the most popular show in the lineup. It gets me enough attention that somebody at one of the bigger stations reaches out and offers me a gig splitting cohosting duties on that station's morning show while the regular cohost is on vacation. All of a sudden I'm doing two shows a day two or three days a week, cohosting in the morning Mondays, Wednesdays, and every other Friday and doing my show for Kent in the evenings. I do that for almost a month. Then the manager at the new station clues me in. The guy I'm filling in for isn't on vacation, he's in a contract dispute with the owners and everybody likes me better than the other guy they've had filling in on the other days and they want me to come onboard and do the cohosting gig full-time. So I do that. It's a better gig, higher profile and more money. Besides that, I don't have much else going on. I'm not playing music with anybody, not going out on the road. I'm around. I sign an eighteen-month contract and I quit doing the show for Kent. For the first time in my life I'm pulling in decent money on a reliable schedule. I pay off my car, move into a nicer apartment. The new gig goes well. I develop a following. The station features me in ads online and on billboards and on the sides of buses. I get recognized more than I ever did when I was playing music. I meet Dave when he gets hired on as a sound tech and we hit it off. The eighteen months go by. I'm sick of waking up early and I hardline the owners over the contract renewal. I want them to give me my own show at a later time. They won't do it, though. They say it's too much too soon. They want me to stay where I am for another two years. I put out feelers and I find another station that'll give me what I want. At first I'm just using it as a bargaining chip, but then it starts to seem like the better option. Dave's been doing regular appearances on the morning show and he and I have a good rapport, and I ask him if he wants to leave with me and be my producer-slash-cohost. He says sure. It's an easy decision, he says. It's a step up for him, something interesting for the resume, and it doesn't really matter if it goes nowhere. He can always go back to doing what he was doing before. It's not like he's married, not like he has kids. So we leave. We sign on at WXYY and we build the new show together. We find our voice, figure out our rhythm. We work out bits and produce content. People respond. The concept evolves. I turn thirty, turn thirty-one. Our contract expires and we renew. Dave tells me that I've got to stop paying rent, got to start investing in my future. He helps me find a house, helps me talk to the bank. I sign the papers and get the keys. I get some decent furniture, get a real bed and a new couch and a nice table. I get a solid stereo, organize my albums, arrange my guitars and my amps. I sit there before or after work and

I put on music and I play along like I used to when I was first learning, when I was just starting out. I turn thirty-two, turn thirty-three.
Our audience is growing. Our contract expires again and we renew
again. I turn thirty-four, turn thirty-five, turn thirty-six. Suddenly
somehow I've been working just in radio—not working part-time at
the Kent station when I'm not on the road but doing a radio show as
my full-time gig—for longer than Counter was even together. It seems
impossible, seems fucked up. I still feel like that guy, still feel like
that guy's future is somewhere out ahead of me. But I've never heard
of anyone starting a band in their mid-thirties that actually did anything, that actually went anywhere. Everyone my age is doing what
they do, what it feels like they're going to do. I turn thirty-seven, turn
thirty-eight. Now it's like a joke, somehow. It doesn't make any sense,
but there it is. There's no undoing it. I still play my guitars, but not as
much. Most nights I watch TV, go to bars, waste time online. I turn
thirty-nine. The show is doing better than it's ever done. The numbers are solid, the sponsors are happy. It's great, I guess. It's what
we've been working for. Mostly I don't think about it. I don't think
about my life. I don't think about how long it's been since anything,
or what it means. Then one day Dave tells me that we have to come
in early, that there's a meeting for the show runners, and when I get
to the station there are streamers in the hallway and a sheet cake in
the common room with a pair of faces and a microphone and a set of
dates like on a tombstone all done up in colored frosting, and Kyle
the intern wants me to tell him how it feels.

AND THIS whole time, through all of this, Logan just keeps getting
bigger. A lot of this you may already know. After the self-titled album
comes *Past the Point* and after that comes *USAhole,* and after that it's
just a whole different thing. After that he might as well be a fucking
astronaut, as far as there being any similarity between what he did
with me in Counter and what he's doing now. Double platinum,

album of the year. What Stage at Bonnaroo, feature story in *Rolling Stone*. He does the whole thing. He gets the whole deal.

And it's funny. If I was Danny or Paul or anybody else, I might have been able to ignore it. Or I might have been able to keep some distance, at least. Instead, with the way things are, every time there's a news item about Logan or the band, or there's an announcement from the label, or there's some bullshit secondhand rumor that somebody heard from somebody whose cousin's roommate is a road-ie for the band, I'm in the booth the next day vomiting it back out. That kind of frivolous, faux-insider, pop culture bullshit is my stock-in-trade, now. It's my job to repeat and comment. When he calls out Bush at the VMAs. When he says that thing about domestic democra-cy building on *Larry King Live*. When he gets thrown out of the Viper Room for throwing a drink at some girl. When he gets the DUI in D.C. When he gets arrested at LaGuardia for unprescribed opiates, coming back from the European leg of the *Crosstalk* tour. All of the rumors and speculation about what really happened behind the scenes, when they cancel the show in Toronto. When the release date for the next album gets pushed back, then pushed back again. The statement from the label saying that Logan is suffering from exhaus-tion, that the Loose Ends are going on hiatus so that he can focus on his health, that everyone in the band and at the label wishes him a full and speedy recovery and hopes to have him back in the studio by the end of the year. The announcement of the new album's new re-lease date, and then the redaction of that announcement. All of the random shit after. The thing where the rest of the band backs Billie Joe Armstrong at a rally for Obama late in the 2012 election. The thing where some production company hires Logan to write a musi-cal about the life of Trotsky, then decides that they can't work with him, then gets sued by Logan's management for breach of contract. All of the judgements and proceedings for all of it. It all goes in through my eyes and ears and comes back out through my mouth. I have a strange kind of million-mile-removed front-row seat for all of it. I'm right there, but I'm nowhere close.

PART
FOUR

SO THAT'S it. We're up to what I already told you about, up to Bethany and Chad and Dave's idea and the rest of it. We're up to me calling his mom and writing the email, up to me sending it off. We're up to me doing my life, doing the show and running errands and dealing with Bethany and all the rest of it, while really all I'm doing is waiting to see if I'm going to hear something back.

I wait a day, wait two days, wait three. I check my spam folder, check the address on the email in my outbox against the one I wrote down. I think about calling his mom again and double-checking the spelling. I don't do it, though. I feel like me writing down the wrong address probably isn't the issue. I wait four days, wait five. Chad wraps up his face-to-face meetings and starts circulating. He hangs out by the booth, hangs out in the hallway, lingers in reception. He tells everyone to ignore him, to pretend that he isn't there, but then he jumps into conversations. He stops people in the hall and he asks them what they would change if they ran the station, asks them what they see as the station's biggest strengths. He asks them how what they do at the station contributes to those strengths. He tells us all not to worry, tells us that it's all one big brainstorming session right now, that nothing is being decided. Nobody's buying it, though. People are sending out resumes, working their contacts. They're taking turns on the equipment, recutting their reels.

Not Dave and me, though. We're still waiting. We wait six days, wait seven. It's been eight days since I sent the email when Dave finally looks at me over the console and says, "All right, so what's the move, here? What do you think?"

We're in the middle of a show. We're on a break. We've got forty-three seconds before we're back on.

"You want to talk about this now?" I say.

Dave shrugs. "Just briefly," he says. "What's your feeling? What are we doing, here? Do we move on, do we reach out again, do we try another avenue, what? You tell me."

I dump my headphones, push back from the desk. I stare up at the clock and I watch the seconds tick by. I don't know what to tell him, don't know what's worth doing. I honestly feel exhausted by the thought of doing anything. I shrug and lean back in. "He's probably got a ton of stuff just sitting in his inbox," I say. "He's probably got some assistant who's at least a week behind, sorting through all the shit that he gets. Let's give it a few more days. If we haven't heard anything in a few days I'll reach out again. Or we can figure something else out."

We've got thirty-four seconds until we're back from the break. Dave just looks at me.

"A few more days," I say. "Okay? We can figure it out then. Let's just give it a few more days. Can we give it a few more days? Can we not try to solve this thing right now, right this second?"

Dave frowns, shakes his head. "What?" he says. "What are you yelling at me for? Have I said anything? I haven't said anything. I haven't said shit. I think it's a fair question, at this point." He holds up his hands. "But okay," he says. "Sure. Fine. Let's give it a few more days. What do I care? Let's give it another week. Let's give it two weeks. Hell, let's give it six months. Then we can really dedicate ourselves. We won't even have to do the show, then. We can sit around all day and wait."

"I hear you," I say. "Okay? I get it. But I'm talking about three days. I'm talking about today, tomorrow, the day after. That's it. That's all I'm talking about."

"Fine," Dave says. "If we haven't heard anything by the day after tomorrow you reach out again or we come up with a new plan and we start taking steps. And by *plan* I don't mean us *planning* to wait some more."

"What?" I say. "What the fuck does that mean? What do you think? Do you think I'm glad we haven't heard from him? Do you think I'm glad that he hasn't gotten back to me? Is that what you think?"

"Calm down," Dave says. "What are you getting so worked up for? I don't think anything. Calm down."

"Listen," I say, "this was your idea. I did what I said I would do. I told you I couldn't promise anything. So don't act like this is me dropping the ball, because I never wanted to hold the ball in the first place."

Dave is staring down at the controls, turning knobs and pushing sliders, nodding. "Sure," he says. "No, you're right."

"I know I am," I say. "I know I'm right."

Dave looks up from the controls, looks at the clock, looks at me. He holds up a hand with the thumb folded in and the four fingers splayed. He keeps looking at me as he starts curling the fingers in, as he starts counting them down.

I lean in, put the headphones back on. "That's cute," I say. "Really, I mean it. Nicely done. Really fucking cute."

BETHANY ISN'T waiting, though. She isn't waiting on anything. She's full steam ahead, on everything. The thing now is that her first appointment with the doula that Katie told her about is coming up and she really wants me to go, really really really wants us to go and meet this person together. The thing is, though, I just can't see the necessity. What even is there to say, at this point? Don't drink and don't smoke and take your vitamins. Even I know that. I don't see why we have to drive all the way down to Akron and pay out-of-pocket to be told something that even I already know. And as far as me meeting this person goes, I feel like there are going to be literally dozens and dozens of opportunities for me to meet her throughout the entire rest of this thing. I don't see why it has to happen right now, right in the middle of all of this other shit I've got going on. And she didn't even check with me first. She didn't even check with me before she made the appointment, didn't check to see if that time and everything works for me, and now she just expects me to be there. It's like, Seriously? You're already living in my house. You're already rearranging all my shit, rearranging my whole life. You're scheduling my appointments now, too?

So I don't go. I don't tell her first, don't tell her about not seeing the point and all the rest of it. I just go along and then on the day of the appointment I tell her that I have to go in early, that I should be back in time no problem, and then I leave and I kill an hour and a half driving around, doing bullshit, and then I call her and I tell her that I'm caught up in something, that I'm not going to make it back in time, that she should just go without me.

I figure it'll be just one more thing, that it won't be that big a deal, but it is. It really upsets her. That night she hits me with it as soon as I walk in the door. How I promised. How she was counting on me. How she needs more from me, needs to feel like she's got a partner in this whole thing.

I haven't put my stuff down yet, haven't even taken off my coat.

"Wait," I say. "Hang on a second. What are you even talking about, you need more? I've done everything. I've done everything else. Everything you've asked for I've either done it or I've said I would do it or I've said we could do it. You want to change my office around, fine. You want to sell my car, fine. So how about maybe you stop for one second and you think about everything I am doing, before you start accusing me of not doing enough? When I can't make it to the first fucking appointment with the fucking doula who we're probably going to see a hundred more fucking times before this whole thing is over?" Then I stop my-self. I'm sort of yelling, now. I take a breath. "Look," I say, "they told me I needed to be there. You know how it is. You know how fucked up that situation is right now. What am I supposed to do? If they tell me to be there then I kind of need to be there."

She doesn't engage with that, though. She shakes her head. "I told you that this was important to me," she says. "I told you that it was important to me that we both meet her. That we meet her to-gether. If you told me that something was important to you, that there was something you wanted to do that was important to you, I would do it. I would honor that."

I laugh at that, though. I look at her and I laugh. "Seriously?" I say. "That's seriously how you want to do this? That's what you're going to use on me right now? Okay, then. How about this: It's *important* to me that I don't do anything to give anyone an excuse to fire me, okay? That's *important* to me. Am I using the right words, now?"

She comes right back, though. It surprises me. She never yells, never really even raises her voice.

"Why are you being like this?" she says. "I don't understand why you're being like this. It's not like I asked you for something crazy. It's not like I asked you to build me a mansion or move to another country or something. I asked you to come with me to a twenty-minute appointment in the next town."

I barely hear the last thing she says, though. I'm already talking again, already talking over her. "No," I say, "you're not asking for anything crazy. You're just asking me to orbit my entire existence around you and whatever you need whenever you decide that you need it. No, you're right, that's totally reasonable. One hundred percent. Absolutely. Anybody could see that. Anybody would agree with you."

She doesn't say anything to that. She just stands there looking at me. She stands like that for what feels like a really long time. Then she looks down. She crosses her arms and shrugs. "I've got to be up early," she says. "I've got the first class tomorrow. I'm going to bed."

I laugh. I'm not even trying to be mean, I'm just surprised. "Wait," I say. "What? Are you joking? We're talking. We're in the middle of talking. You're just going to leave? Just like that?"

I'm moving as I say it, following her as she goes past me and out of the kitchen. I follow her as far as the doorway, stand at the edge of the living room carpet. I watch her cross the room and disappear down the hall. I stand there as she goes into the bedroom, stand there as the door clicks closed.

"Seriously?" I say. "This is really how you want to do this?"

That's it, though. After that nothing comes back. After that there's just nothing.

I GO into the fridge and I get what's left of a six-pack that's leftover from back when I used to buy beer and I go and I sit out on the back patio. I've still got my coat on, but it doesn't help much. I get cold fast. I don't care, though. I kind of like it. I like that it sucks. It feels right, somehow. I sit there drinking the beer and getting colder and colder and more and more pissed off. I think about all the things I should have said to her, all the things I could have and might have and would have said if she hadn't walked away. I think about her growing up in the suburbs with parents who supported her, with older siblings who treated her like she was somebody special and wonderful, like everything she did and said and felt was interesting and important. I think about her college where all of the professors listened to what she had to say, about her little yoga circle where everybody is supportive and nurturing. I think about all of this and then I think, Fuck you, already. Where do you get off? What the fuck do you even know? Your whole life you've been floating on a cloud of support and affirmation. Every single thing you've ever done you've had people telling you how wonderful it is and how great you are. How about you go out and experience the world that everybody else experiences, the world where nobody gives a shit. How about you do that and then you come talk to me. How about then you come back and talk about what you're entitled to. About how you're entitled to more. You child. You don't know a fucking thing.

I go around and around like this until all the beer is gone. Then I go back inside and I curl up on the couch. I lay there shivering for a long time. I've only got my coat and the one little blanket that Bethany put on the back of the couch for decoration. All of the other blankets are in the closet in the bedroom, and I don't want to deal with going in there and getting one. So I lay there with my coat pulled tight around me and that stupid half blanket covering just the middle of me, just the lower part of my shoulders and my torso and the upper part of my legs. Between that and how pissed off I am I feel like I'm never going to be able to fall asleep, but then I do. I sleep really hard, actually. I sleep hard enough that I don't hear her get up and come out into the kitchen, don't hear her make tea and toast, don't hear her putting on her coat and shoes. It takes her closing the front door and starting her car to actually shake me out of it. I get up and I go into the kitchen and I stand there at the sink with her dishes drying on the rack next to me and her blanket still wrapped around my shoulders and I watch through the window as she backs out onto the street and drives away.

I GO take a shower and then I go in and I change my clothes. Then I come back out and I check my phone. I'm thinking that she might have called while I was in the shower, that I'll have a voicemail from her, but there's nothing. So I check my email. I'm not really expecting anything, not really looking for anything specific, I'm just checking it the way you do, out of habit, but there in with the spam and the mailing list bullshit there's a new email and lo and behold, miracle of fucking miracles, it's from Logan.

It says, Hey Dex, it's been a long time.

It says, Sure, why not? I'm overdue for a visit home anyway.

It says, I'll have my guy book it and send you the details.

It says, Talk to you soon.

And 'stunned' doesn't even begin to cover it. I'm fucking floored. I'm gobsmacked. It's been nine days. Despite what I said to Dave, at this point I'm pretty fucking far past holding my breath. I write back and I say great, amazing, fantastic, thank you so much, and then I call Dave and I tell him. I haven't actually thought past the fact that he got back to us, but when I tell Dave he gets all amped up, and that gets me all amped up, and the next thing I know we're up at Sam Ash and we've dropped almost four hundred dollars apiece on microphones and mixers and recording software and other random shit for a podcast that doesn't even exist yet, that doesn't have a date set with its first guest or any guarantee that he'll even show up, that doesn't even have a fucking name.

We stand there in the parking lot with the cold wind blowing hard against us and we stare down at the bags and boxes arranged in an expensive little cluster in my trunk and I say, "Fuck me."

Dave shrugs. "Spend money to make money," he says.

"Sure," I say. I'm watching the wind knock around the free edges and the handles on the plastic bags, watching it lay them out flat one direction and then the other. "The thing is," I say, "Bethany has all of this really specific, really expensive baby shit that she wants to buy, and I've been telling her we can't do it yet because I don't have the cash on hand, and if she finds this shit it might be kind of bad."

Dave has his hands shoved deep down in his pockets, has his shoulders up and his chin buried down in his collar. He shakes his head by moving his whole body, by moving as one solid unit. "Can't help you there," he says. "Different deck, same boat. Katie's car has needed new tires for six months. At least you don't have kids running around getting into everything, finding all the shit they're not supposed to find."

I can't argue with that. I turn back to the cluster. The sound of the plastic whipping back and forth is like the sound of something cracking. "Fuck me," I say again. There's nothing else to say. I reach up for the edge and I pull the lid closed.

I STAY out. I run around, kill time. Then I go to the station and I do the show. Then I go home. Bethany's there. She's sitting at the kitchen table watching something on her laptop and eating a bowl of noodles. She looks up at me when I come in, raises her chopsticks, but then she turns back to the screen without saying anything.

I move around behind her and I look over her shoulder. Inside the little video window she's got pulled up some woman is talking, gesturing, pointing at a list of herbs, but Bethany's got her earbuds in so I can't hear what the woman is saying.

I go into the refrigerator and I get some food and I go sit on the couch. I turn on the TV, find some nonsense to watch. I keep the volume where it is. It's not loud but it's not quiet, either. I expect her to come out and say something, expect her to ask me if I can turn it down, but she doesn't. Instead she comes out and she goes down the hall into the bedroom and she closes the door. A while later she comes out and she goes into the bathroom, and I hear her brushing her teeth, but after that she goes right back into the bedroom and she closes the door and she doesn't come out again.

THIS KEEPS up all weekend, keeps up through Monday, even. Bethany goes in to cover classes, goes off somewhere, I don't know where. When we're both at home we avoid each other. Or maybe it's more like she avoids me. Whenever I come into a room she goes out. If I sit down to watch what she's watching she gets up and leaves.

I don't worry about it. Or I choose not to. I've got other shit to think about and I let myself think about it. On Saturday I get another email from Logan and it's his itinerary and it's all happening a lot faster and a lot sooner than I was expecting. He's flying in on Monday, staying with his parents Monday night, and then he's going to give me a call on Tuesday morning. He wants to get together and do the podcast sometime Tuesday.

I go over to Dave's and we brainstorm questions, brainstorm name ideas, register a website. We hook the new gear up to my laptop and we install the programs, check the mics, set the levels. We run test interviews with Dave's kids, ask them silly questions. We argue over bits we've done in the past, argue over which specific tone and voice and attitude is the one we want to keep. We go back and forth and back and forth.

"Look," Dave says, finally, "it's your show. It's your name. Whatever you want this to be, whoever you want to be, that's fine."

"Okay," I say, "you say that, but then I tell you that I don't like something and you tell me I should do it anyway."

He holds up his hands. He's got Jaimie, the two-year-old, in his lap and she's knocking on the side of his face with her little clenched fist. Dave is wincing away each time she does it. He closes the eye on that side and he looks at me with the other as he shakes his head. Jaimie's fist hits his nose, hits his ear.

"That's not what I'm saying," he says. "I'm just telling you what I see from the outside. I'm telling you how I think we play to our strengths. If you feel differently about it, that's fine."

"You're the one who told me the whole punk rock thing was

dead in the first place," I say. "You're the one who told me to dig it a grave and bury it."

Dave reaches and he takes hold of Jaimie's hand, very gently. Jaimie laughs and starts in with the other fist.

"Yeah," Dave says, "as a lifestyle. As a way of operating in the world. I didn't mean the persona. The persona is our whole thing, here."

I lean back in my chair and I pull my hands over my face. For the nine days we were waiting the whole thing was about whether or not we would actually hear anything. The whole thing was about it maybe not happening at all. Now that it's moving forward I'm freaking out, a little. We've been at it for two days and we've still only come up with six or seven questions we both agree on and the more I read through them the dumber they seem.

I sigh, sit forward, drop my hands. "Fine," I say. "You know what? I don't care. I don't care and I don't know, so you tell me. Whatever you think we should do is fine. However you think we should approach it is fine, because I honestly just don't know anymore."

Dave is holding both of Jaimie's hands now and Jaimie isn't happy about it. She's bouncing in his lap, kicking at him with the little heels of her little sneakers. Dave looks at me.

"Things a little rocky at home?" he says.

"You have no idea," I say.

Jaimie bounces harder, kicks harder. Dave winces, frowns at her. Jaimie starts to cry. Dave looks back at me.

"Oh," he says, "I think I might have some."

I COME home from these sessions at Dave's, come home from work on Monday and I find Bethany reading in the living room, find her watching docs we said we were going to watch together. I find her making food for just herself. Wherever she is, whatever she's doing, when I walk in the room she leaves. She goes into the living room or she goes into the kitchen or she goes into the bedroom and she closes the door.

It's fucked up. I'm not indifferent. But what am I supposed to do? Am I supposed to roll over, apologize, get down on my knees and beg?

I sleep on the couch, sleep on the recliner in my office. I wake up stiff, wake up sore, wake up feeling tweaked from how I was laying. I try to stretch it out, try to work it out with my fingers. It doesn't really help, though. I think, I've got to get to class. I haven't been to the studio, haven't done any yoga at all, for probably two weeks, now. I missed one class and I thought I would catch the next one and then I missed that one, too, and it just went like that. It was one thing after another, one day after another. It's been long enough now that I'm not even sure when the last time was, exactly, not even sure which class it was. It isn't good. I know I should be going, know I need it. It just feels like there's so much else to worry about. But I also know that that's exactly why I should be going. That that's exactly when you need it the most. I think, After Logan. Once we get done with Logan I'll get back. Once we get this thing launched. I think, We just need to get this thing on its feet. Once we do that I'll get back to it. Once we do that I'll have some time. I'll get everything sorted out then.

THEN IT'S Tuesday. We get everything set, arrange everything, clear the whole day. Dave works it out with his sister for her to come over and watch the kids if he needs her before Katie gets home from her shift, and he sets it up with the station manager for her to put on one of our pre-recorded sick day shows if we don't end up making it in. Bethany's got classes on Tuesdays, and she's been hanging out at the studio a lot of the rest of the time anyway, so that's set. After she leaves I go out and I get everything from my trunk and I bring it all into my office and I arrange it how we had it at Dave's house, arrange the mics and the board and everything, so that it's all ready for Dave to plug in and get going when we get the call. Then I go and I dig through the boxes in my closet and I find some old photos of us, some old show fliers, and I set them all out on the desk. I find my copies of our albums and I load one of them into the stereo, and then I run out to the store down the street and I get one of those boxed-up coffee cakes and some more beer and I bring it all back and cut up the coffee cake and set it out on a plate. I make a pot of coffee and while it's brewing I go around the house and I neaten up. I line up all the shoes in the front hallway, put the clean dishes away, straighten up the pillows on the couch. I do everything to get the house ready for him to come over and then I go take a shower and I change my clothes and I go back into my office and I sit there with my phone and I wait for his call.

And it doesn't come. He hasn't called by eleven and he hasn't called by noon and he still hasn't called by one. By two o'clock I've eaten four or five pieces of the coffee cake and I've finished off almost the entire pot of coffee and I'm feeling gross and jittery and pissed and I'm about halfway convinced that he never even got on the plane in the first place, that he totally bailed, that he's sitting somewhere in L.A. right now not giving a fuck about me, not even thinking about me, or about any of this. That it's some kind of rockstar dick swinging, some kind of big final Fuck You for anything I ever said or did that he didn't like.

And it's crazy, maybe. It's too much. It's too big a leap to make. At the same time, though, it's hard to just dismiss. Because it would be kind of perfect, somehow. It would be perfect if that was how this played out. If this whole thing ended up with him fucking me over yet again, ended up with us spending all of this time and energy and money for nothing, ended up with me sitting here like an asshole, waiting for a call that isn't coming.

It's stupid. I know it's stupid. I know I should just call him. I have his number. It was in his last email. At the same time, though, part of me feels like, What good would it even do? Because how would it even go? Either he's here and I end up looking like a tool for being all panicked and desperate, or he's not here and I end up looking like a tool for believing what he said in the first place. As long as I don't call it's still neither, could still work out being neither. As long as I don't call he could still call me first. Once I call it's over, though. Once I call it's one or the other. And, honestly, part of me feels better not calling. Part of me feels vindicated, somehow. The longer I wait the more it's like, See? I told you. I told you he was an asshole. You didn't want to hear it, you thought he was so great, but I knew. I knew the truth and now you know it, too. Now here it is, spelled out across our lives in giant fucking letters.

THE POINT is that by the time my phone finally does ring I've been going around like this, stewing down in this shit, for the better part of two hours, and I'm ready to just go off. I'm ready for this to be Logan calling me from L.A. to straight up laugh at me and I'm ready to just let him have it, ready to tell him what a prick I think he is and what a prick I've always thought he was, ready to tell him that I think his music sucks and that he's overrated, that he's a fifth-rate Robert Smith and that he's only successful because his fucking fan base is a bunch of fucking posers who wouldn't know originality if it kicked them in the fucking teeth. But the thing is, it isn't Logan. It's Bethany. And it's just really bad timing. I've got all of this momentum going already, and there's been all of this shit going on with us, so in my head it's like, Great. Fucking fantastic. What's it going to be this time? Some shit about my chakras being closed? Some shit about how my heart's refrain should be one of thanksgiving? Some shit about some passage from some book that you just read that talks about our exact situation, some passage from some book that now of course I also have to read? So I pick up and I say, "Yes? Hello? What? What's up?"

She isn't calling about my closed chakras or my heart's refrain, though. She isn't calling about a book I have to read. She says my name, and it's one of those things where right away I can hear it in her voice that something is really, actually wrong.

I stand up. Or it's more like I was sitting and now I'm standing, now I'm moving, now I'm going around my desk and out into the living room and toward the front door and I don't remember starting, don't remember deciding to do it. I'm talking, too, talking loud into the phone, and I'm saying, "Bethany? Bethany, what happened? What's wrong? What happened?" even though in that moment I'm sure I know what happened, sure I know what's wrong, sure I know what it is, because what else could it be? What else could it be, that would make her sound like that?

It isn't that, though. The thing is, it isn't that. Instead, it's one of the craziest things I've ever even heard of.

"Oh my God," she says. "Dex, it's Chi. A plane, a fucking airplane, just crashed into Chi's building."

I'm already into the front hallway, already pulling on my coat. I stop with one arm in, let it go, leaving it hanging. "Wait," I say. My heartbeat is so loud in my ears that I'm actually not even sure I heard her right. "What?" I say. "Say that again. Tell me what you just said. What did you just say?"

"An airplane," Bethany says. "An airplane just flew into Chi's building. They're talking about it on the news."

It isn't registering. My mind is still somewhere else, still on the last thing. Coffee and pastry dough and frosting are all churning in my stomach, are all rolling over and knocking against the catch at the bottom of my throat. I swallow it down and take a breath. "Okay," I say, "hang on. I don't understand. I don't understand what you're telling me right now. Go back. An airplane."

"An airplane," she says again.

"Not anything with," I say, but then I don't finish the thought.

"Not anything with what?" she says.

"Nothing," I say. "I just thought. It doesn't matter. Go back to what you were saying. What are you saying? Who is Chi?"

"The doula," Bethany says. "Katie's doula. The doula in Akron. The one we had the appointment with. The one I wanted you to meet."

I'm still somewhere else, though. My mind is jumping around, jumping from one thing to the next. What she's saying goes in but then it's like it gets stopped before it starts to mean anything, before it starts to make sense. Like there's something else in the way, something else holding the center of my attention and demanding that I focus on it and nothing else. And again: maybe if I hadn't been sitting there getting fucked up on caffeine and white flour and processed sugar and whatever weird cocktail of stress hormones gets dumped into your bloodstream when you just let yourself go on fantasies of catastrophe for the past four hours I wouldn't have jumped right to the worst possible thought, the worst possible conclusion. As it is, though, what she's telling me plugs right into some sense or memory or sense of a memory or memory of a sense of the realization that everything from before is over, now, that life from here on in is going to play out inside of whatever bizarre, alternate-future afterworld is left, inside of whatever the fuck things look like now.

"And what?" I say. "You're telling me that an airplane flew into her building? You're telling me there was some kind of attack?"

"Attack," she says. "Attack? Like an attack?"

"Yes," I say, louder. "Like as in somebody attacked us? As in somebody flew an airplane into a fucking building?"

"Oh my God," she says, "I didn't even think of that. They haven't said anything about it being an attack. They keep saying the police are going to make a statement, but they haven't yet."

I'm almost not even listening. I'm back across the living room and I'm back in my office and I'm at my computer and I'm googling *terrorist attack Ohio* and *plane attack terror Akron* and *Ohio terror-*

ism. I'm not finding anything, though. Everything that's coming up is old, is about stuff that was suspected and thwarted, is about raising and lowering the terror alert level, all from months and years ago. "I'm not seeing anything about it online," I say. "What are you watching? Where are you finding coverage?"

"It's just the local news," she says. "I don't know, it's just the local news site." Then she says, "I'm really worried. I've called her like six times and she isn't answering."

I click over to one of the local news sites and I find a live feed. The scene isn't anything like what I imagined. The building isn't some big, free-standing tower. It's one of those ones in a little apartment community, the kind with a bunch of four- and six-unit buildings all laid out along a stretch of road. The building the plane hit is split down the middle, and big flames are shooting out through the gap in the roof, and firemen are running around and spraying it with their hoses, but the whole scene already feels pretty well contained. It doesn't feel like an attack. Compared to what I was expecting, it doesn't feel like much of anything.

"Dex," Bethany says.

"Yeah," I say. "No, I'm here."

"I'm really worried," she says again.

I sit back. I feel exhausted, sick. I feel like she scared the shit out of me for nothing. "Yeah, well," I say, "I mean, you can see what it's like over there. She probably just doesn't hear her phone. Or probably she had to leave in a hurry and she didn't take it with her. Or probably she's not even there. Think about what time it is. She's probably got a patient or a client or whatever."

"But that's what I'm saying," Bethany says. "She meets people in her apartment. If she was with somebody then she would have been at home."

I lean back in, scroll down, start clicking through the photo gallery. Whatever hit the building couldn't have been very big.

There's nothing in the wreckage that's recognizable as anything from a plane, as far as I can see, and the buildings on either side of Chi's look pretty much untouched. I close the window and sit back. I wonder if Logan tried to call me while I've been on the phone, and I just didn't hear the beep.

"Well," I say, "I honestly don't know what to tell you."

She doesn't say anything for a minute. Then she says, "What are you doing right now? Are you doing the show?"

"Yes," I say. "Or, no. I'm working on this thing with Dave. This other thing. I'm supposed to do this other thing with Dave. Why?"

"It's just that I really feel like I should go down there," she says. "Can we do that? I mean, can you come down with me?"

I kind of scoff at that. I don't really mean to, it just comes out. "I mean, no," I say. "No, I can't. I'm right in the middle of something. I'm right in the middle of this thing with Dave." Then I say, "You don't need me, though. Drive down there yourself. If you want to go down there then just drive down yourself."

"I know," she says. "I would just feel better if you were with me. I would feel better if we could go together, that's all."

And it's not that I'm oblivious to what's happening. It's not that I'm blind to the fact that this is some sort of olive branch, or something. But what am I really supposed to do? I can't just drop everything. And at this point, who the fuck is Chi to us, anyway? Bethany's only had one appointment. It all feels like somebody else's shit. It all feels like too much. Like if she actually wants to extend an olive branch then it shouldn't be contingent on me driving all the way down to fucking Akron. For all she knew I was in the middle of doing a show. But I don't want to make a fight where there isn't one, either.

"Look," I say, "I can't. I really can't. I'm right in the middle of this thing. But there probably isn't anything you can do down there anyway. I mean, you're looking at the same thing I'm looking at. The police have that whole area blocked off. I'd be surprised if you could get anywhere close."

"Yeah," she says. "No, you're right." Then she says, "You think she's all right though, right?"

And honestly, I don't think anything. I'm honestly not even thinking about it. I'm thinking about Logan again, about needing to call Dave and tell him something, about what I'm going to say. That all feels way more pressing, all feels way more important, than this.

"I mean, sure," I say. "Sure, she's probably out somewhere and she doesn't hear her phone. She probably doesn't even know that anything happened."

"Okay," Bethany says. "I'm going to keep trying her. I'll let you know what happens. I'll let you know what I hear."

I HANG up with her and I call Dave. He picks up right away.

"All right," he says. "Are we doing this? Are we good to go?"

"I haven't heard anything yet," I say. "He hasn't called."

"That's not a good sign," Dave says. "Have you tried him?"

"No, I haven't," I say. "I'm trying to avoid looking desperate."

Dave laughs. "I've got news for you," he says, "we are desperate. If this doesn't come together I'm going to end up working at Katie's brother's car dealership. And not in sales, either. I'm talking in the back, with a vacuum. I'm talking fucking detailing."

"I hear you," I say, "I just don't know what to tell you."

"All right," he says. "So what do you want to do?"

"I don't know," I say. "If I don't hear something soon I'll try him. Let's give it an hour. If I'm going to beg, at least give me an hour to prepare myself."

"Sure," Dave says. "It's good to be prepared." Then he says, "Be honest with me, though. Why do you think he hasn't called?"

"I don't know," I say. "It could be anything. I don't know his life."

"Right," Dave says. "But I mean, if you had to guess. If you had a gun to your head and they wanted you to come up with your top five explanations."

"I couldn't begin to imagine," I say. "Honestly."

"Sure," Dave says. "I get that. But I just mean, you don't think he bailed, do you? You don't think he would do that, just not call and not show up? After we made plans and everything? You don't think he would do that, right?"

"I honestly have no idea," I say. "I have no idea anymore, what he would or wouldn't do."

I HANG up with Dave and I wait some more. Logan hasn't called by two-thirty and he hasn't called by two forty-five, when Bethany calls back.

"I still haven't reached Chi," she says. "I'm really worried. I really feel like I need to go down there. Will you please go down there with me? Is there any way we can go down there together? Is there any way that Dave can manage without you?"

And I honestly feel like, at this point, it really doesn't fucking matter. Our sick day show is already up and running. If we aren't getting together with Logan then I've got nothing better to do.

"Sure," I say. "Fine. I'll work it out."

"Great," she says. She sounds so relieved. "Thank you," she says. "Thank you thank you."

"It's fine," I say. "I'll see you at home."

"Great," she says again. "I'm leaving right now. I'll see you soon."

I GO in and I pack up all of our shit. I take the mics and the cables and the board and everything and I put it all into this big duffel bag I have and I put it back in my trunk. I put the photos and everything back in their boxes and I put the boxes back in the closet. I feel like with the way things are going it's pretty much guaranteed that now, once I've put everything away and I have something else I said I would do, Logan is going to call, but he doesn't. There's still nothing by the time Bethany gets home.

I'M STANDING in the kitchen, watching for her through the window. When I see her pull in I go out. She meets me in the driveway. She's got her phone in her hand.

"Will you drive?" she says. "I want to keep trying her."

"Sure," I say. "Yeah. Sure. Fine."

We get in my car.

"Thank you for doing this," she says. "I really appreciate it."

I'm going to tell her it's fine, that it's no big deal, but when I look over at her she's already got the phone pressed to her ear again. So I don't say anything. I face the wheel, turn the key, start the car. I pull us out onto the road. And that's how it is the whole way. Either she's trying Chi's number or she's on her screen, clicking around. I assume she's checking for more news, but I don't really know. Apart from her telling me where to go and when to turn we don't talk. Apart from her telling me where to go and when to turn she doesn't say shit to me. It takes us almost an hour to get where we're going, but it feels like it takes even longer.

I'm right about the police. The road that runs past Chi's building is closed off way down at the end. From the roadblock you can't even really see the site. I find a place to park down a side street and we walk over. It's strange. Walking along the road you can hear the hoses and the firemen yelling to each other back and forth, but you can't really see anything. The angle is wrong. All you see is the smoke-haze and the firetrucks and the lights. Then you come around and it's like it's all there all at once. The big smoldering vacancy. The pile of brick and cinderblock and stuff that might have been fixtures or furniture, but now it's too charred and mangled to tell what it was. The whole thing lit by the banks of work spots they set up in the street and the red from the firetruck lights going around and around. And on either side the other buildings looking fine, looking like nothing happened. It's almost surreal. For a second we just stop and stare.

"Fuck," I say. "Fuck me."

Bethany has her hands up to her mouth, the empty one and the one still holding her phone. "Oh my God," she says. "Oh no."

People are coming over to us. One woman goes right past me and takes Bethany up in a big hug. She's pretty much the most pregnant woman I've ever seen. She has to lean and reach way out over her belly to get her arms around Bethany.

"It's so awful," I hear her say. "I can't believe it. It's so awful."

"So they know?" Bethany says. "It's for sure?"

The woman nods into Bethany's shoulder. "Yeah, honey," she says. "They know for sure. For sure, they know."

More people are coming over, crowding in. I didn't notice it before, or maybe with everything else going on it just didn't register, but almost all of the maybe fifteen or twenty people standing around on our side of the street are women and almost all of them are either visibly pregnant or holding babies. They're all moving in close, all surrounding Bethany, all talking at once, crying and reaching in. It's bizarre. They just move past me like I'm not even there. Like it's just understood that I'm not part of this thing. I stand there for a minute waiting for somebody to notice me, but nobody does. They're all focused on Bethany. So I cross the street. I go over to where a couple of cops are leaning against a cruiser. I figure maybe I can get some information about what happened. The cops stand up when they see me coming. The nearer one holds up a hand.

"Sorry," he says. "We can't let you any closer."

I stop. I'm as close as I'd want to be, anyway. I'm all the way to them, pretty much. And it's funny. Up close I can see how young they both are. From across the street it was hard to tell. I nod.

"Sure," I say. I point at the building, at the wreckage. "I was hoping you could tell me what happened," I say.

The other cop, not the one who told me to stop, shrugs. "What makes you think they tell us anything?" he says. He waves a hand at the site. "See it?" he says. "Now you've seen everything we've seen. Now you know everything we know."

He meant it as a joke, but from this side of the street there actually is more to see. From up close I can see things I couldn't see before, can see hundreds and hundreds of pieces of things scattered all over the lawn. Over the one cop's shoulder I can see a chunk of black plastic that looks like part of a TV or a microwave, maybe. Next to that is a piece of wood that might have been a table leg or part of a railing. Most of it is too small and too damaged to be recognizable as anything, really.

I turn back to the cops. "Come on, guys," I say. "My girlfriend's doula lives in there. She's freaking out, and the news hasn't said anything. We drove all the way down from Cleveland Heights. You can't tell me anything else about what this is?"

I point over to where I left Bethany. Between the closeness of the bodies and how everything is backlit by the work spots I can't actually make her out. She's somewhere in the cluster.

The cops are looking.

"A doula," the one says. "That's what, like a midwife?"

"Yeah," I say. "I mean, I think it is. I never actually met her. We only had one appointment so far, and I missed it."

Both cops laugh.

"Shit," the other cop says. "How'd that go over?"

"About as well as you'd expect," I say.

The cop who told me that they couldn't let me any closer laughs at that until he laughs himself out. He hoots and wipes his eyes. "Look," he says, finally, "we really don't know anything you don't know already from watching the news. Some small aircraft clipped some power lines and crashed. No survivors from the plane, one resident killed. One resident home at the time."

"Right," I say. "So that's it? It was just an accident?"

The cop nods. "Just an accident," he says. He cocks his head to the side. "Why?" he says. "You think somebody did this on purpose?"

I shrug. "I don't know," I say. "You never know anymore."

The other cop shakes his head. "Just an accident," he says. "Just one of those freak things." Then he frowns, leans in. "Hey, listen," he says, "can I ask you something?"

"I mean, sure," I say.

"You and your lady," he says. "You guys are doing what, like a home birth? I just mean, that's why people use a doula, right?"

He's looking at me hard. The other cop is, too.

"I don't know," I say. "We haven't really talked about it. It's early, still. We haven't talked about it. Like I said, we only had the one appointment so far. So it's early. And we haven't. There's a lot of stuff we haven't figured out. There's a bunch of stuff we haven't figured out yet."

The cop blows his breath, shakes his head, looks at his partner. "Shit," he says. "Because I mean, to me it's like, How does that even work? I mean, not the baby part. I get the baby part. I mean all the other stuff. Like, do you do it in the bathtub, or something? Or do you just lay out some towels? And does the doula actually deliver the baby? Or does she train you to do it? And like, who cuts the cord and everything?"

He looks at me. They both look at me. I shake my head.

"I don't know," I say. "I mean, like I said, we only had the one appointment, and I missed it.

The cop who's asking shudders, makes a face, looks back at his partner. "Honestly," he says, "I don't know if I could do all that." He looks back at me. "I mean if it was an emergency or something, sure," he says. "But on purpose? Like setting it up like that? Having that be the plan?"

"Right," I say. "No, I'm with you. But it's really not my call."

The other cop frowns. "Okay," he says, "but you're the one who's going to be there, right?"

"Yeah," I say, "I'm the one who's going to be there."

The other cop shrugs. "Then I'd say it's at least a little bit your call," he says. "If it was me, you can bet your ass it would be my call."

WE'VE BEEN talking over the noise from the hoses, but now the hoses stop. We all turn to look. There isn't much to see. Most of the building is a charred pile. Part of the front wall is still standing, but that's about it. The windows look in on nothing. Without the hoses going you can hear all the water running off and down the street into the storm sewers. I thank the cops and I jog back over to Bethany. Most of the women seem to be standing around where I left them, but the cluster has broken up enough for me to get through.

"Where were you?" Bethany says, when she sees me.

I nod across the street. "I was talking to the cops," I say. "I wanted to see if they could tell me what happened."

The other women are all listening.

"What did they tell you?" one of them asks me.

"They said it was just an accident," I say. "Nobody thinks it was any kind of attack or anything. They said it was just one of those freak things. The plane hit some power lines and then it crashed, and that's it."

I shrug. They're all still watching me. Some of the babies are crying

"That's it," I say again. "That's all they would tell me. It seems like that's all there is."

Nobody says anything back to that. We stand there watching the firemen. One truck's team gets finished loading and drives off. Other firemen are walking through the site, raking through the rubble. I take a step away from the group and I check my phone. I figure that maybe with all the noise and confusion and everything I could have missed Logan's call, but I didn't.

WE STAND there for a while, and then the women start splintering off. One of them says she has to go get dinner started and it's like a cue to the rest of them. They all start saying what they need to do, where they need to be. I stand there with Bethany while she says her goodbyes and then we walk back to the car. I get in and I close my door and I turn to her and I say, "So what was that all about?"

She's settling in. She buckles her seatbelt, looks at me. She frowns. "What was what all about?" she says.

"That," I say. "All of those women. The way they all huddled in around you. It was like something out of a nature documentary, or something. It was like watching one of those big flocks of birds in Africa, or something. Like when they all turn together."

I'm trying to make a joke, sort of, trying to maybe lighten things, but it isn't working. Bethany frowns again, shakes her head.

"They're all women that Chi was working with," she says.

"And what," I say, "they all felt compelled to come down here, when they heard what happened?"

She nods. "Chi was a special person," she says. "She meant a lot to people. She helped a lot of people."

I don't know what to say to that. I turn and I face the front, turn the key, start the car. I turn the knob and the headlights come on and shine on lawn edges, driveway ends, mailboxes, empty road. I pull the lever and I put it in drive, pull away from the curb. "Well," I say, "I'm sorry I didn't get to meet her."

"Yeah," Bethany says. "Me, too."

And some part of me knows that it's not a dig. Some part of me knows that. At the same time, though, there's this other part that's like, Seriously? Fucking seriously? After I drove you all the way down here? After I stood around and waited for you and talked to the cops and everything? "Yeah," I say, "right, okay. But again, to be fair, it's not like you checked with me before you made the appointment. It's not like you checked with me to make sure I didn't have anything

147

else going on. And besides, I mean, I couldn't have known this was going to happen. How could I have known this was going to happen? I couldn't have known. Nobody could have predicted this. I thought I was going to meet her. I thought I was going to have a lot of chances to meet her. I thought that by the time things really got going I was going to be seeing her all the time. So I mean, how was I supposed to know? I couldn't have known. I didn't. I couldn't have."

I look at her. She's looking at me. Her expression is confused, surprised even. She shakes her head.

"What?" she says. "I know. I know that. What are you saying? I know that. Of course you couldn't have known. You *were* supposed to have a lot more chances."

I'm nodding now, nodding along as she talks. "Right," I say. "Okay, so you agree with me then. You agree that it wasn't my fault, my not meeting her. You agree with me on that."

She pushes herself up, turns in her seat, turns so that her one leg is up on the seat cushion and her back is against the door. "What are you even saying?" she says. "I don't understand what you're saying right now. What are you saying? I'm not accusing you of anything."

I barely let her finish, though. I'm already talking again, talking over her. "Right," I say. "No, totally. Absolutely. You're not accusing me of anything. Sure. It's my mistake."

She starts to say something back to that, but then she stops herself. Out of the corner of my eye I watch her press her palms to her forehead, watch her push her fingers up into her hair. I watch as she drops her hands into her lap, watch as she holds them up again, the palms out.

"Look," she says. "I'm not accusing you of anything. I'm not. I'm really not. I don't want you to admit anything or deny anything or apologize for anything or feel like you have to defend anything. I really don't. I don't want anything. I'm not asking you for anything."

We're off the street, up the ramp, onto the highway, now. The dark ahead is punctuated by taillights. The bare tree branches reaching up look like cracks in the edge of the deep purple sky. I nod, keep nodding.

"Right," I say. "No, totally. Of course not. Whatever you say."

AND THAT'S it. She turns in her seat, turns to face the window, turns her back to me, and we don't say anything else the whole rest of the way. At one point I see her move to put her hand to her face, and I have the thought that maybe she's crying, but it's hard to really tell. I can't see her face, can't see her reflection in the glass, even. She could be just tired, could be just rubbing her eyes. In any case she doesn't make any sound. Traffic is heavy headed north and it takes a long time to get home, takes even longer than it took us to get down. It's after seven, fully dark, by the time we pull in.

She opens the door and gets out. I turn off the engine but then I don't move to get out. I stay where I'm sitting. She looks at me. Or I guess what I mean is, I can feel her looking at me. I don't look. I keep staring straight ahead, keep looking out to where the driveway ends against the edge of the yard. I can see the few trees at the back of the lot, can just make out the back of my neighbor's house. The light is on in an upstairs window, but the rest of the house is dark.

She closes the door. I turn and I watch her walk away, watch her go up the walk, watch her open the door and go inside. I watch the windows light up and go dark as she moves from the entryway to the kitchen to the living room, and then out of the living room to somewhere I can't see. The bathroom, probably. It couldn't be anywhere else, really. It's not a big house, and anywhere else the light would show.

With the engine off it gets cold fast inside the car. Before the lights go off in the living room I can already see my breath. I don't do anything about it, though. I don't move, don't start the car. I just sit there. I wish I had a cigarette, wish I hadn't thrown them all out, even the emergency reserve pack I used to keep in the glove com-partment, when Bethany moved in. I think about driving to the gas station down the street to get some. I don't do it, though. I know it won't change anything. I take out my phone and I make the call.

IT ISN'T Logan who answers, though. It's some woman.

"Who is this?" she says.

I figure I've got the wrong number. I figure he either gave me the wrong number on purpose or it's what his mom said, that he had to change it again. And, honestly, I'm not even upset. Honestly, at this point, it just seems funny. At this point it's almost just funny, because what did I expect? What else did I really expect?

"Sorry," I say. "I've think I've got the wrong number. Sorry to bother you." And then I hang up.

THE THING is, though, it wasn't a wrong number. I'm sitting there in the driveway trying to work myself up to calling Dave and telling him what happened when the woman calls back.

"Did you just call me?" she says. "Did you just call this number?"

"Yeah," I say, "but I was trying to reach someone else."

"Who were you trying to reach?" she says.

"Logan?" I say. "I was trying to reach Logan Hazelette?" I feel kind of stupid even saying it.

"No," she says, "great. You're right. You've got the right number. This is Logan's phone." She's talking fast, rushing the words. "What's this about?" she says. "I mean, what is this regarding?"

"We were supposed to do an interview?" I say. "I have a podcast? We were supposed to get together today and do an interview? He was supposed to call me?"

She repeats what I said. She's relaying the information to some-body else. She listens to whatever they say back. I can hear someone talking in the background, but I can't make out what they're saying.

"Right," the woman says. Then, to me, she says, "You were supposed to do the interview how? Were you doing it over the phone or was he supposed to be there? Was he supposed to be there in person to do the interview?"

"Yes," I say. "I mean yeah, that's what he said. He said he would come here. He said we could do it here."

She relays that, too. She waits. "I don't know," she says. "Why don't you talk to him? Do you want to talk to him? You talk to him. You ask him." Then there's the sound of the phone being handed over and a man's voice says, "Hello? Who is this?"

"Dex," I say. "This is Dex."

"Dex," the man says. "You were supposed to do an interview with Logan today? Logan was supposed to come to you, to your facility?"

"Yeah," I say. "I mean, that was the plan. That was what we talked about." Then I say, "Why? What's going on?"

He doesn't answer that, though. "Okay," he says. "And where are you located?"

"Cleveland," I say. "I'm in Cleveland."

"Okay," he says. "Cleveland. Ohio? You're in Cleveland, Ohio?" He doesn't sound surprised. He doesn't sound anything. He's just confirming the information.

"Yes," I say. "Why? Where are you? Where's Logan?"

He doesn't answer me. I can hear the woman's voice in the background, the speed of the words and the pitch and the volume, but I can't make out what she's saying.

"I know," the man says to her. "I'm working on it." Then to me he says, "Listen, when you set this whole thing up, who made the arrangements? Did you book his flight and hotel and everything, or did he do that?"

"He did it," I say. "Or he said he was going to have his guy do it. He said he had a guy who would do it. I don't know. I didn't ask. I don't have a budget. He was doing me a favor. I know him from before, from when he lived here. He's from here. He was going to come home and see his parents. He was going to stay with his parents and do the interview and whatever. It was going to be a whole visit-back-home thing. I mean, that's what he told me. That's what he said."

"Okay," the man says. "He was going to stay with his parents. Have you called them? Have you checked to see if they've seen him?"

"I mean, no," I say. "I haven't called anyone. He was supposed to call me. I was waiting for him to call me. This is the first call that I've made."

"Okay," the man says again. He isn't talking to me, though. "Do you have a number for his parents?" he says. "Do you know where to find it? Find their number and try them." Then, to me, he says, "Thanks. Thanks a lot. You've been really helpful. We really appreciate it, and I know Logan really appreciates it."

He waits for me to say something. I don't know what to say. The whole thing is so bizarre.

"Yeah," I say. "I mean, sure. Sure, no problem."

"And listen," the man says, "if Logan does get in touch with you, will you call me at this number and let me know? See if you can get him to tell you where he's staying, anything about what his plans are, anything like that."

"I mean, yeah," I say. Then I say, "But okay, wait a second. What's up? What's going on? Is Logan all right?"

But the man doesn't answer that, either. He moves right past it. "Just promise me that you'll call back if you hear from him," he says. "Okay? Can you please just promise me that?"

"I mean, sure," I say. "Yes. Whatever. Fine, I promise."

"Great," says the man. "Thank you."

"And will you have him call me?" I start to say. "If you reach him first, will you have him call me?" but in the middle of me saying it my phone beeps to tell me that the man already hung up.

I GO inside. Bethany isn't in the living room or the kitchen. The door to the bedroom is open a crack, but the lights inside are off.

I go into the kitchen and I grab the new six-pack from the fridge and I go into my office and I close the door. I put on the headphones and I put on some Social Distortion and I settle into the big, shitty, faux-leather recliner I have in there and I crack the first beer and I check out. I wake up early the next morning with the headphones quiet and the vinyl pads on the big cans stuck to my cheeks and the second beer I opened half-finished and warm against my side where it's tucked in between me and the armrest. I get up and I go out and Bethany is gone again. She's not in the living room or the kitchen or the bedroom or the bathroom, and when I finally look outside her car isn't in the driveway.

I go back into the bedroom, look in the closet, and while I'm doing that my phone rings. I'm thinking it's probably going to be Dave, thinking that maybe it's going to be Bethany, but I'm wrong on both counts. It's neither of them. It's the man from last night, the man with Logan's phone.

"Hello?" he says. "Dex? Is this Dex?"

I'm kind of surprised. How could I not be surprised? "Yeah," I say. "It's me. It's Dex. What's happening? Did you find Logan?"

"I'm still working on it," the man says. "I took the redeye in. I'm down at baggage claim. Should I rent a car, or do you want to come get me?"

I guess it's pretty clear, what he's saying, but somehow I'm still not following. I just woke up and my brain isn't really fully operational yet and besides, who does that? Who takes the redeye cross-country on seven hours' notice? "Wait," I say, "what? What are you talking about? Come pick you up for what?"

"I thought you might want to help me find Logan," the man says. "I thought you said you guys were old friends, or something. Didn't you tell me that? That you guys knew each other back in the day?"

"Right," I say. "Yeah, no, right. We had a band. We were in a band together, before Logan went to L.A."

"Great," the man says. "So you'll come get me, then?"

And I'd like to say that I really thought about it, that I thought about wishing him luck and hanging up and then calling Bethany, and finding out where she is, and going to her there, and apologizing for last night, apologizing for what I said, and trying to make things better, but I don't. Honestly, I don't. When I walked in and saw that all of her clothes were still in the closet I kind of put the whole thing on the back burner. I kind of put the whole situation out of mind. "Sure," I say. "Yeah, sure. I can be there in half an hour."

"Great," the man says. "I'm going to go find a coffee. Call me back at this number when you're outside."

PART
FIVE

I CHANGE my shirt and I put on deodorant and I brush my teeth and then I go out and I start for the airport. I call Dave from the road.

"What the fuck?" he says. "I called you like fifty times."

It's true. He did. The whole time we were down in Akron and the whole ride back my phone was buzzing, and every time I saw that it was just Dave I let it go. I felt like I couldn't really go into it with him with Bethany in the car without probably then having to explain everything to her, too. Or at least that's what I told myself.

"I know," I say, "but listen. My day went to complete shit after I talked to you. It was pretty much the most fucked-up day ever." I tell him all about Chi and the crash and about Bethany making me drive her down to Akron and about calling Logan's phone and who answered and what they said, and about the man calling this morning to tell me he'd flown in on the redeye. "And so that's what I'm doing now," I say. "I'm driving to the fucking airport to pick him up. Okay? So that's what I'm doing. That's the situation. That's where we're at."

"Wait," Dave says, "what? Hang on. Who flew in?"

"This guy," I say. "The guy who has Logan's phone."

"Okay," Dave says, "right, but who the fuck is this guy? And why the fuck does he have Logan's phone? And why did he fly all the way across the country just because you told him that Logan was supposed to be here?"

"I don't know," I say. "I didn't ask him."

"You didn't ask him," Dave says, "but you're on your way to the airport to pick him up."

"Yes," I say. "Look, don't ask me. I did the thing that I thought was maybe a step in the right direction, in terms of making this thing actually happen. What do you want me to do? Do you want me to not go get this guy? Do you have a good idea for something I should do instead?"

"No," Dave says. "You're right. Or I don't know. No, I don't have any better ideas. Fair point."

"Thank you," I say.

"What do you think this means, though?" he says. "This whole thing, I mean. This guy flying out."

"I don't know," I say.

"I know you don't know," he says, "but what's your sense?"

"I don't have a sense," I say. "I've told you everything I know. You know everything I know, now. Your sense is as good as mine."

"Fuck," Dave says. "All right. I guess just call me when you know something, then?"

"Sure," I say. "Absolutely."

"I mean it," he says. "Don't leave me in the fucking dark again."

"I won't," I say. And then I hang up.

I TAKE the exit, pull around the loop. I stop in front of baggage claim and I call Logan's phone. The man answers. I tell him that I'm here and where I am and what I'm driving. A minute or so later I spot him coming out. It's funny. I pick him out right away. He looks just like he sounds on the phone. Ask anybody who's worked a show with a call-in segment and they'll tell you. It's like a sixth sense you develop. On the phone this guy had this kind of thick, nasally voice, like when you have a cold and you can't breathe through your nose, and he looked just like that. Kind of heavy, kind of short, two-day beard growing over not much of a chin, thinning salt-and-pepper hair combed straight back, wraparound sporty sunglasses. I wave and he spots me and comes over and we shake hands.

"Dex?" he says. "It's Dex?"

"Dex," I say. "Dexter. Most people call me Dex. I go by Dex."

"Great," the man says. "Richard Dubowitz. People call me Ricky. You should call me Ricky."

"Ricky," I say. "Great. Ricky. Great."

"Thanks for coming," he says. "I'm sure you've got plenty of other things you'd rather be doing."

"It's fine," I say. "It's no problem. It's great, actually. Really you're helping me. So thank you. Thank you, for your help."

The traffic cop stationed on the stretch in front of the building is blowing his whistle and waving to me to keep it moving. I start back around to the driver's side. Ricky's in no hurry, though. He sets his coffee on the hood, leans against the car, holds up a hand as he looks at me over the roof.

"Hang on," he says. "Let's take a second, here. I need for us to get on the same page about a couple of things, before we run off and start doing stuff."

I look back at the cop but he's turned, now, focused on some-body else. I close my door, lean on the roof. "Okay," I say, "get on the same page about what?"

He won't just come out with it, though. He pushes his fingers up under his sunglasses, pulls them down through the stubble on his cheeks, rubs the corners of his jaws as he works his chin around. "Christ," he says. "Don't you hate that, when your ears won't pop? It's my least favorite part of flying. Every time, no matter what."

I can feel the cop working his way back around to me, can hear the pitch of his whistle changing as he turns. "Yeah," I say. "No, totally. Yes. Sure."

Ricky yawns, nods. He holds up a hand. "All right," he says. "It's like this. I appreciate that you're Logan's friend and I appreciate that you're willing to come out and help me look for him and everything. But what you have to understand is that whatever happens, and whatever I tell you about Logan and his situation, it's all completely off the record. Whatever happens, and whatever I tell you, you don't talk about it on your podcast, you don't tell your girlfriend, you don't talk about it to journalists, you don't make any deals to publish the story, nothing. You can tell your dog and you can tell your houseplants and that's it. Got it? Do we understand each other?"

I laugh at that. Or I kind of snort. "Tell my houseplants," I say. "No, sorry, I guess I don't understand. The whole reason I'm here is to have Logan on my podcast. If I don't have a podcast then there's no reason for me to be here. I mean I'm concerned that Logan is missing, or whatever, but if there's no podcast then I kind of feel like whatever this is doesn't involve me."

Ricky waves that away. "I'm not saying you can't have him on your podcast," he says. "Of course he's going to be on. Absolutely. We're going to find him and he's going to do the interview and it's going to be great. That's what you want and that's what I want and I know that, despite appearances, that's what Logan wants. And you guys can talk about whatever. You can talk about the old times and what you're both working on now and whatever you want. But what I'm saying is, this part stays out of it. This part, and anything I tell you about Logan's situation, cannot be discussed." He leans back from the roof. He lifts his coffee, shrugs with it halfway to his mouth. "Come on," he says. "Imagine if it was you. You wouldn't want this out there. You know how people are. It would be embarrassing. You can understand that, can't you?"

The cop is blowing his whistle at my back. Ricky keeps looking at me. I can see my doubled and distorted reflection in the lenses of his sunglass, but I can't see anything underneath. I shrug.

"Sure," I say. "Sure, I can understand that."

Ricky shrugs again. "Of course you can," he says. "All I'm really saying is, Logan needs a friend. So be his friend. If you're here as Logan's friend then you're welcome. That's all I'm saying. If you're here as a member of the media, then this is where we shake hands and part ways."

The cop is yelling at me, now, yelling the make and model of my car, yelling for me to move. Over our heads planes are coming in and going out.

"No," I say, "I'm Logan's friend. I'm here as Logan's friend."

"Great," Ricky says. He seems genuinely relieved. "Understand," he says, "I don't really want to say these things. But you have to appreciate the situation. Some people—and I know I'm not talking about you, here—but some people would see this whole thing as an opportunity. They'd see it as a chance to advance their own careers, and it would be at Logan's expense."

"Sure," I say. "No, I can see that. I can see how that would be an issue. How someone might see it like that."

I open my door. I figure that's it, that we're good to go, but he's still not finished. He takes off his sunglasses and he starts cleaning them on the front of his sweater. He looks at me while he does it. His eyes are small and kind of sunken and bloodshot from the flight. Or I assume it's from the flight. I don't really know. Maybe they look like that all the time.

"I really appreciate you understanding," he says. "It makes my life so easy. You can't even imagine the hassles I've had in the past. People who say they'll do one thing and then they do something else. Then lawyers get involved and it becomes this whole other thing. It snowballs out of control. It just goes on and on. And for what? Life's too short for that shit. Right? I mean, don't you think?"

He finishes cleaning his sunglasses, but he doesn't put them back on. He keeps looking at me.

"Sure," I say. "Yes. I hear you. I get you. I got it."

He nods. He holds up the glasses, sights them against the gray sky, slides them back on. "Great," he says. "It sounds like we understand each other."

"We understand each other," I say.

Ricky opens his door. "Great," he says. "Then let's go."

WE GET in, head out. The lane loops around and then I turn at the light, accelerate up the ramp, get back on the highway.

"What's the plan, here?" I say. "Where am I going?"

Ricky has pulled a notebook from the outside pocket of his roller bag and is flipping through it. "I spoke to Logan's parents after I hung up with you," he says. "His mom told me that he showed up there Monday evening, stayed for maybe an hour, and then told them that he had to run out for an hour and he never came back. He took his mom's car. She told me that she and Logan's dad spent half of Tuesday driving around looking for it. They found it parked out behind someplace called The Cornwall Inn."

I laugh. I actually laugh at that, laugh out loud. I know The Cornwall. It's a shitty dive bar out on the edge of the town where Logan grew up. Logan and I used to go there and get drunk and fuck with the locals after we had dinner with his parents. "I know that place," I say. "Shit, I'm surprised it's still there." Then I laugh again. All of a sudden I'm remembering something Logan did once, something he said to the bartender that made the bartender throw a dish rag in his face. It's funny. Not what he said, but just the fact that I'm remembering it. Or it's just bizarre. You don't think about something for years and years and you more or less forget it, and then something happens and all of a sudden there it is. You sort of stumble across it and it's all still there.

Ricky flips the notebook closed, drops it in his lap. "She told me she went inside and asked around," he says, "but nobody she talked to had seen him. Or what she said was that nobody there had been there on Monday night. I got the sense that she didn't really press the issue." He reaches down and pulls the handle, pushes the seat back. He folds his arms on his chest. "She said she'd call me if he shows up back at home," he says. "Until that happens, I'd say our first move is to go over there and see if we can't find a bartender or a manager or somebody who was there, who saw him."

"Sure," I say. "That makes sense."

Ricky shifts in the seat, turns to face the door. "Great," he says, over his shoulder. "If you're good then I'm just going to leave you to it. I slept like shit on the plane. Just wake me up when we're there."

"Sure," I say again. Then I start to say something else—something about what Dave said, about who is he, anyway? And why does he have Logan's phone? And what's his deal, that he's going to fly all the way out here at the drop of a hat?—but then I don't. It's like I don't want to piss him off, or something. Which is ridiculous. I know it's ridiculous. But by the time I decide that it's ridiculous, and decide to just say fuck it, and let him fuck off and take an Uber if he feels like I'm asking too many questions, it seems like he's already asleep.

I'M PRETTY sure about where I'm going, but when I get off at the exit and get going down the side streets I get all turned around. I haven't been to The Cornwall in years, since back when I went there with Logan, and landmarks have changed. Buildings have been renovated and gas stations have been torn down and businesses have closed and new ones have opened. I drive down one street after another, looking. Finally I see a building and a tree that I think I recognize, and I turn the corner and there it is.

It's strange to see it. It's strange to be back. I park and I get out and then I sort of just stand there. Ricky gets out and he comes around to my side and he looks around and then he looks at me.

"I know," I say. "I know what you're thinking."

He shrugs. "I'm not thinking anything," he says. He holds up a hand. "After you," he says.

WE GO inside. It's all the same. Same low lighting, same junk on the walls, same bad pin-striping on the mirror behind the bar. There's the same eight-by-ten riser tucked in the back corner and the same cracked green vinyl on the barstools and the booth seats. I think about going over and checking to see if the jukebox is the same, too, if it's all the same early-90s garbage pop and old sad country, but I don't do it. Ricky's already moving to the bar, already waving the bartender over, and I fall in behind him. The sleepy-looking third-shifters from the cabinet factory or wherever, sitting in a little cluster down at the end of the bar, don't even look up.

Ricky takes off his sunglasses, puts a big grin on his face. "Hi there," he says to the bartender. "I'm hoping you can help me. I think a friend of mine was in here on Monday night? I'm wondering if you saw him."

He goes into his jacket pocket and he comes out with his phone and he starts scrolling. He finds what he's looking for, holds it out to the bartender. The bartender shakes his head without looking.

"I wasn't here on Monday," he says. "You want to talk to Steve."

Ricky sets the phone on the bar, leans in, looks at the bartender and then past him, over his shoulder. He's still wearing the same big, friendly grin. He shrugs. "Okay," he says, "is Steve here?"

The bartender looks from Ricky to me and then back at Ricky. He shakes his head again. "I think he's coming in this afternoon," he says. "You could come back this afternoon. Try to catch him then."

Ricky drops the grin, winces. He shakes his head. "That's not going to work for us," he says. "We're in a real time crunch, here." His tone is concerned, now. He looks at me. I nod at the bartender.

"Yeah," I say, "we're really in a time crunch."

"I don't want to give you a hard time," Ricky says, "but it would be a lot better for us if we could meet up with him this morning." He shrugs, looks around, looks back at the bartender. "We don't even need to meet him here," he says. "We can meet him somewhere else. Do you have a number for him? Or an address?"

The bartender looks away, looks down, starts moving things around behind the bar. "I don't know," he says. "I mean, that's not really how we do things. That's not, I mean, we don't give out that information." He glances at Ricky, looks back down. "Come back this afternoon," he says. "That's all I can really tell you."

Ricky doesn't take his eyes off the bartender. "Sure," he says. "No, I get that. I do. But the thing is, this is kind of a special-circumstances situation. I don't need to bore you with the details but the upshot is that I just spent five and a half hours on a plane flying out here from L.A., just so I can try to locate this friend of ours." He laughs. Like, *How crazy is that? Have you ever heard of anything so crazy?* He picks his phone up off the bar, checks the time. "And now," he says, "I've got about ten and a half hours before I'm supposed to get back on another plane and fly back. And when I do that, I need to have him with me. I've got his ticket and everything." He laughs again. "It's crazy," he says. "I know. It's nuts. But what can you do? When your buddy needs your help, you've got to do what you can."

The bartender is looking at us again, looking back and forth between us. Now he shrugs and looks away. "I don't know," he says. "I mean, like I said, you can come back this afternoon. Otherwise I don't think I can help you."

Ricky keeps his eyes on the bartender, but the bartender won't look at him. Ricky nods.

"All right," he says. He goes into his pocket and he comes out with his wallet and he lays a twenty on the bar. He coughs and clears his throat. "Do you have any bottled water back there?" he says. "That fucking dry airplane air. I'm dying here."

The bartender looks at Ricky, looks down at the money. "Sure," he says. "No problem." He goes down into the cooler and comes up with the bottle and he sets it down in front of Ricky. Ricky takes it and starts drinking. The bartender takes the bill and holds it up.

"I'll get your change," he says.

Ricky's still drinking. He waves what the bartender said away with his free hand. He lowers the bottle. "That's all right," he says. "We're all good, here." He drains the bottle and twists the cap back on. "That was great," he says. "Thanks. I really needed that."

The bartender looks at him, looks at me. Then he nods. "You know what?" he says. "I think there's a number for Steve on the board in the office. Let me go check and see. Hang on a second."

"Sure," says Ricky. "Take your time."

The bartender goes away. Ricky leans on the bar. I look around at the guys down at the end. One of them is holding an empty glass, leaning up off his stool, looking after the bartender. The others don't seem to give a shit about what's going on. The guy with the empty glass slumps back down, turns back to the others.

The bartender comes back with a slip of paper in his hand. "This is what's back there," he says. "I don't know if it's current. I don't know if it's his home number or his cell or what." He sets the paper on the bar, pushes it across to Ricky. "That's all I've got," he says. "That's all I can tell you. If that doesn't get you anywhere then coming back this afternoon is your best bet."

Ricky takes the paper, looks at it. "This is fine," he says. "This is great. Thank you."

The bartender shakes his head, holds up his hands. "Don't thank me," he says. "I didn't do anything. You found that number yourself. You got it out of the phonebook. You went in the office and got it yourself. I didn't give it to you."

Ricky's already dialing, already turning, already moving toward the door. "Sure," he says. "Sure, that's exactly what we did."

I stand there. I don't really mean to, it just happens. It's not like I'm torn. It's not like I want to stay and have a beer, or anything. But it also sort of feels like we're leaving really fast, like we just got here. It's weird. I haven't thought about The Cornwall in a really long time, and it feels weird to come all the way out here and then just turn around and leave again. Or maybe I just need a second to process being here. Ricky's already through the door, though, already outside, so I nod to the bartender and I go out after him.

He's wandered off across the parking lot. I go and I stand by the car and I wait. A minute later he comes walking back. He's holding the phone to his ear with his shoulder and he's writing something on his palm.

"Great," he's saying. "Terrific."

"Was that him?" I say.

Ricky lets the phone slide down his chest to his waiting hand. He shakes his head. "I talked to his mom," he says. "She says he's still asleep." He holds up his hand, shows me his palm. "I've got an address, though," he says, "if you're still up for it."

"Sure," I say. "Sure, I'm up for it."

Ricky's already walking around, already trying the handle. He looks at me over the roof, points down. "Great," he says. "Unlock the door, then. Let's get to it."

WE GET in, get back on the road. The address is even farther east. It's out of the town proper, out past a lot of strip mall plazas and landscaping supply yards and empty farmland.

We don't put on the radio, don't talk. There's nothing to do but look at it all. It's kind of embarrassing, somehow. After a while I say, "Pretty much like back home, right?"

Ricky looks at me. He doesn't even give me a look, really. He just faces me. He's got his sunglasses on again, so all I really see when I look at him is my own reflection.

I hold up a hand, wave it at what's going by outside. "I just mean, it's not exactly the bleeding edge out here," I say.

Ricky looks around, looks out the window, shrugs. "I don't know," he says. "It's not bad. I could see living here. Simplify things. Get a little plot, build a little house."

I laugh. I think he's joking. "Yeah," I say. "Get a truck. Find a nice girl. Settle down. Work your way up at the feed supply."

He snorts at that. "Shit," he says. "You have any idea how far half a million dollars gets you in L.A. real estate? You know what a million gets you? Ask Logan, when we find him. It gets you jack shit." He turns back to the window, points. There's a big stretch of rutted-up field going by. Behind that a bunch of bare trees go all the way back to the gray clouds. He says, "That kind of money goes a long, long way around here."

I laugh again. "I mean, yeah," I say, "but that's because there's nothing here. There's nothing happening here. And the things that do happen here nobody gives a shit about. The people who live here don't even give a shit. Nothing that happens here matters."

Ricky holds up his hands. "Look," he says, "all I'm saying is, it doesn't seem like a bad place. There's a lot to be said for living someplace a little bit quiet. There's nothing wrong with that. And besides, I wouldn't say that nobody cares what happens here. Some-body must care, if you've got Logan Hazelette flying in to do your podcast. Logan must care. He must think it matters."

"That's different," I say. "Logan's from here. His parents still live here. And we have history. And besides, Logan just proves my point.

We played the same music for years and got fucking nowhere. Then he went out there and within a year he's this huge fucking star." Then I laugh again. "And anyway," I say, "he blew me off. Would we be out here looking for him if he actually gave a shit? If what I was doing was really so fucking important?"

He starts to say something, stops. He holds up a hand. "Listen," he says. "I'm not here to tell you your business. I don't know your life and I don't know your deal with Logan. But if I were you, with the way things are, I wouldn't take anything Logan does or says too personally."

I'M GOING to say something back to that—something about how I have this tendency to take things that derail my whole entire life kind of personally—but right then the app on Ricky's phone says that it's time to turn, that the destination is coming up. I turn down a side street and I park at the curb and we get out. The house is pretty nice. It's not big but it's well kept. The leaves are all raked and the hedges along the front are trimmed and there's even one of those autumn-themed flags hanging from a pole next to the front door. We go up the walk and up the steps and Ricky knocks and a few seconds later Steve's mom answers the door. I don't know what else to say about her except that she's exactly right for the house. She fits it perfectly. Or I guess it fits her. She opens the door but she leaves the storm door closed. Ricky takes off his sunglasses.

"Hi," he says. "I called? We're hoping to talk to Steve?"

Steve's mom looks at us through the storm door, looks from Ricky to me and back to Ricky again. "What's this about?" she says.

"We just need to talk to him," Ricky says. "We've got to ask him about something that happened at the bar the other night." He holds up two fingers. "Two minutes," he says. "I promise."

Steve's mom doesn't say anything for a minute. She just keeps looking back and forth between us. Then finally she gives a little nod toward the side of the house and she says, "Steven's room is in the basement. There's an entrance around the side, there. You go down the stairs. You'll see it."

Ricky gives her a big smile. It doesn't look right on him. It doesn't work with his face. On his face it looks like a grimace. "Great," he says. "Thanks a lot. Thank you very much."

He starts back down the steps, but she stops him.

"I like to give people the benefit of the doubt," she says. "But I'll tell you what I told Steven, when he moved back in here. I don't tolerate drugs, and I'm not shy about calling the police. I'll do it just like that." She snaps her fingers. "I will," she says. "You ask Steven."

I laugh. I actually laugh at that. To go from this whole standoff thing we're doing to that just seems funny. "It's not like that," I say. "We just need to talk to him."

She isn't having it, though, isn't interested. She's holding up her hands, talking again. "It doesn't make any difference to me," she's saying. "I've said all I have to say." She brushes one palm against the other, brushing them off. "As far as I'm concerned," she says, "the subject is closed." Then, before I can say anything back to that, she takes a step back and she closes the door.

After she's gone I kind of just stand there a second. It's like I'm stunned, or something. I don't know what I was expecting, exactly, but it wasn't that. Ricky's already off the step, though, already moving around the house, so I go down and I go after him. We go around the corner, over to where a set of concrete steps lead down to a little landing and a door. We stand shoulder-to-shoulder in the little cinderblock phone booth and Ricky knocks. Nothing happens and so after a minute he knocks again, harder, with the side of his fist.

"All right," I say, when nobody answers after the second knock. "Hang on a second. Help me out, here. I'm confused. Did that woman actually give you her address? Did she actually tell you where she lives? I mean, because she thinks we're drug dealers, or something. She thinks we're here to sell Steve drugs or do drugs or something."

Ricky doesn't look at me, keeps facing the door as he shrugs. We're so tight in the space that I feel it as much as I see it. "She doesn't think anything," he says.

"She thinks something," I say. "She thinks whatever you told her. What did you tell her?"

He shrugs again. "What does it matter?" he says. "We're here, now. What difference does it make?"

"I don't know," I say. "It feels like it makes a difference."

He turns to me. In the tight space his face is practically right in my face. Or with the difference in our heights it's more like it's right in my chin, right in my throat. "Look," he says, "I asked if he was here, she told me he was asleep, I told her it was important, she told me I could leave a message, I told her we would just swing by, and then I called my friend and I had him do a reverse lookup of the number to get the address, okay? So she doesn't think anything, okay? She's got nothing to think about." He pushes his sunglasses up on his head. "Are you going to be like this about everything?" he says. "Is this how this day is going to go? You're going to make me explain everything I do?"

He looks at me, keeps looking at me. I'm going to keep looking at him, but then I don't. I look down, look back at the door. I shrug. "Fine," I say. "Never mind. I don't care. It's fine. Whatever."

"Great," he says. "Wonderful." He reaches up and he pounds on the door again.

"So what are we going to do if this guy won't talk to us?" I say. "Or if he didn't even see Logan?"

He shrugs again. "I don't know," he says. "How should I know?"

"Fine," I say. I put my collar up and I close my jacket tight around me and I hug it in place. The little space down at the bottom of the stairs is like a walk-in cooler and all I've got on is this kind of leather motorcycle jacket that Bethany got for me from some vintage shop and it isn't enough. It looks really cool but the liner is long gone and the zipper doesn't work and the leather has never really softened back up. I stomp my feet, jump up and down. "Come on," I say. "Fucking wake up already. Jesus Christ. Fuck."

RICKY HAS his fist raised to knock again when all of a sudden the door opens and Steve is standing there in sweatpants and socks and an oversized Buckeyes teeshirt scowling at us and saying "Yes? Okay? Hello? Hi? Can I fucking help you with something?"

And Ricky just steps inside. It's pretty slick, actually. He just steps in, just slips past Steve. And it's funny. Right away Steve's hands go up, like he's going to try to block me if I try to come in, but at the same time he's tracking on Ricky as Ricky moves farther into the room. "What the fuck," he says. "Fucking stop. My man, stop. Get the fuck out of here. Get out."

Ricky's moved into the middle of the room where there's a little seating area, a couch and a couple of chairs around a coffee table. "We're really sorry to bother you," he says. His voice is totally calm, totally natural. "We need your help with something. Hopefully this'll only take a minute."

Steve's still standing between us, still trying to track on both of us at the same time. "No it fucking won't," he says. "It won't take a minute, it won't take a second, because you're fucking leaving right fucking now."

Ricky sits down in one of the chairs, leans back, raises his hands and lets them fall. "Come on," he says. "Let's not make this a big pain in everybody's ass. Help us out and we're out of here. Two minutes. Promise."

Steve's eyes are on me but he's talking to Ricky when he says, "Help you with what?"

"I just need to know if you saw somebody," Ricky says. "I need to know if a friend of mine came into the bar on Monday night. That's all. You tell me yes or no and then we're out of here."

Steve just stands there for a minute looking back and forth between us, and then he sort of straightens up. He keeps his eyes on me as he backs out of the doorway. I go in. Standing outside and looking in it was hard to make out much besides the furniture. Inside with the door closed behind me I get the full experience. It's exactly what you'd expect. Low drop ceiling, bad florescent lighting, ugly carpet. Bad paneling on the walls and those shitty hollow-core doors. And the smell. That same stale basement smell of air freshener covering mildew and weed smoke. A little kitchen area off to one side. A big old TV in a big old TV cabinet against one wall and the couch and the chairs. Steve moves around and takes a seat on the couch facing Ricky.

"Sure," he says. "Why not? Come in. Make yourselves at home. You guys want anything? I can make some coffee. Or you want breakfast? I've got cereal. I might be out of milk. My mom might have some. I could run up and see if she's got any."

Ricky shakes his head. He's got his phone out again and he's scrolling through. "Thanks very much," he says. "We're fine."

I'm still standing just inside the door. Steve turns to look at me and then he turns back to Ricky and he nods.

"Great," he says. "Terrific. In that case, why don't you go ahead and tell me what the fuck you're doing here, and what the fuck you want."

Ricky nods. He finds what he's looking for on his phone and he holds it out to Steve. "We're looking for a friend of ours," he says. "We need to know if you saw this guy in the bar on Monday night. Anything you can tell us—if you saw him, if you talked to him, if you saw him leave with anybody—that would all be really helpful."

Steve doesn't take the phone though, doesn't look at it. He looks at me again and then he looks at Ricky and he says, "Come on, man.

What is this? You come to my place and you get me out of bed and you come busting in here and you want to know if I've seen this guy? I mean, what? What's the deal? Does this guy owe you money, or something?"

Ricky's still holding out the phone. "Just look at the picture," he says. "Either you saw him or you didn't see him. You tell us you did or you tell us you didn't and then we're out of here and you can go back to sleep."

Steve sits back, shakes his head, laughs. "Man, fuck you guys," he says. "I'm not telling you shit, so why don't you just get the fuck out of here and let me start my morning in peace?"

Ricky doesn't let him finish, though, doesn't let him get it all the way out. "Look," he says, "here's how it is. Either you look at this photo and you tell me what I want to know, or I go upstairs and I tell your mom that you just sold me enough weed to manage my glaucoma for a week. That everybody around here told me you're the guy to see." He picks the phone up again and holds it out. "In case you're confused about what this is," he says. "In case you think that us being here is the most inconvenient thing that can happen to you this morning."

For a second Steve doesn't move. The two of them just sit there, looking at each other. Then Steve sits forward. It's funny. It's like at the door. It's like he just gives up. Like he just accepts it. He waves a hand at the screen.

"Sure," he says. "Sure, I saw this guy. He said he grew up around here and he hadn't been back in a while. He said he used to hang out at The Cornwall back when he lived here." He sits back again, looks at me over his shoulder, looks back at Ricky. He holds up his hands. "All right?" he says. "We good? You got what you want? You leaving now?"

Ricky puts the phone back in his pocket, but other than that he doesn't move. What I mean is he doesn't make any move like he's about to get up, like he's about to leave. "I need to find him," he says. "I need your help. I'm worried about him. I flew all the way out here from L.A. to find him and make sure he's okay."

Over the back of the couch I see Steve shrug.

"I mean, he seemed okay to me," he says. "He seemed fine."

Ricky nods. "That's good," he says. "I'm glad to hear that. But I still really need to talk to him. So if you heard him mention any plans, or you saw him leave with anybody, it would be really helpful if you could tell me."

Steve doesn't say anything for a minute. Then he sort of groans. He sits forward, leans his elbows on his knees. "Come on, guys," he says. "I told you what you wanted to know. I answered your questions, so can't you just leave? I don't know you and I don't know this guy and I really don't want to get in the middle of anything, okay? I already told you what you wanted to know, okay? So how about you just leave? Now? Please?"

Ricky starts to say something, but I get there first. I come around and I stand next to the other chair and I say, "Listen, man. Whatever you think this is, it's not that. Logan, the guy in the picture, he and I go way back. The thing he said about how he used to hang out at The Cornwall? Most of the time that was with me. He's in town to see me. The whole reason we're looking for him is we were supposed to get together and he never showed up and he never called. Then we found out that he went to the Cornwall on Monday night and we went there and the guy there told us that we should talk to you so we came here."

It's weird. I really thought that if I explained things, if I sort of cut through all of Ricky's pseudo-tough-guy third-degree bullshit, that that would do it, somehow. That that would help. That we would be able to talk like normal people. But it doesn't work at all. Steve just looks at me like he's even more confused, now. It doesn't help that it sort of sounds like nonsense, coming out.

"I've got a radio show," I say. "I'm on the radio. What I mean is, we're not bad people. I mean it's not like we're bad people who are after him, or something. I have a show on the radio. That's the whole reason Logan's even here in the first place. He's supposed to do a thing for my show. I'm Dex Foster."

Steve's whole demeanor changes. "Seriously?" he says. "Oh, no, totally. Man, I listen to your show all the time." He looks at Ricky and then he looks back at me like he can't even believe it. "That's so crazy," he says. "You're Dex Foster? That's fucking crazy." He's getting excited. "That's so funny," he says. "You know I actually called in to your show one time? I was on the air and everything."

"No shit," I say. "About what?"

He shakes his head. "Man, I don't even remember," he says. "Some sports thing, or something. Something about the Cavs, maybe. It was a long time ago. I mean it was probably five or six years ago. And you hung up on me pretty fast." He laughs.

"Yeah," I say. "Well, sorry. That's just the show, you know?"

He waves it away. "Sure," he says. "Totally. I got it. It's cool."

Ricky's been sitting back through all of this, but now he sits forward again. "Great," he says. "So we're good? You'll help us out?"

Steve cools again. He looks down, looks away. "Man, I don't know," he says. "I mean, who am I to say? It's not my place. It's not my place to make those decisions for other people. I mean, right? Like, people are always going to do what they're going to do, right? Everybody's got their own path. Everybody's got to find their own truth, and just because something is truth for me doesn't mean it's truth for them, right?" He looks at me, looks down again. "It's about respect," he says. "Like, fundamentally. Like we've all got to respect each other's journeys."

He looks at me again. His look is searching for something, but whatever it is it doesn't seem like he finds it before Ricky goes into his jacket pocket and he brings out his wallet and he lays two twenties on the coffee table. He holds them there with his fingers and he says, "All right, how about this? There's forty bucks in it for you if you can help us out."

Steve looks at the bills and then he looks at me and then he looks at Ricky. For a second I think he's going to say something about, Didn't Ricky hear him? Something about, Didn't Ricky hear what he just said? But he doesn't. He looks down and he shrugs and then he nods at the bills and he says, "A hundred. I'll tell you for a hundred."

I almost laugh, but then I don't. There's just no time. Ricky is already talking again. He's already making the deal.

"What?" he's saying. "What will you tell me for a hundred? What do I get for a hundred? I don't want to just hear that you saw him. I need something really useful. Something that helps me find him."

Steve is nodding. "No, totally," he says. "I can do that. I can tell you when he left, who he left with, what they were talking about, where they were going." He's counting them off on his fingers. "Or I can tell you where they were probably going," he says. "But, like, ninety-nine percent sure that's where they were going."

Ricky keeps his finger on the bill as he shrugs. "Okay," he says. "Go ahead. Tell me."

Steve looks at me, then at the money, then back at Ricky. "All right," he says. "That guy, your friend, he asked me if we served anything besides booze. I told him that we didn't, but that there was a guy there who did. I introduced them, and they left together."

Ricky shakes his head. "That's nothing," he says. "What am I supposed to do with that?" He's talking loud, now, talking fast. "What's the guy's name?" he asks. "Where can I find him? Where did they go?"

Steve holds up his hands. "Jesus Christ," he says. "I don't know his real name, okay? Everybody calls him Yammer. I don't even know the guy. Honestly, I'm trying to keep clear of that whole scene." He looks at me like he's looking for support, for understanding. "I don't get involved," he says. "This guy hangs around the bar, I work at the bar, sometimes people come in looking for shit and I point them in his direction, that's it. That's all I do. That's the extent of my involvement."

Ricky's not having it, though. He shakes his head again. "I don't hear an answer," he says. "Where? Where can we find him? You have to tell me where we can find him, otherwise it's no deal."

"All right," Steve says. "I'll tell you. Just calm down, okay? Just keep your voice down. I'll tell you. You guys have to swear that you won't say shit to my mom, though. Because it would seriously be my ass."

Ricky's whole demeanor softens. He nods. "Sure," he says. His voice is quiet, back to normal. "Sure, we won't say anything." He looks at me. "Right, Dex?" he says. "We promise." He looks back at Steve and shrugs. "Why would we say anything?" he says. "We just want to find our friend. Beyond that, none of what happens here has anything to do with us. None of it is any of our business."

"Okay," Steve says. "Okay. All right. So the guy who owns the Cornwall, Tom, he's a really good guy. I mean, I owe him a lot. He's helped me out a lot. And he's not what you think. He's just being practical. There's not really any money in that place. It's hard. And people are going to do these deals anyway. If he kicks them out they'll just do it in the parking lot and if he kicks them out of the parking lot they'll do it in the woods. It's not going to stop anything. So Yammer throws Tom a commission and Tom throws us a commission for pointing people in Yammer's direction. It works for everybody." He's looking down at the floor, looking down at his hands, glancing at us and then looking down again. "Seriously, though," he says, "I swear to God, I don't even fuck with that shit anymore. I smoke a little weed because I have anxiety and agoraphobia, but that's it. And that's basically a medical thing. Other than that, as far as that whole scene goes, I don't have anything to do with it. I just point him out to people who ask. That's it. That's all I do."

Ricky looks from Steve to me and then back to Steve again and he shrugs. "So what?" he says. His voice is loud, now, load again. It's louder than it was before. "You're going to introduce us to Yammer?" he says. "You said you were going to tell me where they went. You said you were going to help me find my friend."

Steve puts up his hands. "Jesus Christ," he says. "Can you cool it with that shit? Please? My mom is right upstairs."

"Tell me, then," Ricky says. "Tell me what I want to know and we're gone. We're out of here the second you tell me."

Steve shakes his head. "I can't," he says. "I can't introduce you to Yammer. I don't know where he is when he's not at the bar, and he doesn't come in until late. But I can tell you where they went. Or I can tell you where they would have gone. Because see, this one time, back when I first started working there, when I first moved back, this one time I went out with Tom and Yammer and those guys after the bar closed. To meet the guy. Yammer's guy. But we're talking one time and one time only. And I only went because I had to. I had to show those guys that I was cool with everything. So I'm thinking that if Yammer had what your friend wanted then they wouldn't have left, right? They would have done the deal and Yammer would have come back. But he didn't. So I'm thinking that your friend must have wanted something Yammer didn't have on him. So they would have gone to see the guy."

He looks at Ricky. Ricky shrugs.

"Sure," Ricky says. "That makes sense." His voice is quiet, relaxed. He shrugs again. "Great," he says. "Give us the address and we'll get out of your hair."

Steve looks down, shakes his head. "That's the thing," he says. "I don't know it. I never knew it. Tom drove us. I remember basically where it is, what neighborhood and everything, but I'd have to actually see the house to know which one it was."

He looks at Ricky again. I'm looking at Ricky, too. For a second

Ricky doesn't move. Then he pushes the bills across the table and he lifts his finger.

"All right," he says. "Forty now, the rest when you show us the house." He stands up. "Go get changed," he says. "We'll wait for you in the car."

Steve doesn't even take the bills. He looks from Ricky to me and back to Ricky again. "Wait," he says.

Ricky isn't waiting, though. He's already across the room, already opening the door and going out. Steve turns to watch him go and then he turns to me. His look is confused, pissed. His look says he wants me to do something, wants me to solve this. I give him a thumbs up. I don't know what else to do. He's just sitting there, looking at me.

"Great," I say. "Okay." Then I go out, too. I pull the door closed behind me. It's a relief to be outside. After the basement the cold air feels good in my lungs. I go up and across the lawn. Ricky is waiting by the car.

"Jesus," I say. "Were you, like, a cop in a former life?"

He doesn't answer that, though. He's working his hands over each other, blowing onto them. His breath makes a little cloud. "Unlock the fucking doors, already," he says. "Let's get some fucking heat going. I'm fucking freezing."

I UNLOCK the doors and we get in. I start the engine and I crank the heat and we sit there, me with my jacket wrapped tight around me and Ricky hunched forward in his seat and with his hands up over the vent.

"Look," I say, after a while, "if you want me to do something other than what I'm doing then you need to tell me. You've got to tell me if you want me to play good cop or bad cop or something. You can't just put me into the middle of stuff and assume that I know the fucking script." I say, "And anyway, what I said worked. Your forty bucks wouldn't have done shit if I hadn't said what I said."

Ricky holds up his hands. He doesn't look at me, though. He's still hunched over, still leaning into the dash, still huddled close to the vents. "Sure," he says. "Absolutely. No argument here."

And it doesn't sound like he means it, but what the fuck do I know? It sounds like he's just saying it to get me off his back, but how would I really know? It's not like I know him, not like I know what it means when he says things one way or another. So I don't argue the point. I take out my phone and I send a text to Dave saying that we're working on it but that we're making progress and I'll call him soon. Then I start writing one to Bethany. I don't finish it, though. I don't end up writing anything at all. I'm still trying to figure out what to say, and how to say it, when Steve comes walking up.

He comes across the yard wearing a big baggy sweatshirt with the hood up and his hands in the kangaroo pocket and he comes over to the passenger door and Ricky rolls down the window.

"Okay," Ricky says. "Everything all set? You ready to go?"

Steve doesn't answer him right away, though. He looks off down the street, shrugs. "See," he says, "the thing is, I've kind of got a bunch of stuff I need to do today? And then I need to head into work at two? So I don't really think I'll have time to look for this place and get back here and still do everything."

Ricky doesn't say anything for a second, and then he nods. "Okay," he says, "what time do you need to get back?"

Steve looks down, shrugs again. "I don't know," he says. "Maybe eleven? Noon at the latest."

"That's no problem," Ricky says. His tone is casual, inviting. "We'll definitely have you back before then," he says.

Steve doesn't move, though. "Right," he says, "okay, but you don't really know where we're going. You don't know how far we're going, so you can't really know how long it's going to take. I mean, you can't really promise that we'll be back. You see what I'm saying?"

But then he stops talking, because Ricky is opening his door and getting out.

"Listen," Ricky is saying, "I promise that we'll have you back, okay? You have my word. All we need from you is to know which house it is. You point out the house and if we're short on time we'll bring you back here and then we'll just go back ourselves, okay?" He's moving around behind Steve, sort of corralling him into the passenger seat. "Ride up front," he's saying. "You ride up here where you can see."

Steve gets in. He doesn't really do it like he wants to but he doesn't protest, either. Ricky closes the door and gets in back.

"All right," he says, once he's in. "We set? Everybody good? Steve, you tell Dex where to go."

WE GET on the road. It takes us maybe twenty minutes to get where we're going, and apart from Steve telling me where to go and when to turn nobody says anything. The neighborhood Steve takes us to looks like it was nice not too long ago. The lots are big and the houses are decent, but a lot of the places look like nobody is taking care of them anymore. There are newspapers and phonebooks in driveways and branches down in yards, empty garbage cans that have fallen over and been left out. We go past one house with its garage door stuck halfway open and another where the cable dish has been blown or knocked or pulled down and left hanging from where the cable snagged on the gutter. There are cars in some of the driveways and lights on in some of the windows, but just as many of the places look empty.

We drive around for ten minutes, looking.

"Okay," I say, finally, "so which one is it?"

Steve is leaning forward in the seat, looking. He shakes his head. "I don't remember all of these side streets," he says. "I remember it being just one main road all the way through."

Ricky reaches between the seats and pats Steve on the shoulder. "You're doing great," he says. "Just take your time."

We keep going. I drive up and down the different streets, some of them more than once. Steve keeps thinking he recognizes a street name or a tree or a mailbox, but it always turns out to be nothing.

"Jesus Christ," I say, finally. "If it's here, we've definitely passed it by now. We've probably passed it twice. If you didn't recognize it any of those times you're not going to recognize it the next time, either."

Steve is tapping his feet, drumming on his knees with his fingers. "I just don't remember it being this many streets," he says.

"Shit," I say. "How fucked up were you? I mean, how sure are you that this is even the right development?"

"I'm sure," Steve says. "I'm like, ninety-nine percent sure. Ninety-nine point nine percent." Then he sits up. "Wait," he says. "Slow down. That's it. That one." He points and laughs. He's bouncing in the seat. "That's it," he says again. "Holy shit, that's it. That's totally it. That's the house."

I pull over and park. The house is a white ranch with a detached garage and a newer-looking minivan in the driveway. It's definitely one of the nicest houses on the street. Or at least it's in the best shape. The lawn is mowed and the leaves are raked. Somebody even pulled the garbage can back up from the curb.

"Are you sure?" I say.

"Totally," Steve says. "Absolutely. One hundred percent."

Ricky reaches between the seats, pats Steve on the shoulder again. "Great work," he says. "Really terrific."

I shut off the engine and I open the door. Ricky is getting out, too. Steve leans across my seat.

"Wait," he says, "so you guys are doing this now? You're going to go talk to him now?"

I lean back down. Ricky does, too.

"Yeah, Steve," Ricky says. "Yeah, we were."

Steve twists in the seat, cranes his neck to look at Ricky around the headrest. "Okay," he says, "but see, the thing is, you told me you'd take me back? You said that if I showed you the house then you'd take me back? You said that you wouldn't do this now. That you'd take me home and then you'd come back and talk to him."

Ricky doesn't let him finish, though. He holds up a hand. "Steve," he says. "Listen to me. Don't worry. We'll be five minutes. We're going to go inside, talk to this guy for five minutes, and then we'll come right back out and take you home, okay?"

Steve is squirming in the seat, trying to get a better angle on Ricky. "Yeah," he says, "okay, but see, the other thing is, I'm not really sure I want this guy knowing that I told you where he lives? Like I would really prefer it if nobody knows that I had anything to do with this? So it would be a lot better if nobody sees me here?" Then he says, "Guys?" because while he was saying the last thing Ricky stood up out of the doorway.

I stand up, too. I look at Ricky over the roof.

"It's going to be fine," Ricky says. "Just stay here and nobody will see you. I promise, nobody will know that you had anything to do with this."

IT FEELS like Steve's probably got something to say to that, too, but he doesn't get the chance before Ricky steps back and closes the door. I close mine, too. We start toward the house. Across the street and onto the lawn I look back. I can see Steve slouched down in the seat, with his hood up and the top of it pulled down to cover his eyes.

"Shit," I say. "Steve seems kind of nervous."

It's a joke, or it's supposed to be a joke, but Ricky doesn't laugh. He doesn't acknowledge it at all. He climbs the front steps and he rings the bell. I go up and I stand next to him and a second later the door opens. The woman who's standing there is young-looking and small and she's holding a baby and the baby is asleep and the woman is looking at us like we better have a really, really good reason for ringing her doorbell.

Ricky takes off his sunglasses. "Hi," he says. He almost whispers it. "We're really sorry to bother you," he says. "I just got in from out of town, and my friend told me that I could get some supplies here? Some things I couldn't bring with me on the plane?"

The woman looks from Ricky to me and then back to Ricky again. She's rocking the baby, shifting her weight from side to side, but her eyes are angry and she's gritting her teeth at us like there's something she wants to say, something she wants to yell, but can't because of the baby. She steps back and closes the door. She does it really softly, but it's pretty clear that's not what she wanted to do.

With the door closed I laugh. I look around and I laugh. It's all just so ridiculous. It's like, How did I even get here? I turn to Ricky. "Okay," I say, "so now what?"

Ricky's got his sunglasses off and is rubbing his eyes. He drops his hands, and blinks up at the bright gray sky. He looks at me. "Just give it a second," he says.

I laugh again. "Give it a second," I say. "Give what a second? Even if this is the right house, don't you think that was her way of telling us to fuck off?"

Ricky holds up a hand. "Give it a second," he says, "because she knows that if she doesn't come back I'm going to ring the doorbell again. And she doesn't want me ringing the bell again, does she? No she doesn't, because she just got that baby to sleep. So right now she's putting the baby down, and then she's going to come back, or her guy or somebody is going to come see what we want, because nobody wants me to ring the bell again, and nobody wants us standing out here for the neighbors to see. Okay? So that. Give that a second."

I snort at that. "Neighbors," I say. "What are you talking about? What neighbors? Look at this place. Have you looked at this place?"

Ricky doesn't respond to that, though. He's not even looking at me anymore. He's turned back to the door. "Just wait," he says. "Okay? Just wait because I told you to. Wait because I said so. Okay? Will you just do that, please?"

I'm going to say something back to that—I don't know what, exactly, but something—but I haven't come up with it before the door opens again and the man standing there says, "Goddamnit, would you come inside already? Before the whole fucking neighborhood sees you."

WE GO inside, into the front hallway.

"Thanks for meeting us," Ricky whispers. "We know you must be busy."

The man is tall and thin and he's got a salt-and-pepper goatee and a shaved head that you can tell from the follicle stubble is more necessity than decision. He gives us his best I'm-not-somebody-you-want-to-fuck-with look and he whispers, "I'm not meeting you. That's not what this is. This is me getting you the fuck off my fucking doorstep while I figure out what the fuck I'm going to do with you."

Ricky nods and holds up his hand. "Sure," he whispers. "Absolutely. Your house, your rules. You call the shots."

The man gives Ricky another warning look but it's like Ricky doesn't take it, somehow. It's like he just isn't buying into the man's whole thing. He just keeps looking at the man with the same blank, earnest expression on his face. The man turns to me.

"Explain this," he whispers. "Fucking now."

I hold up my hands. "Hey, man," I say, "I'm just the driver." I say it in my normal voice, though. The man winces.

"Fuck," he whispers. "You want to try to keep your fucking voice down?"

"Shit," I whisper back. "Sorry."

We stand there for a minute, listening. There's nothing, though. The man turns back at Ricky.

"Look," he whispers. "This isn't how this works. This isn't fucking Target. I don't deal with the public. You can't just show up like this. I can't have random people coming here. If you come here then you need to be with somebody, and even that has to be under special circumstances. And I'm talking about a rare set of fucking circumstances. You understand me? So I need you to fuck off back to wherever you came from and not come back, okay? Otherwise I'm going to have to do something."

Ricky isn't having that either, though. He steps back so he has room and he starts taking off his jacket. He holds the collar with his chin while he folds in the sleeves, holds it against his stomach and lets it drop into another fold. "I know," he whispers. "I understand completely." He takes a step forward, takes another step, starts moving farther into the house. "But we really need your help," he says. "They told us that sometimes Yammer brings people here, and time is kind of a factor, and so here we are."

The man has his hands up. He's stepping back, though. It's like it's not even a decision. Ricky keeps crowding him and he keeps moving to make space and then Ricky crowds him again. He shakes his head.

"Yammer didn't tell you how to find me," he whispers. "Yammer knows better."

Ricky keeps moving forward as he nods. "Right," he whispers. "No, you're right. Yammer didn't tell us."

I'm right behind Ricky. Off to our left the hallways opens up into the living room. There's a big flatscreen TV on the far wall showing some daytime talk show with the volume turned all the way down and under that there's a little pile of toys, a few dolls and some other stuff. Next to it there's a doorway leading onto a hall.

"Stop," the man whispers, louder now. "Fucking stop."

Ricky stops. "It wasn't Yammer," he whispers.

The man shakes his head again. "I don't care who it was," he whispers. "You can't be here."

"Look," Ricky whispers, "we're just trying to find our friend. Someone told us that he might have come here with Yammer on Monday night. We're hoping that you saw him and that you can tell us something that'll help us find him. Tell us about that and we're out of here."

The man is only partly paying attention now, though. He holds up a hand, takes a step through the wide doorway and into the living room. We all stop and listen. A second later I hear it, too. Somewhere down the hall the baby has started crying.

The man's whole demeanor falls. He raises his hands, presses them to his eyes, lets them drop. He looks at us. "All right, fuck it," he says, in his regular voice. "Just come downstairs, okay? We can talk downstairs."

WE FOLLOW him down the hall and into the kitchen, and then through a door and down a set of stairs into the basement. The basement is nice. It's nicer than the living room, actually. There's an even bigger flatscreen and a couple of high-end-looking leather couches set up around a pretty high-end-looking coffee table. There's a short bar with a mirrored back and a really nice stereo setup in a really nice custom buildout.

The man sits down on one of the couches. He sits like he's really glad to be sitting, like this whole thing has worn him out. I stop at the bottom of the stairs and I lean against the post. Ricky takes a lap around the room, nodding at stuff.

"This is nice," he says. "This whole place. Nice setup."

The man perks up. "You like it?" he says. He sits up. "You know I actually grew up in this house," he says. "Down here was my playroom, back when I was a kid."

186

"No shit," Ricky says.

The man shakes his head. "No," he says, "no shit. This was a pretty decent neighborhood, back then. That whole real estate bubble thing kind of fucked everything up. You know." He makes a circle in the air with his finger. "One of those vicious cycle things," he says. "Property values dropped and people started to leave and nobody moved in and property values dropped some more because of all the empty houses and so other people left, and on and on." He shrugs. "Gina and me bought this place from my mom straight cash," he says. "Private sale. Just so she could get out. We paid the old price, too. I won't even tell you where the valuation's at now." He shakes his head. "They say it's coming back," he says, "but shit. I mean, you drove through. You saw."

Ricky nods. "We saw," he says. Then he shrugs. "These things are cyclical," he says. "You're through the worst of it, anyway."

The man thinks about it, shrugs again. "I don't know," he says. "Maybe." He looks at me, then back at Ricky. He holds out his hand. "I'm Josh, by the way," he says. "Upstairs that's Gina, and our son, Tristan. And we have another daughter, Maddie. She's five. She's at preschool right now."

Ricky steps in and shakes Josh's hand. "Richard Dubowitz," he says. "People call me Ricky. You should call me Ricky." He nods to me. "That's Dex," he says.

Josh is making a point, though. He holds up the hand Ricky shook. "What I'm saying," he says, "is that I need you to understand why I can't have random people showing up at my house, knocking on my door in the middle of the afternoon, looking for shit. There's a reason I do things the way I do things. It's about distance. It's about sustainability."

Ricky moves around the table, takes a seat on the other couch. "Sure," he says. He holds up his hands, looks at me and then back at Josh. "Hey," he says, "we get it. You've got to be smart. You've got to think about your family. I mean, it's all about them, right? Everything we do we do for them. Am I right?"

Josh nods. "No," he says, "that's it. That's exactly it. It's all about them."

"I completely understand," Ricky says. "And look, let me just say, on behalf of both of us, on behalf of Dex and myself, we want to apologize. We're sorry, okay? We're sorry. We were going on the information we had, and clearly we listened to the wrong guy. But I swear to God, Josh, we didn't come here to cause you or Gina any problems. Okay? You have my word."

Josh looks at us, looks from Ricky to me and then back to Ricky, and then he sits back. He waves a hand in the air, waves away what Ricky said. "Forget it," he says. "Don't worry about it." He pulls a hand over his face. "Look," he says, "you have to understand. I hate being that guy. I don't want to be that guy. This is a people business. It's built on relationships. I don't want to have to be some hardass. That's not me. But you've got to be careful."

Ricky is nodding. "Sure," he says. "It's a lot of pressure, being in charge. Being that guy. Looking out for everyone. Keeping an eye on everything all the time."

Josh snorts as he shakes his head. "And people think it's this whole other thing," he says. "Like it's just cash and fucking partying all the time." He points up the stairs. "Shit," he says, "you saw what I got in the driveway. You see what my life is." He shrugs, looks at me. "Anyway," he says. "Fuck that shit. You didn't come here to hear me complain." He holds out his hands, the palms up and open. "What do you guys need?" he says. "If I don't have it I can get it. I can have it here in less than an hour."

Ricky unfolds his jacket, goes into the pocket, takes out his phone. "We're not here for any of that," he says. "We really are looking for a friend of ours. They told us that he might have been here a few nights ago with this guy Yammer? We're just hoping that you can tell us where they went, or anything that might help us find him." He finds what he's looking for on the phone and holds it out to Josh. Josh glances at it and laughs.

"Shit, man," he says. "You don't have to show me no picture. I have everything The Loose Ends ever did. I'm talking live, studio, import, everything." He's counting them off on his fingers. He holds up the hand, the fingers spread. "I saw them like five times," he says. "Shit yeah he came here. He sat right where you're sitting. Apart from my kids being born it was the fucking highlight of my fucking life."

Ricky puts the phone away, spreads his hands wide. "That's great," he says. "So, what? He came over here and you guys partied?"

Josh's face falls a little. He shakes his head. "No, man," he says. "With the kids and everything we keep a pretty strict policy about on-premises usage. We're strictly supply, not venue."

Ricky is nodding. "Right," he says. "So they left. Did they say where they were going?"

Josh shakes his head again. "No," he says, "but I sort of just assumed they were going back to Yammer's place. That's kind of what it seemed like, from how they were talking. That was my impression."

Ricky is still nodding. "Great," he says. "I guess we need to talk to Yammer, then. Do you have a number for him?"

Josh laughs at that. "Yammer's got a different burner every other week," he says. "I stopped trying to keep track. He calls me when he needs something. I can tell you how to get to his place, though. It's kind of a hike, but I can tell you how to get there if you want to go."

Ricky keeps nodding as he says, "Sure, Josh. Sure, that would be really helpful."

"No problem," says Josh. "Just give me a second."

He gets up and goes over to the bar. Ricky sits back into the cushions. I take out my phone and I check my messages. There are a few from Dave asking me what's going on, but there's nothing from

Bethany. I think about writing something to her, just asking where she is or what she's doing or what's going on later, just anything, but I don't do it. Or at least I still haven't done it by the time Josh comes back. He's got a piece of paper in his hand and he holds it out to Ricky. Ricky stands as he takes it.

"It's kind of rough over where Yammer lives," Josh says. "I don't mean rough like scary, I just mean it's kind of rough. So just, you know. Fair warning."

Ricky folds the paper and slides it into his pocket. He holds out his hand. "We really can't thank you enough," he says.

Josh shakes his hand. "It's no problem," he says. "When you find Logan, tell him I said what's up. Or tell him I said thanks for shopping, or whatever. Or come back anytime." He laughs.

Ricky is already moving around the couch, already headed toward the stairs. I fall in behind him. Josh stands at the bottom while we go up. Ricky opens the door, softly.

"Hey," Josh says, "one more thing." His voice is low again. Louder than a whisper, but lower than it was with the door closed. "Who told you about this place?" he says. "Who told you where to find me? It wasn't Yammer, so who was it?"

Ricky stops in the doorway, turns, leans on the railing. "It was Steve," he says. "The bartender over at that bar. The whatever it's called. The Cornwall Inn. Steve the bartender told us."

Josh smiles a tight, lipless smile. "Steve," he says. "That little motherfucker." He holds up a hand. "All right," he says. "Thanks. Thanks for the heads up."

WE GO up into the kitchen and back down the hall. Off somewhere beyond the living room I can hear Gina singing some lullaby. The words are too low to hear but the melody is coming through. It's something that I know, somehow, something that I recognize but can't quite name. I have the feeling that it's going to come to me any second, that she's just about to get to the part that I know, but then we're already down the hall and going out and then Ricky pulls the door closed behind us and I can't hear her anymore.

"You really are something," I say. "I've got to hand it to you."

Ricky is two steps ahead of me. He's pulling his jacket back on, zipping it up and putting up the collar.

"You know anywhere around here where we can get some food?" he says. "I haven't eaten since L.A., I'm fucking starving."

"Sure," I say. "I'm sure we can find something."

WE CROSS to the car and get in. Steve is yelling at us before we even have the doors closed.

"What the hell?" he's saying. "You said five minutes. That wasn't five minutes." He's looking back and forth between us, twisting around in his seat. "You fucking promised," he says. "You guys fucking promised me."

I'm starting the car, looking at the wheel, so I miss the beginning of what happens next. I hear one door open, then another, and when I look up Ricky is outside the open passenger door and he's got ahold of Steve, got one hand on his arm and the other gripping the hood of his sweatshirt, and he's pulling. Steve is yelling, holding on and bracing his feet in the well, and Ricky is grunting and cursing. Then all of a sudden it all lets go and Steve is sprawled out on the grass and Ricky is stumbling back onto somebody's lawn. Ricky slips in the snowy mud and almost goes down, but then he catches himself and he comes striding back. Steve is up and kneeling where he fell and for a second it looks like Ricky is going to charge right through him, but then Ricky sidesteps around him and maneuvers himself into the passenger seat. He reaches for the door handle and he gets ahold of it and he tries to close the door, but Steve is in the way. Ricky lets go of the door and he turns in the seat and he starts sort of kick-pushing at Steve's haunch with his heel. The first two times Steve manages to sort of block him but the third one gets through and Steve topples back over. Ricky goes for the handle again and he gets the door closed and he locks it. He settles himself in the seat, pushes strands of hair back from his forehead. He's breathing heavy through his nose. He goes into his pocket and he comes out with the piece of paper Josh gave him and he hands it to me.

"Here," he says. "This is where we're going next."

Outside the window Steve is getting up. He reaches and he tries the door handle, and then he slaps his muddy palms against the window. "Hey," he says. "Hey, asshole. Hey." He slaps his hands against the window again, against the door, against the roof.

Ricky doesn't look at him. He has his phone out now and he's typing, scrolling, searching. He shakes his head. "I don't see anything around here," he says. "I see a bunch of fast food and that's it."

Steve has stopped hitting the car. Now he's bending down to look in, glaring at Ricky through the mud-smeared glass. I roll down the rear window on that side and I lean back in my seat and I say, "You should probably just get in the car, man. I'm pretty sure Josh and Gina don't want you hanging around in front of their house."

For a second Steve doesn't move, doesn't give any indication even that he heard me. Then he stands up. He puts his hands in his sweatshirt pocket and he turns, like maybe he isn't going to get in. Like maybe he's going to walk home or stay here just to spite us.

"Come on," I say. "Don't be an asshole."

He can't keep it up. What's he really going to do, anyway? So he opens the door and he gets in the back. "I'm not the one being an asshole," he says. "This guy. This fucking guy's the asshole." He hits the back of Ricky's seat with his palm.

Ricky doesn't react at all. He keeps looking down at this phone. I find Steve in the rearview, watch him cross his arms and sink down in the seat. I watch for a second longer to make sure he's not going to do anything else and then I face the front and I put it in gear and I pull away from the curb.

I DRIVE us back to Steve's mom's house, park out in front. Steve doesn't get out, though. After a second I turn around and look at him. He's just sitting there, looking up at the house.

"Is your mom going to give you a bunch of shit about this?" I say.

He shrugs. "The fucked-up thing is," he says, "it doesn't even matter. It doesn't matter what I tell her. She'll just assume."

"That sucks," I say.

He shrugs again. He's still looking at the house. "It would be one thing if she got it," he says. "Like it would be one thing if she understood how it is. Then we could at least talk about it like people. But she's got all of these fucked-up ideas about everything. When she was a kid she had some uncle who quit drinking by joining the church, and it's like that's it for her. Like it's all just about character and willpower and being a good person. Like, Just say No. It's a fucking joke."

"So why don't you move out?" I say. "I mean, shit, you couldn't pay me to live with my parents. I'd rather live in my fucking car."

He shakes his head. "It's not that simple," he says. "She spent a bunch of the money from my dad's life insurance to send me to this clinic in Minnesota. She needs somebody renting that room. If I moved out she'd have to find somebody else, and I don't really want that. I don't really want just some random stranger living in my mom's basement."

"I don't know," I say. "It still seems like a hassle."

He looks at me. "She's my mom," he says. "What can you do?"

Nobody says anything for a minute. Steve turns back to the window, but he doesn't make any move to get out. Ricky finally looks up from his phone.

"Okay," he says. "Here we are. We're here. I thought you were in a big hurry to get back. I thought you had stuff you needed to do."

Steve mumbles something back to that, something I don't quite catch. Ricky leans his head to one side.

"What?" he says.

Steve clears his throat, speaks up. "The money?" he says. "The rest of the money? The other sixty you owe me?"

Ricky goes back to his phone. "The deal was a hundred if you helped me find my friend," he says, "and I still haven't found my friend."

Steve shifts, leans, sits forward. He pulls himself up so he's almost up between the seats. "Wait," he says. "That's not what you said. That wasn't the deal. You said forty up front and the rest when I showed you where he went, and I showed you. I showed you. I did what I said. I did the deal."

Ricky won't answer him, though, won't even look at him. I don't, either. I kind of can't. I look down at the wheel, look down at my hands. After a minute I feel Steve sit back.

He laughs. "Fine," he says. "You know what? Fine. Fuck it." He opens the door and gets out and then he slams the door behind him, slams it hard enough that the whole car shakes. He leans down outside Ricky's window and he presses both middle fingers against the glass and he says, "Fuck you guys. Fuck both of you. I hope you never fucking find him. And I hope your show gets fucking cancelled." Then he turns and walks away.

I watch him cross the lawn, watch him go around the hedge, watch until he disappears down the stairs.

Ricky holds up his phone. "I'm seeing Subway and I'm seeing McDonald's," he says. "Between those two I don't give a shit. It's your call. Right now I could really do either."

WE GO to the Subway. It's one of those ones that's built in a separate little space inside a gas station convenience store. Ricky orders a veggie footlong and the girl mashes everything into the bun and wraps it up. I get a Coke. I'm not even remotely hungry. My stomach has been kind of knotted up and sour all morning. We sit in one of the little two-seater booths along the front window and I watch cars pulling in and filling up and driving off while Ricky eats.

"So what's our plan, here?" I say, finally. "We go see Yammer and he tells us where he left Logan and we go there and we find him and that's it?"

Ricky works something out of his teeth with his finger, looks at it, puts it back in his mouth and swallows. He shrugs. "I don't know," he says. "I don't know how it's going to go. You know as much as me. You know everything I know." He looks at me. "Why," he says, "you need to be somewhere?"

It's starting to get kind of late in the day for me to be this far from downtown if I'm planning on making it back in time to do the show.

"I mean I need to be somewhere eventually," I say. Then, because of how he's looking at me or because it's Logan or because of I don't even know what, I shake my head. "I'm good for a while, though," I say. "I'm good."

Ricky nods. "Great," he says. He goes back to work on his sandwich. I finish the Coke and I start chewing the ice.

"My girlfriend's going to be so pissed at me," I say. "She was pissed before, but now it's going to be a whole other thing. I didn't tell her about any of this. I didn't leave a note, or anything. I just left." I laugh. "Whatever," I say. "She'll get over it."

Ricky chews and swallows. "Why don't you call her?" he says.

I watch a big man climb down from a big truck, watch his two big kids work their way down from the running board to the pavement. I shrug. "It's a whole thing with her right now," I say. "I think we'd just end up getting into it if I called her. I'll see her later. I'll deal with it later. It's fine. I'll deal with it later."

Ricky nods. "How long have you guys been together?" he says.

I have to think about it. "Six months?" I say. "Or seven? Six or seven months?"

Ricky chews a bite, tongues it into his cheek, holds up a finger. "Good communication," he says. "Good communication is the foundation of all strong relationships."

I laugh. "You sound like you've been reading the same shit my girlfriend reads," I say.

Ricky swallows and shrugs. "You can do what you want," he says, "but if I were you I would call her."

And maybe he's right. Maybe I know he's right, even. And maybe if our conversation was the only thing going on I would have done something about it. Maybe I would have called her. But the thing is, it's not. The thing is that right in the middle of him saying that the big man with the truck and his kids come inside, and right away they start making just a ton of noise. Right away the kids start running up and down the aisles, yelling and grabbing things off the shelves, and the man starts yelling for them to come back and cut it out and be quiet. And I'm not going to try to talk through all of that. I'm not going to try to consider anything with all of that going on. And I let that sort of cover the fact that maybe I don't really have an answer for him. I let that kind of be the end of it. I let it die somewhere between the man telling one kid to put some beef jerky back and him telling the cashier that their mother spoils them. I chew some more ice and I watch them go out and I watch them load up and drive away. Then I turn back to Ricky and I say, "How's your sandwich?"

He shakes his head. "Terrible," he says. "It's really unbelievable. And people wonder why the rest of the world hates us."

I laugh. I think he's joking. It seems like a ridiculous thing to say. "Why," I say, "because we make shitty sandwiches?"

He isn't laughing, though. He shakes his head again. "Because of this," he says. "This place. That guy. His truck. His kids." He points with the sandwich, takes another bite. "Forget the Rockies," he says. "Forget the Grand Canyon and the D.C. Mall. This is what they should put on the postcards."

"Okay," I say, "but so what? I mean, what's your point?"

Ricky nods. He sets the sandwich down and he points at me with both hands. "That," he says. "That's my point. That right there." He leans back, spreads his arms. "Things are the way they are," he says. "Right? I didn't make the world this way, and I don't bear any responsibility for it being like this." Then he sits forward again. He reaches across the table and he pulls the straw and the lid it's threaded onto out of my cup and he holds it up between us. "Like this," he says. "You see this? You know what this is?"

"It's a straw," I say. "It's my straw."

Ricky shakes his head. "Wrong," he says. "It's plastic. It's polypropylene that somebody refined out of crude oil and mixed with some coloring agent and formed into this little lid and this little tube. And do you have any idea where that crude oil came from? For this shit that isn't even a necessary part of you drinking your drink?"

"Jesus Christ," I say. "I don't know. Fucking Texas."

Ricky is rolling the straw between his fingers, spinning the lid. "Sure," he says. "Sure, it's possible. Depending on the price per barrel and the import policies in effect at the time it was produced, there's a chance that it came out of the ground somewhere on this continent. Then again, there's also a pretty good chance that it came out of the ground somewhere else. There's a pretty good chance that it came out of the ground someplace not so nice, someplace where, for example, the government has been known to deploy its military against its civilian population. Someplace where they don't talk about things like due process and basic human rights. Someplace where we know all of this is going on and we still don't do a fucking thing about it, because why not? Because of this." He sets the straw and the lid down on the table between us.

197

The lid makes a circuit around where the end of the straw is touching the table, rolls against my cup and stops. Ricky leans forward. "Now the question," he says, "is do you actually give a shit that any of this is going on? And the answer is no, of course you don't. Not because you're a coldhearted person or because you're an asshole, but just because it doesn't have anything to do with you. Right? It's all happening somewhere else, somewhere thousands and thousands of miles from your life. You haven't killed anyone. You haven't deployed military-grade weapons against your own people. You haven't chased and burned people out of their homes. You didn't do any of that. You're just here drinking your drink." He sits back. "And that's why," he says. "Because to the rest of the world America and the rest of the modern West means wanting what we want when we want it and not really giving too much of a shit about how we get it. It means being casually ambivalent about the repercussions of our casually entitled way of life."

I pick up the straw, thread it out of the lid, dig it back into the ice. "So what?" I say. "You think that the fact that you're saying all of this makes you better than me? What do you think fueled that plane that you took to get here? What do you think has been fueling my car this whole time, while I've been driving your ass around? How do they make the parts for that phone you're always checking?"

He doesn't rise to it, though. He shakes his head. "I'm not saying I'm better," he says. His voice is still low, still even. "I'm saying the whole Western world is headed for a reckoning, and this right here is us sprinting toward it with open arms. This right here is a monument to everything that's hastening its arrival." He picks up the sandwich and takes a bite, but then he makes a face and he spits it back out onto the wrapper. He reaches and he brings the wrapper in around everything, the sandwich and what he spit out and the used and unused napkins and the open and unopened mustard packets, and his squeezes it all into a big wad. Then he stands up. "All right," he says. "That's it. I'm done here. Let's go."

WE GO out and we get back on the road. Ricky reads Josh's directions, but other than that we don't talk. Yammer's place isn't so much a place as it is a trailer in a park, one of a couple dozen single- and double-wides set along a loop of dirt road behind a chain-link fence. I drive in through the open gate, past the wooden sign with the rules and the cluster of chained-up garbage cans. Josh's directions have the wrong trailer listed, but the neighbor whose door we knock on points out the right one. It doesn't look too promising. There's no car parked next to it and no lights on inside, and no one answers when we knock.

"Maybe the neighbor knows where he went," I say. "Maybe she knows when he's coming back."

We go back and ask, but the neighbor doesn't know anything. Ricky shows her the picture of Logan on his phone, asks her if she's seen him around with Yammer, but she just shakes her head.

"We keep different hours," she says. "You could ask his sister. She works over in Parkman. Maybe she's seen him."

"Thanks," Ricky says. "I think we're going to stick around here and see if we can't catch him, if it's all right with everyone."

The woman shrugs. "Suit yourself," she says. "No one here's going to bother you. Most people are at work anyway."

WE GO back and we sit in the car and we wait. We wait for almost an hour, but nobody shows.

"I can't do this forever," I say, finally. "I've got other shit I need to do. We've got to try to move this along."

My phone has buzzed a half-dozen times while we've been sitting here, but I haven't looked at it. I haven't even looked to see what time it is.

Ricky sits forward, rolls out his neck. "All right," he says. "Let's try the sister. See if that gets us anywhere."

We go and we get the details from the neighbor. Yammer's sister works for a welding and fabrication company thirty minutes farther east. Ricky leaves his number, asks the neighbor to call him if Yammer comes back.

"Or you could ask him to call me himself," he says.

The neighbor looks away, shakes her head. "Like I said," she says, "we keep different hours."

"Sure," Ricky says. "Thanks all the same."

WE GET back on the road. I turn on the radio, tune it to our station. I catch the end of a song by The Specials and then I listen through one by Iggy and the Stooges and then Dave comes on with the station identification and to say that I'm out with the flu and that he'll be filling in, taking calls and playing requests.

"Shit," I say.

Ricky's laying back in the seat with his sunglasses on and his hands in his lap. He doesn't move, doesn't sit up. "What?" he says.

"This is supposed to be me," I say. "This is my show. I'm supposed to be on right now. This is supposed to be me."

Ricky lifts his head and listens. Dave is reciting some news item, something about some stupid thing some celebrity said in some interview.

"Fuck," I say. "I can't believe I did that." I really almost can't. It sounds stupid, maybe, but right then it's like I can't even understand how it happened. Like I went through some kind of time warp or the day just evaporated, or something. Like I had time and I had time and then all of a sudden I didn't. Like it went straight from being okay to being way too late without anything in between. I pull a hand over my face. "Jesus Christ," I say, "I must be losing my fucking mind." I look at Ricky and I say, "I just thought we were going to have time." It sounds stupid, saying it out loud. I turn back to the road. "Or, I don't know," I say. "I don't know what I thought. I guess it doesn't matter what I thought."

Out of the corner of my eye I see Ricky lay back. "It sounds okay," he says. "It sounds like they've got it covered." Then he says, "Is it bad? Is it a big problem, you not being there?"

I'm thinking about how pissed Dave must be, thinking about how it'll be if Chad is listening. I snort. "I mean, yeah," I say. "It sure as shit isn't good."

I LEAVE it on. Dave is in the middle of "Killing an Arab" by The Cure when the signal starts to go. There's another station pushing in on the same frequency. It's strange. I've never driven out to the edge of the broadcast range before. I've never been out to see where it stops. There's nothing out here, just empty fields and wooded lots and a few little houses and sheds and barns. The other station is playing an ad for a special someplace is running on snow tires. More and more of it is coming through, the words getting clearer between the static bursts. I reach up and I twist the knob, turn the radio off.

It almost doesn't matter, at this point. We're almost there. The next turn is ours. I park in the gravel lot and we get out and go inside. The woman at reception has to go out onto the shop floor to find Yammer's sister. She takes a pair of safety glasses off a hook on the wall as she goes through the door. The reception area gets loud with the machine sounds and then quiet again as the door swings closed.

We wait. We pace around. Our sneaker soles squeak on the concrete slab. There's bad burned coffee in a maker in the corner and there are gray metal folding chairs along one wall, and a little table with old copies of *Us* and *People*. Finally the door opens again and the receptionist comes back with Yammer's sister. Yammer's sister is tall and thin and she's wearing blue coveralls with her name on a sewn patch on the breast pocket. She pulls off the big noise-suppressing cans she's wearing and she lets them hang around her neck while Ricky tells her why we're here.

She shakes her head. "I don't really see him very much," she says. "He only calls me when he needs money. I couldn't even start to tell you where to look for him." She looks at us like she's trying to decide whether it would be worth it, trying to explain what we're in for with her brother. She shakes her head again. "Sorry," she says. "I'm sorry you came all the way out here for that."

"It's all right," Ricky says. "We appreciate you taking the time."

SHE GOES back through the door and we go back out and we stand at the car and we look at each other over the roof.

"Well, fine," I say. "What do you want to do now?"

Ricky leans on the car and yawns. "I don't know," he says. "Work our way back, maybe. Go by the trailer park and see if Yammer's back yet. If not, maybe we go back over to that bar and see if we can catch him there. That's all on the way back, right?"

"Sure," I say. "It's all on the way."

WE GET in and we get back on the road. I leave the radio off. There are still no lights on at Yammer's, and the neighbor still hasn't seen him. We give it another fifteen minutes and then we head out, head back to The Cornwall. It's still early, but it's already a different scene from before. There are ten or twelve cars and trucks in the lot, and inside is loud with the noise from the jukebox up against the noise from the TVs up against the noise from the people talking. Steve is at the bar and he sees us come in and then he pretends that he didn't see us. The other bartender looks us over when Ricky asks about Yammer, shakes her head.

"I haven't seen him," she says. "It's still a little early for him."

Ricky takes out a pen, writes his number on a napkin. "Can you have him call me if he comes in?" he says. "I really need to talk to him." He takes out his wallet and he puts a five on the napkin and he slides it across.

The bartender is leaning in with her head turned, listening. She nods. "Sure," she says. "Sure, no problem." She puts the napkin and the bill into her pocket. "You guys want anything to drink?" she says.

Ricky looks at me. The jukebox is playing some shit pop country song that I've never heard before. The guy next to me is talking loud to the guy on the other side, practically yelling. I shake my head. Ricky holds up a hand to the bartender. The bartender nods, turns her attention to somebody else. We work our way to the door. It's a relief to get outside. Ricky has his phone out and pressed to his ear. He walks out across the parking lot, loops around, comes back.

"Okay," he's saying. "Thanks anyway." He pockets the phone. "Logan's parents," he says.

"Still nothing?" I say.

"Still nothing," he says.

WE GET back on the road, get on the highway. Ricky calls around and finds a hotel, tells me where to go. I pull up in front, pull up to the curb in front of the big automatic doors, and he gets out.

"So what's the plan?" I say.

Ricky is leaning in, collecting his bag. "I'll call you in the morning," he says. "Right now that's all I've got. That's all the plan I can come up with right now."

"Fine," I say. "I'll talk to you in the morning, then."

"Talk in the morning," he says.

Then he closes the door and he turns and he wheels the bag inside. I watch him go, sit there after he's gone. I have this feeling, I'm not sure how to describe it. Like I just got back from Mars, or something. Like I just got back from outer space and I need a second to remember how things are here on Earth. Or maybe I'm just stalling. Maybe I'm just avoiding what I have to do next and I'm trying to tell myself that it's about something else. I don't know. I can't just keep sitting here, though. I can't sit here forever and there's no point in me going in to the station. There's only an hour left of the show and there'll be even less left by the time I actually get there and me showing up now will only fuck up Dave's cover story.

So I go home. Bethany is there. She's sitting on the couch, sitting cross-legged with her feet up on the cushion and her back against the armrest, reading. I go and I sit at the other end of the couch and I stare straight ahead at the dark TV, at the empty wall.

"Where were you?" I say. "Where did you go? I was up pretty early and you were already gone."

I look at her. She keeps looking down. She marks her place and she closes the book and she keeps looking down at the cover. The cover shows some kind of tree-woman. The tree-woman's arms reach up and become leafy branches. Her feet root down into the earth. Bethany shrugs.

"One of the women from yesterday sent out an email to everyone on Chi's mailing list," she says. "She wanted to see if we all wanted to get together. People asked to do it early."

I turn back to face the TV. I can see my reflection, but it's strange and distorted and from the angle I'm at I can't see her. I nod. "Ah," I say. "Got it. Okay."

"I was going to text you," she says. "I ended up kind of rushing around. I had to go right to the studio. And, I don't know."

She stops herself. I wait, but she doesn't finish the thought.

"You don't know what?" I say.

"I don't know," she says again. "You seemed pretty annoyed by the whole thing."

I let my head fall back into the cushion and I stare up at the ceiling. I rub my eyes and I pull my hands over my face.

"I'm not annoyed," I say. "There's just all of this other shit. There's all of this shit with work. I'm not annoyed. I'm just tired."

She doesn't say anything for a minute. Then she says, "The police released a statement. They said the same thing you said. That it was just an accident. That the pilot got too low and hit some power lines. He just lost control and crashed. They don't know why."

I nod without lifting my head. "Wow," I say. "Shit. That's crazy."

"It's just so stupid," she says. "It's just like, For what? For what reason did this have to happen?"

It's funny. The whole way back from the hotel I was thinking about how this was going to go, about sitting here and really hashing it out. Now, actually sitting here with her, it's like I can't keep focused. My mind keeps jumping around, keeps jumping off onto other things. While she's telling me about the police statement I'm thinking about Ricky, about Logan, about what I'm going to say to Dave.

I shrug. "These things just happen," I say. "Shitty things happen. They don't need a reason."

"I don't accept that," she says. "I refuse to accept that."

I rub my eyes again. I'm thinking about the equipment in my trunk, about us maybe driving back out to that trailer park, about this whole thing just dragging on and on and on. I roll my head to the side and look at her.

"Okay," I say, "fine. Why don't you tell me, then? You tell me the reason. What's the reason? You tell me why it happened. You tell me the reason things happen the way they happen."

She looks surprised, confused. She starts to say something but then she stops. She shakes her head. "I don't know," she says. "That's not, I mean, that's not what I'm saying." She stops again. She pushes her hands up into her hair, holds them there, holds her hair all bunched up high on her head. Then she lets it go. "What's happening right now?" she says. "What are you doing? Are you mad at me? Is that what's happening? I don't understand what's happening."

"I'm not mad," I say. It comes out loud, though, comes out louder than I meant it to. "I'm not mad, I just don't know what you want me to tell you. What do you want me to tell you? I don't know what you want me to tell you."

She shakes her head again. "Nothing," she says. "I don't want you to tell me anything. I don't want you to say anything."

I let my head roll back. I stare up at the ceiling again. "Great," I say. "I won't say anything, then."

We don't say anything for a while. I sink back into the cushions and close my eyes. It feels good to close my eyes. I feel like I could fall asleep right here, like this. I know I can't let myself, though. I know I can't because the show is going to be over soon, and when it is I really need to call Dave.

"Why are you being like this?" she says, finally. "Can't you just tell me that it's going to be okay, or something? Can't you just pretend?"

I don't open my eyes, don't look at her. I raise my hand and I let it fall. "It's going to be okay," I say. "Okay? How was that? Do you feel better now?"

"No," she says. Her voice is loud, angry. It's a surprise. I look at her. She shakes her head.

"Look," she says, "I don't know what's going on with you, but if talking about Chi makes you so uncomfortable—"

I don't let her finish, though. I laugh. I laugh right in the middle of what she's saying.

"Uncomfortable?" I say. "It doesn't make me uncomfortable. Talking about Chi doesn't make me uncomfortable. Talk about her all you want. Go ahead. I don't care. Talk."

But she's talking, too. She's still talking. She's matching my volume. "Then why are you being like this?" she's saying. "If talking about her doesn't make you uncomfortable then why are we even fighting about it?"

"I don't know," I say. "I didn't start it. It wasn't my idea."

She doesn't say anything back to that. She just looks at me. She's got her mouth set in an angry little line. Like she's holding in all of the things she wants to say, but won't. Then, she gets up. I think she's going to walk out, going to go close herself off in the bedroom again, but she doesn't. She comes around behind the couch and she puts her arms around my neck and with her face down close to mine she says, "You have to talk to me, Dex. Please. I need you to talk to me. Please tell me what's going on with you."

I reach up and I unclasp her hands and I take her arms from around my neck. I sit up and then I stand up and I turn and face her. "I've got to call Dave," I say. "There's some stuff. Some stuff for the show. I didn't get to talk to him about it today."

She doesn't say anything for a minute. She just looks at me. We stand there, looking at each other. Then she nods. She holds up her hands.

"Okay," she says. "You do whatever you need to do. I won't bother you. I'll leave you alone."

And I don't say anything. I don't say a fucking word. I go around and I go into my office and I call Dave. I tell him about Ricky and about running around all day looking for Logan, make up some bullshit story about my phone being dead.

"It's fine," he says, finally. "It was fine. I handled it. It would've been nice to have some warning, but whatever."

"Yeah," I say. "I mean, same here. I wasn't trying to spend the whole day on that shit. That wasn't my vision for how the day was going to go."

"All right," he says, "so what's the plan now?"

"I don't know," I say. "Ricky said he's going to call me in the morning. Beyond that, I'm not sure there is a plan."

"Right," Dave says. "But you're doing the show tomorrow, right?"

"I'm planning on it," I say. "I'm not planning on not doing it."

"Right," Dave says again. "But what I'm saying is, You're going to tell this guy that you need to be back, right? You're going to make it known that the plan needs to include you being back in time to do the show, right?"

"Yes," I say. "Yes, I will make it known."

"Great," Dave says. He doesn't really sound like he thinks it's great, though. He doesn't sound like he thinks it's anything.

"Did Chad notice?" I say.

Dave snorts. "Did he notice?" he says. "Yeah, I think he probably noticed. He was running around, but I think he would have had to be in a fucking coma to not notice that one of his hosts didn't show up."

"Shit," I say.

"Shit is right," Dave says. "Just be there tomorrow."

"I will," I say.

"And find Logan," he says.

"I'm working on it," I say. "What do you want me to say?"

"Nothing," Dave says. "You're working on it."

"Yes," I say, "I'm working on it."

"Great," Dave says again. "I'll see you tomorrow, then."

"Yes," I say, "I'll see you tomorrow."

PART
SIX

I STAY in the office. I only go back out to get some food and to pee, and by then Bethany has gone to bed. Or at least she's gone into the bedroom. Coming out of the bathroom I think maybe I hear something, think maybe I hear her talking on the phone, think maybe I hear the sound of someone's voice coming through a little phone speaker somewhere under the sound of the toilet running and the water draining in the sink, but when I stop and wait and listen I don't hear anything else. The rest of the house is dark, and there's no light coming from under the bedroom door.

I sleep in the recliner again and I wake up early the next morning feeling stiff and shitty and I go online and a couple of my pop culture forum trolls have sent me emails with links to articles and Logan's name is in the headlines of all of them. There's a picture circulating on the tabloid sites and the news aggregators of a man on a gurney being wheeled through a doorway. The angle is bad and there's somebody's arm in the foreground blocking part of the man's face, but even still you can see the inside of the man's right forearm and you can see what looks like Logan's Counter tattoo.

I call Ricky. "Have you seen this?" I say. "Have you seen this thing? Have you seen this picture they're saying is Logan?"

"I was asleep," Ricky says. "I haven't seen anything."

"There's a picture," I say.

"Right," Ricky says. "No, I got that part. Hang on." I hear him moving around, hear him typing, and a minute later he comes back and he says, "Are you seeing anything about where this is? Anything about what hospital?"

I'm clicking around to different sites, scanning articles. "No," I say, "I'm not seeing anything like that." Then I say, "But so what? I mean, it's got to be one of the ones out by where we were yesterday, right?"

I can hear him typing again.

"Who know?" he says. "It could be. Or it could be that he got on a bus and he's in D.C. or Atlantic City or some other random place."

I don't want to hear that. Or maybe it's more like I need to not hear it. "Come on," I say. "Come on, that's not what happened. He didn't get on a bus. He's still here. I know he's still here. He wouldn't leave. Why would he leave? He didn't leave. He's here. I'll bet you a thousand bucks he's still here."

"All right," Ricky says. "All I'm saying is, let's see if we can't get a little more information before we go running around to every hospital in the tri-county area."

"Sure," I say. "Fine. Okay. Sure."

"I'll make some calls," Ricky says. "Let me see what I can find out. I'll call you back. Give me five minutes. Or ten. I'll call you back in ten minutes."

"Great," I say. I'm standing, now, moving out of the office. "That's great," I say. "You make some calls, I'm going to start heading your way. I'll call you when I'm downstairs. You can let me know what you find out then."

I GO down the hall and into the bedroom. I need to change my clothes. I've slept in the same pants two nights in a row. Bethany is still there, still asleep. I try to be quiet, but she wakes up.

"What are you doing?" she says. "Are you going somewhere?"

"It's a work thing," I say. "That thing I was supposed to do with Dave. I've got to go out for a while."

She frowns. "What time is it?" she says.

"It's early," I say. "Go back to sleep."

She sits up, yawns, looks at her phone. Then she looks at me. "What time do you think you're going to be back?" she says.

I'm digging around in my dresser, looking for socks. I shake my head. "I don't know," I say. "I don't really know what this is going to entail. I may have time to come home before the show, but I may not. I don't know. I won't know until I know."

She doesn't say anything for a minute. Then she says, "I need to talk to you, at some point today. I need for us to just make it a priority and set aside some time."

I've found fresh socks, put them on. I'm finished and I'm ready to leave. "Okay," I say. "We need to make it a priority. Okay. Does it absolutely have to happen today? Because I really don't know what my day is going to look like. I'm not really in a position to promise anything. So yes, we can make it a priority, but does it have to be today?"

She's looking at me, watching me. "It would be good to do it today," she says. "It would be better if we did it today."

And it does seem a little weird, maybe, but what the fuck is normal anymore? What the fuck of what she's been asking of me lately has had anything to do with normal? So it doesn't even register. It doesn't make me wonder. It doesn't make me think. My mind is off on other shit. I'm thinking about getting to the hotel, about which hospitals are out by where we were yesterday. I'm thinking about calling Dave and telling him.

"Okay," I say. "Well, like I said, I don't know what to tell you. I literally don't know what this day is going to look like. I can text you when I know something, but that's about all I can promise right now. Okay?"

She doesn't answer me, though. She doesn't give any sort of indication that she heard me. She's not even looking at me anymore. She's looking down, now, looking at the covers at the foot of the bed, looking at nothing.

"Okay?" I say again. "Bethany? Okay?"

She comes back. She looks at me. "Can't you just stay?" she says. "Can't this thing wait? Can't you just stay and talk to me?"

I shake my head. "I have to be there," I say. "I have to go."

"Five minutes," she says. "Just stay five minutes and talk to me. They can wait five minutes."

I've already moved into the doorway, though. I'm already moving out into the hall. "I can't," I say, "I'll call you later. I'll text you when I know something." And then I go all the way out. I go down the front hallway and I put on my shoes and my coat and I leave. I get in my car and I drive to the hotel and I call Ricky from the lobby and I sit there drinking coffee from the breakfast buffet until he comes down.

"How'd you sleep?" I say.

"Like shit," he says. "Let's go."

We go out to the car.

"I was right," I say. "My girlfriend is super pissed at me. She really didn't want me to come this morning. She wanted me stay so we can talk about our relationship."

Honest to God, I have no idea why I say this.

Ricky frowns. "So?" he says. "Why didn't you stay, then?"

And I don't really know what I was expecting him to say, but it wasn't that. "I don't know," I say. "Because I need to find Logan. Because I thought you needed my help finding Logan. I thought we were doing the thing. I mean, do you not want my help?"

We're standing at the car, now, talking over the roof. Ricky shrugs and looks off across the parking lot.

"I mean, yeah," he says. "Sure, yeah."

I lean on the roof, hold up a hand. "Wait," I say, "what are you saying right now? I didn't stay and talk to her because I thought we were doing this. Are you saying that I shouldn't have done that? What are you saying?"

Ricky turns back, tries the door handle, looks at me. "I'm not saying anything," he says. "I'm saying relationships are hard. Sometimes you've got to make sacrifices."

I shake my head. "No," I say, "that's not what you're saying. It doesn't feel like that's what you're saying. It feels like you're saying something else."

He doesn't say anything back to that. He looks down, looks at the hotel, looks off across the parking lot. Then he looks back at me. "All right," he says. "You want to know what I'm saying? I'm saying that if I were in your shoes, and I'd just spent the last twenty-four or forty-eight or however many hours trying to track down a bingeing addict, in the hope that when I find this bingeing addict he's going to be in any sort of condition to do an interview with me, I think I might take a second and step back and really think about my expectations and my priorities. I might really take a second and stop and think about where I'm putting my energy. I might think about where my energy and my attention and my focus are going to do the most good." He's been leaning on the roof but now he pushes himself back. He raises his hands. "That's all," he says. "That's all I'm saying. You do with it what you want. You take it or leave it. Listen or not."

The thing is, though, I barely hear him. I barely hear what he says. After the first part I can barely hear anything over the noise inside my head, over the rushing hissing sound in my ears.

"So you're telling me I shouldn't bother," I say. "You're telling me that I'm kidding myself if I think this interview is going to happen. You're saying that even if we find him it isn't going to happen. Is that what you're saying?"

Ricky sets his hands back on the roof, the fingers spread. "What I'm saying," he says, "is that if that is Logan in that picture, and he is in the hospital because of something he got into with whatever the fuck he got from our friend Josh, then just from a purely practical standpoint I might be concerned about his ability to give any sort of worthwhile interview, let alone his willingness or desire to do so at any point in the immediate future." He leans back, pulls his hands off the roof, lets them drop and hang by his sides. He shrugs. "Come on," he says. "I'm not telling you anything you don't know already, right? All of this has occurred to you, hasn't it?"

And what am I supposed to say to that? Just what the fuck am I supposed to say to that?

"Yeah," I say. "No, of course. I mean, of course I've thought about it. I've thought about that. Absolutely. I totally thought of that."

For a second it seems like he's going to say something else, but then he doesn't. We just stand there for a minute, looking at each other over the roof of the car. Then he turns and he looks off across the parking lot again and he shrugs. He looks back at me.

"All right, then," he says. "So let's go."

WE GET in, get on the road. Ricky tells me where to go. He's got a lead. A friend at dispatch in L.A. called someone at dispatch somewhere else who called someone at dispatch in Cleveland. The hospital he sends us to is even farther east than Yammer's place, even farther out than where Yammer's sister works. It takes a long time to get there, and when we finally pull in there isn't much going on.

"Are you sure this is the right place?" I say. I point at the empty stretch of curb along the front of the building and I say, "Shouldn't there be news vans and stuff? Shouldn't there be reporters and cameramen and people around, if he's really here?"

Ricky leans and looks up at the building. "I don't know," he says. He sits back and shrugs. "I guess we'll find out."

WE GO inside, in past the cop working security and over to the reception desk. Ricky does the talking, but the woman won't give us any information. She says it's against hospital policy for her to discuss matters regarding any patient with anyone outside that patient's immediate family.

"Can you just tell us whether he's here or not?" I say. "You don't have to let us see him, we just need to know whether or not he's here. We've been looking for him for two days."

The woman levels her look at me. "It's against hospital policy," she says, "to discuss matters regarding any patient with anyone outside that patient's immediate family."

"Thanks," Ricky says. "We'll get out of your hair."

WE GO back out, back past the cop. We stop just outside and we stand there on the sidewalk and I say, "Well, shit. What are we supposed to do now?"

Ricky has his sunglasses off and he's rubbing his eyes, mashing the palm heels into the sockets. "All right," he says, "just give me a second. Just hang on."

I step off the sidewalk and out into the parking lot and I turn and look up at the building. It's like a joke. It's just floor after floor of identical little squares, identical little windows.

"Fuck," I say. "We're never going to find him. Look at this place. He could be anywhere. And we don't even know that he's here. He's probably not. They probably transferred him someplace better as soon as he came in. He's probably in some private room in the main campus downtown, or something."

I'm kind of rambling. Ricky stops rubbing his eyes and holds up his hands.

"All right," he says. "Just cool it, would you? Don't freak out. There's more than one way into this place. We just need to find someone else to talk to."

WE GO around and along the side of the building. Down by the far end a man and a woman wearing coats over their scrubs are smoking by a side door. Ricky waves as we walk up. He points at the cigarette the man is holding and he says, "Any chance you've got another one of those?"

The man looks from Ricky to me and then back to Ricky. He goes into his pocket and he brings out the pack and he flips back the lid. Ricky takes one.

"Thanks," Ricky says. "Shit, I haven't smoked in probably ten years. There are times when you just need a cigarette though, am I right?"

The man holds out a lighter. Ricky leans into the flame. He blows a long thin plume of smoke and grins.

"Goddamn," he says. "Nothing like it, am I right? Sometimes you just need a cigarette."

The woman laughs.

Ricky laughs, too. "What?" he says. "Am I doing it wrong? I'm a little out of practice."

The woman shakes her head. "It's not that," she says.

Ricky shrugs, "Okay," he says, "what, then?"

The woman narrows her eyes at him, waves her cigarette back at the building. "What are you here for?" she says.

Ricky pulls on the cigarette, blows smoke at the sky, watches it go. Then he drops his gaze and looks at her. "It's my old man," he says. "He's not doing too good. The doctors aren't sure what more they can do for him."

He sells it pretty well, but the woman just laughs again. Ricky shrugs.

"All right," he says. "How about my cousin, then? My sister's cousin? My cousin's wife? My neighbors's sister's kid?"

The woman is nodding. She turns to the man. "See?" she says. "What did I tell you? Didn't I tell you? That's what I thought." She turns back to Ricky. "Two hundred," she says. "Each. Two hundred each."

Ricky frowns. He looks at me, looks back at them, shakes his head like he doesn't understand. "Two hundred," he says. "Two hundred for what?"

The man speaks up. "You're reporters," he says. "Right? You're here because of that singer?"

Ricky gives them a big guilty grin. He holds up his hands. "Shit," he says. "All right, you got us. Busted."

The woman slaps the man's shoulder. "What did I say?" she says. "I told you. What did I say the second they came around the corner?"

The man nods. "You're right," he says. "When you're right you're right."

Ricky leans against the building. "So he's here, then?" he says. "The singer? He's in there?"

The woman shakes her head. She holds out her hand. "Two hundred," she says. "Two hundred, each."

Ricky makes a big show of considering it. He looks off across the lawn, looks up at the sky. "Look," he says, finally, "you have to understand the situation. I'd be going out of pocket. My editor only wants two hundred words, and I can get two hundred out of what I've got now. I can get two hundred out of what's online and the fact that I'm standing here with you and you're basically telling me he's inside. I need more if I'm going to sell him something. If I can sell him something more then maybe it's worth it. If I can't do that then it's all on me, you understand? It's money out of my pocket." He makes a show of considering it some more. He looks at me, shakes his head. He turns back to the woman, nods at the building. "Who else has been up there?" he says. "How many other reporters?"

The woman shakes her head. "None," she says. "None that I know of. You're the first, as far as I know. And I've been here all morning."

Ricky nods. Then he shrugs. "Still," he says. "Like I said, that's a lot of money for something I don't really need."

Nobody says anything for a minute, and then the man says, "Okay, so what do you need?"

Ricky shrugs again. "I don't know," he says. "I mean, for that kind of money we'd want real serious face time with him." He turns to me and laughs. "Shit," he says, "for that kind of money we'd want to have breakfast with the guy."

They don't laugh. They look at each other. Then the woman nods. She turns back to Ricky.

"Sure," she says. "Sure, we can do that."

The man backs her up. "We can get you up to his room," he says. "We can do that for sure."

It's what he asked for, but Ricky lets them wait for an answer. He draws on the cigarette, breathes smoke, stares off across the lawn. The man watches him. The woman holds up her hands.

"Fine," she says. "You don't want the deal? It's no skin off my back." She drops her cigarette, toes the butt into the little concrete pad. "Somebody else will come along," she says. "You're not the only ones who can figure out where to look. There'll be somebody else along any minute now, and they'll be more than happy to take the deal." She takes her ID badge out of her pocket and she swipes it in the lock. The indicator light flips green. She turns back to Ricky. "I know who took that picture," she says, "and I know what she got paid for it. For what we're offering, two hundred apiece is a good price. Two hundred apiece is generous."

Ricky nods. He takes a last drag on the cigarette and he flicks the butt out onto the lawn and he takes out his wallet. He pulls out a stack of bills and he counts out four hundred in twenties and he holds half in each hand. He says, "I'm making this deal on the condition that you can't offer it to anybody else. I need exclusivity. Otherwise it's not worth it for me."

The woman shrugs. There's a smile pulling at the corners of her mouth. Her eyes are on the money. "Sure," she says. "No problem. Absolutely. Fine by me."

Ricky holds out the money. They pocket it. The automatic lock has already reengaged and the woman swipes her card again and we go inside. We go down the hall to the elevator and we go up a few floors and then we follow them down another hall to a security door. We wait outside while the woman goes in. She comes back maybe thirty seconds later and lets us through. The man stays behind.

"Good luck," he says. Then the door closes. We go after the woman. Up ahead the hall opens into the main area of the ward. The nurses' station forms the inside corner where the hall turns. The rooms are all along the outside wall. We go down and we stop in the bend. The nurses' station is empty but I can hear people off in the rooms, can hear things being wheeled toward us down the hall, around the next bend in the space we can't see. The woman points to one of the doors. "That's it," she says. "Once you're inside, stay inside. Don't go in and out. If somebody comes in, or if somebody calls security, we don't know each other. You figured some way in here on your own."

Ricky nods. "Sure," he says. "That's fine."

The woman looks at us, looks at me, and nods. Then she leaves. She goes back the way we came. We go over to the door. Ricky turns the handle and goes inside. I'm going to go in after him, but then I don't. It's like I can't, somehow. I stand there in the hall and I watch the door swing closed. All of a sudden all I want to do is get as far away from here as I can. All I want is to get back in my car and drive and just keep driving. But then I hear footsteps coming down the hall and it sounds like they're coming toward me, coming up behind me, coming after me, and so I open the door and I go in. As it works out I'm there just in time to see Logan open his eyes and look up at Ricky, there just in time to hear him say, "Motherfucker."

THERE'S A chair at the bedside and Ricky sits down. "It's good to see you, too," he says. "Dex and I have been looking all over for you. You wouldn't believe the time we've had. We've been all over the place haven't we, Dex?"

I take a step closer. "Yeah," I say. "All over the place." I hold up a hand. "Hey, Logan," I say. "How's it going, man? Long time no see."

Logan looks at me. It isn't a look of recognition. It isn't an apology. It isn't anything. He says, "How's it going, Dex?" It isn't really a question, though.

I take another step closer. I say, "We drove all over the place, man. We looked everywhere for you. We went to the fucking Cornwall. Ricky even called your mom."

Then I laugh. Like, Isn't it ridiculous that we called your mom? They don't laugh, though. They don't even respond. Ricky's got Logan's phone out and Logan has closed his eyes again.

I take another half-step forward. "I saw you guys on Letterman a while back," I say. "You guys sounded like shit."

They don't respond to that, either. Ricky has Logan's phone to his ear.

"Yeah," Ricky says. "I'm here with him now. I think that goes without saying." He looks at Logan, looks him over. "I don't think so," he says. "We'll call you in a little while, when he's feeling up to it. Okay? Okay." He hangs up. "Amber says she loves you," he says.

Logan nods without opening his eyes. "She say anything else?" he says.

"We can deal with it when you get home," Ricky says. "For now let's worry about you. How are you feeling? Do you need anything? Is there anything Dex or I can do to make you more comfortable?"

Logan has his hands up to his face, now, the palms covering his eyes. There's a thick IV tube running into the back of his left hand. I didn't notice it before.

"Is there anything you can do," he says. "Is there anything you can do? There's one thing. There's one thing you can do. You can fuck off, Ricky. That's one thing you can do. If it's not too much trouble. If you're looking for things you can do. If you're taking requests."

Ricky is only halfway listening, though. He's making another call. "Yeah," he says. "I'm with him. No, he's still his usual, charming self. I don't know. I haven't looked yet. I don't think so. I don't think it'll be a problem. I don't know. Tonight or tomorrow. I'll look and get back to you." He hangs up and pockets the phone, turns back to Logan. "Everybody sends their best," he says.

Logan nods. "I'm sure they do," he says.

Ricky stands up and leans and gets Logan's chart from the holder at the end. He opens the lid and looks it over. "What have we got?" he says. "New verse, same song?"

Logan has dropped his hands, but his eyes are closed again. He shakes his head without opening them. "Hilarious," he says. "I get it. Because I'm a singer, right?"

Ricky flips the lid closed, puts the chart back, sits back down. "I told you before," he says. "I'm not the enemy. I'm not the bad guy, here."

Logan is still shaking his head, rolling it back and forth on the pillow. "No," he says, "I know. You're the good guy, I'm the bad guy, and Amber is the damsel in distress." Then he stops shaking his head. He opens his eyes and he looks at me. "Hey, Dex?" he says. "I'm actually pretty uncomfortable? Do you think you could track down a nurse or somebody and see if you can get me like a morphine drip or something?"

I don't know what to say. I look at Ricky and Ricky shakes his head. I look back at Logan. "No," I say. "I mean, I guess not. Sorry."

Logan nods, waves a hand. It's the hand with the IV tube. The tube snakes back and forth in the folds of the sheet like something alive.

"That's okay," he says. "Don't worry about it. I can get it myself," and then all of a sudden he's reached and he's fished the little call button joystick out of the sheet folds and he's pressing the button. I didn't even notice the joystick laying there and so it takes me a second to even process what's happening, and I guess it's the same for Ricky, because he doesn't make any move until Logan has already pressed the button four or five times. He makes a grab for the joystick but Logan moves it away and so he grabs at the cord and he pulls and the joystick slips out of Logan's hand.

"Goddamnit, Logan," Ricky says. "Really? Do you really have to make everything so fucking difficult? Do you?" Then he stands up. He's had his sunglasses up on his head this whole time but now he takes them off and puts them in his pocket. He combs back his hair with his fingers and he straightens his jacket collar and he coughs and he clears his throat.

I'm watching him do all of this. "Wait," I say, "what's happening? What are we doing?"

Ricky's facing the door. He waves a hand back at me. "Just take it easy," he says. "I'll handle it."

We wait. We wait for long enough that it almost seems like maybe nobody is coming, but then the door opens and a nurse comes in. She stops when she sees us.

"You two aren't supposed to be in here," she says. "How did you get in here?"

Ricky looks at me, frowns, shakes his head, keeps shaking his head as he looks back at the nurse. "We're not?" he says. "I'm sorry. Nobody told us. We just came in. We didn't mean to do anything wrong. We certainly didn't mean to cause you any trouble."

The nurse isn't having it, though. "This is a secure wing," she says. "You couldn't have just come in, somebody had to let you in. I need you to tell me who let you in."

Ricky shrugs. "I'm sorry," he says. "I really don't know what to tell you. Nobody let us in. We just walked in. I swear. I swear on my mother."

The nurse gives him a look, but she doesn't say anything back to that. She turns to Logan. "Do you know these men?" she says.

Logan shakes his head. "I've never seen them before," he says. "I'm really glad you're here, though. I'm in kind of a lot of pain? Could you maybe get me some Dilaudid, or something?"

Ricky laughs. "See?" he says. "He's kidding. He's a big kidder."

The nurse turns back to Ricky. She points at him and she points at me and she says, "You two really can't be in here. This whole ward is immediate family only. Unless you can show me that you're Mr. Hazelette's immediate family, I need you to leave now."

Ricky nods, holds up his hands in surrender. "All right," he says, "all right. But just hang on a second. We're all on the same side, here. We all want what's best for Logan." He takes a step toward her, extends a hand. "Let's go out in the hall," he says. "Let's go out and talk about this for one minute. Just one minute, I promise. Then, if you still want us to go, we'll go. Okay? Sixty seconds. You have my word."

He's moving toward her like he expects her to back up, expects her to move with him, but she doesn't. She stays put. She shakes her head. "I'm sorry," she says. "The policy is the policy."

Ricky is basically right up to her, now. He's still nodding, still holding out his hand. "That's fine," he says. "I understand complete- ly. And in ninety-nine point nine percent of cases I would comply fully. I have nothing but respect for the work you do. But this is that one special case where we have to bend the rules a little bit. And I can tell you why, but you've got to give me one minute to explain."

For another second it really seems like it's not going to happen, but then the nurse folds. She shifts her weight, takes a step back. She holds up one finger.

"Fine," she says. "You can say whatever you want for one minute, but then you both have to go."

Ricky is following her out into the hall. "Sure," I hear him say. "Of course. Absolutely. That's fine." And then the door swings closed, and I can't hear him anymore.

AFTER THEY'RE gone I just sort of stand there. I don't know what else to do. I don't feel like it really matters what I do. I feel like any second now she's going to come back in and tell me that it's time for me to go. I feel like any second now she's going to come back in and tell me that hospital security is on their way.

It keeps not happening, though. She keeps not coming in.

I look back at Logan. He's got his eyes closed again. I go over and I stand behind the chair that Ricky was sitting in and I just sort of look at him. He doesn't really look all that great. He's thin and his color isn't good. His skin, the actual skin itself, looks thin. I can see muscle strands or tendons or ligaments or whatever, see nodes of veins or nerves or something along his neck and across his temples and in the hollows under his eyes.

Or maybe it's not that. Maybe that's not what I'm seeing. I don't know what things are. I don't really know.

I say, "I was kidding before, that thing I said about you guys sounding like shit on Letterman. You guys sounded fine. You sounded good."

He doesn't respond to that. He doesn't nod, doesn't shrug. He doesn't open his eyes.

I move around and I sit down in the chair.

"I don't get it," I say. "Why did you even come here? I mean, were you ever actually planning on doing the podcast? Because if you were, then I mean, what the fuck? And how was I even supposed to get in touch with you? And if you weren't, then why come? I just mean, help me out, here. Help me understand. Tell me what's going on. I've been driving around with that guy Ricky for the past day and a half. I think at this point you can at least tell me what this is. I feel like you owe me at least that much. I've got better shit to do, you know. I've got better shit to do than run around looking for you. I've got a life, here. I've got a whole life and I've got plenty of other shit on my plate right now. I don't need to be doing this."

And I don't mean to but I get kind of worked up, saying all of that. I get kind of loud. I have to catch myself, have to shut it down. I take a breath and I hold it for a five-count, blow it out and hold for a five-count, the way they taught us to do in class. And it works. I'm not expecting anything, really, I'm just doing what I know I ought to do, but it really, actually, works. After a few breaths I start to feel better. After a few breaths the whole thing just starts to seem funny to me. It starts to seem too perfect to be anything but funny. I shake my head, hold up my hands.

"You know what?" I say. "Whatever, man. Whatever. It's fine. I'm good. It's fine."

He opens his eyes, then. He opens his eyes and he looks at me. Then he looks up at the ceiling and he shrugs.

"There's just a lot going on in L.A. right now," he says. "A lot of bullshit. It felt like a good time to get out of town. You sent me that email and it seemed like an okay idea. I hadn't seen my folks in a while. It felt like it was probably time to come see them. They're not getting any younger."

I wait for him to say something else, something more, but he doesn't. He just lays there.

"Yeah?" I say. "And? That's it? That's the deal? Just came into town to see the folks?"

He doesn't say anything back to that, though. He doesn't respond at all. He blinks twice, slowly. On the third blink his eyes stay closed.

I laugh again. I lean back in the chair and I stare up at the stupid pinpoint patterns in the stupid panels in the stupid drop ceiling, at the spray of big and little dots in the sea of white squares, and I laugh. It's all just so ridiculous. This whole era of my life. This huge chunk of years, and the huge chunk that came after. And now this. I close my eyes and I press into them with my fingertips, watch the dot spray pattern repeat itself in red-tinged photo-flash negative inside my skull.

"Sure," I say. "Sure, of course. You've got to see the folks. It's always good to see the folks."

WE SIT there some more. Or I sit and Logan lays. The nurse keeps not coming.

I check my phone. There's nothing from anybody. I think about texting Bethany, about taking a picture of Logan and sending it to Dave, but I don't do it. I don't know why I don't, really. It's like everything just feels pointless, now. I put my phone away.

I wonder what Ricky is doing, wonder if he's coming back, wonder what happened to him and if I should go and try to find him.

I look at Logan. He's just laying there. Like he couldn't care less. Like it doesn't really matter to him whether I'm there or not. Like, as far as he's concerned, me being there is pretty much the same thing as nobody being there at all.

I sit up, sit forward. I lean in.

"All right, listen," I say. "I know you don't really give a shit, but just because I'm here, and just so you know, I'm not still mad about Counter. I don't hold it against you, or whatever. I get it. I mean I get it, now. I get that you had to do what was right for you. I get that you had to do what was right for your life." I say, "I mean, I don't think you needed to say all of the shit you said, but I can understand the sentiment. I can understand what went into that decision." I say, "So, I mean, whatever. For whatever that's worth. For whatever that's worth to you."

Honestly, if you asked me now, I'm not even sure I could tell you why I said it. I'm not even sure I could tell you where it came from. I wasn't thinking it before I said it. I wasn't thinking anything close.

He opens his eyes and he looks at me. His look is confused, annoyed. Like he doesn't understand what I'm saying or why I'm saying it. Like he doesn't understand why I'm still here bothering him, doesn't understand why I'm still taking up his time with this shit.

He says, "What?"

I can barely look at him. I shrug. "You know," I say. "I'm just saying. Just so you know."

His face twists into a sneer. It's funny, almost. It's the same face he's making in the main picture in the liner notes for *Past the Point*, the same look I saw him give a thousand times to restaurant managers and club owners and waitresses and cops. It's the same look I saw him do onstage three nights a week for years. He shakes his head.

"Are you fucking kidding me?" he says. "What are you talking about? Is this why you invited me here? Is this what this is?"

"No," I say. "That's what I'm saying. I'm saying this isn't that. I'm saying I'm good. I'm good with what happened. I'm not, like, trying to have some big moment, or whatever. That's what I'm telling you. That's what I'm saying." Then I say, "Hey, look, this wasn't even my idea. This whole thing was my producer's idea. I didn't want to do this in the first place."

I wait for him to say something back to that, but he doesn't. He just lays there, staring up.

I hold up my hands. "You know what?" I say. "Fine. That's fine. You don't want to talk about it. That's fine." I stand up, push the chair back.

"I'm going to check in with Ricky," I say. "I'm going to see what Ricky's doing." I start moving toward the door. "It was really good to see you," I say, over my shoulder. "Good luck with everything. Really. Best wishes." I put my hand on the handle but then I stop and I turn back and I say, "You know what? Fuck that. Fuck that, and fuck you. I take it back. I take back what I said. I still think you're an asshole. You were an asshole then, and you're an asshole now. If anything you're an even bigger asshole now."

He shakes his head, rolling it back and forth on the pillow. He raises a hand, beckons me. "Sure," he says. "Go ahead. Get it out of your system. You've been saving it up. Now here's your big chance."

I'm moving back toward him, now. "Hey, listen," I say. "You don't know me. You don't know what this is. You don't know what I've been doing."

"No, sure," he says. "You're right. This isn't that. This is different. It's that I just don't understand. It's that I haven't seen your side of things."

I'm standing behind the chair, now. I'm leaning on its back. "I'm not talking about my side of things," I say. "I'm talking about what happened. I'm talking about facts. I'm talking about historical events. I'm talking about what you did and what you said when you did it."

"Fine," he says.

"You didn't need to say all of that shit," I say.

"Okay," he says.

"You know what I'm talking about," I say.

"Honestly, I don't," he says, "but either way."

I laugh. I laugh at that. It's just so preposterous. "Are you fucking kidding me?" I say. "You don't remember? All that shit you said about how Danny and Paul and me were all going to end up as a big nothing if we didn't come out to L.A. with you? How we were all going to be nobodies? You really need me to say it? You remember. You know what you said."

He's got his hands up and he's rubbing his eyes. "I don't," he says. "I really don't remember that." Then he drops his hands and he looks at me. "That's what I said?" he says. "That's really what I said?"

And here's the thing. I'm all fired up. I'm ready to keep going, ready to shout it out with him. But he doesn't even say it as a challenge. He says it like he's really asking me, like he really wants to know. Like he's almost worried now that he might have said it, almost worried that he can't remember if he did. And all of a sudden it's like I can't even look at him. I can't meet his look. I look down and I shrug.

"I mean, yeah," I say. "Or, I mean, maybe that's not exactly what you said. Those might not have been your exact words. That might not have been your exact phrasing, or whatever, but that's basically what you said. That's the point you were making."

He doesn't say anything back to that. He doesn't say anything for a while. I look at him. He's not looking at me anymore, though. He's looking at the ceiling again, but it's not like how it was before. It's not like he's checked out. It's like he's thinking. I go around the chair and I sit down. He looks at me.

"What I remember," he says, "is that Danny was done and Paul was right behind him, and neither of us had anything really keeping us in Ohio, and we had a lot of good material that we weren't getting in front of the right people." He says, "What I remember is pretty much taking it for granted that you would want to go. That we were going to go out there together. I remember really not wanting to go out there by myself. I don't think I would have bought the ticket if I thought I was going to have to go out there by myself."

"Okay," I say, "but you didn't go out there by yourself, did you? You went out there with Jade."

He snorts at that. "Jade," he says. "Are you joking, man? Jade bailed within a month. Some other guy in some band looked at her and that was it."

I sit forward, lean my elbows on my knees, hold up my hands. "Okay," I say. "Let me see if I've got this. Let me make sure I'm getting this right. In your recollection of things, you didn't break us up?"

He sneers at that, too. "Broke us up," he says. "What are you talking about? We were already broken up. Paul and Danny were both done. There wasn't a band to break up. That was practically the whole reason I thought it made so much sense for us to go."

I've still got my hands up. I shake my head. "You told us you were leaving at a band meeting," I say. "How would we have had a band meeting if we didn't have a band?"

He gives me a look. "Come on," he says. "We knew that Danny was done. We had already talked about it. The whole conversation at that point was about what we were going to do when Danny finally freaked out or quit or whatever. That's what the meeting was about. It was about where we were and what we were going to do going forward." He frowns, shakes his head again. "The other stuff I don't remember," he says. "I don't remember saying you were going to be nobodies. I don't remember saying you were going to be a big nothing if you stayed." He shrugs. "I mean, I'm not saying I didn't say it," he says. "I don't remember thinking it. I don't remember that being part of my thinking. But I guess I could have. I mean, maybe. Maybe I did. I don't know. "

I sit back. I start to say something and then I stop. I start and I stop again. I really don't know what to say. I feel like there's nothing to say. I laugh. It's just ridiculous, somehow. I stop laughing. I reach up and I rub my temples, rub my eyes, rub the corners of my jaw. I hold out my hands and I let them fall.

"You know what?" I say. "All right. I don't know. You remember what you remember and whatever I remember is, I mean, at this point, what does it matter? I guess it doesn't even really matter. I guess it's not going to change anything. I guess it doesn't really make any difference."

And I really mean it, too. Right then, sitting there with him, it really feels like it doesn't make any difference at all.

He doesn't say anything back to that. He doesn't say anything for maybe half a minute. I feel like maybe I pissed him off, somehow, like maybe me laughing pissed him off and he's not going to say anything else and that he's done, now, but then he shrugs.

"For what it's worth," he says, "I wouldn't say that you missed anything worthwhile."

I laugh again. I think he's kidding. "Oh, no?" I say.

He looks at me, shakes his head. "No," he says. "Trust me. It's not what you think. It's not like what it was when we were playing. It's something else. It's a whole other thing."

I nod. "Sure," I say. "Sure, I can believe that. I can definitely believe that. Getting paid a shitload of money to play Madison Square Garden and the Greek Theater and wherever, that would be different. That would be different from how it was when we were playing."

He doesn't engage with that, though. He's making a point. He shakes his head again. "That's what I'm saying," he says. "We don't play music. We *produce content*. We *design and deliver product*." He waves a hand in the air. "Hey, guys," he says, "write us something with a really aggressive hook. Audiences are really responding to aggressive hooks right now. And make it about having a positive self-image. Having a positive self-image is really big right now. And see if we can't get a lot of bass in there. The guys making this season's car commercials like a lot of bass." He drops the hand, looks at me. "It's a big crock of shit," he says. "It's nothing. It's a big nothing. It's nothing you'd want."

"Yeah, well," I say. "I guess that's easy for you to say."

He's been facing me, laying with his head turned, but now he turns back. He stares up at the ceiling and he doesn't say anything for probably a full minute. Then he clears his throat and he says, "All right, listen. I want to tell you something. Last winter I had this big plan that I was going to go off somewhere and really get my shit together. I was going to get away from everything and everyone I knew and the whole scene in L.A. and all of my bad habits and just meditate and get clean and try to get back in touch with whatever I was before everything got crazy. I knew this guy who had this place he was going to let me use, this little house down along the coast in El Salvador. He had this idea that El Salvador was going to turn around and become the next Costa Rica and then it didn't and the place kind of just sat there. It doesn't really matter. The point is, this house is on this little inlet where water runs in from the ocean and forms a river, and across the river there's this island. And this island is pretty much undeveloped. Like there's no running water, no electricity, no real roads. But all of these people live there in these little tin shacks. And all they do is, every day they go out in these dugout canoes that they make themselves and they fish. And every day I would go out and I would sit on the dock behind this house and I would watch these people go up and down this river, fishing. And I'm all fucked up, sick and throwing up and fucking freezing even though it's a hundred and ten fucking degrees out. And every day they're going up and down and up and down and up and down. And then one day I'm sitting out there and I have this moment of, I don't even know what you'd call it. Not clarity, exactly. But it was like all of a sudden I could see myself seeing. I could see my brain processing what I was seeing. I could see the thoughts I was having and how they were making me see the things I was seeing in the way I was seeing them. I mean, on a level that was different than just normal self-awareness. This was a whole other thing. And what I realized is that I'd been sitting here watching these people for days and days without ever really seeing them. I'd been seeing something that wasn't really what was out there, it was just a projection of my reality and my value system. Like I would look at them and I would have this baseline sense of, 'Oh, shit, look at these poor people. They don't have anything.' As if what these people really wanted was a 6 Series or a house in Malibu. As if what they really wanted was a five-thousand-dollar watch. As if what any of them really wanted out of life is any of the shit that I had. It was like thinking that the birds or the squirrels or the fucking bobcats wanted any of that shit. All of a sudden it all seemed so fucking ridiculous. Me, sitting there thinking that these people were poor because they didn't have oceanfront property in Southern California. As if that wasn't a completely fucking irrelevant concept. As if the concept that you would acquire and possess land and property wasn't totally nonsensical. Do you see what I'm saying?" He turns his head and he looks at me. There are tears in his eyes. He laughs. "And it was like, what are we doing?" he says. "What the fuck are we all doing? All of this made-up shit. All of this propaganda about what we want and who we want to be and what we all want to own. This ideology that we accept and internalize and integrate and that then becomes our reality. It was like I could see it. It was like I could really, finally see just how absurd it all was. How absurd I am." There are tears running over the bridge of his nose, now, running down his cheek and into the pillow. "Do you get what I'm saying?" he says. "L.A. isn't someplace else. Everywhere is just another franchise location. We just pump out the content. We articulate the message. You want to know about playing Letterman? Or Madison Square Garden? The fucking Greek Theatre? It's not sweetness and light, man. It's not the Universe opening itself up to you and holding you close and telling you that you're good and special and loved. It's just another ad, man. It's all just another fucking pitch."

He's been getting louder and louder, building and building, but now he stops. He squeezes his eyes shut, clenches his jaw. Veins stand out across his temples, along his neck, under his eyes. Then he lets it go. His face goes slack. He shakes his head.

"Shit," he says. "Sorry." His voice is different. It's suddenly hoarse, condensed. It's suddenly small in the space. "Sorry," he says again. "I'm sorry if I'm not making any sense. I'm not really thinking very clearly right now. They've got me on these fucking SSRIs, and they make it hard for me to, to, to really say things the way I want to say them."

He opens his eyes and he looks at me. His eyes are red, swollen, tired.

"It's cool," I say. "I mean it's fine. You're fine."

He lets his head roll back and forth on the pillow. He stares up at the ceiling. "Sorry, man," he says again. "Sorry about all of this. Sorry for, you know, whatever. I'm just sorry."

I don't say anything back to that. Neither of us says anything for a while. Then I push back the chair and I stand up.

Standing beside the bed and looking down at him he looks really small, laying there.

"I'm going to let you get some rest," I say.

He looks up at me and nods. "Okay," he says. He waves toward the door. "Talk to Ricky," he says. "Set it up with him. Maybe tomorrow?" He looks around. "Maybe you can just bring your stuff in here," he says. "Just set it up and do it here."

For a second it doesn't even register, what he's talking about.

"Oh," I say. "I mean, are you sure? Are you still okay to do it? I mean, you still want to do it? Do the whole thing?"

He holds up his hands. "I'm here," he says.

"Okay, then," I say. "Great. I'll set it up with Ricky."

"Okay," he says. "And ask him to come in here, for a second. Tell him I need to talk to him."

"Sure," I say. I step over to the door and I turn the handle and I move backwards into the doorway. "Sure," I say again. "No problem. I'll do that. Okay." And then I turn and I go out.

RICKY'S THERE at the nurses' station. He's talking to the nurse who came into Logan's room, the one who told us to leave. They're both laughing.

Ricky waves when he sees me. "Hey, Dex," he says. His tone is easy, casual, inviting. "Everything all right?" he says. "You guys catch up?"

I go over to them. I nod. "He says he wants to talk to you," I say. "He asked me to ask you to come in."

Ricky nods. "Sure," he says. He doesn't make any move toward the room, though. "Let me ask you this," he says. "How does he seem? I mean, how does he seem to you?"

He's looking at me. The nurse is looking at me, too. I shrug.

"I don't know," I say. "I mean, I really couldn't say. I haven't talked to him in a long time. I don't know what normal is for him anymore."

Ricky nods again. "Okay," he says.

"He told me to talk to you about doing the podcast," I say. "He said we could do it tomorrow. He said we could just set everything up in the room, do it here."

"Sure," Ricky says. "That can work." He turns to the nurse. "Lynn will let you in," he says. "Won't you, Lynn?"

Lynn gives him a look. "Don't go speaking for me," she says.

Ricky laughs. "Come on," he says. "Don't you know who this is? This is Dex Foster. You've probably heard him on the radio. Your boyfriend probably listens to his show."

Lynn laughs at that. She looks at me. "You're Dex Foster?" she says.

"Yeah," I say. "I am. I'm Dex Foster. That's me."

She nods. "I've heard your show," she says. She looks back at Ricky. "All right," she says. "Don't tell anyone I told you this, but there's a little buzzer outside the door. You can ring in on that. Just tell whoever's working that you're part of Mr. Hazelette's faith community, and that you're here offering spiritual support. They'll let you in." She points a finger at me. "But I'm serious," she says, "don't tell anybody I told you."

"Sure," I say. "I won't. No problem. Thanks."

She looks down, shuffles some papers on the counter. She waves a hand. "That's okay," she says. "Don't worry about it."

I turn back to Ricky. "You're staying here, right?" I say. "I mean, you don't need a ride?"

Ricky shakes his head. "Right," he says. "No, I'm good. Thanks, though. And thanks for all the help."

"Sure," I say. "Sure. It was nothing."

I GO back out, go back through the security door and down the elevator and out through the side door. I go back around the front of the building and over to my car and I get in and I call Dave. He answers on the first ring.

"Tell me something good," he says.

"I saw Logan," I say. "We found him. I talked to him."

"Holy shit," Dave says. "That's amazing. Fucking fantastic."

"Right," I say. "Fantastic."

"So," he says, "How was it? How did it go?"

"Honestly?" I say. "It was weird. It was very, very weird."

"That's okay," Dave says. "Weird is okay, right? Weird can be good. Weird can be interesting."

"Sure," I say. "I guess weird can be good."

"Okay," he says. "And so how much did you get? Do you think you've got enough?"

"No," I say. "I mean, I didn't get anything. I was only in there for a few minutes. He's in the fucking hospital. It's a whole involved thing. There was this nurse that kept trying to kick us out. And he's all fucked up. He's recovering. We're supposed to get together tomorrow. I'm supposed to come back and do it tomorrow."

"Ah," Dave says. "Got it. Okay." Then he says, "Well, either way, right? The main thing is that you found him."

"Right," I say.

"So you're doing that tomorrow," he says, "and so you'll be in today, right? You're good to do the show today?"

"Yeah," I say, "I'm good. I'm leaving now and I'm going to run home and then I'll be in."

"Great," Dave says. "Fucking great. I'll see you later, then."

"Sure," I say. "I'll see you soon."

I HANG up with him and then I text Bethany that I'm coming home and then I get back on the road. It takes me almost an hour to get back, but it feels like it takes even longer. It feels like it takes forever. Ten minutes into the drive I check my phone and there's nothing from her and five minutes later I check again and there's still nothing, and after that it's every two or three minutes for the whole rest of the way and every two or three minutes for the whole rest of the way there's still nothing.

I tell myself that it doesn't mean anything, that she's probably just in class, but it doesn't really help. My mind is working, now. I'm thinking all kinds of things. I'm thinking about all the fit, sensitive, emotionally-available poser douchebag assholes at the yoga studio who all want to sit with her and drink tea and put a hand on her arm while they listen to her talk about her problems. I think about her ex in Chicago, about how far along in the drive she'd be if she left right after I did. I don't mean to—I don't even want to—but I kind of can't help it. I can't stop. It's like someone in the next room playing the same shitty song over and over again at top volume, and the more I try to just ignore it the more it's there. It's bizarre, almost. It's extreme. But being there with Logan and watching him spin out it was like it hit me all at once. It was like it hit me all at once how it's been with us for the past week, how it's been with us for the past however many weeks. It was like this sort of fog I'd been living and operating inside of had lifted, for a second, and I could finally see just how badly I was fucking up.

I go to the studio, but her car isn't there. I circle the lot twice and I still don't see it, cruise around the block and check the street parking. I check my phone again and there's still nothing. There's still nothing since I checked it two minutes ago. So I go home. I don't know what I'm going to do if her car isn't there, but it is. It's right where it was when I left. I park and I go inside. She's there at the kitchen table, doing something on her computer. She folds the top down when I walk in. I go and I sit down across from her.

"I went by the studio," I say. "I thought you'd be in class." I say it in a rush. I feel out of breath, feel like I ran here from the studio. I feel like I've been running all morning.

She nods. "No," she says, "you're right, I should be. I called off. I called in sick."

"Oh," I say. "Are you sick?"

She doesn't answer me. She looks down, shrugs. "How'd your thing go?" she says.

I can feel my heart beating in my chest, feel the blood pulsing behind my eyes. "My thing," I say. "Fine. My thing went fine." Then I say, "I texted you that I was coming home."

She looks up at me. "Oh?" she says. "I didn't see it. My phone's in the bedroom. Sorry."

I shake my head. "It's fine," I say. "It doesn't matter." Then I say, "Look. Listen. Look. Here's the thing. I've been a dick. I don't know if it matters to you that I realize it, now, but I do. I didn't before. I mean I did but I didn't. But I do, now. I really do. And I'm sorry. I've been fucked up and I'm sorry." I say, "I've had this thing with work, and I didn't really see what it was doing to me. I didn't understand how much it was messing with my head. It was like I was in this mental fog of just stress and weird shitiness. And I couldn't tell how things were anymore." I look at her. "But it's over, now," I say. "Or it's not over, but I get it, now. I can see it, now. I couldn't see it before, and so I couldn't do anything about it. It was like I couldn't get my head above water enough to see what anything was or where I was or what I should be doing. But I do, now. I don't know what it's worth to you, me saying that, but it's the truth."

She doesn't look at me. She's got her hands folded on the table-top and she looks at them while I talk. When I'm finished she nods. She still doesn't say anything, though. We just sit there like that. Then she looks at me and she says, "I want to ask you something. Can I ask you something?"

"Yeah," I say. "Sure. Anything."

She nods. She's got her mouth set now in that way she does when she's upset or nervous, the lips pulled in and pressed together in a thin, indecipherable line. She looks down, nods again, looks up at me. She says, "When I called to tell you about Chi, you said you thought I was calling about something else. What did you think I was calling about?"

I can't look at her. I look down and I shrug. "I don't know," I say.

"Did you think something had happened?" she says. "I mean, to me? To us? Did you think something had happened to us?"

I shrug again. "I don't know," I say. "I mean, yeah. Maybe. I thought, maybe. You sounded really upset. Until you told me what it was I thought that maybe something had happened."

I look at her. She's still looking at me. She nods.

"And how did you feel?" she says.

"How did I feel?" I say. "I don't know. Scared. Shitty. How was I supposed to feel?"

"I mean, were you upset?" she says. "Would you have been upset, if it had been that?"

She's still looking at me. I look back at her. And I could say a lot of things, but I don't. I could but I don't. I shrug.

"Honestly," I say, "I don't know."

She looks down. She nods. Then she sits forward. She says, "Look, I'm glad you're here, because I need to talk to you about something. I've been thinking about it, and I think that maybe now would be a good time for me to go visit Hannah. It might be a good time for me to go and stay with her for a little while."

It takes a second to register, what she's saying. "Hannah," I say. "Hannah. Hannah, who? Wait, what? You mean Hannah your sister?"

She's nodding, now. "Hannah," she says. "Hannah my sister."

"Wait," I say, "you mean in Paris? You mean you're going to go stay with Hannah in Paris?"

"Yes," she says. "I'm going to go stay with Hannah in Paris."

"For how long?" I say. "I mean, what's a little while?"

She shrugs. "I don't know," she says. "My ticket's for ten days, but that's just because we needed a return date for the ticket. Hannah said we can change it. She said we can play it by ear. We're going to play it by ear."

"Okay," I say. "Okay. Right. Okay." I look at her. "Sorry," I say. "It's just. It's just that this isn't what I was expecting. It isn't what I was expecting you to say."

"What were you expecting me to say?" she says.

"Nothing," I say. "I mean, not nothing. But not that. Not Hannah. Not Paris."

She looks down, looks at her hands stacked together on the tabletop. She shrugs. "We've been talking about me coming to visit for a long time," she says, "and I haven't done it, and I just figured that pretty soon it's going to be harder to get over there, and it seems like you're so busy right now anyway, and I just realized that if I was going to do it then I needed to stop putting it off and just make it happen. And when I told her about everything that was going on with us and with Chi and everything she said she'd split the ticket with me." She shrugs again, looks at me. "So I'm going," she says.

"You told her what was going on with us?" I say.

She shrugs again, nods. "She's my sister," she says. "I tell her a lot of things."

I don't know what to say to that. I lean back, let my head tip back, stare up at the ceiling. I pull my hands over my face and I let them drop into my lap. I sit forward and I look at her. "Look," I say, "it's just a stupid fight. We just had a stupid fight. You don't have to leave the country because we had a stupid fight."

She shakes her head. "It's not like that," she says. "It's really not. It's all, I mean, it's all just been a lot, lately. I know it's been a lot. And it's like, here you were. You had your whole life. You had your own space and your whole routine and everything, and then I came in and I started telling you what to do and how to be and what to eat and what things were going to be like, and everything." She shakes her head again. "It's like, Oh look," she says. "Here's Baby Bethany, bossing everyone around. Telling dad he's Captain Hook and telling mom she's Tinker Bell and making all the dinner guests be Lost Boys. Isn't she funny. Isn't she cute."

"I was a mess, though," I say. "I was a train wreck before you moved in here. I was a complete disaster."

"That's not the point," she says. "The point is that you were you, and it wasn't my place to come in and try to change that."

"That's not," I say. "That's not what this was. And anyway, I mean, it's not like that's a bad thing. What you're talking about isn't a bad thing. I'm so much better, now. My life was shit before. My life is so much better because of you."

I mean it, too. I've never said it before, never even thought it. As soon as it's out of my mouth, though, I know. As soon as it's out of my mouth I know that it's absolutely, irrefutably true.

"Look," I say, "don't go. Don't go stay with Hannah. Don't do it."

She doesn't say anything back to that, though. She looks down at her hands.

I laugh, then. I don't know why. I don't think anything is funny. It's like I don't know what else to do.

"I don't understand," I say. "I mean, what? All of this is because of Chi? Because I didn't go to our first appointment with Chi?"

She looks up at me, then. She frowns and shakes her head. "It isn't that," she says. "It's the whole thing. It's the whole dance we're doing. The dance we're both doing."

"But it doesn't feel like that," I say. "It feels like this is about me and something I did. Something I did or didn't do or did wrong. It feels like this is you punishing me for my bad behavior."

She shakes her head again. "It's not," she says. "It's really not. We both did this. I did this as much as you did. Where we are right now is something we both did. And this is me taking responsibility for my part in that. This is me acknowledging the fact that I'm not blameless, here. And if I'm going to do something about it then I really feel like I need to get some distance and sort of take stock of myself and my behavior and see what I can do differently going forward to make this actually work. Because it doesn't, right now. It just doesn't. And it needs to." She's been sitting forward, leaning on the table, but now she sits back. "This will be good," she says. "I really think this will be a good thing. I really do."

It's not an argument. She's not making a point. It's already done. She's just summing up.

I close my eyes, pull my hands over my face and let them fall.

"Well, shit," I say. "When's your flight?"

"Eleven," she says. "Heidi is giving me a ride."

I laugh. I'm just surprised. "What," I say, "you mean tonight? You mean eleven o'clock tonight? Jesus Christ, Bethany."

"Eleven tonight," she says. "Hannah worked it out. Her company has some special account with one of the airlines."

"Jesus Christ," I say again. I don't know what else to say. Then I say, "Look, don't go with Heidi. I'll drive you. At least let me drive you to the airport. At least let me do that. Don't just leave. Let me drive you. Don't have Heidi drive you. I'll drive you."

She thinks about it. She nods. "Okay," she says. "Sure. Okay."

"Great," I say. "Thank you. Jesus Christ. Thank you."

SHE GOES into the other room to call Heidi and I sit there at the table. I don't know what to do. I don't know what to feel, even. I'm almost too surprised to be upset, too surprised to be anything. It doesn't even seem real, somehow. It feels like she's going to walk back in and ask what I want to do for dinner, ask me when I'm going to finish packing up my office. But then she comes back in and she says, "We should probably leave by eight-thirty. Eight forty-five at the latest."

I have this sense that if I can just figure out the right thing to say, and if I can make it come out the way I want it to come out, and if I can have her hear it the way I want her to hear it, then I can fix this. I can make her change her mind and stay. It feels close, like it's right there on the tip of my tongue. It feels like, if I can just get started, I'll find my way there.

But I don't. I open my mouth and all that comes out is, "Eight-thirty. Okay. Sure. Eight-thirty. Got it."

AND THAT'S it. That's all there is to it, because after that I have to leave. I have to go to work. I go in to the station and I run into Chad in the hallway and he asks me if I'm recovered, asks me if I'm feeling better, and it takes me a second to remember what the fuck he's even talking about.

"Oh," I say. "Yeah, right. Totally. Much better, thanks."

Chad puts a hand on my shoulder, squeezes. "That's great," he says. "I'm glad to hear it." Then his expression changes. He looks concerned. "Listen," he says, "I need to talk to you guys at some point in the next couple of days, okay? When you're back to feeling one hundred percent?"

"Okay," I say. "Sure. No problem."

Chad nods. "Great," he says. "Just drop by the common room at some point in the next day or two."

"Sure," I say again. "I'll let Dave know."

He gives my shoulder another squeeze, lets go, hurries off. I go find Dave and I tell him.

"Fuck," Dave says.

"Yeah," I say. I almost don't care, though. It's like I can't, somehow. It's like I've reached my daily limit.

Dave is rubbing his forehead. "So what do we think?" he says. "Do we think this means what I think it means?"

I shrug. "I really don't know," I say. "I guess we're going to find out."

WE DO the show. We take some calls and we play some music and we do our little schtick. It's nothing special. It's nothing memorable. It's just another show. Then it's over and I go home. Bethany's there in the bedroom, packing. I go and I sit in my office. I have this vague notion that I'm going to really start organizing, that I'm going to have something to show her when she comes to get me, that when she sees how much I've done she'll think twice about leaving, but in the end I don't get anywhere. I sit there looking through old fliers and polaroids and whatever else is on the desk, shuffling it all around from one pile to another, until it's time.

I carry her bags out to the car. I let her get settled before I put it in gear. I pull out and I merge into traffic.

I have that same sense that there's some perfect thing to say, some perfect thing that will make her change her mind, make her cancel her ticket, but then we're to the airport already and I still haven't figured out what it is.

We get her stuff out of the back and we pile it on the sidewalk and then we stand there in the loading zone, her with her bags and me with my hands in my pockets.

"I'll call you when I get there," she says.

I look at the bags, at the sidewalk, at the car, at the wall of glass running along the front of the building. I look everywhere but at her.

"Great," I say. "Okay. Sure."

"I'll miss you," she says.

I look at her, then. "You don't have to miss me," I say. "Don't go. You won't miss me if you don't go."

She shakes her head. "This'll be good," she says. "You'll see. It's good to get some space once in a while. We probably haven't done it enough."

There's nothing else. She steps forward and she kisses me and then she hugs me for a long time. Later on I'll tell myself that I remember how it was—how her cheek felt against mine, how her hair smelled, all of those things—but the reality is that I don't. The reality is that that memory is something I cobbled together later, something I postulated about, something I made up when I wanted to remember and I couldn't. When I thought back and all I could remember was feeling shitty and stupid and pissed. When all I could remember was barely hugging her back.

I remember letting her go, though. I remember that just fine.

She gathers up her stuff, puts on her backpack, goes inside. I watch her through the glass, but I can't for very long. Once she starts toward the ticket counter she goes behind a column and then behind a section of opaqued glass, and I can't see her anymore. I'm going to move, going to walk down along until I see her again, but the cop is already blowing his whistle at me. So I get back in the car and I leave.

I DRIVE home and I drink four beers in front of the TV and I fall asleep watching bullshit, and in the morning I drive back to the hospital. I still have everything in the car, all of the equipment that Dave and I bought, the microphones and the headphones and the board it all plugs into. I have pictures, too, pictures of us playing gigs and hanging out. I have it all together in the black duffel bag in my trunk.

Nobody hassles me. I act like I know exactly where I'm going and nobody questions it. I go in past reception and I ride the elevator up to Logan's floor and I press the button to be let onto the ward and somebody buzzes me in. I nod to the nurse at the nurses' station and he nods back and then he goes back to what he was doing. I go down the hall and I open the door and I go into Logan's room and Logan isn't there.

I call his phone. It goes straight to voicemail. I call it three more times and it's the same thing. On the fourth try Ricky answers.

"Hey," I say. I practically yell it. "I'm here at the hospital," I say. "Logan's not here. He's gone. He's not in his room. He's missing again."

"Calm down," Ricky says. "He's not missing. I've got him. He's right here."

I sit down on the bed. I kind of collapse onto it.

"Oh thank Christ," I say. "I was freaking out. I seriously don't think I have it in me to run around looking for him again." I laugh. I'm just so relieved. "Okay," I say, "so where are you? Are you at the hotel? I've got all my stuff. I'm ready to go. Tell me where you are and I'll come to you."

Ricky doesn't say anything for a minute. Then he says, "I don't think it's going to work this time, Dex."

I know what he's saying. I think on some level I knew the second I walked into the room. Some part of my brain is just refusing to see it, though. Some part of my brain, the part doing the walking and the talking, the part making the phone calls, isn't listening to the part that knows.

"You don't think it's going to work this time," I say. "You don't think it's going to work. What does that mean, Ricky? What does that mean, you don't think it's going to work? It's all set up. I've got everything here with me. I've got all of the equipment here with me. I spent the last two days helping you find him, Ricky. What do you mean you don't think it's going to work?"

Ricky doesn't say anything back to that, though. I can hear noises in the background, people talking and things beeping and a message going on a public address system.

"Ricky?" I say. "Where are you right now? Are you at the fucking airport, Ricky? Did you take Logan to the fucking airport?"

He doesn't say anything back to that, either.

"Okay," I say. "That's fine. I can come there. I'll come there and we can do the interview there. We can do it in one of those lounges, or something. Logan can get us into one of those lounges, right? He's got some special V.I.P. status, right?"

"It's Dex," I hear him say. "I know. I know that. I'm telling him."

"Is that Logan?" I say. "Is Logan right there with you? Let me talk to him. Put him on the phone. Put Logan on the phone, Ricky. Put him on the fucking phone. Goddamnit, Ricky, put Logan on the fucking phone."

He won't do it, though. "Logan can't talk right now," he says. "He appreciates your concern, but this isn't a good time. If you're ever out in L.A. and you want to set something up, feel free to reach out then."

I'm up off the bed, now, up and pacing around the room.

"Feel free to reach out?" I yell into the phone. "Feel free to reach out? If I'm ever out in L.A., you fucking asshole? If I'm ever out in L.A.? Fuck you, Ricky. Fuck both of you."

A nurse comes in, then. It isn't the nurse I saw on the way in and it isn't anyone I recognize from yesterday. She stops in the doorway and she says, "What are you doing in here?"

I hold up a hand. "Just hang on for one second," I tell her. Then, to Ricky, I say, "Put Logan on the phone, Ricky. I'm fucking serious. Put him on the phone. Put that asshole on the phone. I swear to God, Ricky. You fucking owe me. Logan owes me." I'm yelling as loud as I can, now. "Put him on the phone," I yell. "Put him on the fucking phone."

He doesn't, though. He hangs up on me. I'm not sure exactly when. I only notice it after I stop yelling, and by then I have other things to worry about.

The policemen who come and stand in the doorway tell me to lay down on the floor, to put my hands on my head. They have their hands on their guns. They cuff me and they take me down to the cinderblock office they have in the basement and they make me explain what I'm doing there.

"I'm here to interview a patient,"I tell them, over and over again. "Go look in the bag. Look in the bag, and you'll see."

They won't look in the bag, though. Or at least not right away. The bag is part of the reason the nurse called them, apparently. The bag made them all think that maybe this was something else. They tell me later that they actually called in the local bomb tech to evaluate the situation. They tell me this as part of the list of reasons they would be justified in filing charges against me.

"Disturbing the peace," they say. "Inciting a panic."

They're trying to intimidate me, but it doesn't really work. At this point I almost don't care what happens. The only thing waiting for me when I get out of here is the phone call I have to make to Dave.

"I didn't disturb the peace," I tell them. "I was on the phone by myself in a closed room. You all are the ones who freaked out. I told you exactly what was in that bag. I've been telling you this whole time. It's not my fault that you don't fucking listen."

EVENTUALLY THEY let me go. They have to. Apart from me being in an area of the hospital I'm not technically supposed to be in they don't really have anything on me. They emptied my pockets, took my wallet and my keys and my phone, and by the time they give it all back I have a voicemail from Bethany telling me that she's landed and she's with Hannah and they're heading back to Hannah's apartment and she'll try me again later. I call her back but she doesn't answer and I don't leave a message. I don't really know what to say and besides that, I'm still right in the middle of everything here. I'm on my way back upstairs to collect my stuff. The policeman who's escorting me scans us through the security door and he walks me down to the room and he follows me inside. The bag is where I left it but it's open, now, and everything has been taken out and spread across the floor. It's a mess. I pack it all up, pack up the microphones and the board and the cables and the pictures. Then the policeman escorts me back downstairs. He follows me across the lobby and he stands outside the entrance and he watches to make sure as I go out and I get in my car and I leave.

It takes hours. Not the packing up, but everything. The drive out and the detention and the interrogation and the drive back. By the time it's all finished the whole morning and part of the afternoon is gone. By the time it's all finished I have to go straight to work. I drive down to the station and I go inside and Dave is there, waiting for me in the downstairs lobby.

"So?" he says. "How'd it go?"

I can't even look at him. I shake my head. "It didn't go," I say. "I showed up and there was nobody there. That asshole Ricky spirited him away. They were already at the airport by the time I called. They're on a plane back to California by now. I had all the recording shit with me in a duffel bag. The nursing staff thought I was a fucking terrorist, or something. They thought I was there to shoot the place up. They called security on me. They took me down to this little bullshit holding cell office thing they have in the basement and they held me there for like three fucking hours."

Dave is frowning, shaking his head. "Wait," he says, "what? Are you kidding? You're kidding. Tell me you're kidding."

"I'm not kidding," I say. "Trust me, I wish I was kidding."

Dave pulls a hand over his face. "Fuck," he says. "What the fuck?" He looks at me. "After all of this shit," he says. "After everything. After everything you did."

He's pretty worked up, but I can't match him. I'm not there any-more. I was a few hours ago, but I'm not now. Now I just feel ex-hausted. I feel like I could lean against the lobby wall and close my eyes and just fall asleep right there. I feel like I could fall asleep against the wall and stay there for a month. The custodians could just come and sweep around my feet.

"There's something else," I say. "Bethany's gone. She left. She went to stay with her sister. She says she thinks we need to spend some time apart."

Dave's whole demeanor changes. "Oh shit," he says. "Shit, man, I'm sorry. I didn't know it was like that. I mean, I didn't know you had all that going on. You should have told me. I mean you could have told me. You didn't need to do all of this bullshit with Logan. I could have driven that guy around. You should have told me."

I shake my head, shrug. "Honestly," I say, "I don't know that it would have made any difference. Things have been kind of fucked up with us for a while."

"Still," Dave says, "I'm sorry." Then he says, "Look, why don't you go home? I can cover for you."

Maybe he's just offering to be nice, but right now I kind of don't care. Right now all I want is to go home and put on a movie and lay on the couch and check out. Right now I can't even imagine making it through a whole show.

"Seriously?" I say. "Are you sure?"

He shrugs. "Yeah," he says. "Sure. I'll tell everybody your flu came back. I'll tell them you came back to work too soon. That you weren't really better yesterday."

"What about Chad?" I say.

He pulls a face. "Fuck Chad," he says. "That guy's going to do whatever he's going to do. He knows what we are, or he can sure as shit find out. I don't see how what we do or don't do today is going to make any difference."

I'm going to say something back to that—I'm not sure what, but something—but then I don't. Dave puts a hand on my shoulder and he starts leading me to the door, and I let him.

"Look, don't worry," he says. "We'll figure something out. I'll call you tomorrow. We'll talk tomorrow and we'll figure something out. It'll all work out. You'll see. With this and with Bethany. Trust me. One day we're going to look back on this and it's going to seem like nothing. We're going to wonder why we were so worried."

We're through the door, now. Or at least I am. Dave's stopped in the doorway. I turn to face him. I'm going to say something—something about how I'm sure he's right, maybe, or something about I don't even know what—but then he steps back and the door closes between us and I still haven't said it. I stand there and I watch through the glass as he crosses the lobby to the elevators and then I turn and I walk back to my car and I drive home.

I put on a movie and I lay on the couch and I sort of drift in and out. I put on another movie when that one ends and I drift some more. By the time that one ends it's dark out. I think about getting up and eating something, about making dinner or ordering in or going out, but in the end I don't do it. I haven't eaten all day, but somehow I'm not really hungry. I put on another movie and somewhere in the middle of that one I fall all the way asleep. I sleep like I never sleep anymore, sleep like I haven't slept in months, sleep like disappearing, like dissolving into nothing. I wake up with the DVD menu screen showing again, with the little snippet of theme song playing over and over, and my phone buzzing in my pocket. I figure it's Bethany, calling me back. I don't even look at the screen before I answer.

PART
SEVEN

FULL AND honest, yes? Full and honest. Okay. Okay okay okay.

I PIECE it together, later. Later I piece together some semblance of a timeline. I piece together a version of events. I have her itinerary, have the news reports. I have the message she left me. There are things I learn and things people tell me and other things I assume. There are things I just imagine. For some things, there's nothing else I can do.

Bethany has a layover in New York, and another one in London. She gets into Paris late Friday afternoon. Hannah picks her up and they go back to Hannah's apartment on the rue de Charonne. I don't know for sure how long they're there but probably it isn't very long. Probably it's just long enough for Bethany to drop her bags. After sitting on planes and in airports for so long I'm sure she wants to be out and moving, walking around. After talking about it with Hannah for so long I'm sure she's ready to be out in that city.

I'm sure she's hungry, too. I don't know what she would have found to eat at any of the airports and I can't imagine that she would have touched anything they offered her on the plane. La Belle Équipe is right around the corner. They walk over and get a table, get one of the tables you want, one of the ones set out on the sidewalk out in front. One of the ones that's like something out of what you picture when you imagine a charming Paris bistro.

They sit and they talk. I imagine them talking, imagine whole conversations. I imagine Hannah's questions and concerns, her excitement. I imagine the plans they make for the trip and after, imagine everything down to what food they order and what the waiter looks like. I can't help it. There are so many blank spaces in what I know, in what I can ever know.

Or maybe it's not that. Maybe that's not what it is. Maybe I imagine the things that I hope are true. In my imagination they're so wrapped up in their conversation, in their happiness at being together, that they don't even notice the black sedan circling the block. They don't even notice it when the sedan stops, when the two men with Kalashnikov rifles get out. In my imagination they don't even have time to turn, don't have time to be scared, don't have a chance to feel anything but that happiness, before the two men open fire.

YOU KNOW the rest. Or you can look it up. You can read the reports. How that attack was just one in a coordinated series. How diners were similarly gunned down at other cafés, at Le Carillon and Le Petit Cambodge and Café Bonne Bière and La Casa Nostra. How, at Le Comptoir Voltaire, a man placed an order before detonating a suicide vest. How other attackers detonated suicide vests outside the international football match being held at the Stade de France. How that explosion drew a crowd inside of which a second attacker detonated a second vest. How the crowd that gathered after that explosion was similarly attacked. How men with assault rifles entered the Bataclan theatre during a rock concert and began firing indiscriminately into the audience. How all in all one hundred and twenty people were murdered and hundreds more were wounded. How it was what British Prime Minister David Cameron called the worst terrorist attack in Europe for a decade, and the worst act of violence in France since the Second World War.

I DON'T know anything about it. I haven't listened to the radio or turned on regular TV, haven't looked at any news or social media or anything on my phone since I left the station. And people know it's happening, Dave must know it's happening, but why would anyone call me? Dave only knows that Bethany left, that she went to stay with her sister. He doesn't know where that is. He doesn't have any reason to think that it's Paris. So why would he call? He doesn't call. Nobody calls. For hours and hours I don't know. For hours and hours it's going on, it's already happened, and I don't know. I watch a couple of movies and then I fall asleep and then my phone buzzes me awake. I figure it's Bethany, but it's not. She's got her phone set up so that you can reach her in-case-of-emergency contact even with the home screen locked, and her in-case-of-emergency contact is me. The policeman's accent is thick and because I haven't heard anything about the attack it takes me a long time to understand what he's saying.

Or maybe it isn't that. Maybe it's something else that keeps me from understanding, that makes me make him repeat himself over and over and over. In my memory he tells me at least a dozen times, but now I feel like that can't possibly be right. Maybe it is, though. I don't know. The truth is that I barely remember it at all. I don't remember hanging up. I don't remember anything I said.

Everything becomes strange, becomes like a dream, becomes like that dream where you're stuck in slow motion and it's already too late. I get my passport and I put on my coat and I walk out the door. I drive to the airport and I buy a ticket. I ask the agent to book me on the next flights, whatever they are. Apparently this sends up some sort of red flag, though, me flying internationally one-way without booking ahead. Or maybe it's just that I'm flying to Paris like that. Maybe it's just that everyone is on high alert. The person checking tickets at security radios in to someone, and then two TSA agents come and they pull me out of line. They take me into a little room with a table and a few folding chairs and they let me wait for thirty minutes before somebody comes to ask me what the nature of my trip is, to ask me why I'm going to Paris.

They make me say it again and again and again. They look at me like they don't believe me, not even a little bit, when I tell them. Then somebody decides that it's all right and they let me go, just like that. They take me back out and they put me in the front of the security line and they send me through.

It doesn't matter, really. I've got nothing better to do. Even with the hour I wasted with them my flight, my first flight, doesn't take off for another two hours.

I wander around the terminal, wander through the stores. I buy a bagel and I eat a few bites and then I carry the rest of it around for a while before I throw it away. I stand by the big windows and I watch the planes coming in and taking off. I think I do that for a long time, but it's hard to tell. It's hard to tell how much time is passing, how much time has already passed. I'm not asleep but I'm not really awake, either. I go over to my gate but it's not my gate yet. I wander around some more and I come back and it's still not my gate. I wander around some more and when I come back it is. I hang around, take a seat, stand back up, pace around. I wait for them to start boarding. I stand in the queue, scan my ticket. I board the plane and I find my seat. We sit there forever while everyone gets settled, while everything gets set. Then we push back from the gate and we go wait on the tarmac. Finally it's our turn. The world outside the window accelerates to a blur and then falls away.

I've got another four hours in Boston. I sit in one of the restaurants and I watch the news crawl along the bottom of the screen on the TV behind the bar. There's nothing there, though. There's nothing new. It's the same shit over and over. I eat three bites of the hamburger I ordered and then I let the waitress take it away. I drink another coffee, pay the check, go to the bathroom. I look at myself in the mirror, splash some water on my face. I feel like right now I just need to get there, like everything else can happen once I get there. I wait in the seating area, wait for my boarding group to be called, wait in the line. I wait for the people to move, wait for the woman in the aisle seat to stand up so that I can get into my seat.

I sit and I stare out the window. I drift in and out. The world goes dark and then sometime later it goes light again. Nothing else has changed. Outside it's still open empty ocean in every direction.

IT'S EARLY Sunday morning when we land. I clear customs and I get a cab, but I have no idea where to go. My phone doesn't work internationally and when I borrow the driver's phone to call the number the policeman called me from I get a prerecorded menu and a list of options that I don't understand.

I tell the driver to take me to the main police station, to the police headquarters. It's all I can come up with. We wind our way through the busy city. It feels like it takes forever, but probably it doesn't. Probably it's only twenty or thirty minutes. The radio is set to some talk station, and people keep calling in and shouting, but it's all in French and I don't understand any of what's being said.

Finally we get there. I get out and I give the driver all the cash I have. I haven't changed any bills and I don't know how much the ride costs. It doesn't seem to matter much. Or at least the driver seems satisfied. He takes the money and he gives me some bills back and he drives away.

I go in. Inside is crowded with people yelling and crying and rushing around. It's almost overwhelming. I don't know who to talk to, don't know what talking to them is going to accomplish. I make my way to the front desk but the man there doesn't speak English. He points me to a bench. I go and I sit and I wait for a long time. Or maybe it just feels like a long time. There's so much going on, so much noise, so much confusion. Finally someone comes and asks me in English what I'm doing there. I tell him what happened, tell him about the phone call I got. He nods. He tells me to follow him and he takes me back to a little partitioned-off area and he asks me a series of questions while he types my answers into his computer.

He asks one question after another after another. I keep thinking he's finished, keep thinking he's got to be finished, keep thinking that this has to be it, that this question has to be the last one, but it never is. He just keeps going.

I have this growing, gnawing sense that time has gotten away from me, that I'm wasting time when I'm already late, that I need to be somewhere else, need to be doing something else, and instead I'm here filling out this form with this policeman who clearly can't help me, who clearly doesn't know what the fuck he's doing, who clearly doesn't know a fucking thing about anything.

"Why?" I say, finally. "Why do you want to know? What difference does it make?" I stand and I look out over the partition at the rest of the room and I say, "Is there anyone here who can actually help me? Is there somebody here who can help me, and not just waste my time with this bullshit?" I turn back to the policeman. I lean over the desk and I yell in his face. "I need to see her," I yell. "I need to see her right now, do you understand me? Right fucking now."

I can't see her, though. They can't let me see her. We're not married and we aren't related, and without this documentation they have no way of knowing who I am. They have no way of knowing if I have anything at all to do with her.

"You called me," I say. "I didn't call you. You called me."

It doesn't matter, though. It isn't proof of anything. Besides that, the policeman I'm talking to isn't the one who called. He has no way of knowing if what I'm telling him is true.

I have to appreciate their position, he tells me. Times like these, stressful times like these, sometimes they make people do strange things. People want to involve themselves. It can make a difficult situation even worse. This is why the protocols exist, he explains. At times like these, it's more vital than ever that the protocols be maintained.

Her family has been contacted, of course. And of course I'm free to speak with them. He's certain that it is all as I say it is, certain that they will grant their permission for me to attend the identification with them.

"There's nothing else," he tells me. "I'm very sorry. There's nothing else I can do."

Sitting at the desk, sitting down behind the partition, the noise from the rest of the station is dampened, somewhat, but standing up you get it all. It's just wave after wave of unintelligible sound. And it's too much, finally. All of it—the call and the interrogation and the flights and the questions and the noise—it's all finally too much. It's like it all hits me all at once. I sit back down. I kind of have to. All of a sudden I just feel totally exhausted. I turn back to the policeman.

"Is there a hostel nearby?" I say. "Or a cheap hotel?"

The policeman looks at me with concern. He nods. He pulls out a pad, writes down a name, tears off the sheet. He holds it out to me.

I take the paper and I look at what he's written, but it doesn't compute. The little marks he's made don't mean anything to me.

"Where is this?" I say. "Can I walk there from here?"

He nods again. "Oh, yes," he says. "It's very simple." He explains the way, tells me what streets to turn down and what landmarks to look for. Halfway through I realize that I'm not listening, realize that nothing he's said so far has stuck with me. I don't stop him, though. I don't ask him to repeat himself. I wait until he's finished and then I thank him and I stand up and leave.

I GO outside and I stand there on the sidewalk. It's getting on toward late morning, and people are out. They're walking, driving, moving past me in all directions. They're waiting at corners and buying things in shops, talking on phones and reading magazines. For a second I just stand there and I watch them. I get kind of hypnotized by it all. It's just so strange. It's so strange, how normal everything seems. But I realize too that maybe it's not normal, that maybe it only seems normal to me because I don't know what normal looks like here. Maybe it only seems normal because I don't know how it's different from how it would be. It only seems normal because I don't know what anything means.

I WANDER around for an hour, looking for the hostel. I never find it. Instead I end up in front of a hotel that's nicer than any hotel I've ever stayed at in my entire life, and I'm so tired and so sick of looking that I go inside and I book a room. I just don't care anymore. I go up to the room and I lay down on the bed with my clothes on and I sleep for something like fifteen hours, and when I wake up it takes me a second to remember where I am and what I'm doing there.

I GO down to the hotel's business center and I send Bethany's parents an email telling them where I'm staying and what my room number is. Then I go out. I feel wide awake, feel like I need to do something, feel like I'm going to go crazy if I just sit in the room doing nothing. I walk around and I find a mobile phone store and I try to see if I can make my phone work internationally, but the sales-

259

people I talk to only speak enough English to make it clear that they want me to buy a new phone and sign up for a new plan. So I leave. I walk around some more and then I walk back to the hotel and I check my email. It's been over an hour, but there's still nothing. I check at the front desk to see if there are any messages for me, but there's nothing there either. So I go back out. I walk back to the police station. I have this idea that if I talk to somebody else I'll be able to get somewhere—I'll be able to get something done—but it doesn't happen. Nobody will tell me anything, nobody can do anything for me. I leave and I go back to the hotel and I check again and there's still nothing. I'm out of ideas, now, but I can't sit still. I leave again and I wander around. I see the Eiffel Tower and Notre Dame and the Louvre. I don't mean to. I'm not sightseeing. I'm just wandering around, just killing time, just moving for the sake of moving. It all feels faked, somehow. It all feels like some absurd dream. These are things out of movies, things out of some other life, some other life that's a million miles from mine. It can't possibly be real, can't possibly be right, that I'm standing in front of them. But there they are.

I haven't eaten since I don't even remember when. Since the three bites of hamburger in Boston. I'm not really hungry but I don't have anything else to do. I go into a café and I eat a sandwich, or part of a sandwich, and I drink a few cups of coffee. Then I start back. I get turned around, though. I get lost. I go down one street after another. I keep thinking that the next turn is going to take me back to something I recognize, but it never happens.

I walk past a space where the front is all windows, where I can see all the way through the lobby and past the reception desk to the glass wall and the yoga class going on in the studio space inside. I stop and I watch, watch the class go from down dog to chaturanga to up dog to chaturanga, and then I open the door and I go in. I don't really think about it first, I just do it. I ignore the girl at the front desk when she calls to me and I go straight through into the studio. I kick off my shoes and I drop my coat and I get down into down dog, get down and do what everyone else is doing. I let my head hang, let my neck elongate. I reach my hips toward the ceiling and I root down through my palms and I try not to notice how the energy in the room has shifted, try not to notice that the teacher has stopped talking. I try to pretend that it's all all right, that if I just wait it out it'll pick back up and keep going. I try to pretend that I don't feel everyone stopped and waiting to see happens now, don't feel everyone waiting to see what the crazy man is going to do next.

The teacher comes over and she kneels down next to me and she says something I don't understand, something in French. I bend my knees and I come out of the pose. Kneeling there on the floor I can see the class and I can see that everyone else has come out of the pose, too, that they've all moved slightly away, that they're all sitting watching me.

I hold up my hands. "I'm sorry," I say. "I didn't mean to interrupt. I didn't mean to disrupt the class. I just thought maybe I could join in for a little bit. I thought maybe I could just hang out here in back." I turn back to the teacher. "I'm sorry," I say again. "I know. I get it. I know that's crazy. I know that's not what you're supposed to do. I know that's not how you join a class."

The teacher doesn't say anything. She just looks at me. She's an older woman and she's wearing her straight gray hair in a long braid that hangs over her shoulder and when I see how she's looking at me it's like I can see what she's seeing. It's like I can see myself, see what I'm doing, see what I've done. And I can't even look at her. I have to look away. I feel so fucking stupid.

"I'm sorry," I say again. "I'm sorry. I'm really sorry." I can feel my face getting hot, feel my eyes starting to water. I sniff and I blink it back. I look at her. "You probably don't even understand me," I say. "You don't even know what I'm saying."

She nods. "I do," she says. Her voice is soft and her accent is distinct but the words are very clear. "Please," she says. "These people need this class. With everything that has happened, these people need this space."

I nod. I look around at the class and then I look back at her. "No," I say, "I know. I totally know. Believe me, I know. I really, really know."

She nods again. She's still looking at me, still looking at me with that same look. "Please," she says again.

I look back around at the class. No one has moved, no one has made a sound. They're all just watching me. I stand up, hold up my hands.

"I'm sorry," I say, for what feels like the dozenth time. "I'm sorry, everybody. Please. I'm sorry. I'll go. Have a good class."

Then I go and I get my jacket and I fumble into it. I kick my feet into my shoes. I take two steps toward the door and then I stop and I turn back. I put my hands together in front of my heart and I bow. I want to let them know, somehow. I want to show them how it is. In that moment I really, really need to know that they understand. I need to know that, even though we all agree that I need to leave, now, they understand. But I know it's ridiculous, too. I know it doesn't matter. I know it's too late. When I straighten back up and look at them nothing has changed. They're all still watching me like before. I turn and I go back out into the lobby and I pull the mashed backs of my shoes out from under my heels and I wipe my eyes and I leave.

I FIND my way back to the hotel. The next turn actually takes me back to someplace I recognize. I walk in through the big fancy front doors and Bethany's family, her parents and her brother, are there. They're standing at the desk. It's strange to see them. It's like how seeing the Eiffel Tower was, somehow. Her brother sees me first, comes over and shakes my hand.

"Thanks for being here," he says. He puts a hand on my shoulder and he leads me back to his parents. "Mom, Dad," he says, "you remember Dex."

Bethany's father is finishing with the concierge. Bethany's mother shakes my hand.

"Thank you for coming," she says. Her voice sounds like something small and dried up, like the voice a husk or a dead leaf would have if it could talk. "We all appreciate you being here," she says.

"Sure," I say. "Sure, no problem. I mean, of course."

The concierge is handing over the little folder with the keycards. Bethany's brother takes it from his father and he reads the room number aloud. He looks at his parents.

"Okay," he says. "Let's get you guys settled in."

I HELP them carry their bags to their room. I talk the whole way. I can't help it. It's like I can't shut up. I tell them about getting flagged by TSA, about getting detained and interviewed. I tell them about going to the police station and waiting and getting lost. I ramble on about how nice the hotel is, about how all the sights are really close, about how I walked past the Eiffel Tower and the Louvre and Notre Dame without even meaning to. I don't know what I'm saying or why I'm saying it. Finally we get to their room. Her parents take their bags and go inside. Her brother holds the door for them and then he turns back to me.

"The police are expecting us first thing in the morning," he says. "I'll tell the front desk to call your room when we're heading over."

"Okay," I say. "Sounds good."

He points. "I'm just next door," he says. "You can call me if you need anything. I'm going to be up late, so don't worry."

"Okay," I say. "Thanks."

He nods. "Okay," he says. "I'm going to make sure these guys get settled." He holds out his hand. "Thanks again for coming," he says. "We all appreciate it. I know our parents really appreciate it."

I shake his hand. "Sure," I say again. "Sure, yeah. No problem."

He lets go and he goes in and the door swings closed. I stand there in the hall. I think that maybe I'll be able to hear something, that maybe they'll say something about how they appreciate me being there or they wish I hadn't come, something definitive, and I'll be able to hear it, but there's nothing. It's a nice hotel, and out in the hall you can't hear anything from inside. Or maybe they're just not talking. Maybe there's nothing to say.

I GO back to my room. I lay on the bed and I stare up at the ceiling. I don't feel tired at all, but there's nothing for me to do. I lay there for hours. It's like how it was on the plane. I drift in and out. The room goes dark and then it goes light again. I get up and I get undressed and I take a shower and then I get dressed again in my same clothes. There's nothing else to do. I don't have anything else with me. I don't have another option. I go down to the lobby and I sit in one of the big chairs in the little seating area they have off to one side of the room and I wait. I wait while they set up the breakfast buffet and then I go in and I pick through it. I eat a few slices of melon and I drink a couple cups of coffee and then I go back out. I wait for twenty minutes and then I go back to the room to pee and then I come back and I wait some more. Finally Bethany's brother comes down. He doesn't see me. He goes over to the desk and he talks to the concierge and the concierge picks up the phone and makes a call. A few minutes later Bethany's parents come down. I get up and I go over, then. Bethany's brother sees me and nods.

"Oh, great," he says. "I was just about to have them call you."

"No need," I say. "Here I am."

"Here you are," he says. He nods toward the door. "I had them call a cab for us," he says. "It's waiting outside."

"Great," I say. "After you."

WE GO out and we get in the cab. Bethany's father sits up front and the rest of us climb in back. Bethany's brother gives the address. The driver starts off. He winds his way through the early morning traffic. Nobody says anything. Then we're there. The driver pulls up to the curb in front of the building and we climb out and Bethany's brother pays and we go inside.

Bethany's brother talks to the policeman at the front desk. The policeman nods. He calls to another policeman who shows us through to the room where we're going to wait for the policeman who's going to take us where we need to go.

The room is like something out of the DMV. There are a few folding chairs and a water dispenser and posters on the walls with instructions for what to do in different emergencies. If someone is choking. If someone is on fire. If someone has a weapon. Bethany's parents sit and her brother stands and I pace around. Nobody says anything. Bethany's father puts his hands together, the palms together and the fingers pointing down, and squeezes them between his knees. Her brother crosses and uncrosses his arms, puts his hands in his pockets and takes them out again. Her mother just stares ahead at nothing.

Then the policeman comes. We follow him out to a waiting car. Bethany's father has Bethany's mother sit in front and he climbs in back with Bethany's brother and me. It's a tight fit but it's fine. We don't have far to go. A few minutes later we're in front of the building. The policeman parks and shows us inside. We follow him down a flight of stairs and down a hallway to a security door. He gives the names to the guard and the guard checks them against his list and then he lets us through. Inside the policeman gives the names again, to the attendant. The attendant nods. He goes over to the wall of doors and he opens two and he pulls out the drawers. The sound of the bearings rolling in the runners is impossibly loud. The walls and the floor are all tile and there's nothing to dampen it, even a little.

Bethany's mother makes a little sound somewhere down in her throat, something between a cough and a gasp and something else. Bethany's father looks and then he looks at the attendant and he nods six or eight fast little nods, like someone trying to shake off a sneeze. Her brother puts an arm around his mother's shoulders. The attendant pushes the drawers back in and closes the doors. The sound the doors make as they close is the sound of a vacuum sealing, the sound of something collapsing into nothing. The policeman turns to us.

"Okay," he says. "Okay, that's it. It's done."

He takes a step toward us, toward the door. His arms are spread wide. He's guiding us out.

I think about her inside there, alone and cold, in where I can't get to her or touch her or hold her or tell her about the stupid thing I did at work, the stupid thing I said, the stupid thing I thought was just so fucking clever. In where she can't write in her journal or get more books to read, where she can't attend any more classes or workshops or seminars. Where she's going to miss everything, the entire future, forever.

And then something else is happening, something else is there, and it's like all of a sudden I can see him, can see my kid. And he isn't this issue, this thing that's happening to me, this collection of stresses and fights between us. I can see him for what he is, see him for what she'd been telling me he was all along, see him as this new becoming, this new being manifesting itself through her and through me, a branching off of the river of the creative force inspiring everything, the creative force that at every new moment inspires the entire Universe into being, manifesting itself into the world through us. For one second I can just see it, can see all of it. For one second it's so blindingly clear. And then it's gone. Just as quickly it's gone. As soon as I see it it's gone, and in its place is the knowledge that it's gone because it's really gone, because it's already gone. In its place is everything he'll never be and never do, everything we'll never be and do together, all the moments that he'll never have with Bethany and that she'll never have with him. And it's like I feel it all at once, how perfectly annihilated they are. It's like I feel all at once how they've vanished from all the warm, soft places where their beingness had pressed up against mine.

And then somebody is yelling, and somebody is calling for help, and somewhere far away there is the shudder of impact and the feeling of pain as I punch and kick and flail, as I drive my fists and elbows and feet and head into tables and desks and doors and walls. There's a burning in my throat and a ringing in my ears as my mouth screams wordless sounds. And then people are coming and people are there, and arms are holding my neck and my arms and my waist and my legs, and voices are in my ear telling me to stop, telling me to calm down, telling me to breathe.

THERE ARE forms to sign, and her father signs them. Then the policeman drives us back to the station. There's no reason for it, though. There's no reason to go back. There's nothing else for us to do. We walk down the street to a café and we sit at a table outside and nobody says anything. My knuckles are already starting to swell and stiffen and turn colors and I sit there opening and closing my fists, feeling the pain as something very small and far away and unimportant.

Bethany's father clears his throat. "I guess I'll have to call the embassy," he says. "Or, I don't know. I don't know what you do. I don't know what we do about getting back. About getting everything back."

"Didn't they tell you?" her brother says. "I mean, didn't they explain when you signed those papers?"

Her father doesn't look up. He shrugs, waves it away. "I don't know," he says. "They might have. I don't know."

"I'll do it, dad," he says. "Don't worry about it. I'll take care of it."

Their father doesn't look at him, either. He waves that away, too. "I'll do it," he says. "It'll give me something to do. Something productive."

NOBODY SAYS anything for a while. We sit there, waiting. Finally the waiter comes. He's young and he speaks to us in English without us having to speak to him first or tell him that we're Americans. He says, "Not a very good time to visit Paris." He says it as a sort of apology.

To no one in particular Bethany's mother says, "I don't think I'm going to get anything. I'm not very hungry."

"You should try to eat something," Bethany's brother says. "Even something small."

"He's right," says Bethany's father. "You haven't eaten anything since the plane."

"Order something, mom," Bethany's brother says.

Bethany's mother holds up her hands. "Fine," she says. "I'll have whatever you're having. What are you having?"

Bethany's father hasn't really looked, either. He picks up the menu. "I don't know," he says. "One of the sandwiches, I guess. Ham. Or chicken salad."

Bethany's mother nods. "That's fine," she says. "Whichever one it is, just order two."

Bethany's brother says, "You could get one of each."

268

Bethany's mother is looking at her hands, folded in her lap. Without looking up she says, "That's fine. I don't care. Whatever you want to do is fine."

"One of each," Bethany's father says to the waiter. "One ham and one chicken salad."

"And ham for me," says Bethany's brother.

The waiter nods. He turns to me. "And for you?" he says.

"Sure," I say. "Chicken salad. Yes. Okay."

THE WAITER takes our menus and he goes away and we sit there. We sit there for probably three minutes and nobody says anything. Then I sit forward and I say, "I'm sorry. I'm sorry about before. About making a scene. Or whatever you want to call it. I'm sorry."

Nobody says anything back to that. Nobody even looks at me. Bethany's father coughs. I keep going.

"I'm sorry if me being here is making this worse," I say. "I'm not trying to make this worse. Please believe me, the last thing I want to do is make this worse. That's the absolute last thing I want to do. If you guys want me to go, I'll go. If you want me to not be here. If you'd rather I wasn't here. If you'd rather just figure things out without me here."

Nobody says anything back to that, either. Then Bethany's mother looks at me. It might be the first time she's actually looked directly at me since they arrived. She shakes her head.

"We would never tell you not to be here," she says.

Bethany's father clears his throat, then. Bethany's mother looks at him. He looks at her and then he looks at me.

"But maybe you're right," he says. "Maybe it would be better."

Bethany's mother looks down at the table. Bethany's brother is watching his parents. Bethany's father looks at her brother. Her brother turns to me.

"It's not that we don't appreciate you being here," he says. "We do appreciate you being here. We know it wasn't easy for you to get here. We appreciate how much you care about Bethany. It's just that this is more of a family time."

I nod. "Sure," I say. "No, I get that. I totally get that. I hear you. I mean, of course. Yes. I hear you."

Nobody says anything for a minute. Then Bethany's father starts to say something. He stops himself before he gets it out, though. He looks at Bethany's brother and then he looks back at me and he laughs. He holds up his hands and he looks around at his family and he says, "You see? You see what I'm talking about? Do you see now? This. This is exactly what I mean. This is what I'm talking about." He looks at me. "Why are we talking about this?" he says. "We shouldn't be talking about *you*. We shouldn't have to talk about *you*. This isn't about *you*. This doesn't concern *you*."

I look at Bethany's brother, at her mother. Neither of them is looking at me, though. They're both looking down, looking somewhere else. I look back at Bethany's father.

"No," I say. "That's what I'm saying. I'm saying that if you don't want me to be here then I'll go. That's exactly what I'm saying I'll do. I'm not trying to make this about me. I'm really not. Honestly. I'm not trying to do anything."

Bethany's father laughs again. It's the most humorless laugh I've ever heard. There are tears in his eyes.

"You're not trying to do anything?" he says. "You're not trying to do anything?"

"No," I say, "I'm not. I'm not doing anything. What do you think I'm doing? What do you think I'm trying to do?" I say it like a kid, like a teenage punk, like how I used to argue with my parents when they would accuse me of things. I see myself doing it but I can't stop it. Or maybe I can and I don't. Maybe I just don't. "What am I doing?" I say. "Tell me what I'm doing, then. If I'm doing something then tell me what I'm doing. I'm not doing anything."

Bethany's mother holds up her hands. "Please," she says. "Please, stop this. Both of you. You have to stop this."

I stop. We both stop. We sit back. Nobody says anything for a minute. Then Bethany's father sits forward again.

"Look," he says. His voice is quiet, now, under control. "We do appreciate you flying all the way over here. And we do appreciate the fact that you and Bethany cared about each other. But the five or six or however many months you two were together doesn't give you the right to insert yourself into this. Can't you see that? Put yourself in our place. Take one minute and try to imagine that something like this has happened to you, and instead of being allowed to process it you have to spend your time dealing with some stranger, somebody you've met once in your life. Does that seem right to you? Do you think that's right?"

Later on I realize that really I could say the same thing—that something like this has happened to me, that instead of being allowed to process it I'm being forced to spend my time dealing with strangers, people I've only met once in my life—but at that moment it doesn't occur to me. It doesn't occur to me because something else occurs to me instead. It doesn't occur to me because that's the moment when I realize that Bethany didn't tell them. That to them I'm not the person that Bethany is going to have a kid and a life and a home and a future with. That to them I'm not the father of their grandchild, I'm just some guy that their yoga hippie daughter is shacking up with. I'm just some random stranger who showed up and talked to them about the Eiffel Tower and the Louvre, who lost his shit and caused a scene at the worst moment of their entire lives.

I stand up. I go into my pocket and bring out the change the cab driver gave me at the police station and I lay it on the table.

"I'm sorry," I say. "This is all the cash I have. I can pay you back whatever I owe for the sandwich the next time I see you. Or I can send you the money." Then I say, "I'm sorry. I'm really sorry. I really am. I'm so sorry. I'm sorry for everything. If I can do anything, if you can think of anything I can do, please let me know."

Then I turn and I walk away. I make my way between the empty tables, past the waiter coming with our food, and I leave the café.

I WALK back to the hotel and I check out. I don't go back up to the room. There's no point. There's nothing there. The bill I charge, the receipt I sign, is for hundreds and hundreds of dollars. It's for more than I spent on a month's rent in some of the places I lived when I was starting out. It's for more than I spent on a month's rent for our place in Nashville. It doesn't seem to matter much. I take the train to the airport and I get a flight leaving at six the next morning. There's nothing earlier that makes any sense. Nothing that's available would get me home any sooner. I would be sitting for hours in London or Boston or New York instead.

I wander around the terminal. I walk past the restaurants and the stores and the gates. I go and I stand at the big window and I look out at the tarmac. I watch runway workers and baggage handlers moving around below me, four or five stories down. I go and I stare at the big board, at the flights coming in and the flights going out. I think about not going back, about changing my ticket and flying somewhere else, anywhere else. I think about landing somewhere and finding a new place to live, a new job, a new life. I think about the station filling my time slot and the bank repossessing my house, about how in six months or maybe a year there would be somebody else living there, maybe some other family. There would be somebody else's bed in the bedroom and somebody else's couch where my couch is now, somebody else's TV in somebody else's TV cabinet. Somebody else's life filling all the rooms. I think about all the shit I've held onto, all the collected artifacts of me, and I think about the bank or whoever they hire for that sort of thing coming in and taking it all and selling it off or donating it or throwing it away, think about all of it scattering into Salvation Army stores and other people's houses and trash cans and dumpsters and landfills and fires, all the teeshirts and show fliers and demo tapes and rare imports and all the other shit, too, the shit that's just the shit of everyday life, the cereal bowl I always use and Bethany's favorite tea mug and the yoga mat she keeps in the corner by the front door and all of the clothes she didn't bring to Paris. I think about all of it drifting apart, all of it moving farther and farther in every direction until eventually each thing loses sight of every other thing, until no one would ever guess or imagine that these things had once been together, had once been connected, had once made a life.

I DON'T know if leaving was the right thing. Sometimes I still think I should have stayed, should have insisted that I had a right to be there, should have told them about Bethany being pregnant. The rest of the time, though, I feel like there wouldn't have been much point. The rest of the time I feel like it would have been unpleasant for everyone and it wouldn't have made any difference.

And it did seem like, apart from the paperwork, there wasn't much left to do.

But then again, maybe that's just what I want to think. Maybe that's just what I hope is true. On the plane I imagine Bethany's mother getting in touch, imagine her reaching out at some point after everything has calmed down and telling me that she regrets how they handled things, that they were all upset and not thinking clearly, but it never happens. At the funeral she hugs me, and they let me stand in the receiving line, but nobody asks me to speak and there's no discussion of me coming with them to scatter the ashes.

BUT I'M getting ahead of myself, now. I'm mixing things up, getting things out of order. Let me go back. Full and honest. Here it is. You're welcome to it. It's all yours.

273

I LAND in Cleveland on Wednesday afternoon. I don't go home. I go to a bar. It isn't a bar I know, isn't a bar where they know me. It's just some random bar. I'm six time zones ahead or behind and I feel exhausted and wide awake at the same time, and my idea is to drink until I don't feel that way anymore. It never happens, though. It doesn't work. Eventually the bartender has to just cut me off. I go out and I sleep in my car. No one bothers me. I wake up Thursday morning with cars and people going by, with the whole world still happening. I'm somewhere between still drunk and the worst hangover I've had in years. I turn on my phone. I turned it off in Paris when I realized that it wasn't going to work and I haven't had it back on since and now I've got something like twenty-five or thirty missed calls and text messages from Dave asking me to call him, asking me what's going on, asking me where I am.

I don't call him. I go to a diner and I order breakfast and I sit there staring at it. Then I go home. I can't think of anything else to do. I shower and I shave and I change my clothes. Then I go back out. I still can't think of anywhere to go, can't think of anything to do, but I need to be somewhere else. I drive around, drive in circles. I end up at the mall. I wander around looking at clothes and shoes and people. Outside the Foot Locker a couple of guys recognize me and they want a picture, and because I'm taking a picture with them other people notice me. Or at least they notice what's going on. A lot of them don't seem to really know who I am, though. Or maybe they just don't care that I'm me. It seems like a lot of them only come because they see other people coming. Most of them go away without asking for a picture. After that I go to the movie theater and I watch twenty minutes of something and then I go into another theater and I watch another twenty minutes of something else. I leave the theater and I go to the food court and have a coffee. It's all not enough. I leave the mall and I find another bar. I don't make it very far, though. After last night the smell alone makes me nauseous. I make it through half a beer and then I leave and I go get back in my car. Sitting there in the parking lot I start crying, start punching at the steering wheel and the ceiling, but my knuckles are all fucked up and the jolt of pain I feel hitting them again is such a shock that it stops me in my tracks. So I wipe my eyes and I drive home. I turn on the TV and I lay there on the couch. Eventually I sleep.

TIME PASSES strangely. The days drag on and on but then suddenly somehow whole weeks have gone by. I don't go to work, don't answer my phone. I don't come to the door or check the mail. Mostly I sleep. When I'm awake I have this constant feeling that I'm forgetting something, something important, this feeling that there's somewhere I need to be and something I need to be doing, but I can't quite remember what or where it is. I can't quite figure out how to start.

HER BROTHER calls. I don't answer but I listen to the message. It's about the funeral, the date and time and location. I make a note, find my suit. On the day I get dressed and I drive to Pittsburgh. There are people there that I recognize, people from the yoga studio. They hug me and tell me how sorry they are. I don't know what to say to them, don't know what I'm supposed to say. The truth is that I'm sorry I came. I don't know what I was hoping for, but whatever it is this isn't it. This all feels pointless. I'm glad when it finally starts winding down, when it feels like I can drift off and leave.

Bethany's brother catches up with me on my way out to the car. I think maybe he's going to talk to me about the service, about Paris, think maybe he's going to apologize for how they've handled things with me, for how everything's been, but that's not it. He puts a hand on my shoulder and he looks me in the eye and he tells me that their mother wants all of Bethany's things, all of her clothes and her computer and her books and her journals and whatever else is in the house, and he's told her that he would take care of it. He tells me how, once things settle down, he's going to fly to Cleveland and pack everything up in Bethany's car and drive it all back here.

"You understand how it is," he says. "She's Bethany's mother. It means a lot to her, and right now dad and I are just trying to do anything we can to help her get through this." He gives me a look, gives my shoulder a squeeze. "It would just be really, really helpful if you could just not make it an issue," he says.

I think about telling him to fuck off, to shove it up his ass, to get his fucking hands off me. I think about pushing him away, swinging at him, telling him that if he comes near my house then he'd better come ready for a fucking fight. For a second it really feels like it's all right there, like it's really going to happen, like that's really what I'm going to say when I open my mouth and start to speak.

But it's not. It's not and it doesn't. None of that happens. Part of it is that I know it won't make any difference, know that even if it comes right down to it he'll just get the cops or a lawyer or somebody to come push me around instead. I know that either way he'll get what he wants. The bigger part of it, though, is that I'm just so fucking tired. I've barely mustered enough energy for this day, for all of this standing here and shaking hands and being hugged, for all of this listening and nodding and acting like a human being. So I nod. "Sure," I say. "Sure, it's fine. It's no problem. It's fine."

He gives me a little smile, gives my shoulder another squeeze. He takes his hand away. "Okay," he says. "Okay. Great. Thanks for understanding. I'll text you when I work out the details."

Then he turns and he walks away. I watch him go, watch until he's inside. He never looks back. I go and I get in my car and I drive home and I fall asleep on the couch, still in my suit.

I HANG out, hang around, kill time. I drift from room to room. I don't shower, don't shave, don't comb my hair or change my clothes. I live on dry cereal and ramen and coffee and microwave popcorn. I watch day become night become day become night.

I read articles, first-person accounts, translations of police reports. I read the Wikipedia page over and over on the off chance that there's been an edit or an addition since the last time I checked. I wake up crying, wake up confused, wake up gritting my teeth so hard that my jaw aches for hours afterwards. I punch a hole in my office wall, clip a stud, watch my barely-better hand swell up and turn purple again. I blast Rancid and Cro-Mags and Fugazi at two in the morning until my neighbor comes over and pounds on my door. I turn it down until his light goes off and then I turn it up again. I leave it up until he comes back, until he yells, until he threatens to kick my ass. I leave it up until he calls the cops.

I walk into rooms and I stand there trying to remember what I was looking for, trying to remember what I was going to do.

I go to the gas station and I buy more food, buy chips and a few boxes of Kraft macaroni and cheese and milk and beer and cigarettes. I smoke inside, smoke in my office, fall asleep on the couch with a lit cigarette in my mouth and wake up with it burning a hole in the cushion.

I zone out, drift off. I come back to find that I'm standing in the bedroom doorway, that I'm standing by the bed, that I'm standing halfway inside the part of the closet she used to use.

I CALL my parents. My mom answers.

"It's me," I say.

It takes her a second to figure out who that means.

"Dexter," she says, finally. It isn't really a statement but it isn't really a question, either. She says, "Your dad's not here. He ran to the store. He'll be back in a few minutes. Or he'll be back in a little while."

"That's fine," I say. "I didn't call to talk to him. I mean I don't need to talk to him. That's not why I called."

"Oh," she says. "I see. Okay."

It feels like maybe she's going to say something else, or maybe I'm just hoping that she will, but she doesn't.

"How are you?" I say.

"Fine," she says. "We're fine. Things are fine. How are things with you?"

And I'm going to tell her. I'm going to say it, going to dump it all out like the week's garbage all over the kitchen floor, the crushed containers and the chicken bones and the egg shells and the coffee grounds and the milk carton dribbling the last little bit that wouldn't quite come before, dump it all out and let her see it, let her deal with it, let her clean up the mess she's made, the mess she's made of me, the mess she's let him make of me, but then I don't. I don't do it. I take a breath and I say, "Fine. I'm fine. Things are fine."

"Okay," she says. "Well, good. That's good. I'm glad to hear that."

Then we just sit there. We sit there for probably half a minute, neither of us saying anything.

"So," she says, finally, "what's new with you?"

"Nothing," I say. Then I say, "Listen, mom, I have to go. Take care of yourself." And then I hang up before she can say anything back.

DAVE COMES by. He comes around back, comes around to the sliding glass door off the patio. It's the only reason I let him in. I've been pretending I'm not home when people come to the door, but Dave sees me through the glass.

He has all of my stuff from the station, all the little random shit I've left there over the years. He has it all packed up in a box.

I don't have anything to offer him. I don't have any real food and I already drank all the beer. I make coffee and we sit there drinking it. I don't even have any cream.

"I'm sorry," I say. "I mean. For not calling and not showing up, and everything. For not letting you know. Not keeping you in the loop. And, just, I don't know. Just sorry."

He shrugs. He waves it away. "Listen," he says, "don't worry about it. Given everything, I'm the last person you need to spend any time worrying about." He sips his coffee, shrugs again. "For what it's worth," he says, "I honestly don't think it actually made a whole hell of a lot of difference. I think the reality is that the die was cast the minute the station sold. I think we could have stopped showing up after that first meeting with Chad or we could have worked our asses off and done the best shows of our lives, and we'd still be right where we are."

I nod. I can't think of anything to say. I can't even really focus on what he's telling me. I drink a mouthful of coffee and it's hot and it burns my tongue and then it burns my throat and then it burns all the way down. I don't care. It's like it's happening to someone else, to something else, to some inanimate object, to a funnel or a piece of drainpipe. It's like it's happening a million miles away.

"So," I say, "are you finding stuff to do?"

He nods. "Sure," he says. "I've got a few sound tech gigs lined up. Odds and ends. Freelancing. I've got some contacts I'm trying to work. Katie's picked up a few more shifts, in the meantime. We're figuring it out. We'll be all right."

"Great," I say. "Good. I'm glad. That's good."

He nods again. He sips his coffee. Then he leans his elbows on the table and he laughs. He shakes his head. "I just keep thinking about how close we were," he says. "It's like, Fuck. We were right there. With everything that's happening now, it could have been so huge."

I don't know what he's talking about. I haven't been keeping up with things. I haven't even checked my email. I shake my head. "What?" I say. "What happened?"

He looks at me, frowns. "Seriously?" he says. "Man, I know you've been off the grid, but I thought for sure you'd heard." He goes into his jacket pocket and comes out with his phone and he starts searching, starts scrolling through. "The Loose Ends are back together," he says. "They announced it a few days ago. They're doing a new album and a big tour and everything. Here, look. Look at this."

He holds out the phone. I take it and look. The article he's got pulled up shows a headline about the reunion and a promotional photo of them all standing together with their arms around each other's shoulders, all of them smiling. Logan looks like they've made him up to look healthier than he actually is. Everyone else just looks older and puffier.

"They're saying it's going to be huge," Dave says. "They're projecting it to out-sell all of their previous tours. We're talking about hundreds of millions of dollars, worldwide. They're saying that the new album could be complete shit and it wouldn't even make any difference. Apparently the pre-sale activity has been insane."

I hand back the phone. "I guess that explains why they made such a big deal about finding him," I say.

Dave snorts. "I'd say it does," he says. He looks at the screen again, shakes his head. "The fucking lifestyles of the rich and famous," he says. "Fuck me."

I LEAVE the stuff Dave brought where he left it. It sits there on the kitchen floor. I walk around it. I don't look at it, don't think about it.

I hang out, kill time. I start to feel antsy, start to feel like maybe I want to go to a yoga class, but I don't want to see those people. I go for a run instead and I make it maybe three-quarters of a mile and then I give up. I feel like I'm dying, feel like there's no air left in the world. I walk back to the house with my hands on my head and my sides aching and the already-sweat-soaked streaks on my sweatshirt going cold down my back and my front.

I lay on the couch and I watch stuff that Bethany TiVo'd. I watch some stupid baking show and some stupid show about veterinary emergencies. I watch the first few minutes of one of the documentaries I promised her I would watch and then I turn it off and I don't go back to it. I fall asleep and I wake up and I fall asleep again.

THEN, BETHANY'S brother comes. He shows up in an Uber with a stack of packing boxes and a shopping bag full of duct tape. I let him in. I show him where everything is. I get Bethany's bags, the ones she didn't take to Paris, the ones she used when she moved in here, out of the crawlspace. I help him pack. We're together all afternoon. And it's funny, almost. It's the first time we've really spent any time together alone, and we kind of get along. And it turns out that he lived in Cincinnati back in the late nineties, and he actually saw Counter play.

"Wow," he says, when we make the connection. "No, totally. I totally saw you. I saw you a few times, actually. I saw you at Frank's Tavern and I saw you at The Riverside and I think maybe one other place. Or maybe I saw you at Frank's twice. I think the first time it was just kind of random, but the second time I made a point of seeing you. You guys were really good." He laughs. "God," he says, "that feels like a lifetime ago. I haven't been to a concert in probably ten years. I haven't been to a concert since Maddie was born, so we're talking at least ten years. Which is crazy." He shakes his head. "Seriously, though," he says, "you guys were great. You were really great."

"Thanks," I say. "Really. That means a lot."

It doesn't, though. He's right. It does feel like a lifetime ago. It feels farther away than that, even. It feels like somebody else's life.

"I think we were right there on the cusp for a while," I say, "but it never happened. Somehow we just never got over."

He shrugs. "I guess that's the way it goes," he says.

"Sure," I say. "That's the way it goes."

WE CARRY everything outside and we load it into Bethany's car and then we shake hands and I stand there and watch as he drives away. I watch until I can't see him anymore, until I can't see the car, until I'm just watching the place where it disappeared. Then I go back inside. He brought tons and tons of packing materials, dozens of boxes and rolls and rolls of tape, way more than we actually needed, and what's left is still sitting there in a pile on the living room floor.

I get down and I build out the boxes and I keep packing. I pack up my demo tapes and my band teeshirts and my stacks of fliers. I pack up the framed photos I have of me with different people I interviewed back at the station at Kent, the pictures of twenty-something-year-old me with Henry Rollins and Tim Armstrong and Steve Jones. I pack up my records and my tapes and CDs. I go through the kitchen and I pack up the plates and the cups and the silverware and the pots and pans. I go through the bedroom and I pack up my clothes, pack up my shoes, pack up the bedding. I go through the living room and all the closets. I carry it all outside and set it out on the lawn, out in the snow, all of the boxes, and then I take the bed and the dresser and the couch and the chairs and the kitchen table and the TV and all the little throw pillows that Bethany bought and the rug she helped me pick out and I drag it all out there, too.

It's late, well past dark and freezing cold, by the time I'm finished. I go back inside and I sit on the floor in the empty living room and I stare at the empty walls, at the little faded halos around where things used to hang, at the empty hall closet and the empty place by the door where she always left her yoga mat, at the empty kitchen cupboards and the empty shelves and all the rest of it, and then I close my eyes and I breathe deep, breathe down through my throat chakra and my heart chakra and my sacral chakra, breathe down into the raging center of the impulse I have to tear through the house, to drive my arms and legs and head and body with as much force as I can summon through whatever stands in my way, to beat my shattered self against the immovable physical realities of this stupid world until there's nothing left, nothing left of any of it, nothing left that anyone would recognize, not even me.

AND THEN I leave. I leave everything on the lawn and I leave the doors unlocked and I get in my car and I start driving. I drive past downtown, past Oberlin, past Sandusky and Toledo. I cross the state line into Indiana and I sleep for a few hours at a truck stop outside South Bend. I cross Illinois, stop for food at a diner out-side Davenport, sitting at the counter with a half-dozen salespeople from Evansville. I roll through Des Moines and Omaha and Lincoln. Somewhere west of North Platte my car starts overheating and I have to pull over and leave it on the roadside and hitchhike to the next town. The kid who picks me up smokes three cigarettes down to the filter in the ten minutes we're on the road. He drops me off at the first garage we pass and I thank him and I go inside. The mechanic slides out from underneath a cargo van when I ring the bell. He nods when I tell him what happened, when I explain. He goes and he gets a jug of something down off the shelf and then he leads me out to his truck and he drives me back. Back at my car he takes my keys and he pops the hood and he unscrews some cap I've never messed with and he empties the jug into whatever tank or reservoir the cap goes to. He comes back screwing the cap onto the empty jug and he hands me his keys and he tells me to follow him. Then he goes back and he gets in my car and he pulls out into traffic. I start the truck and I pull out after him. We do forty the whole way, hugging the shoulder. Back at the shop he finds the crack in the radiator. He can epoxy it, he tells me, but it'll take eight hours for the epoxy to set.

"We'll be closed by the time it's ready," he says. "You'll have to pick it up in the morning."

"Can't I just pay you now and have you leave it out in the lot, or something?" I say. "If you leave it out in the lot I can just come by later and get it. You can just leave the keys in it. I don't care."

The mechanic looks at me. "I mean, sure," he says. "It's your vehicle. I can do whatever you want me to do with it. But even if I get in there and get it all worked out in the next hour, that epoxy isn't going to be set until the middle of the night."

"That's fine," I say. "Really. It's fine."

The mechanic keeps looking at me. Then he shrugs. "Okay," he says. "Whatever you want. It'll be out back. But unless you want to have this happen again, I'd strongly suggest you give it the full eight hours."

I THANK him and I pay and I leave. I walk along the road until I hit the town. The town isn't much. A hardware store and a McDonald's and a coffee shop and a drug store and a few other random little shops. I wander around, kill time. I go into the coffee shop and I get a coffee and I read the paper. It's the same thing everywhere. In Belgium the terror watch level is still at four, the highest level. Police in New York are on high alert heading into the holiday season. I walk through the hardware store and the drug store, buy a toothbrush and some toothpaste, brush my teeth in the drug store bathroom. I go into the McDonald's and I order one of the combo meals and I eat it. I'm not even hungry, I don't even want it, but I eat it anyway. I've still got hours and hours to kill. I leave the McDonald's and I leave the town center and I walk around the neighborhoods. I walk past house after house and driveway after driveway and mailbox after mailbox. Everything is very quiet. No one is out. My footsteps crunch in the snow where it's been packed down on the sidewalk. I figure eight hours is the manufacturer's most conservative estimate and that in reality it's probably ready a lot sooner and it's probably fine now and will definitely be fine by the time I make it back. I turn around and I try to retrace my steps, try to head back in the direction I think

I came from, but I get turned around. I go down a different street than I meant to, a different street than I did before. It's ridiculous. It's a tiny town, but in the dark every residential street looks the same. It takes me almost an hour to find the main street again.

I walk back to the garage, find my car parked behind the building. The doors are open and the keys are in the ignition. I start it up and I pull out of the lot, stick to surface streets until the temperature gauge rises and holds at the midpoint. Then I circle back. I find the ramp and I get on the highway and I move into the left lane and I hit the gas. All night long it's me and the semis, running through a lot of flat empty nothing. Around dawn I start to drift and so I get off the highway and I sleep for a few hours on the side of some random state road in eastern Colorado. I wake up to a trooper knocking on my window and asking to see my ID, asking me where I'm headed, telling me I can't sleep here. He makes me stand by the car with my hands out of my pockets and visible while he calls everything in. Eventually he lets me go, lets me off with a warning. He tells me to use a designated rest area next time. I thank him and I tell him I will and then I get back on the road, but I have to pull over again before I reach the highway. I feel nauseous, unsteady, adrenaline sick. I pace around with my hands on my head trying to catch my breath, trying to release the tightness running like a band around my ribs and up into my throat. I'd been fast asleep, lost in a dream. I was back in Cleveland, back in the house, back in my life, but everything had changed. The house had mutated, expanded, grown hallways like vines or roots or branches that stretched for miles, that wove their way around and around and back on themselves. I was looking for her, was sure that she was somewhere just up ahead, but around each corner all I found was more hallway, always more hallway. I was still looking when the trooper's knuckles rapping on the glass exploded into my awareness and brought me back, brought me fully awake, with my heart jackhammering in my chest and the pulse running up my throat and into my jaw, with it throbbing under my tongue and inside my brain and in the hollows behind and around my blinking, staring eyes.

I GET it together. I get back on the highway. I watch the Front Range rise up out of the plains like a mirage, like a cartoon sunrise. I've never seen anything like it. I've never been this far west. Touring with Counter we never made it past Kansas City. I push through into Utah and I sleep at a campground in the Fishlake National Forest. I wake up to mountains and water and trees and the smell of trees. I cruise across the corner of Arizona and the southern tip of Nevada, through Las Vegas and then over the state line into California.

The temperature gauge starts creeping up again outside Baker. I make it off the highway and I pull into a gas station, but the kid working there can't help me. The gas station isn't a garage, it's just a gas station, and the kid doesn't know anything about cars. I ask him if there's a garage nearby, but he doesn't know that either. He goes into the office and he comes back with a phonebook and he hands it across. The first place I call tells me it'll be a hundred dollars just for the tow, and the second and third places aren't much better. I'm dialing the number for the fourth place when another customer comes over and asks me what the trouble is, asks me which way I'm headed.

I tell him. He nods.

"Well," he says, "I can't help you with the car any, but if you want a ride I can give you a ride."

I FOLLOW him out, get in his car. I don't really think about it. I just go. Once we're out on the road he starts talking. He tells me everything, his whole life's story. For miles and miles, through Barstow and Victorville, he goes on and on. How for most of his life he was a sinner. How he blasphemed and transgressed, harbored lust and envy. How he committed wicked acts. How then he met a man who changed it all, a man who was more than a man, a man named Jesus Christ. How once he invited Jesus into his heart he was made clean again, made whole. How once he invited Jesus into his heart he was filled to overflowing with God's perfect love.

He looks at me. "And what about you?" he says. "Have you found faith?"

I shake my head. "I never really got into religion," I say. "It was never my thing. I wasn't raised with it, or anything. It just wasn't part of my life." Then I say, "I was doing a lot of yoga there, for a while. I got kind of into the whole prayer-mindfulness-spirituality part of that. So that's kind of something."

He nods. "Sure," he says. "That's a good thing."

"Yeah," I say. "It's a lot of the same stuff. Be more aware, be more tolerant, be more peaceful. Try to be a better person."

"Sure," he says again.

"I don't know," I say. "I guess maybe I didn't get that into it. I could've been a lot more dedicated. I could've been more disciplined about it. I think I was kind of a bad yoga person. I didn't really put all that stuff into practice the way I should have. The mindfulness and the tolerance and all that stuff. I had all of this other shit going on that I think I kind of let myself get caught up in. I didn't take it all to heart the way I should have."

He shrugs, shakes his head. "Faith is a journey," he says. "We're all sinful creatures. It's just our nature. Knowing the path doesn't mean you don't stray, it just means you know when you have and you know how to get back. But it's never a one-shot deal."

"Sure," I say. "That makes sense."

He nods again. He looks at me. "You know it doesn't matter to Him," he says. "You want to call it Christianity or Sun Worship or Yoga or Native American religion. It's all one thing to Him. You know that thing they say, Look at the big picture? That's Him. He's the big picture. He's the ultimate big picture. I mean, look." He waves a hand at the road, at the desert, at the billboards, at the sky. "Look," he says again. "You see it? It's not nothing. There's something, and there's something, and there's something else. Right? You see it. It's all there."

"Yeah," I say, "I see it."

He looks at me, considering. Then he shakes his head. "No, you don't," he says. "You don't see it. But you will. When you want to you will. When you're ready to see it you'll see it. That's the beautiful thing. He's always there. You don't even have to look for Him. As soon as you open your eyes, there He is."

I look out at the road, at the other cars, at the rocky hills and the scrubby plant life going by.

"Sure," I say. "Him and everything else."

He laughs at that, laughs like he understands. He shakes his head again. "It's a bitch," he says. "Don't think I don't know it. In a world like this one? Shit. It's a wonder they don't bar the door."

WE CROSS the city limits. He asks me where I want to go. I don't have any idea. I tell him to drop me someplace near the water. He drives me to the Santa Monica pier. He stops at the gate and he puts out his hand and he asks me to pray with him.

I put my hand in his. He closes his eyes.

"Dear Lord Jesus," he says, "please watch over this man and protect him on his journey. Please visit Your Holy wisdom upon him. Help him discover the path to Your door."

He squeezes my hand and lets it go. I thank him for everything and I open the door.

"God bless you," he says.

"Okay," I say. "Thanks again." Then I get out and I close the door and he drives away.

I cross the parking lot, take off my shoes, walk down to the water. I walk out away from the pier, out away from the noise from the rides and the games. I walk until I can hardly hear it at all and then I sit down in the sand and I watch the waves coming in.

I sit there for a long time, sit there for hours, sit there until the sun sets in front of me, until all I can see of the waves are the slivers of reflected light that shine on their faces as they rise and the tendril of foam along the shore where they break. I sit there until the park on the pier shuts down, until the lights on the rides and the games all blink off. I sit there until I'm freezing cold. Then I get up. I walk back to the parking lot and I brush the sand off my numb feet and I put my shoes back on and I leave the beach.

I need to find somewhere to stay, need to find a motel or something, but my phone is dead and my charger is back in my car in Barstow. I find a CVS and I buy a new charger and I find a Starbucks and I plug it in. The cheapest place I can find in the area is almost two miles away, but it doesn't matter. I don't have anything else to do. I wait until I've got enough of a charge to get me there, or what I hope is enough of a charge to get me there, and then I leave and I start walking. My phone dies when I'm less than a quarter mile away and I have to walk around the block and finally ask somebody before I find it. The guy at the front desk wants to know how long I'm planning on staying and I tell him maybe one night, maybe longer, and he tells me he may not be able to extend the hold if I don't book in advance. I tell him to make it two days to be on the safe side and he swipes my card and gives me a key. I go up to the room and I lay down on the bed and I stare up at the ceiling. I don't really know how long I lay there, but it feels like a while. Eventually I fall asleep.

I KILL time. I walk around. I walk down to Venice, down to the Beach Cities. I walk out on the piers and I stare out at the ocean.

I stand there and I try to really see it, really get my head around it all, but I can't do it. Hours and hours later it still just seems absurd, still seems impossible, somehow: that out beyond this water there is more water, that there is water beyond water, water going out and out and out. And that under the water, too, there is water: water all the way down, water gliding densely over water, water massing under water. And in time: that going back and back there is water, this same water, this same water rolling onto the shores and rising into the clouds, this same water falling on the hills and the mountains and the plains and the deserts, this same water running and pooling and finding its way back again and again, over and over, without record or memory, forever.

And that of course it's not impossible. That of course it's no more impossible than anything else that seems impossible, and is, no more impossible than any other incomprehensibility. It is no more impossible than any of the other ancient and indifferent constants upon and before and beneath whose physical and temporal vastnesses we live and work and postulate our little theories about what this is and how it's done, upon and before and beneath which we and all of our clever notions rise and fall, flash and fade, appear and disappear again from being.

And that within that instant, that so-small-as-to-be-nearly-non-existent interval between rising and falling, flashing and fading, is all of the self-regarding, all of the choosing and pursuing and making and destroying, all of the thrashing and shouting and claiming, all of the elaborate chasing-your-own-tail we call being a person. And that it is me, finally—that it has to be me, can only be me, the frantic and spastic and desperate and ultimately ridiculous act of me, enacted within this fraction of a fraction of a fraction—that is strange, improbable, unlikely, absurd. That of course in the contest for authority between oneself and infinity there is no contest. That I've got it wrong, somehow, have always had it wrong, have always had it all wrong anytime I thought I knew anything at all.

MY CREDIT cards have been going, one by one. The one I used to buy the plane tickets goes at a gas station in Indiana, the one I used at the hotel in Paris goes at a grocery store outside Des Moines. I used the last one to check into the motel, but when I go to extend my reservation on the third morning it gets declined. I tell the guy that it's an issue with the card, that I just need to call the company and sort it out and that if he'll let me keep the room for another night I'll pay him once it's fixed, but he shakes his head. It's not his decision, he tells me. If I can't pay for the room some other way then he's going to have to ask me to vacate.

He walks me back to the room and he stands there while I get my stuff together. It doesn't take very long. I've only got a few things. There's my coat and my hat and the phone charger I bought and another toothbrush. I pack it all into a plastic grocery bag that's left-over from whatever I bought last and the guy from the front desk holds the door.

"Sorry," he says.

"Don't worry about it," I say.

I hand him the key and I go out. He turns off the lights and he closes the door and locks it. Standing there on the exterior corridor overlooking the parking lot he turns and looks at me. He looks like he's maybe twenty-five, like this is just a job he's doing while he tries for some other kind of life, like in the short time he's worked here he's never had this happen, never had to do this part of the job.

"Do you have somewhere else you can go?" he says.

"Sure," I say. "I can call some people. It's fine."

He looks down at the key in this hands, turns it over. He nods. "Okay," he says.

"Listen," I say. "Relax. It's not your fault. It's my fault. It's my own stupid fault. You're just doing your job."

He looks at me again. He looks relieved. "Okay," he says again. "Thanks. Thanks for that."

"Sure," I say again. Then turn and I leave him there. I don't know what else to say to him and I don't really care. I go down the poured-concrete staircase and across the parking lot and I leave the motel.

MY PHONE is paid through the end of the month. I think about calling Dave, about asking him to send me some money, but I don't do it. I think about calling my parents, about asking them. I dial the number and I call Logan, but all I get is the recorded message saying that the number I'm trying to reach is no longer in service, that I need to check the number and try again.

I WALK. I walk along the beach, walk back down to Venice, walk along the canals. I find a grocery store and I get a donut and a coffee and I walk around putting stuff into a cart until the donut and the coffee are gone. I get cleaned up, or as cleaned up as I can get, in a gas station bathroom. I sit in a coffee shop and read a newspaper that somebody left until the barista tells me I need to buy something or leave.

I wander around a bookshop, reading parts from different books. I wander around a record store. I sit outside a bar and I listen to the band starting up, listen to their first few songs.

Then it gets dark. I make my way back to the beach, find a spot under the pier, hunker down in the sand. I close my eyes and I try to sleep. All night long there are sounds, shapes, movements in the dark. There are whispers close by and whispers farther away. There is the sense of a decision being made, the sense of it having been made. There is a kind of twilighting that mimics sleep. The sound of the waves mixes with the noise from the cars mixes with the distant engine noise from the planes coming in and out of LAX. I drift off and come awake in the dark, drift off and come awake with the sky going pale, drift off and come awake with the sky blue and bright beyond the pilings and people around, people going by, people out walking and jogging and walking their dogs.

Nobody stops or looks at me. Everyone moves past. I get up and I leave the beach. I stand there on the strip and I shake the sand out of my clothes and I wonder what the fuck I'm going to do.

I'M COMING down. I don't know how else to describe it. It's like I've been high for a month, fucked up for a month, and now all of the things that happened and that I did and that at the time seemed distant and unreal and unimportant and somehow disconnected from me and any coming consequence are all sinking in, all at once. Standing there on the strip still half-asleep and with sand in my clothes and caked to my skin I start thinking about my car, finally, start thinking about finding a phone number for that gas station in Baker and figuring out what happened to it, if it's still there and where it got towed if it's not, and how to get it fixed. I start thinking about contacting a realtor and trying to figure out how to get my house listed and sold before the bank steps in, start thinking about who I can stay with back in Cleveland and where I can find a cheap apartment and who's got furniture I can have. I start thinking about who I know at what stations, about who I can talk to and where I can work and what I can do. It feels like there's still time, maybe, like there's still something there, still a network and a following and a name. It feels like there's still enough pieces left to put back together into some semblance of a life, into some semblance of the life I had before. I just need to get my shit together and start right now and really, really try.

But it's strange, too. Standing far outside of everything it's like I can see it all, finally: can see that thing, that life, that person, see it for all its various threads, see those threads stretching back through time, see them acting and being acted upon, pushing and resisting and yielding to and opposing and overcoming in a fantastic perpetual forward tumbling until finally the thing is and always must be understood only and always as the culmination, see too that this culmination is itself only one strand inside the greater culmination, the overall, the all that is the All, and the culmination that is me is both of this All and in the All, both composed of and composing, both part and product, can see how easy it would be, finally, to step back into his life, to become him again, his thoughts and habits, his likes and dislikes, his opinions and attitudes, his story and everything that goes along with it.

And that's it. That's where I am, that's what I'm thinking about, that's what I'm trying to sort through, shake off, get my head around, when Jonathan finds me.

PART
EIGHT

I DON'T notice him at first. It seems like one second I'm there alone and the next second he's there with me, making some joke about one of the dogs that somebody is walking by. Then he introduces himself. He asks me what I'm doing. I tell him I'm not doing anything. He nods. He asks me if I'm hungry. I tell him I'm not. He nods again.

"Okay," he says. "Well, come with me anyway. I hate eating by myself." He points off down the strip. "There's a great place," he says. "Right down there. Two minute walk. You should come with me. It'll be fun."

I look where he's pointing, look back at him. I sort of laugh. "I don't get it," I say. "What is this?"

He frowns, shrugs. "You don't get it," he says. "What don't you get? It's breakfast. There's nothing to get."

"Right," I say. "Okay, what I mean is, Why?"

He shrugs again. "I told you," he says, "I hate eating alone." He turns and takes a few steps away, stops and turns back. "Come on," he says again. "You're going to love this place. It's my favorite breakfast place. It's the best."

I don't move, though. I shake my head. "I can't," I say.

He frowns again. "You can't," he says. "Why can't you?"

I don't look at him. I look out across the beach, look out at the water. I shrug. "Because," I say, "I've got stuff to do. I've got a lot of shit that I've got to do."

He's coming back. "Oh," he says. "No, sure, that makes sense. I mean, you look busy."

I look at him, now. He's grinning. I nod.

"Right," I say. "Anyway, nice meeting you."

His expression changes. "Come on," he says again. "Don't be like that. I'm teasing you. You know I'm teasing you."

He keeps looking at me. I laugh. I can't help it. It's just funny. The whole thing is just funny. I nod again.

"Sure," I say.

He looks relieved. He takes another step closer. "It's fine," he says. "Come have breakfast and then you can go do whatever you've got to do. You need a solid breakfast if you've got a lot to do. You don't want to be running around on an empty stomach. That's the worst."

I shrug. "Yeah," I say, "you're right."

He holds up his hands. "Great," he says. "So we're good, then? You're coming?

I don't answer him. I look off across the beach, look out at the people, look out to the water again. I'm thinking about calling Dave, about asking him to wire me some money, asking him to wire me enough money to cover a bus ticket back to Baker and whatever tow bill there is and whatever the repairs are going to be and gas for the drive back. I'm thinking about asking him to wire me enough money to cover a bus ticket all the way back to Cleveland, if that's what it's going to be instead. I'm thinking about how I really need to start, really need to get going, really need to not waste any more time, here on this beach or in this city.

I am hungry, though. I haven't eaten anything since the donut and coffee I scammed from the grocery store yesterday morning.

I turn back at Jonathan. He's still looking at me. He's waiting for an answer. He holds up his hands.

"What?" he says. "What's the problem? It's breakfast. It's eggs and bacon and hash browns and coffee. Who doesn't like eggs and bacon and hash browns and coffee? How can you not go for eggs and bacon and hash browns and coffee?"

I GO with him. We walk down to the spot and we get a table and Jonathan orders.

"I know," he says. "You're not hungry. But just in case. Just so I don't feel rude eating in front of you. If you don't want to eat it then they can just box it up."

"Sure," I say. There's no chance of that, though. Sitting there with everyone around us eating, smelling food and hearing him order, I'm sure I've never been so hungry in my entire life.

The waiter brings our coffees. Jonathan pours cream into his, stirs in sugar.

"Really, though," he says, "what are you doing?"

"I'm on a road trip," I say. "I've been meaning to get out to L.A. for a while."

He tries the coffee, stirs in more sugar, tries it again. "A road trip," he says. "Where'd you start from?"

"Ohio," I say. "I started in Cleveland."

"Wow," he says. "Cleveland. That's a long way. How're you finding the traffic out here?"

I look away, look across the room and out the window, look out at the beach and the water. I shrug. "It's fine," I say. "It's traffic."

"Sure," he says. "It's like anything else. You get used to it."

I look back to him. He's still looking at me. Like he knows, already. Like somehow he already knows. That sounds crazy, maybe, but that's really how it feels.

"My car broke down in Baker," I say. "I left it at a gas station. Some guy gave me a ride into the city."

He doesn't register the change. He nods. "Wow," he says again. "You're hitchhiking. Geez, you don't hear about people doing that much anymore."

"No," I say, "I guess you don't."

He thinks about it, frowns. "It seems kind of dangerous," he says.

"Yeah," I say, "it's probably not a great idea."

He nods again. "So where are you staying?" he says.

I kind of snort at that. "Why?" I say.

He shrugs. "I was just wondering," he says. "You hitchhiked into town, you don't have a car. I figured you've got to be staying someplace nearby."

I'm holding my coffee. I set down the mug, lean in. "All right, listen," I say. "I appreciate you bringing me here and everything, and not to be rude, but what's your deal?"

He frowns, shakes his head. "My deal?" he says. "I don't know. I don't know that I understand the question. What's my deal with what?"

"With this," I say. "With bringing me here. With this whole thing."

He shrugs. "You looked hungry," he says.

"I looked hungry," I say.

"Yeah," he says, "you looked hungry."

I sit back and I look around, then I lean back in and I say, "Look, I don't really want to say this, but you're kind of making me say it."

He leans in, too. "What?" he says. "You don't want to say what?"

"I'll stay for breakfast," I say, "but I'm not going to fuck you."

He shrugs again. "Okay," he says. "I'm not going to fuck you, either."

He doesn't sound offended. He doesn't sound anything. He keeps looking at me. And I laugh. I laugh loud enough that the people at the tables around us stop talking, stop eating, for a second. I don't really mean to, but I kind of can't help it. It's just so bizarre. I sit back, pull my hands over my face, let them fall into my lap.

"Okay, fine," I say. "So this is what, then? Some kind of Jesus thing? I'm your good deed for the day?"

He thinks about it, shrugs. "Okay," he says. "Sure. If that's what you want to call it. If that's what makes sense to you."

I snort at that. "What makes sense to me is you being a fucking cop," I say. "What makes sense to me is you busting me for vagrancy or some shit."

He laughs at that. "If I was a cop," he says, "do you think I'd buy you breakfast first?"

"Yeah, right," I say. "No, probably not."

He's still laughing. He shakes his head. "I promise you," he says, "that's not what this is."

He doesn't say what it is, though. He doesn't say anything else. He stops laughing and he looks at me. And it's too much, somehow. It's finally just too weird. I set my mug down and I stand up.

"All right," I say. "This has been great and everything, but you're catching me at the end of about the most fucked-up month of my entire life, and right now I think what I really need to do is just head home and start sorting some things out before they get any worse. So I think this is where I say, Thanks for the coffee, and I go. So, thanks for the coffee."

He doesn't get up, doesn't protest, doesn't even raise his voice. He just keeps looking at me and he says, "But if you leave now, you'll never know."

And maybe it's bullshit. Maybe it's a con, a cheesy sales tactic, a baldfaced manipulation designed to keep me on the hook for God-only-knows what. Part of me knows this. But there's another part of me that's just about done, that's just about at its wits' end, that's tired and out of ideas. There's another part of me that's willing to hear him out, because what the fuck do I know, anyway? I've been steering the ship for all of this time, and look where it's gotten me. So I turn back and I lean on the back of the chair and I look at him and I say, "What? I'll never know what? What won't I ever know, if I leave now?"

He doesn't rise to my level, though. He keeps where he is, keeps even. He looks back at me and shrugs. Like it's obvious, has always been obvious. Like it's been obvious all along, what this is.

"You'll never know whether I can help you find some answers," he says.

I SIT back down. Our food comes and we eat. He asks again where I'm staying. I tell him the truth, tell him about the motel, about my card being declined, about sleeping under the pier. He nods. He tells me he has a spare room, tells me I'm welcome to it until I figure out what I'm going to do. I don't know what to say. He tells me it's not a big deal. He pays the bill and we go out to his car.

His place is up in the hills. He shows me the room, gives me some clothes, gives me a towel and a razor. I take a shower and I shave for the first time in weeks, the first time since before Paris. Afterwards my reflection looks strange to me. I stand there staring at it, turning my chin back and forth and pulling at my cheeks. Then I get dressed. I put on the clothes Jonathan gave me. I gather my old clothes up in a pile. Standing there finally clean and holding the clothes I can smell how they actually smell, can smell how I must have smelled to Jonathan and everyone else on the strip and in the restaurant. I dump the pile in the trash and I tie off the bag. Then I go out and Jonathan gives me the tour. There's no TV and no internet but there are shelves full of CDs and tapes and records, shelves full of books. He tells me to make myself at home. I thank him and I tell him I may just go lay down, that I didn't get much sleep last night. He tells me it's fine, that he'll see me later. I go in and I lay down on the bed. I feel like I might not be able to fall asleep, like it might all be too weird, but then I'm waking up and it's hours later. I get up and I go out and Jonathan is there and he's got lunch made and waiting. We sit and we eat and we talk about music, about the bands we've seen and people we've met. I tell him about different groups that Counter played with and opened for, different people I interviewed on the show. He tells me his stories. He's seen everybody, met a lot of people, hung out at a lot of parties.

"I was pretty heavy in that scene for a while," he says. "A long time, actually. You might not think it to look at me now."

I nod. He's right, I wouldn't. His whole demeanor, his whole deal here, feels a million miles removed from all of that. I ask him what changed. He shrugs.

"It started getting to be not good," he says. "I could see where it was headed. People I knew were killing themselves in incredibly unoriginal ways. And I had some close calls. Nothing too dramatic. Just those things where you sort of look back later and realize that it could just as easily have gone the other way. That it didn't have to work out. Still, I didn't know what to do about it. That's the thing people don't realize. It's like you forget any other way of being. Breaking out of it becomes very difficult. You feel like you need to learn how to do everything all over again. How to feed yourself, how to buy groceries, what to do with your nights, what to do with your days, how to talk to people about something other than getting high." He shrugs again. "I wasn't doing a good job of any of that," he says, "and then I ran into this guy I hadn't seen in a while, and he took me out to breakfast, and he told me what he'd been doing, and where he'd been, and it was like something finally just clicked."

"Something clicked," I say.

He nods. "Something clicked," he says again. "Seven years sober. It'll be eight in March."

"Wow," I say. "Great. Good for you." Then I say, "I know what you mean, though. How you sort of get adapted to your situation and that adaptation keeps you there. How you feel like you wouldn't even know how to be if you weren't being that thing in that place. You wouldn't know what to do with yourself. Like you almost have to dump everything and start over again from nothing."

Jonathan's nodding. "Exactly," he says. "It's like you're a baby again. Like you're brand new in the world."

"So this guy," I say, "your friend. He was in what, A.A.?"

Jonathan shakes his head. "Not that," he says. "The thing he was involved in and that he got me involved in isn't really even addiction-focused. Sobriety isn't the point, it's just one of the things that happens in the Process." He sets down his fork. "It's a whole thing," he says. "I can give you some books about it, if you want. But the basic idea is you start off by looking at your life and looking for patterns. The idea is that each of us is basically just a collection of habitual ways of dealing with and relating to our surroundings and the things that we come into contact with and the things that happen to us. Like each of us has our own personal playbook that we run plays out of. And ninety-nine point nine percent of the time we aren't even thinking about these plays. We're almost not even conscious of them. To us, running these plays just feels like us being ourselves. And we go through life running these plays over and over again with the sort of vague sense that this is what it is to be a person. But the problem is that for some of us, I'd even say a lot of us, maybe even most of us, these plays aren't all that great. For a lot of us they're just good enough to get us through our day-to-day lives without anything too bad happening. They're just good enough to keep us from getting fired or getting our asses kicked or having our wives or our husbands or our girlfriends or whoever leave us. But within this there's no question of us *evolving*. There's no push to say, No, wait, stop, let's look at this. Let's really look at the plays we're running and let's see if they're working and if they could be working better. There's no question of us growing and changing and improving and maybe one day even transcending into a higher plane of being. Like, take me. With me, everything was about this feeling that I was outside of everything. Like real life was happening on the inside, and I was on the outside, and the way for me to get on the inside was to have the drugs. And then once I was inside I would still feel like I was outside, and so I would take the drugs so that I would have the feeling that I was part of what was happening. That was how I got away from feeling that I was on the outside. And I'd feel all right for a little while and then I would come down and I'd feel like I was on the outside and the whole process would start over again. So for me, once I realized that it was all about this feeling of being outside, that these plays I was running were all about dealing with this feeling, I started really seeing how the drugs weren't solving the problem. I saw how they were just sort of numbing the symptoms without ever treating the underlying issue. And that's when I really started to say, Wait, hang on a second, why am I even doing this?" He laughs. Then he stops, waves it away. "Sorry," he says. "That's a lot. I know that's a lot. And I'm maybe not doing the best job of explaining it. Like I said, I've got books you can look at if you're interested. Or there's actually a meeting tonight, too, if you want to go to that. If you're interested in going to that. I was planning on going. You could come with me."

"A meeting," I say. "A meeting of what?"

He shrugs again as he picks up his fork. "There's a community of people who are involved in this work," he says. "We get together, talk, share our stories, that sort of thing. We support each other. They're good people. I think you'd enjoy meeting them." He takes another bite, chews and swallows. "Come with me," he says. "Just come check it out and see if it speaks to you. If so, great. If not, it's no big deal. Either way it should be interesting."

"I don't know," I say. "I mean, don't get me wrong. I think it's great that you've found something that works for you. But I'm just not really into all that."

He cocks his head to the side. "You're not into what?" he says.

I shrug. "I don't know," I say again. "Groups. Group stuff where a bunch of strangers get together and talk about their feelings. Where everybody has this big experience and they all feel like, Oh, wow, what amazing people. What strong, beautiful people these people are, all sharing their truth." Then I stop myself. I hold up my hands. "Sorry," I say. "That came out wrong. I didn't mean to be shitty. That's not what I meant. I just mean. You know what I mean. You know what I'm saying."

Jonathan nods. "Sure," he says. "I know what you're saying. Trust me, I understand where you're coming from. But let me propose something to you. What if you thought about it more like going to a show? Why do you go to a show? You go because you love the band or you love their sound or you love one of their songs. And you could just sit at home listening to their album, but you don't want to just sit at home listening to their album. You want to go to where they're playing and you want to be there with those people making that music and with other people who feel the same way about that music that you do. You want to join your feeling with a bigger feeling than what you get just sitting in your house or singing along in your car. Right?"

He's looking at me. I shrug again.

"Sure," I say. "I mean, I guess. I don't know that I would put it that way, but sure. Okay. Sure."

He's nodding. "Okay," he says. "So that's basically what this is. It's a moment for like-minded people to get together and share in a collective sense of openness and respect and pursuit of whatever Truth our little brains can wrap themselves around." He holds up his hands. "And that's it," he says. "It's nothing more than that."

He's still looking at me.

"Right," I say. "I mean, okay. I get that."

He keeps looking at me. Then he shrugs. He looks down at his plate and he picks up his fork. "Well, like I said," he says, "either way. It's up to you."

I DON'T go with him. I hang out and I listen to his albums. He's got everything, got obscure bands and rare imports that I've never even heard of. He's got enough random stuff that I think he might even have one of Counter's albums, but he doesn't. Or at least I still haven't found it by the time he gets home. I'm still standing by the shelves, still looking, when he walks in.

I go over to the stereo and I turn down Joy Division live at Birmingham University. "Sorry," I say. "I hope it's all right."

He waves a hand. "No," he says. "Like I said before, make yourself at home."

"This collection is pretty incredible," I say.

"Thanks," he says.

"How was the meeting?" I say.

He nods. "It was good," he says. "It was really good. You should have been there."

"Yeah?" I say. "You guys feel all the feelings?"

He nods again. "We did," he says. "We felt all the feelings." He goes over to the couch, sits down. "What about you?" he says. "You feel all the feelings here? You commune with the great God of rock 'n' roll?"

I snort. "Sure," I say.

He doesn't engage with that. He points at the CD I'm holding. "What've you got there?" he says.

I show him. It's *Wonderful* by the Circle Jerks. He nods.

"You know Zander Schloss gave me that album," he says. "Not that

305

copy. The cassette. It's over there somewhere. I saw him at a party right after it came out. He just had this one copy they'd given him. He had it in his pocket to show people, I guess. I told him I was going to run right out and buy it and he just gave me his."

"Wow," I say. "I interviewed Greg Hetson one time, when he was touring with Bad Religion. I never met Zander, though."

"He's great," Jonathan says. "Funny guy. Talented musician."

I go over and I sit down in the chair facing him. "So do you still see any of those people around?" I say. "Like, do any of those people ever show up at your meetings?"

"What people?" Jonathan says. "You mean famous people?"

"Yeah," I say. "I mean, you said before that it was a guy you knew from the scene who got you involved."

He shakes his head. "The people who come to the meetings are just people," he says. "They're not famous. And that guy who told me about it, he wasn't famous either. He was just a guy."

"Oh," I say.

"No," he says, "if you came to a meeting you'd be the most famous person there."

I laugh at that. "Being on the radio in Cleveland doesn't make you famous," I say. "It doesn't make you actual famous, it only makes you Cleveland famous."

He raises his eyebrows at that. "Oh, no?" he says. "I grew up out here, so you're going to have to explain to me how Cleveland famous is different from actual famous."

I shrug. "You know," I say. "It's just Cleveland famous. People in Cleveland know you, but that's it."

"Right," he says. "But you live in Cleveland, don't you?"

"Right," I say. "I live in Cleveland. I was living in Cleveland, before I came out here."

"So you're famous in the place where you live," he says. "People you interact with on a day-to-day basis know who you are."

"Yes," I say, "okay, technically. Technically a lot of the people I interact with in Cleveland know who I am."

He holds up his hands. "I don't know," he says. "To me, it kind of sounds like you're famous."

"Okay," I say, "maybe you can make some sort of semantic argument about it, but there's a difference. You know there's a difference. We can sit here and pretend that it's the same, but we both know that it's not the same. We both know that where I'm at and where an actual famous person is at are not the same place. We both know that where I'm at and where Henry Rollins is at are two very different things."

He sits forward, then, leans his elbows on his knees. "Okay," he says. "So you tell me, then. You tell me where he's at. Tell me where you think Henry Rollins is at. Tell me what you think life is like for Henry Rollins that makes it so different from what life is like for you."

I laugh at that. "It's different," I say. "What do you want me to say? It's just different. You know it's different."

He doesn't accept that, though. He shakes his head. "But how?" he says. "Tell me how it's different. Tell me specifically how it's different."

And it's funny. It feels like the kind of thing you would never have to justify thinking, the kind of thing where there are a hundred reasons it's a valid thing to think, a valid conclusion to come to, but sitting there in Jonathan's house with him watching me and waiting for an answer I can't even come up with one. I shake my head, raise my hands, let them drop. "It's just different," I say. "I don't know. It's better. It's just better. You know what I'm talking about. You know what I mean. He's done things. He's done things that people care about. People actually care about the work that he's done."

Jonathan nods. "And nobody cares about the work that you've done," he says.

"Exactly," I say. "Nobody cares about the work I've done."

He's still nodding. He sits back. "Okay," he says. "Got it." Then he sits forward again. "You want to know what I think?" he says.

I laugh again. I shrug. "Sure," I say. "Sure, go ahead. Why not? What do you think? Tell me what you think."

"I think that you think that being famous, that being actual famous, means never feeling bad," he says. "I think that you think that being actual famous means feeling good and happy and fulfilled all the time."

It takes me a second to untangle that. I frown and shake my head. "You think that I think that being famous means feeling happy and fulfilled," I say. "So do I think that being famous means feeling fulfilled? That's the question?"

"The question," he says, "is what do you think the experience of being actual famous is? Do you think it's some sort of magical state of constantly feeling good and fulfilled?"

I shake my head again. "I don't know," I say. "I don't think so. I mean, I don't think I think that. Or, maybe I do. Maybe a little bit. Not fulfilled. Fulfilled isn't the word I'd use. Maybe it's more like I feel like, yeah, I think that when you're famous there's a baseline sense of feeling valued or like what you've done with your life is worth something. Like what you do is worth something. I don't know. So maybe, yeah. Maybe fulfilled is the right word. Maybe I do think that I would generally feel a lot better if I had a sense that anybody gave a shit. That I'd done something with my life that was worth people giving a shit about. I don't know if that's exactly what you're talking about."

"What I'm talking about," he says, "is this collective fantasy we all have about what it is to be rich and famous. About how when you're rich and famous you don't have any problems, you're never self-conscious, everybody loves you, you feel great about everything you do and everything you've ever done, you don't have any regrets, nobody ever gets mad at you, and on and on." He's counting them off on his fingers. "Everything unpleasant just dissolves before it gets anywhere near you," he says. "Right? That's the idea, right?"

"I guess," I say. "I mean, sure. For the sake of argument, sure."

He holds up his hands. "Hey, look," he says, "if I'm wrong, please tell me. If I'm off base then tell me. I'm trying to understand the difference. I'm trying to understand what you're telling me. I'm trying to figure out exactly what you think the difference is between what your life is like now and what you think it would be like if you were actually famous."

"Okay," I say, "I get it. Point made. Rich and famous people have problems, too."

He shakes his head. "But that's not my point," he says. "My point isn't that they have problems, my point is that *they have the same problems*. They're just also rich and famous." He sits back. He waves a hand in the air. "Which, on the balance," he says, "might mean that they actually have more problems."

He keeps looking at me as he lets that hang. I hold up my hands.

"Yeah," I say, "okay, well, you'll have to forgive me if I don't feel especially bad for them."

He shakes his head. "That's not what I'm saying, either," he says. "I'm not saying that you should feel bad for them. Or, if you are going to feel bad for them, you shouldn't feel bad for them about that. You should feel bad for them because they're the most tricked. They got tricked worse than anybody."

I don't get that. I shake my head. "Wait," I say, "what does that mean? What are you saying?"

He sits forward again, sets his elbows on his knees, spreads his hands. "I'm saying we all have this dream," he says. "We have this collective dream about the special, separate, magical world that these rich and famous people operate in. It's the same dream that makes rich and famous people want to become rich and famous in the first place. But at the end of the day it's just a dream. At the end of the day it's just another illusion inside the big illusion."

"The big illusion meaning L.A.," I say.

He looks around, makes a circle in the air with his finger. "The big illusion meaning this," he says. "The big illusion meaning all of this. What this is and what we're supposed to do while we're in it and what's good and what's bad and where we think we're trying to get to. The big hamster wheel and everything that keeps us on it."

"The big hamster wheel," I say.

"And look," he says, "just because I understand something about it doesn't mean I'm off it, or anything. Living down here you're always going to get caught up. You're going to have moments where you forget your eternal nature and you start thinking that all of this is the really real thing. You have to realize what you're up against. You have to realize that the entire machinery of the culture we live in is here to present its philosophy and convince us that it's the one Truth. Up to and including powerful incentives both positive and negative. Up to and including fabulous prizes and the threat of eternal exile and the threat of corporal punishment." He shrugs. "And even that would all be a different thing," he says, "if it wasn't also kind of fun to get caught up in it. Right? It's fun to make believe. Like going to the movies. It's fun to get invested in storylines and characters and get dazzled by all the noise and the lights and the action and forget that it's all pretend."

"So you have the meetings," I say.

He nods. "Exactly," he says. "That's exactly it. That's exactly why."

I shake my head again. "I don't know," I say. "I don't know how caught up in everything I feel. I don't know how caught up in everything I've ever felt. I certainly didn't start out trying to get famous or thinking I was going to get famous. All of that happened later. It only became really important later. It was a different thing, in the beginning. Music and everything was a different thing. It was the one place in my life where I didn't have to act like everything was fine and life was fine and I was fine. Where I could be totally honest about how fucked up everything felt. I think it was maybe more like what you're talking about with the meetings. I feel like it was a way for me to not buy in. It was a way to get off the hamster wheel."

He's nodding. "Sure," he says, "but then what did you do? You bought into another culture."

"Maybe," I say, "but even still, it was a culture that was all about tearing down the stuff that you're talking about."

He shakes his head. "I'm not talking about a specific set of cultural structures," he says, "I'm talking about the entire concept of cultural structures. Not a specific hamster wheel. All hamster wheels."

"Right," I say, "that's what I'm saying. That's what it was about. It was about tearing all that down."

He nods again. "Ah," he says. "Okay, I get it. You weren't that kid singing into his comb in the bedroom mirror."

"Right," I say.

"You were a true believer," he says. "A Young Turk. A little punk rock jihadi."

I stop. I wasn't even doing anything, wasn't even about to do anything, but I still stop. "What?" I say.

"You know," he says. "Tear it down, set it on fire, destroy the institutions of oppression. Drag down the great Satan of Western Consumerism." Then he stops, too. His face changes. "What?" he says. "What did I say?"

I shake my head. "Nothing," I say. "It's fine."

"Wait," he says. "Hang on. You seem upset. Are you upset?"

"I'm not upset," I say.

"I didn't mean it as a putdown," he says. "I didn't mean. I just meant." He stops again, scoots forward on the cushion. "I'm sorry," he says. "I'm sorry if I upset you."

"It's fine," I say again. I can't look at him, though. I get up and I go over to the shelf and I put the Circle Jerks CD back in its place. Then I move over past the CDs and the cassettes and the records to the books. I say, "So all of this stuff you're talking about, you've got some books about it? You said before that you had some books I could look at, if I was interested."

I turn and I look at him. His look has changed. He looks relieved.

"Sure," he says. He gets up and he comes over. He scans the titles and he pulls one down. "This is a good one," he says. "Start with this. If it speaks to you then there are some others I can give you."

He holds the book out. It's one of Teacher's. I take it and I look at the cover. The cover shows the outline of a person floating above a field full of flowers. The sun in the sky behind the outline is shining out from where the outlined person's heart would be.

"Thanks," I say. "I'll take a look and let you know."

He nods. "Okay," he says. Then he yawns. He puts a hand on my shoulder. "I think that's about it for me," he says. "I'm going to turn in. Goodnight. Sleep well."

"Sure," I say. "You, too. And thanks again."

HE GOES out and I stay for another few minutes, looking through his albums. Then I go in and I get in bed and I open the book. I'm not really all that interested—I mostly asked about it to change the subject—but I'm not all that tired, either. I figure I'll read a few pages and that'll be enough, that after that I'll start to get sleepy, but I don't. I read the introduction and then I read the first chapter and then I just keep going. I'm seventeen pages in and then somehow I'm forty pages in and then somehow I'm sixty-seven pages in. Suddenly somehow I've got a hundred pages to go, then eight-three, then seventy-one. By the time I finally can't keep my eyes open anymore the alarm clock on the bedside table is showing that it's after three and I've got less than forty pages to go.

I GO out in the morning and I stand in the kitchen drinking the coffee that Jonathan made and reading until I finish the book. Jonathan's been in and out the whole time and when he sees the book sitting there on the counter he stops and comes over.

"All done?" he says.

I nod, yawn, rub my eyes. "I was up until three, reading it," I say. "I actually thought I was going to finish it last night, but I got too tired."

He nods. "And?" he says. "What'd you think?"

I shrug. "Honestly," I say, "I don't even know. I don't know what I think."

He's still nodding. "I know the feeling," he says. "Pretty incredible, right?"

"It was really something," I say.

Jonathan nods toward the living room. "There are more," he says. "There's a whole bunch. They're all in there on the shelf by where this one was. You can help yourself."

"Thanks," I say. "I think I'm going to need a minute to digest that one."

Jonathan reaches and he pulls the book across the counter. He picks it up and he turns it over and he looks down at the author photo on the back. "Teacher is a very special being," he says. "I feel very lucky to be here on this planet at the same time that he's here. I feel very privileged to have met him and heard him speak. I feel very privileged to be part of his work."

"Oh," I say. "I didn't realize that you actually knew him."

He nods, frowns. He's still looking down at the photo. "When I first got involved he was doing more public appearances," he says. "Speaking at colleges and symposiums and things like that. He doesn't do that very much anymore. His organization bought some land up north maybe ten or twelve years ago and he's mostly up there, now. If you want to hear him speak you pretty much have to go up there. But it's not like before. You have to be part of the organization or somebody who's part of the organization has to bring you. It's not just open like it was before. It's not open to the public."

"Sure," I say.

He sets the book down and slides it back. He looks at me and shrugs. "Sorry," he says. "I get a little bit excited when I talk about him. You want to change the subject? Let's change the subject." He leans in, leans his elbows on the counter. "What are your plans for today?" he says. "What are you trying to get into?"

I shake my head. "I don't know," I say. "I need to make some phone calls. I guess how that goes is going to determine everything else."

He nods, stands up. "Okay," he says. "Well, let me know if I can help. Let me know if you need a ride somewhere or anything. Otherwise I'm going to be in and out all day. If I'm headed out and I don't see you I'll leave my number on the fridge. Otherwise, like I said, make yourself at home."

HE LEAVES and I go out onto the back patio and I call Dave. He picks up on the first ring.

"Where are you?" he says.

"California," I say. "I'm in L.A. I drove out."

"You drove out," he says. "Jesus Christ, man. I went to your house. I called you like a hundred times. I was going to call the cops, or something."

"I needed to clear my head," I say.

"You needed to clear your head," he says. "Okay, terrific. Is it clear, now?"

"I don't know," I say. "I think it's more clear." Then I say, "The thing is, I can't get back. My car broke down and all my credit cards are getting declined and I don't have any cash."

"You don't have any cash," Dave says. "You're calling because you don't have any cash. You're calling because you need money."

"Sorry," I say.

"It's fine," he says. "How much do you need?"

"I don't know," I say. I explain the situation. "So I have to get back to Baker," I say, "probably pay to get it out of some impound, pay to get it towed to wherever somebody can fix it, pay to have it fixed, and then pay for gas to get back."

"Okay," Dave says again. "So a few hundred dollars? A thousand?"

"I don't know," I say. "I mean, probably. Can that work? I'll pay you back. And if it's not that much I'll give you back whatever's left."

"Shit, man," Dave says. Then he says, "You know people are picking through your shit. The garbagemen won't take a lot of it. It's just sitting there. You could have sold some of it, or something. If you were just going to leave it all there anyway."

"Yeah," I say. "I guess I could have done that."

"Okay," Dave says. "Fine. You don't want to talk about it? That's fine." Then he says. "Do you have anyone else you can ask? I just mean, I'm definitely good for a few hundred, but a thousand is a lot for us right now. Can we sort of go into a pool with somebody else? Can you ask your parents, or anything?"

"I mean, sure," I say. "Sure, fine, I'll ask my fucking parents. Never mind. Thanks for your help."

"All right," Dave says. "Calm down. Forget I said it." Then he says, "We can take it out of the savings. Take it out of the kids' braces fund, or something. I'll work it out."

"Thank you," I say.

"When do you need it?" he says.

"As soon as possible," I say.

"Fuck," he says. Then he says, "I'll see if I can get it done over lunch. I should be able to get it done over lunch. Okay? Does that work for you? Or is that not soon enough?"

"That would be amazing," I say. "Thank you."

"It's fine," he says. "Just get it together, all right? You're giving me a fucking ulcer."

"I will," I say. "I am."

I CALL my bank, google options, look into instant cash sales. I find a local realtor and I call and I explain the situation. There are terms to finalize, forms to sign. It's really better if I'm there in person, they tell me. There's only so much we can do over the phone. It's exhausting trying to sort it out, exhausting talking to people and reading through everything on my little phone screen. I google Western Union and I find a location and then I go inside and I ask Jonathan if he can give me a ride. He says he's got to run into town anyway. We go out and we get in his car.

"So how's it going?" he says. "You making progress?"

"Some," I say. "I don't know. There's still a lot. I kind of made a mess of things."

He nods. "And now you're trying to clean it all up," he says.

I shrug. "I mean, yeah," I say. "I don't know what else to do. I'm sure you don't want me staying in your guest room forever." Then I say, "I mean, why? You think I shouldn't?"

He shrugs. "I don't know," he says. "Obviously I don't know the specifics of your situation. But it does sort of seem like, if you went through all the trouble of unmaking the life you had back there, there was probably some reason. You know. There was some sort of unacknowledged need expressing itself."

I turn and I look out the window, watch storefronts and people and palm trees twined with Christmas lights glide by. I shake my head. "I don't know," I say. "Everything I did made sense to me when I was doing it. It all felt like it made sense at the time. So I don't know. I don't know what that means. I don't know if it means anything. I mean, maybe I just went kind of crazy for a little while."

"Sure," he says. "That's always a possibility." Then he says, "You should Process it."

I don't understand what he's suggesting, though. I don't know that term. "I am," I say. "I'm trying to process it."

"No," he says, "I mean you should Process it. You should run it through the Process. What I was telling you about. What we were talking about over lunch."

"Oh," I say, "right. Got it."

The truth is, though, I don't know what he's talking about. There's been so much already, between our conversations and Teacher's book. On top of that, I'm only halfway paying attention. My phone is telling me that the Western Union is coming up and so I'm watching out the window, watching the buildings, looking for the sign.

"It's really helpful," Jonathan says. "It can really help you clarify things. It's a really effective way to get in touch with your own feelings about things. To separate out what's true from what's background noise."

I spot the sign, then. I point. "There," I say. "There it is."

Jonathan slows and pulls in. He finds a spot and parks.

"I should only be a minute," I say.

He nods. "Sure," he says. "It's fine. I'll be here."

I GET out and I go in. There's no line, no one else waiting. The agent counts out the bills and he slides them into an envelope and he slides the envelope across the counter to me. I put it in my pocket and I thank him and I go out. Jonathan is still sitting where I left him. I go over and I open the door and I get in.

"How'd it go?" he says.

I can feel the money in my pocket, feel the thickness of the bills pressing into my thigh, banded down by the jeans he loaned me. I nod. "Good," I say. "It went fine. It's good."

He nods. "Okay," he say. "So what now?"

I yawn, rub my eyes. I drop my hands and shrug. There's nothing left to do but start taking steps. "I guess I should call that gas station," I say, "see if I can find out what happened to my car."

He nods again. "Anything I can do?" he says.

I shrug. "Nothing I can think of," I say. Then I say, "Are you hungry? I could use some food. You could let me buy you lunch. That would be something."

He grins at that. "I know a great place," he says. "It's right around the corner from here."

"Great," I say. "Let's go."

I GOOGLE around and I find the number for the gas station and I stand outside the restaurant while I make the call. The guy I talk to doesn't know anything, though. He says I'll have to talk to the manager. He gives me a number, but nobody picks up when I call. I call the station again and I ask the guy if he can just go look outside and see if the car is still there. He won't do it, though. He can't see the spot I'm talking about from the counter and he's not allowed to leave the register. He doesn't remember seeing it, he says, but he doesn't remember not seeing it either.

"It's a gas station," he says. "There are always cars around."

"All right," I say. "Can you tell me where it would have gone if it got towed, then?"

"I don't know," he says. "Like I said, you'll have to talk to Dan."

"I tried him," I say. "He didn't pick up at the number you gave me. Does he have another number? Is there another number I could try?"

"That's the only number I have for him," the guy says. Then he says, "Look, I mean, why don't you just come see if it's here?"

"Because I'm in L.A.," I tell him.

"Well then I don't know what to tell you," the guy says. "I'll look for it when I leave work, okay? I'll look and I'll see if it's here and if you call back tomorrow I'll tell you if I saw it, okay? That's the best I can offer. That's the best I can do for you."

"Fine," I say. "Okay. Sure. Great. Thank you."

"Okay," he says. "I'm not in until three. Call back after three."

"Fine," I say again. "Great. I will."

I HANG up with him and I go inside and I tell Jonathan what happened. He shakes his head.

"Not really the answer you were looking for," he says.

"Not really an answer at all," I say.

He shrugs. "So you call him tomorrow," he says.

"I guess," I say.

"What else would you do?" he says.

"I don't know," I say. "Go up there, maybe. Get a bus ticket and go up there and actually see what I'm dealing with. It might be easier than trying to do it all over the phone."

He shakes his head. "You don't want to do that," he says. "You take a bus up there and then you do what, walk around? Try to figure out how to get to whatever lot it got towed to on foot? Try to figure out how to get to wherever you're going to stay while they fix it? You'd be doing most of it over the phone anyway." He shakes his head again. "Don't do that," he says. "Stay here and call the guy tomorrow and figure it out. Then at least you'll have an idea of where to go and what to do." He looks back down at the menu. "And anyway," he says, "if you wait until tomorrow, I can drive you up there."

I'm surprised. I wasn't expecting it. "Wait," I say. "Seriously?"

He shrugs. "Sure," he says. "I've got time tomorrow."

"It's three hours away," I say. "It'd be six hours, roundtrip."

He shrugs again. "It's okay," he says.

I wait for him to say something else, to look at me, but he doesn't. I pick up my menu, but then I close it again and I set it back down on the table.

He looks up at me, then. "What?" he says.

"Nothing," I say. "It's just. I feel like such an asshole. You're being so fucking nice to me."

He frowns. "Hey," he says, "it's fine. It's not a big deal. It's not worth getting upset over."

I nod, wipe my eyes. "No," I say, "I know. It's just. Never mind. I'm good. Sorry. I'm good."

"Well, look," he says, "if you want to make it up to me there is something you can do. There's some stuff I've got to do this afternoon that you can help me with. If it would make you feel better."

I nod. "Sure," I say. "Absolutely. Anything I can do."

He turns back to his menu. "Great," he says. "Let's eat, and then we can get to it."

WE EAT and I pay and then we get back in the car and we drive down to Long Beach. We park in front of a house and we go up the steps and Jonathan knocks. The man who answers the door looks me over and then he hugs Jonathan. He hands Jonathan a set of keys. Then he goes back inside.

We go over to the minivan parked in the driveway and Jonathan unlocks the doors with the keys the man gave him and we get in. Inside is all stripped down. The seats have been taken out of the back and the carpet has been ripped up and there's just scratched-up metal and the hitch points where the seats used to be. Jonathan starts the engine and we drive over to a light industrial complex somewhere in Anaheim. We pull around behind the building and Jonathan backs up to a garage door and honks the horn and somebody inside rolls the garage door up. There are dozens of boxes inside, dozens of boxes for us to load. By the time it's all in the back wheel wells are low over the tires and you almost can't see out of the back window. The man who opened the door has Jonathan sign a form and then we get back in and we leave.

We drive all around the city, delivering what we picked up. We go to people's houses and independent bookshops and health food stores, go to churches and interfaith centers and the administrative offices of community outreach programs. We unload the boxes and we help unpack what's inside. There are pamphlets with titles like,

Are You Looking for Answers? and *What's It All About?* and *Radical Love* and *Militant Peace*. There are fliers for events and lectures coming up at different spots around L.A. There are copies of the book I read and copies of other books by Teacher. The people we deliver to are all excited to get them. They're all excited to see Jonathan. They all thank him, thank me. They tell us to thank Teacher for them. They tell us that they're looking forward to the Solstice Confluence, tell us that they'll see us there.

We're on the road all afternoon. Finally we're down to just a few boxes left. We drive over to a storage unit in Lakewood and we unload them. The storage unit is full of other boxes. Jonathan goes into one and he pulls copies of a couple of Teacher's books and he hands them to me.

"Just so you have them," he says. "Whenever you're done digesting the last one."

"Thanks," I say. "Really. Thank you."

We drive back to Long Beach, drop off the minivan, pick up Jonathan's car, get back on the road.

"What now?" I say.

He checks the time. "I'm supposed to run a meeting in about an hour," he says. "I can drop you back at the house, though."

"That's okay," I say.

He looks at me. "That's okay, what"? he says. "'That's okay' I can drop you back at the house, or 'That's okay' you want to come to the meeting?"

I shrug. "I mean, either way," I say. "Either way is fine. I can come to the meeting. You don't need to drive me back. It's cool. If it's cool then I'll come to the meeting. But either way is fine. Whatever you want to do is fine with me."

He shakes his head. "No," he says, "I mean, that's great. That's great if you want to come. You can absolutely come to the meeting. Absolutely."

"Okay, then," I say. "Great. I'll come to the meeting, then."

WE GO to the meeting. It's in the basement of a community center up in San Marino. And it's funny. I'm actually kind of nervous, I'm not sure what to expect, but once it starts it's all familiar, somehow. It's like the yoga classes, like the workshops I went to with Bethany. There's the same holding of space, the same setting of intention. There's the same call to acknowledge and accept and then release the everyday mind's clinging and resistance, its need to know and control. We arrange our folding chairs into a circle and Jonathan brings the meeting to order, welcomes us, invites us to open our hearts. He guides the meditation, leads the exercise, reads the passage. He moderates the period of sharing and response. Afterwards we stack the chairs back onto the rolling cart and we stand around drinking weak decaf out of styrofoam cups and eating the store-bought holiday cookies that somebody brought and people come over and introduce themselves. They shake my hand, hug me, tell me I'm welcome. They ask how I ended up here, how I heard about the meeting, how I first learned about Teacher, how I met Jonathan. I hug them back, thank them for having me, change the subject. I say something about Teacher, about the meditation, about the reading, about the city. They smile and nod, listen and accept. They don't push. There are other things to talk about anyway. The Solstice Confluence is less than two weeks away, and they're all making plans. Who's got a tent, who's got a cooler, who's got a camp stove, who's got room in their car.

"And what about you?" a man named Leonard asks me. "Are you coming?"

"I don't know," I say. "I mean, probably not. I don't think I'm going to still be around."

The woman he's with, a woman named Wendy, frowns. "Where are you going?" she says.

"I need to go home," I say. "I kind of made a mess of things back home. I really need to get back and straighten it all out."

Wendy shakes her head. "You should stay," she says. "Really. Missing the Confluence would be a mistake. Anything you need to work out, you'll be in a better place to deal with it afterwards."

The other couple standing there with us, a man named Kurt and a woman named Denise, are both nodding.

"It would be a shame to miss it," Kurt says.

"A shame," Denise agrees.

I shrug. "I don't know," I say again. "I mean, the other thing is, I probably can't really afford it, right now. Money's kind of tight until I get back. I can't really afford a ticket, or anything."

Wendy gets excited when I say that. She shakes her head. "But that's the thing," she says. "You don't need a ticket. It's open to anyone in the community."

"They take donations," Leonard says, "but that's all. There's no ticket. There's no charge for anything, once you're there. And if you can't give anything then you give by just being there."

"All the money goes to Teacher's Foundation," Denise says. "It all goes to help grow the Work."

"Jonathan will be there," Kurt says. "Just have Jonathan bring you. He'll bring you."

"I don't know," I say again. "Maybe. I mean, I'll have to see. Like I said, I don't know where I'm going to be. I don't know if I'm still going to be around. But I'll talk to him. I'll talk to Jonathan and see what he says."

"Do that," Wendy says. "Talk to Jonathan. Seeing Teacher, actually being there and hearing him speak, it's an opportunity you don't want to miss."

Leonard is nodding. "It'll change your life," he says. "It changed mine. It changed all of ours."

Denise puts her hand on my arm. "Stay," she says. "Talk to Jonathan. We want you there."

Jonathan is walking up. "Talk to me about what?" he says.

"About coming to the Confluence," Kurt says. "About getting a ride with you."

Jonathan looks at me. "Of course," he says. "Absolutely. If that's what you want to do, you're more than welcome to ride with me."

Leonard turns to me. "See?" he says. "There you go."

They're all looking at me. I shrug again.

"Okay," I say. "Sure. I mean, maybe. Let me figure some stuff out first and let you know. Can I figure some stuff out first and let you know?"

Jonathan nods. "Of course," he says. "Whatever you want. It's all up to you."

PEOPLE START drifting off, start saying their goodbyes, start leaving. We wait around and we walk out with the last few and then we get in Jonathan's car and we head back.

"So what'd you think?" Jonathan says.

"It was interesting," I say. "And everybody seemed really nice. They seem like really nice people."

"They are," he says. "They're the best people."

"They seem pretty keen on me going to the Confluence," I say.

He nods. "The Confluence is a special thing," he says. "I think you'd find it really meaningful." He looks at me. "But I understand, too," he says, "if you feel like you really need to get back."

"It's not that I don't think it would be great," I say. "I mean, it sounds amazing. It's just this other shit. But maybe. I don't know."

He nods again. "Well, look," he says. "You don't need to decide anything right this second. I'll hold the seat for you until you figure out what you want to do."

"Thanks," I say. "Really. Thank you. For this and for everything. For bringing me to the meeting and letting me stay at your place and just, for all of it. I really appreciate it." Then I laugh. I pull my hands over my face, let them drop into my lap. "I don't know what I would have done," I say. "I don't know where I'd even be right now, if it weren't for you. I really don't."

He shrugs. "I'm glad I could help," he says. Then he looks at me. "I want to tell you something," he says. "Can I tell you something?"

"Sure," I say. " I mean, of course."

He nods. He turns back to the road. "We're all where we're supposed to be," he says. "You, me, these people in these other cars, everyone at that meeting. Even Teacher. We're all where we're supposed to be. We're all doing what we're supposed to be doing." He looks at me, looks back at the road. He shakes his head. "The Universe doesn't make mistakes," he says. "I genuinely believe that. I truly, truly believe that. And I know it may not feel like that to you. I know it may not feel like that right now. I know it feels like there's somewhere else you're supposed to be and something else you're supposed to be doing. But let me tell you something. The other morning I woke up an hour before my alarm was set to go off with this feeling like I just wanted to go be by the water. So I got up and I got dressed and I drove down. It was kind of ridiculous. I mean, think about what traffic is like at that time of day. It took forever. And I didn't have a plan. I just went to the first place I thought of. That's the only reason I was even there." He looks at me. "So you tell me," he says. "You tell me what you think that is."

I look at him, keep looking at him as I shake my head. "I don't know," I say.

He nods. "I don't know, either," he says. "But doesn't it maybe sort of seem like somebody does?"

WE GET back to the house. I go in and I get in bed and I start on the copy of *The Mortal Vessel* that Jonathan gave me, but I barely make it five pages before I fall asleep. I start in again almost as soon as I wake up, though. I'm almost done with it by the time I call Baker. The attendant tells me he remembered to look but he didn't see my car. I thank him and I hang up and I try the manager again. I get nothing, though. I spend forty minutes searching around for numbers and calling different towing companies in and around Baker. I wait on hold while people look through records, while they ask around to whoever would have been running the truck that day. I sit on the line and I wait for people to call drivers and get back to me. It takes calling everybody and then calling some of them a second time before I find it.

"It's here," the man says. "Somebody didn't log it right in the computer. But it's here. It's in the lot."

"Great," I say. "So what's the deal with it? What's the story?"

He tells me. There's the cost of the tow and there's the cost per day to have it parked there, and if I need it towed to a repair shop there'll be a charge for that, too.

"Goddamnit," I say. "Did you look at it, at least? Can you tell what's wrong with it?"

"Sorry," he says, "we don't do repairs. We're just towing."

We go back and forth. He knows a garage that can look at it, he says, but I'll want to set things up with them first. The guy's not going to let it just sit over in his lot, either, and if I don't sign off on the repair work then he'll just end up having it towed back. I tell him I'll get back to him and then I hang up and I call the number he gave me for the garage. The owner's in the middle of something, but the guy I talk to says he'll have him call me as soon as he's finished. I wait for ten minutes and then I call again and it's the same thing. I wait for ten more minutes and then I call again. The same guy answers and he tells me that the owner had to run out for a part and he'll be back in a while. I ask him if the owner's got a cell phone and I push him until he gives me the number. The owner's in the middle of talking to somebody when I call him, though. He says he'll call me when he's on the road. I thank him and I hang up and I sit there waiting for that. I wait for five minutes and then I start to call again and while I'm bringing up the number he calls me. I explain everything to him, explain the situation. I tell him about the prior repair and what the problem might be. He tells me how he does things, how he bills hours, how soon he can get to it if I have it brought over today.

"All right," I tell him. "Let me sort some things out on this end and I'll call you back."

"Sure," he says. "Whatever you want to do. It's your call."

There's nothing to sort out, really. It's not like I have any other ideas. It's not like I have a ton of options. Still, it takes me another five minutes of sitting there before I actually make the call. The funny thing is, though, the guy won't do the job. He says I need to pay off what I owe for the prior tow and the storage before he'll do anything else.

"I don't have a working credit card right now," I tell him. "All I've got is cash. I'd have to buy a bus ticket just to get up there to pay you. Let me pay you when it's fixed so I only have to come up there once. I'll pay you and I'll pay for the repairs and it'll be all good."

He won't do it, though. It's the company's policy, he says. It's not even his decision.

"Okay," I say, "I understand all that, but can't you bend the rules a little bit? Just this one time? This is special circumstances. And anyway, the guy'll have my car. Just tell him not to give it to me until I pay you."

"Sorry," he says. "It's not my decision. Get this bill paid and then we'll sort it out. Until then I've got nothing for you."

I HANG up with him and I go back inside. Jonathan is there in the kitchen. He looks at me and he asks what's wrong. I tell him. He shakes his head.

327

"So what do you want to do?" he says.

"I don't know," I say. "Send him a money order, or something. Buy one of those prepaid cards." I sit down at the counter. I feel exhausted. I pull my hands over my face and let them fall. "What I really want is to not think about it anymore," I say. "What I really want is to have this tow truck guy just do his fucking job and help me out and not fuck me around."

Jonathan looks over at the clock on the stove. "I think you're going to miss the post office, as far as sending a money order goes," he says, "but they have those prepaid cards over at Ralph's. I'm supposed to run a meeting over in Temple City. There's a Ralph's over near there. If you want to come with me we can go over early and try to get it sorted out. We can at least get that part done. Then you'll have it. Then no matter what you decide you want to do, at least you're not carrying around a bunch of cash."

I feel like I can't even think about it anymore. I pull my hands over my face again. I shrug. "Great," I say. "Okay. Fine. Sounds good."

WE GO to Ralph's. Jonathan stays in the car while I go inside. I stand in line, wait to talk to somebody, but when it's finally my turn the guy can't help me. There's some confusion about me having an out-of-state driver's license. He says I need to talk to somebody else, a manager or somebody. I stand there while he sends out the page. He has to do it twice before the manager comes. The manager isn't much help either, though. He tells me he needs to check first, needs to make a call.

He makes the call but there's no answer. He looks at me with the phone still pressed to his ear and shakes his head. He lowers the receiver into the cradle.

"The recording says they're only there until five," he says. "You could come back tomorrow."

I have no idea what the problem is, no idea who he could be calling. I'm ninety-nine percent sure I could walk into any other store in Southern California and get this done. But I also feel like I just don't have it in me. I don't have it in me to argue with this guy or explain the situation to Jonathan or figure out where else to go. I don't have it in me to deal with it. At this point it's all starting to feel like it doesn't matter, anyway. At this point it's all starting to seem more funny than anything. I thank them for nothing and I go back out and I get back in the car. Jonathan looks up from the book he's highlighting.

"How'd it go?" he says.

I nod. "It went fine," I say. "I'm all set. I'm good to go."

"Great," he says. He closes the book, starts the car. "One less thing to worry about," he says. "One more thing off the list."

"Exactly," I say. "One less thing."

WE DRIVE over to the meeting. This one's in a church basement. We bring our chairs in like before and Jonathan stands and welcomes us. He invites us to open our hearts, invites us to close our eyes. He tells us to empty our minds, to become aware of our breath, to draw it low into our center. Then he tells us to imagine that we're walking through a dense forest. There are trees all around, trees towering overhead. Everywhere we look, any direction we turn, there are more trees. He tells us to imagine that this forest is our life, tells us to imagine that each tree we walk past is a concern we have about something in our life. One tree might be, How am I going to pay the rent this month? Another tree might be, What's going to happen with my marriage? Or, What will happen with my work situation? Or, How will I get my car fixed?

He tells us to follow his voice, tells us that his voice is leading us through the forest. It's leading us out into a big clearing, out into a field, out into the center of the field.

"Now take a moment," he says. "Look around, in your mind. Look up at the sky. Feel the breeze. Feel the sunshine on your face.

"And now look back at the forest. Notice how all of the trees look small, now. Notice how they can't follow you into your field, how when you're in your field they're far away.

"Now think about those things. Think about which ones still matter to you and which ones don't. Think about which ones you've kept and which ones have stayed in your life out of habit or the social circle you were in or a pressure you felt from the world to be a certain kind of somebody.

"You're free, in your field. There's nothing in your field that you don't want to have there. Nothing can come into your field if you don't invite it. So what do you invite? What do you choose? What matters to you, now? What matters to the true you that stands out in the sun?"

He brings us out of the meditation. He reads a passage from one of Teacher's books. He opens the floor and he invites us to share.

People stand and share. They read from notebooks, read from journals. They laugh, cry, shout, scream. We sit and listen. We hold the space. Afterwards we stand around and it's like before. The weak coffee, the snacks, the whole thing. People introduce themselves, hug me, shake my hand, welcome me. We wait until the last of them leaves and then we go back out to Jonathan's car.

"I'm not dumb," I say, "I get it."

He's steering us down the aisle, steering us out of the lot. He keeps his eyes on the road as he frowns and shakes his head. "Wait," he says. "What? What do you get?"

"What you're doing," I say.

"What I'm doing," he says. "What am I doing?"

"Come on," I say. "You know. You know what you're doing. That guided meditation. That shit about, 'I don't know how to get my car fixed.' I see what you're doing. I'm not an idiot."

He's watching the road. He looks at me, looks back. He holds up a hand. "Okay," he says, "hang on. What's going on? Tell me what's going on with you. What happened?"

And the truth is that I don't really know. I don't know what happened. All I know is that when he said what he said it was like something in me shut down or froze up, like some part of me ejected into the cheap seats and everything down on the floor stopped mattering. Everything happening down on the floor just seemed stupid, all of a sudden. It all just seemed like a fucked-up joke.

I hold up my hands, shrug. "Nothing," I say. "I'm fine. I'm good. I'm totally good."

He looks at me again. "You don't seem fine," he says.

"Yeah," I say, "well, I am. So don't worry."

He doesn't say anything for a minute. Then he says, "Look, whatever you're upset about, whatever it is, I apologize. I didn't mean to upset you. I wasn't trying to do anything, I swear."

I snort at that, though. "Right," I say. "Okay."

WE DON'T say anything else. We don't talk the whole rest of the way. I don't even look at him. I watch out the window. Back at the house I go into the bedroom and I get into bed and I lay there in the dark. I hear him moving around out in the living room, hear him out in the kitchen. Finally he goes in to bed and the house is quiet. I lay there for a long time before I finally fall asleep. In the morning I wake up early and I search around on my phone and then I go out. Jonathan is there in the kitchen. He looks up from his cereal.

"I need a ride to the bus station," I say.

He frowns. "Where?" he says. "I mean, which one?"

I hold out the phone. He looks and nods. He looks back at me.

"You going to Baker?" he says. "Because I'm still happy to drive you. I'm still happy to drive you, if that's where you're headed."

I shake my head. "It's fine," I say. "If you want to drive me somewhere then you can drive me to the bus station."

He nods. "Sure," he says. "Let me just finish this and we can go."

"Great," I say. "I'll be outside."

I GO and I wait outside. It's colder out than it looks. I can see my breath. I cross my arms, stomp my feet, walk around in circles. Finally Jonathan comes out. We go and we get in his car and he drives us down and through the traffic into downtown. He pulls up in front of the station.

"Are you sure you want to do this?" he says. "Honestly, I can drive you. It'll be a lot faster."

I've already got my door open, though. I'm already getting out. "It's fine," I say.

"Okay," he says. Then he starts to say something else, but I don't hear what it is. I don't let him finish, don't let him even really start. I close the door and I cross the sidewalk and I go inside.

I GO up to the counter and I buy the ticket. It's a bunch of tickets, actually. There's a bunch of nonsense I have to go through, a bunch of transferring in and around Barstow. It's going to take forever. On top of that, there's an hour and a half wait for the last leg, for the bus from Barstow to Baker, and my first bus doesn't leave until after three.

I wander around, kill time. I buy a newspaper, buy a sandwich. I buy a music magazine from a newsstand down the street. I think there might be something in it about the Loose Ends' new album, but there isn't. I go and I buy a pack of cigarettes and I smoke a few, standing out on the sidewalk. I go back in and I read the big board with all the different destinations listed. I wander around some more. Finally it's time. I board and I wait and then we pull out of the station. I watch the city go by out the window. I drift off and I wake up and then I drift off again. I wake up in Barstow. There's a lot of confusion about where to go, about whether the next bus is on time or whether it already came and went. People tell me where to go and where to stand. A while later a bus comes. I ride through town to another station and then I wait there. Finally I board the bus out of Barstow. It's already after six. I call the towing company to let them know that I'm on my way, to ask them how to get to their place from the bus stop, but the phone just rings and rings. I try them two more times and it's the same. Outside the desert is so dark that the lit billboards look like they're floating in nothing. Then a while later there are more lights. They float up out of the dark and surround us. We pull into the Baker station and unload. It's after nine. I ask the ticket booth attendant where I can find a motel. The one he sends me to costs forty-eight dollars a night and all night long the guy in the next room has his TV going loud enough that I can hear it clearly through the thin wall and the false headboard and the shitty motel pillow. I wake up early and I eat a stale danish and I drink a few cups of watery coffee from the breakfast bar in the main office and then I call the towing company again and the guy finally answers.

"I'm here," I say. "I'm in town. I'm at some motel by the bus station. How do I get to you?"

He tells me where he is, tells me how to get there from the motel. It's a long way to walk. I tell him that.

"I don't know what to tell you," he says. "Get an Uber. Call a cab."

"How about a pickup service," I say. "I spent all day yesterday on a bus so I could come out here and pay you."

"You came out here to get your car," he says. "I didn't tell you to leave it here."

I'm too tired to argue. I barely slept. It feels like there's no point, anyway. "Fine," I say. "I'll be there as soon as I can."

I GO outside, get oriented, start walking. I stick my thumb out. Nobody stops. I leave it out, forget I'm even doing it. Then a cop drives

333

by. For a second it seems like it's going to be all right, but then pulls into the next driveway and he turns around and he comes back. He pulls up next to the curb and he rolls down his window.

"Hi there," he says.

"Hi," I say.

"What're you doing?" he asks.

"Nothing," I say. "Walking. Just walking."

He nods. "Where are you walking to?" he says.

I tell him. "I was going to call a cab," I say, "but I'm running short on cash. I've got to pay this guy for the tow and for storing my car and then I've got to pay him to tow it over to this garage and then I've got to pay the mechanic, and it's just a whole thing."

He nods again. "You got any ID on you?" he says.

"Yeah," I say. "I mean, yes. Yes, sir." I dig out my license and I hand it over. "I didn't know it was illegal to hitchhike," I say. "I mean, is it illegal? I don't know how it is here. I'm from Ohio. You can see I'm from Ohio."

He doesn't say anything to that, though. He's looking at my license, typing something into some device he's got mounted to the dashboard.

"I'm really sorry if I did something wrong," I say. "I'll stop. I'll just walk. It's cool. You don't have to give me a ticket. I'll stop."

He doesn't say anything to that, either.

"Come on," I say. "Just give me a break. Can't you give me a break? Everything is so fucked up for me right now. You have no idea. I'm just trying to get my car fixed so I can get back home and try to put my life back together. I'm just trying to get home so I can try to fix my totally fucked-up life." Then I stop myself. I kind of have to. I feel like if I keep going I'm going to throw up or start crying or something. I close my eyes and I press my lips tight together and I breathe in through my nose. I draw the breath down into by stomach, down into my diaphragm, make a tightness in my throat as I blow it back out again. I open my eyes, look at him. "I'm sorry," I say. "If it's wrong, I'll stop."

The cop opens his door and gets out. He goes over and he opens the rear door and he turns to me.

"I can't let you ride in front," he says. "It's against the rules. But get in and I'll give you a ride where you're going."

I don't move. I look at him. I point at the open door and I say, "You're telling me that if I get in there you're going to let me back out, right? That's what you're saying, right?"

He shifts his weight, settles it to one side, waves a hand. "Come on," he says. "I'm going that way anyway."

I go over and I get in. He closes the door and he gets back in up front and we pull away from the curb.

"Thanks for this," I say. "Really. Thank you."

He shrugs. "It's not a problem," he says.

I look around at the cage separating the compartments, at the molded plastic interior, and then I sit back and I laugh. It's all suddenly funny, somehow. "Man," I say, "it's been a long time since I rode in the back of one of these."

"How is it?" he says. "About the same as you remember?"

"I guess," I say. "Or, yes and no. Last time I remember my experience being largely defined by my anxiety over what my parents were going to do when they found out."

He laughs at that. "What did they do?" he says.

I shrug. "The usual stuff," I say. "Took stuff away. Tried to ground me. Told me what a disappointment I was."

"That's rough," he says.

I shrug again. "It wasn't the first time they said it," I say. "Technically it wasn't the last time, either."

"Still," he says. "Kids screw up. It's not the end of the world."

I look at him, look at his reflection in the rearview mirror. "How many kids do you have?" I say.

"Three," he says. "Eight, ten, and fifteen."

"Fifteen," I say. "So you know something about it."

He nods as he laughs again. "Oh, yeah," he says. "I know something about it."

HE LETS me out in front of the building. I thank him again and I go inside. The man behind the desk looks up from his phone. I tell him who I am and why I'm here. He nods.

"You made it," he says.

"I made it," I say.

He nods again. "Okay," he says. "You set things up with Pat?"

I shake my head. "I haven't called Pat," I say. "I'm doing one thing at a time."

He turns to his computer, moves the mouse around, watches the screen wake up. "Are we towing it over there for you, is what I'm asking," he says.

"I don't know," I say. "Is it drivable?"

He shrugs. He's still looking at the screen. "I have no idea," he says. He nods toward the door behind him. "Go through there and tell Luke which one is yours," he says. "He'll show you where it is. If you can get it as far as the gate then just come in and pay this bill. Otherwise we'll figure out about getting it over to Pat's."

"Okay," I say. "Thanks."

I go out through the door, out into the dirt parking lot behind the high fence. I find Luke sitting in a plastic lawn chair in the shade of the building and I tell him what the man said and which car is mine. He walks me down to where it's parked, way down at the end of the row. I thank him and I get in and turn the key and the engine turns over but it doesn't sound right. It takes me giving it a lot of gas to get it to move at all. I get it as far as the gate, though. I kill the engine and I get out and I go back inside.

"How far is Pat's place?" I say.

The man shakes his head. "Not far," he says. "A few miles. You think it'll make it?"

"I don't know," I say. "If it doesn't I know who to call."

He laughs at that. "Okay," he says. Then he tells me the total. It's more than before.

"That's not what you told me on the phone," I say.

He shrugs. "It was here another day," he says. "What do you want me to tell you? Technically I should charge you for today, too. Any car that's on the lot after eight a.m."

Again, I feel like I don't have it in me to argue with him. It feels like there's no point. I take out Dave's money and I start counting bills out onto the counter. "No," I say as I do it. "Absolutely. You're doing me a big favor, actually. Really I should be thanking you."

He just shrugs again. I push the bills across the counter. He takes them and he gives me my change. I stuff it all back into my pocket and I go back out. He follows me as far as the doorway. He calls to Luke, gives a thumbs up. Luke nods and he goes around and opens the gate.

"How do I get to this Pat guy's place?" I ask him.

"It's easy," he tells me. He explains the way. I thank him and I get in and I start the car and I pull out through the gate. Out on the road the temperature gauge climbs past the midpoint and the engine starts making noises I've never heard it make before. I slow down, put on my hazards, hug the shoulder as people honk and pull around me. It feels like I'm never going to make it, but somehow I do. I leave it parked in front and I go inside. I can feel the heat coming off the engine from three feet away as I go past. Inside Pat nods when I tell him who I am.

"Where is it?" he says.

"I left it out front," I say.

"You drove it here?" he says.

"I drove it here," I say, "but it certainly wasn't happy about it."

He looks at me. "You driving it here means it's going to need at least half an hour to cool down before I can do much of anything with it," he says. "Probably longer. You should've just had it towed."

"Well, I didn't," I say. "So that's where we are. I don't know what else to tell you."

He looks at me some more. Then he shrugs. He nods to the corner, where a few chairs are set around a coffee table with some magazines spread on top.

"Make yourself comfortable," he says. "I'll get to it when I can."

I GO and I sit and I wait. I wait for what feels like a long time. I look through a couple of the magazines, read parts of a couple articles. I get up and I walk around, look at the shop, look at the certificates on the walls. I go back out and I try to feel whether my car has cooled down any, but I can't really tell. I don't know how hot it was before compared to how it is now and I don't know how cool it needs to be for Pat to do anything with it. I go back inside, sit back down, wait some more.

FINALLY IT'S time. Pat calls me over. I follow him out and we put the car in neutral and we push it inside. Inside he opens the hood and looks around. He goes over and he starts the engine and he stands there, listening.

"See?" I say. "It doesn't normally sound like that. And I don't have any power on acceleration. I have to give it a lot of gas to get it to do anything."

Pat holds up a hand. He's trying to listen. He revs the engine, lets it idle, revs it again. He kills the engine and he gets out.

"So what do you think?" I say.

"I don't know," he says. "Give me a minute and I might know something."

"Okay," I say. "Fine. Great. Fine. Sorry."

I GO back outside and I sit there on the step and I watch the cars going by on the Mojave Freeway. I sit there for what feels like a long time, but maybe it isn't. Then Pat comes out. I think he's going to say something about the radiator, but he doesn't. Or at least he doesn't start there. There's another problem, something much worse.

"So, what?" I say, when he's finished explaining. "I don't understand. You're saying you can fix it or you're saying you can't fix it?"

He shrugs. "No," he says, "I can fix it, it's just kind of to the point where you start to ask the question. That age, that mileage, needing those repairs, people usually start thinking in terms of whether it's worth it. But it's up to you. I can do it, if that's what you want. I'm just saying."

"Right," I say. "Okay, so how much would it be, then? How much are we talking about, all in?"

He talks it through, lists out the issues and the parts and the labor, gives me the number. It's more than I have left of what Dave sent me, more than I had to begin with, before the bus ticket and the tow and the storage fee.

"Jesus Christ," I say. "Fuck me."

He doesn't like that. He crosses his arms. "Look," he says, "I'm just telling you how it is."

"I know," I say. "I'm sorry. It isn't you."

He nods. He holds out his hands. "So?" he says. "You tell me. What do you want to do?"

I laugh. "What do I want to do?" I say. "What I want to do is irrelevant. Even if I wanted you to fix it, I can't afford it." I shake my head. "Is there any sort of budget option?" I say. "Like you can do just enough to get it back to Ohio?

He gives me a look. "Ohio," he says. "Is that where you started from?" He laughs. "Geez," he says. "If you ask me, I'd say you're lucky the thing made it as far as it did."

I barely let him finish. "Okay," I say. "So what, then? Is that a no? No, there's no budget option? Is that what you're telling me?"

He shakes his head. "What I'm telling you," he says, "is that if I were you, and I was trying to get back to Ohio, I'd look into getting a bus ticket or a plane ticket way before I even thought about putting another dollar into that car."

I can't look at him, can't even be near him. I take a few steps away and I rub my eyes, keep rubbing them as I nod. "Well, okay," I say, from between my hands. "Great. I mean, thanks. Great. Okay." I don't know what else to say. I drop my hands and I blink my eyes clear and I look past him, over his shoulder and through the open garage door at my car still sitting up on the lift. "Shit," I say.

He's watching me. He turns and he looks where I'm looking and then he turns back to me. "All right, listen," he says. "I've got a buddy who runs a salvage yard. I can call him and see if he wants to come look at it. He may be able to give you a few hundred bucks for it." He holds out his hands. "I know that's not the answer you were looking for," he says, "but at least it'd be something. It'd cover the cost of the ticket back, at least. I can call him right now, if you want me to. If you think that's something you'd like to do."

I don't think anything. I kind of can't. I shrug and I look at him. "Sure," I say. "Great. Why not? Sure. What else am I going to do? Call him. Let's do it. Sure."

PAT GOES inside to make the call. He comes out a minute later to let me know that the man's on his way. I thank him and I go and sit back down on the step. I feel weird, feel gross and tired and wide awake all at the same time. On top of that, it's getting hot. Walking along the road and riding in the cop's car and dealing with the towing company and then driving and parking and going inside it had all still felt like morning, still felt like the sun was low and the day was cool and just starting. Standing out there with Pat it was like we crossed some sort of vague threshold and it was suddenly full bright hot day. Now everywhere I look there's heat shimmer coming off of something and the sunlight reflecting off the cars and the buildings is so bright that looking at them I have to squint down to almost nothing.

I keep looking, though. I feel like it doesn't matter. I feel like it doesn't matter anymore if my corneas sear and blister, if my eyes bake out of my skull and melt down my face. It doesn't matter what happens, now. I sit there and I stare. By the time the man shows up and asks me if I'm the guy with the car there's a white spot in my field of vision that flashes bright when I blink and takes a really, really long time to go away.

He looks at the car and he gives me a number. I tell him no and he offers me another fifty. I say no to that, too, and he goes up seventy-five. It's his final offer, he says. I shrug and say okay. I fill out the forms, sign over the title. He counts out the money onto the hood. Pat gets down with a screwdriver and he takes off my license plates. He puts them in a manilla envelope and he hands them to me. We all shake hands. Then the man from the scrap yard hooks my car up to his truck.

He gives me a ride back to the bus station. He's going that way anyway. He lets me off in front. I climb down and I go inside. I can see the reflection of the truck and my car hitched up by the front axle all driving off in the glass in the bus station's big door. Then I'm inside and I don't see it anymore. I go up to the window and I buy my ticket. I find a seat and I wait. I wait for hours. I don't do anything, don't think anything. I'm just there. Then the bus comes and I get on.

I RIDE, sleep, make the transfers. I ride and sleep some more. I get into the city and I get a cab. The driver tries to talk to me about something but I don't really listen. Finally he stops trying. He drops me off in front of the house. I get out and I pay the fare out of the cash I got for my car and he drives off. I go up the walk and I knock on the door. There's nobody home, though. I take a seat on the step and I wait. I wait and wait. It gets dark, gets late. I cinch down my sweatshirt hood, stomp my feet, walk around in a little circle to keep warm. Finally I see headlights coming and I go down the walk to meet him. I'm there just as he's opening the door, just as he's getting out. I say his name. It startles him. He drops the box he's holding.

"Shit," I say. "I'm sorry."

His whole demeanor changes, when he sees that it's me. He laughs. "It's all right," he says. "Don't worry about it. It's fine."

I get down and I help him pick up everything that spilled. It's more fliers, more pamphlets. We get it all put back together and he picks up the box.

"Let me get it," I say.

He shakes his head. "It's fine," he says. He picks up his keys from where he set them on the hood and he holds them out to me. "Here," he says, "you can get the door."

I take the keys. I go up the walk, unlock the door. I stand there on the step as he goes in past me. He takes six or eight steps inside before he stops and turns. He looks at me and frowns.

"Well?" he says. "Are you coming in or not?"

HE DOESN'T ask me what happened. He doesn't ask me anything. He gives me copies of Teacher's other books, gives me a notebook and a pen. He leaves it all on a shelf in my room.

I read it all, read everything he's given me. I read *Beyond the Self*, read *Quantum Consciousness*, read *Return*. I read through the days, read late into the nights. I fall asleep with the books still open in my lap, still open in my hands. I dream about snakes, about fire, about the movement of the stars and about strange dark forms rising in vast open spaces. I wake up disoriented, wake up having forgotten where I am and how I got there, wake up with thoughts and ideas and insights that in the dream seemed clear and profound and obvious, even, sliding out of focus and vanishing as the tangible world seeps up and becomes real again.

I go to more meetings, drive out with Jonathan to meetings in Hollywood and Torrance and Culver City and Santa Monica. I arrange the chairs, form the circle, do the meditations. I hold the space, honor the story and the teller, but when it's time to share I don't share. I tell them I'm not ready, tell them I'm working on it, tell them that I need more time.

The truth is that I'm not working on it, though. I'm not working on it the way I'm supposed to be, not working on it the way they think I mean. The notebook that Jonathan gave me, the notebook that I carry around with me and take to all the meetings, is still as blank and empty as it was the day Jonathan left it on the shelf in my room.

"It's not enough," Jonathan tells me, finally. "It's not enough to just be there in the room. You can't sit outside and expect it to come to you. It doesn't work like that. It's not going to come to you on your terms. You have to come to it. You have to make yourself part of it. Nothing is going to happen for you until you do."

We're driving back from a meeting in Culver City. I'm watching the dashboard, my knees, the notebook in my lap go light and dark with each lighted sign or streetlight or big shop window we pass.

"I know," I say. "You're right. I know you're right."

He nods. "Okay, then," he says. "So what's the issue? Tell me. I can help you if you tell me."

And I want to tell him. I want him to understand. I want to explain that it's not about me holding back, not about me standing outside and expecting it to come to me, it's only that I'm afraid: that if I start it I won't be able to stop, that it'll all keep coming and coming until my chest cracks open or my head caves in, until I'm exhausted and empty, broken and destroyed, hollowed out and shattered into a hundred thousand pieces.

343

I look at him. I shake my head. "It's nothing," I say. "I'll do it. I'll go next time. Next time, I promise. Next time I will."

I DON'T go the next time, though. I don't go that time or the time after that or the time after that. I don't go before the Solstice Confluence, don't go before we load up in Jonathan's car and we drive up here.

What can I say? What do I need to say? What is there to say? It's like certain shows, like that first show in that driveway in South Euclid a hundred years ago. There's the same sense of being taken up into some greater momentum, the same feeling of a space becoming a world apart, the same sense that now this separate world is the only world with any meaning or reality, that the former world has fallen away and become something distant and unimportant. For three days and nights I hardly sleep, barely eat, barely drink. For three days and nights I'm lost in the crowd, carried along, pushed and pulled, turned around and back again until finally everything becomes strange, becomes wheeling and unreal, until it all becomes like a dream where everything is disconnected from everything else, disconnected from any concept of its own natural consequence, even, until there is the general sense of the illusory quality of things and the sense that now, in this space, all of the subtle and seemingly immutable laws that distinguish spirit from being, matter from energy, meat from breath, have begun to fade, have begun to lose their permanence, and that now and in this space spontaneous transformations and manifestations are possible, likely, inevitable, even, that now they are just a matter of directed focus, of earnest intention, of releasing what is known and simply and fundamentally letting go.

And then it's time, and I go down and I join the gathering in the field, and He is there, Teacher is there, and what can I say? He is Teacher, He is the One. He is the Door and He is the Path to the Door. He speaks and the world is washed away and made anew. He calls us to raise our voices and our hands and my hands and my voice are raised. For hours and hours, for months and years, for the balance of my life and into what comes after. Until the sun dims and grows cold, until the spinning Universe slows, until the stars and the planets and the moons all slip from their orbits and scatter across infinity. Until the big fire is lit and we gather and dance and sing and exalt in the warmth and the light that it gives.

And then the sky goes pale, and it is the morning of the fourth day, and we leave the embers to go down and stand at the edge of the pond and watch the sun climb through the trees. First there is a glow, then flashes, and then its fullness is visible between the trunks. Then it crests the branches in blinding brilliant life-giving yellow-white, and the turning world slides away beneath me, and I lose myself and fall in the mud and the shallow water, fall amongst the rushes and the reeds and the multifarious life which crawls or slithers or swims or flies away.

They gather around me. They raise me up. They help me walk to the house. They put a damp cloth on my forehead, give me water to drink. They show me where I can shower, show me a room where I can lie down.

I go in and I wash off the mud, wash myself clean. I go in and I lay down on the bed. I'm not thinking I'll sleep, I'm just going to rest my eyes, but then I'm waking up and it's hours and hours later. The afternoon sun is shining in through the window and the field outside is empty. The tents and the cars and the people are gone.

My clothes, the clothes that Jonathan gave me, have been washed and folded and set on the foot of the bed. I get dressed and I go out into the kitchen. People are there and Jonathan is there with them. He introduces me around, introduces me to Bhakti and Ananda and Drishti. He tells me that they've been talking about me, that they've worked it all out, that I can stay here if I want to, stay and work with Teacher, that there's room for me in the dorms.

"So?" he says. "What do you think? Is that something you'd want to do?"

They're all looking at me, all waiting for my answer. My mind is blank, empty, clean. My mind is quiet for the first time in my entire silly life.

"Yes," I hear myself say. "Yes, that's what I want. That's what I want to do."

Jonathan nods. He's got my notebook, the notebook he gave me, there on the table in front of him. He opens it and he sets a pen on the blank page and slides it across the table toward me. He looks at me. "In that case," he says, "there's just one thing you need to do first."

SO I'VE done it, now. Now it's done. Here it is. Full and honest. It's all here.

The money's here, too. What's left of the money Dave sent and what's left of what I got for the car. Do what you can with it. It's not much. It's nothing. But it's yours.

Tell me what to do, now. Tell me what to do and I'll do it. I don't care. Go out and talk to people, run meetings, work in the fields, work in the barn. Work in the print shop, drive a truck, cook the food, clean the toilets. Whatever it is, whatever Teacher wants me to do, I'll do it. I'll be that thing. I just can't be this. I can't be this any more. This little collection of memories and opinions, this jumble of assertions asserting and reasserting themselves, telling and retelling themselves the story of themselves. Defending and fortifying and feeling sorry for themselves. Walking around on two legs and calling themselves a person. I can't do it anymore. This all has to stop. It all has to end.

I'm sorry. That's all I can say. What else can I say? If there's something else to say I'll say it. I'm sorry. That's all that's left. I'm sorry for everything. It's not an excuse. I should have been better. I should have tried harder. It should all have been different. I'm so fucking sorry. If I could take it all back I would. If I could go back and erase myself, go back and erase every place where I brushed up against the world, where me being in the world made any sort of difference, I would do it. In a second. In a heartbeat. I would trade my life for hers, would trade my life for theirs. I would.

What else is there? There's nothing. There's nothing else. Thank you. Thank you for letting me be here. From the bottom of my stupid, broken heart, Thank you. Thank you with all the breath I have left in my body.

So tell me, now. Tell me what to do. Tell me what to do, and I'll do it. Whatever it is, whatever Teacher wants, I'll do it. I'll be that thing. Let me be that thing. I'm ready. I'm yours.

Scott Burr is a graduate of the creative writing program at The Colorado College, where he won the Ebey Prize for novella-length fiction and was a finalist for the Reville Prize in short fiction. His previous novel, *Bummed Out City*, was one of *Library Journal*'s top read books of 2015. His short fiction and novel excerpts have appeared in *Mildred*, *Metonym*, *The Mayo Review*, and elsewhere. He lives and works in Cleveland, Ohio.